D1144589

Richard Montanari was born in Cleveland, Ohio, to a traditional Italian-American family. After university, he travelled extensively in Europe and lived in London.

Returning to the US, he started working as a freelance writer for the *Chicago Tribune*, the *Detroit Free Press*, the *Seattle Times*, and many others. He wrote his first book, *Deviant Ways*, in 1996 and it won the OLMA for Best First Mystery. His novels have now been published in more than twenty-five languages.

Also by Richard Montanari

The Violet Hour

Kiss of Evil

Don't Look Now (*previously published as* Deviant Ways)

The Rosary Girls

The Skin Gods

Broken Angels

Play Dead

The Devil's Garden

The Echo Man

The Killing Room

The Stolen Ones

The Doll Maker

Shutter Man

The Buried Girl

Richard Montanari

sphere

SPHERE

First published in Great Britain in 2019 by Sphere

1 3 5 7 9 10 8 6 4 2

Copyright © Richard Montanari 2019

The moral right of the author has been asserted.

Lines from 'Two Fusiliers' from *The Complete Poems in One Volume* by Robert Graves, edited by Beryl Graves and Dunstan Ward © Carcanet Press Ltd 2000

*All characters and events in this publication, other than those
clearly in the public domain, are fictitious and any resemblance
to real persons, living or dead, is purely coincidental.*

All rights reserved.
No part of this publication may be reproduced, stored in a
retrieval system, or transmitted, in any form or by any means, without
the prior permission in writing of the publisher, nor be otherwise circulated
in any form of binding or cover other than that in which it is published
and without a similar condition including this condition
being imposed on the subsequent purchaser.

A CIP catalogue record for this book is available from the British Library.

Hardback ISBN 978-0-7515-6385-6
Trade Paperback ISBN 978-0-7515-6386-3

Typeset in Janson Text by M Rules
Printed and bound in Great Britain by
Clays Ltd, Elcograf S.p.A.

Papers used by Sphere are from well-managed forests
and other responsible sources.

MIX
Paper from
responsible sources
FSC® C104740

Sphere
An imprint of
Little, Brown Book Group
Carmelite House
50 Victoria Embankment
London EC4Y 0DZ

An Hachette UK Company
www.hachette.co.uk

www.littlebrown.co.uk

For Paloma

luce mia

Rotherham MBC	
B54 030 715 0	
Askews & Holts	18-Feb-2019
AF	£19.99
WAT	

Show me the two so closely bound
As we, by the wet bond of blood.

Robert Graves, 'Two Fusiliers'

Amsterdam

March 22, 1819

On the third day of his madness Dr Rinus van Laar tasted the mouth of the devil.

He stepped from the ruin of his home, into the orchard where the body of his wife, dead these three days past, had begun to soften and color. He remembered the first time he had seen Anna that day by the river, the way the summer sun had brushed her hair with honey. She was now the color of winter.

Anna's killer lay scattered beside her in seven pieces. Six, Rinus amended. He could not remember where he had put the man's head. He longed to look one last time into those feral, lifeless eyes.

As he uncapped the amber vial he considered the aviary snare tucked beneath the eaves. The white bird studied him, watching, waiting, scheming, the thin leather strap tightly coiled around one leg.

Rinus van Laar raised the vial to his lips, let seven drops of mandragora fall onto his tongue. He lay next to his wife, took her cold hand in his own, and beckoned the fire.

At dawn, Rinus van Laar carefully returned the drawings to the leather portfolio. Fourteen sketches by the master, already more than two centuries old.

Seven vices. Seven virtues.

It was this treasure the killer sought. It was in defence of this treasure that Anna had given her life.

He placed the portfolio into the steamer trunk, latched it, and secured the iron lock. He tacked funeral instructions and payment to the front door.

As he prepared to leave, he looked one last time at his wife, and saw the bright green leaf seeking sunlight through the matte claret of Anna's dried blood.

In her virtue there was life.

Six hours later, his infant son in his arms, Rinus van Laar left for America.

Being the true diary and journal of Eva Claire Larssen

July 21, 1868

We left Richmond before dawn. I am riding back wagon with Deirdre Samuelsson and her brother Jonah. Jonah is still small, and thinks of all this as an adventure. Deirdre is my age, just fourteen, and terribly shy due to her stammer.

They say six hundred thousand died in the war. Imagine. Daddy was killed at Manassas. Mama also died from Yankee hellfire, but not right away. Not Sonja Larssen. She held ground three years, and breathed her last yesterday at noon. Our first day's journey took us seven miles.

The dead walk behind us.

August 7, 1868

The rain is endless. We got stuck twice on the road out of Rowleton, where we picked up two weeks' domestic work. Mr Samuelsson had to ask some local boys and their mules to help pull the wagon from the culvert. My sweater got soaking wet, and as the wool dried by the fire last night it smelled of Mama. I cried myself to sleep again.

August 19, 1868

We crossed the Ohio River at Wheeling this morning. Deirdre and I went to the general store and bought nails and tobacco for Mr Samuelsson. He let us buy some fruit, and I had the most delicious pear.

Ohio looks like home before the war.

September 1, 1868

I awoke to the sound of church bells. When I climbed down from the wagon I saw that we were stopped on the crest of a hill overlooking the most beautiful valley I have ever seen.

When I stepped to the edge I saw them for the first time. Two grand houses facing each other across a field of green, houses so important they even have names. Veldhoeve and Godwin Hall. I will be working at one, and staying in the other.

Imagine.

September 2, 1868

All the buildings here are freshly painted and well cared for. The war did not come to this place. When we reached the town square I looked at the plaque.

ABBEVILLE, OHIO. EST. 1790

Perched on top of the plaque was a beautiful white bird, its pearl feathers glossed with early morning rain. I sat on the bench across from it and took out my pencils and pad. This is my drawing.

Although I am not taken by such notions, as I left the square, I could swear that bird was watching me.

Tomorrow morning I will begin work at Godwin Hall. If you are reading this, if the sun now shines where you stand, it means I am long forgotten.

If you are reading this, it means I never made it back home again.

Autumn – The Fire Boy

1

At just after 4 a.m., five days before the flames ended his world for the third time, Will Hardy stood on the corner of Mercer Street and West Houston.

There was a time of day, Will believed, a still and transient moment when an outright silence came to New York City, a time when he could ride his Cervélo through the darkened streets and allow his mind to fill with things other than traffic and stray dogs and noise, or the vagaries and brutal competitiveness of academia.

A tenure-track professor at New York University for the past six years, Dr William Michael Hardy, thirty-eight, was well published in his field of forensic psychology. His work had appeared in the *Journal of Clinical Psychology and Psychological Trauma*, as well as many other peer-reviewed publications. He had lectured at universities in both the US and Great Britain, and was slated to be on a panel on the foundations of psychopathology in Stockholm this coming winter.

He had consulted many times with the NYPD, most recently on the case of a serial rapist hunting the Brownsville section of the city. Because of his work on that case, Will had been profiled in *New York Magazine*, and had twice appeared on the *Today Show*.

By the time Will reached 14th Street the morning sky had begun to lighten, casting a soft lavender radiance onto the buildings.

As he had every morning for the past three weeks, Will rode slowly onto the sidewalk at Union Square, and stopped in front of Barnes & Noble. He checked and reset his watch. Near record time.

He leaned his bicycle against a leg of the aluminum scaffolding, removed his helmet and gloves, and regarded the collection of books on the racks facing the street. His heart still fluttered when he saw the cover, the clever photo of black and white 35 mm movie film curled onto the smooth and seductive curve of a woman's shoulder.

It had been nearly a month, and he still found it hard to believe. Somehow, Dr William Hardy had the No. 13 hardcover on the *New York Times* non-fiction list, a surprise hit called *A Flicker of Madness*. The book was an informal study examining seven classics of film; each, in the author's opinion, a masterful depiction of criminal psychosis.

For Will, the hardest part of writing the book was picking only seven films to feature, in the end selecting, among them, *The Night of the Hunter*, *The Silence of the Lambs*, and Fritz Lang's *M*.

Ego stroked for the moment, as he turned onto University Place, and headed back, he saw the black birds silhouetted against the morning sky. For Will Hardy it marked the beginning of a new day, and led the way home.

Twenty minutes later, Will sat on the bus bench across from the brownstone on Prince Street. Eighty-eight days earlier this had been his home.

He sipped his coffee, looked at the third floor, at the lights coming on, at the shadows essayed on the blinds.

Inside, his wife of sixteen years was just starting her day. The daughter of a New Rochelle surgeon and a concert pianist, Amanda Kyle Hardy worked as a juvenile social worker in the Administration for Children's Services, as well as a counselor for a variety of drug and alcohol dependence facilities. If there was one thing at which she was more proficient than Northern Italian cooking, it was landscape watercolors. At thirty-seven, she was often taken for a woman in her late twenties.

Will glanced at the corner window of his daughter's room. An early riser like her father, Will knew that fifteen-year-old Bernadette – who went by Detta, and then only to her father and mother, as well as a few close friends – had already been up for an hour, making her mother's favorite coffee, toasting the cocoa bread from the Ghanaian bakery on Greene Street, poaching two eggs.

After sixteen years of marriage Will Hardy had awakened one day to find himself blindsided by his own blindness. Somehow he had not seen any of the warning signs of his life and marriage drifting away.

The main reasons, at least as Will saw it, or wanted to believe, were his long hours and dozens of added responsibilities on the tenure track, obligations that kept him away from home for sixty to seventy hours a week, and many times the weekends.

Will and Amanda had been at chilly arm's length all spring, saying things like 'excuse me' when they passed each other in the narrow hallway of the apartment. They'd done much of their communicating, such as it was, via Post-It notes on the refrigerator.

It was Will's decision to move out, not wanting it to get to the point where it would be Amanda's choice. He figured if he moved first, moving back would still be possible.

And all this time Detta Hardy had been the tolerant and reluctant referee, living an only-child's nightmare, the daughter of a psychologist and a social worker, two people who were supposed to fully understand all this.

In the early years of their marriage Will and Amanda had tried to have a second child, seeing every fertility doctor in Manhattan that either of their benefit packages would allow. It was not to be. There would only be Bernadette and for that Will Hardy felt eternally blessed.

He wondered if she was faithfully taking her meds.

2

Located in the heart of Greenwich Village, New York University was one of the largest private non-profit institutions in the country, with centers on the Upper East side, as well as the MetroTech Center in Brooklyn.

On this Monday morning Will's first class of the new year was a forensic core course with thirty-two students. The class was held in a tiered, medium-sized lecture hall with one hundred seats, fitted with a pull-down screen and state of the art video projector.

Psychology of Violence covered, among other topics, case law as it applied to risk assessment and the treatment of violent patients, as well as sexual violence.

Today's lecture was titled *Medium Cruel*, the designation a play on Haskell Wexler's *Medium Cool*.

Will took a deep breath before opening the door to the hall. He had done this many times, and each time, at the precipice of a new year, he felt the same trepidation, the same sense of anxiety and unease, the belief that he was in all ways a fraud, taking his salary under false pretenses.

He opened the door anyway.

'Good morning,' Will said as the last two students hurried in and found their seats. He knew only a handful of the students, but they surely knew him. In addition to his CV and publishing history he had also consulted on the TV police dramas *Brooklyn Steel* and *Station 21*.

At a smaller school, these credits might have made Will Hardy a modest celebrity. At NYU the star-bar was much higher, being the alma mater of Woody Allen, Burt Lancaster, Philip Seymour Hoffman, Neil Simon, and Martin Scorsese.

After welcoming the students to the new academic year, and to his class, Will offered a brief introduction to the lecture.

'We've all seen these TV shows and asked ourselves if they are accurate depictions of not only crime in America, but also of the men and women who fight the good fight. As of this fall season, nearly fifty percent of all primetime drama is about police, fire departments, or medical facilities. Clearly, the interest in these subjects is as high as ever.'

Will lowered the lights, and started the video, a compendium of scenes from popular police TV dramas over the years: *Blue Bloods, Homicide: Life on the Street, Beretta, Miami Vice, NYPD Blue, Cagney and Lacey*, even the original *NYPD*, starring Frank Converse and Jack Warden.

When the lights came up, Will began his talk.

'It seems, especially in western societies, that what happens at eight p.m., on prime time television – where we see no end to gun play, extreme physical violence, and sexual sadism – at eleven p.m. becomes tragedy, with newscasters offering solemn expressions and an earnest, sotto voce recounting of the day's horrors.

'Violence sells deodorant and cell phones and beer and luxury sedans at eight o'clock. At eleven o'clock the news presents the same heinous acts as fact, but this time our reaction is not to immediately jump on Amazon to buy the widgets, but rather to wring our hands and walk around with signs saying *stop the violence.*

'Which is the real culture?' Will asked of the room. 'Prime time or night-time? If violence is truly abhorrent to us all, why do we watch it for three hours every night, reveling in each gunshot, each thrown punch, each citizen violated in some terrible way?'

A hand went up. The student was David Kleinman, a near genius twenty-year-old who had already earned his BA. Will acknowledged him.

'I read somewhere that you worked on *Brooklyn Steel.*'

'That's right.'

'If you don't mind me asking, what, exactly, did you do on the show?'

The truth was Will did quite a bit of standing around, eating craft service, and watching the younger female extras on the show adjust their costumes.

'I answered their questions about procedure and motivation,' Will said. 'To the best of my ability.'

'That show was canceled mid-season.'

Will amended his posture, gearing up for a skirmish. 'It is called show *business*, after all. Sometimes compromises must be made.'

'What sort of compromises?'

Let's see, Will thought. Reality, character, plot, plausibility, motivation.

'Not much,' Will said. 'Once in awhile we discussed procedural aberrations.'

Another raised hand. A pretty young woman named Jenny Barclay, a sociology major from Evanston, Illinois. Will called on her.

'What sort of aberrations?' she asked.

It was a soft grounder.

'Well, on any given prime time cop show, we are usually presented with a crime before the credits roll and the first ad break. Yes?'

Nodding heads. A few students shifted in their seats.

'As the show progresses our intrepid detectives conduct due diligence, and eventually discover where the suspect is working, usually at a loading dock. Cut to our cops spotting the subject from a block or so away. It is at this point they yell the man's name. Invariably, the suspect takes off running, which allows for an exciting foot chase through the streets of Manhattan. Ultimately, the suspect gets hit by a cab, and is triumphantly taken into custody. Cue pithy exit line, roll end credits.'

Will looked at the class. These agreeably cynical students were rapt.

'I submit that it might be better procedure to quietly sneak up behind the subject, and place him in handcuffs. That said, this would not allow for the ubiquitous overturned fruit cart.'

Kleinman again. 'Are there any police shows you *do* like?' he asked. 'Do any of them get it right?'

'I quite like the original *Prime Suspect*. Can't go far wrong with Helen Mirren, can you?'

Silence.

'Then there's Robson Green. Small but mighty. *Touching Evil, Wire in the Blood*, all that.'

Will hit the pedal.

'There used to be a show called *Cracker*. The main character was an alcoholic, degenerate gambler, an unapologetic womanizer called Edward "Fitz" Fitzgerald. Fitz was a criminal psychologist, not unlike your esteemed Dr Hardy. Except for the unapologetic part.'

A few polite laughs.

'The character was played by Robbie Coltrane, who also played—'

'Hagrid,' Kleinman said. 'In the Harry Potter films.'

'Exactly. You know your crime shows.'

'Don't like them, don't watch them,' he said. 'I know my Harry Potter films.'

Will cleared his throat, headed for the finish line. 'I also quite like *Broadchurch*. It's a bit of a soap opera, but I think it's one of the—'

'Those are all British shows.'

Another gauntlet. 'I suppose they are,' Will said, as if this was just coming to him for the first time. He'd spent a year abroad at Oxford and it was there that he began his love affair with British crime shows. Add to this his ten months of DVDs while attached to a British Army Intelligence unit in Iraq, and his tastes were all but set.

'Aside from the ones you were paid to consult on, any American shows?' Kleinman added.

Will glanced at the wall clock. Was he really only forty minutes into his first class of the new semester? Did he really have another three months of this? He looked back at David Kleinman and asked:

'Does *Dragnet* count?'

3

Growing up in Dobb's Ferry, a small town in Westchester County, Will had never considered a life in academia, had indeed been nothing more than an average student of limited attention span and scant ambition. His sports were baseball and basketball; his music was whatever was in the top 40.

Will's father Michael had been a firefighter with FDNY, as well as an outdoorsman, shade tree mechanic and writer, introducing his only son in equal measure to the finer points of tying lures, changing the points and plugs on muscle cars, as well as the works of Jack London and William Trevor.

After ten years working ladder companies in Brooklyn and Staten Island, Michael Hardy was assigned to Rescue Company One. Organized in 1915, the company was called in to incidents where rescue operations were needed, often to rescue injured or trapped firefighters.

It took less than a year for Michael to receive his first commendation for bravery, and less than three years to be promoted.

There were many in the company, and indeed across FDNY, who believed Michael Hardy was being fast tracked to captain.

It all ended on a hot July day in Will's tenth year.

The call came in of a firefighter trapped in the basement of an apartment on 125th Street in West Harlem. Rescue Company 1 responded.

As young Will would learn over the following weeks, his father entered the building through a broken window on the first floor, making his way to the basement laundry room, where the fire had started due to faulty wiring. There Michael Hardy found James Wilton, probationary firefighter, just twenty-three years old, a father with two small children.

When Michael Hardy extracted the fallen firefighter, the barely conscious Wilton told him that there was a baby still trapped in the laundry room. Michael, against his captain's orders, ran back in to the burning building.

It was somewhere on the concrete steps leading to the lower level that a fuel oil tank exploded, the shards of steel slicing through his protective gear like bullets.

It would be an hour before the captain of Rescue Company 1 would learn the truth, that James Wilton had been mistaken. The infant had already been rescued.

Michael Hardy died during surgery that night in Mt Sinai Hospital.

For the next three years, in the wake of his numbing grief, young Will Hardy read everything he could on the causes, nature and characteristics of fire, its mythos and lore. He studied everything he could find at the libraries regarding the mindset of those who started fires, their motives and twisted rationales, often attempting to absorb texts far beyond his reading comprehension level. He learned the difference between the mind of an arsonist and that of a pyromaniac. He learned about the Triangle Shirtwaist Factory fire, the Hartford Circus fire, the tragedy of

19

Our Lady of the Angels. He learned the names Peter Dinsdale and David Berkowitz.

In the next three years, as only child, with no extended family nearby, Will also learned to care for his mother.

Sarah Hardy was a brittle woman, even before the tragedy of her husband's death. A lifelong sufferer of depression, she was often lost for weeks to her moods, but was always there for her family, if only in daily constancy, the mechanics and rote of suburban life.

Each morning Sarah Hardy would rise before dawn, dress for the day as if she were going to an office, artfully apply her makeup and perfume. With breakfast dishes cleared, she would walk to the living room where she would sit for hours, china cup growing cold, the newspaper opened to the Style section, often unread.

After her husband's death Sarah grew increasingly morose and distant, sometimes going days and weeks without uttering a word.

The only times Sarah Hardy would talk, really opening up to her son, was when she came down from her manic states. In those rare moments, late at night, she would tell Will about her childhood, her hopes and dreams as a young girl, her fantasies and fears. In these times Will saw the woman who had lived a life of imagination and insight, a woman who felt the grass beneath her feet, the sunlight on her face.

On the day Will Hardy's world ended for the second time he came home from school a few minutes late. It was a Wednesday afternoon in mid-March. Will found his mother, still in her robe and slippers, sitting on the couch instead of her favorite chair. Her eyes were closed, her hands folded. At first Will thought she was asleep, but his mother never took naps during the day. She barely slept at night.

When Will stepped closer he saw that something was wrong with her makeup. She had applied it too heavily, too hastily. It gave her a spectral, clownish appearance. When he saw the empty pill vials neatly arranged on the end table, their caps orderly placed on the seat cushion next to her, he knew.

He watched for many minutes, waiting and hoping for his mother to draw a breath, to stir, to open her eyes. She did not. In those long minutes Will lost all sense of time and motion. He would later recall standing in the basement at his father's workbench, the smells of natural gas and 3-in-One, the flinty redolence of oil on sandstone.

The first recollection that stayed in his memory was sitting on his bicycle in Gould Park. He remembered riding home as fast as he could, certain that when he arrived he would find himself mistaken, that he would discover his mother in the kitchen methodically preparing their supper, finding that all would be as it was when the day began.

But he did not return to find his nightmare dissolved.

He returned to an inferno.

4

The Palladium Athletic Facility was on East 14th Street. In addition to its deep-water pool, and 3,000 square foot weight room, it housed a lower level with state of the art stair-steppers, treadmills, elliptical trainers, and stationary bicycles.

When Will turned the corner, at just after noon, he saw Trevor standing near the entrance. One of his closest friends, NYPD Detective Trevor Butler was a barge of a man, broad through the waist and chest, with fiery red hair and beard to match.

They'd met when Will was studying at Oxford. Trevor had lectured on the psychology of community policing, a concept in its infancy at the time, and the two men became fast pub mates.

While Will had never considered joining any branch of the armed services – had indeed fully expected to apply to FDNY, only to decide in his junior year in college that he could be of greater service as a behavioral therapist and teacher – Trevor

Butler was a reservist with the Territorial Army. Third generation soldier, third generation cop.

Before the UK military launched Operation Telic, and Trevor was called up, he told Will of an attachment that was deploying with the regular army. Trevor's interest and education in psychological operations placed him in a unit that interrogated captured prisoners in the field, and he put in a word that Will might be a good fit for an American contractor of civilian deployment.

Will had thought the idea insane, but after a few weeks of coaxing from Trevor, along with more than a few bottles of Jameson, he agreed.

What had started as a fast friendship in the pubs of Oxfordshire, became a bond forged on the sand-choked highways of Fallujah.

As Will got closer to his friend, who had agreed to start an exercise regimen with Will as his taskmaster, Will noticed that the big man's hoodie and matching sweat pants still had the price tags on them.

Will tried not to look.

As they warmed up on their stationary bicycles Trevor told Will about some of the cases he was working. As a detective in the 112th Precinct, there was never a shortage of tales.

In turn, Will told Trevor about his first day, specifically about being grilled about *Brooklyn Steel*. Trevor Butler also consulted on the show.

'The student asked me what TV cop shows I liked,' Will said.

'You didn't mention *Broadchurch*, did you?'

'I did.'

'Oy.'

Will laughed. 'What is everybody's problem with that show? I kind of like it.'

'I think it's a David Tennant/*Doctor Who* thing. Once you play The Doctor ... '

While Will was in half-committed training mode for an upcoming triathlon in Lake Dunmore, Trevor Butler was here because of a recent health scare. Doctor's orders to lose twenty pounds and cut out all added sugar.

Will had a *kyokushin* session scheduled for one o'clock. He'd considered inviting Trevor to the full-contact karate class, but decided to take this one step at a time.

As they began to slow, and Trevor could once again breathe, he asked: 'Whatever happened with that kid? The one from the video store. What was his name again?'

'Anthony,' Will said. 'Anthony Torres.'

A few weeks earlier Will received an email from a member of one of his professional organizations, the New York Behavioral Therapy Association. He did not know the sender of the email, but that was not unusual. Along with *curriculum vitae* and publishing history, the organization's registry listed a brief biography and special areas of interest of its members.

The email contained a short case history of a fifteen-year-old boy named Anthony Torres who had recently been arrested for stealing merchandise from a West Village video store. The NYBTA member tagged the email with the note that suggested Will might be interested in taking the boy on as a *pro bono* patient, if time and circumstance allowed.

Will was interested. He immediately called Trevor and had him pull Anthony Torres's file.

If the boy was convicted of this crime, which had the potential to become a strong-arm robbery charge, there was a chance he would be forced to leave his current accommodation, a minimum security group residence called Near Home, and be placed in a much tougher juvenile facility upstate.

Will had not done much patient work in the past few years, but it was clear that Anthony Torres was on the cusp of going deeper into the system, and looked to be heading to Riker's Island. His plight, and specifically his history, got Will's attention.

'Are you going to follow up?' Trevor asked.

'I already did,' Will said. 'I talked to him on the phone for an hour last week.'

'Wow,' Trevor said. 'Most of the kids I collar don't say two words.'

'He's a smart kid. Probably fronting most of his thug behavior. I'll let you know in the next few days.'

'How so?'

'I'm meeting with him this afternoon.'

Abandoned on the steps of New York Hospital at the age of eleven months, Anthony Torres entered the foster care system, being placed with his first permanent family at two. The boy seemed to thrive. The father was a lineman for Con Ed; the mother was a seamstress who took in work from department stores.

When Anthony was seven, a case worker for ACS noted bruises on the boy's arms. An investigation uncovered a pattern of abuse from Anthony's older foster brother, a boy named DeAndre. The adult DeAndre Tillman was serving a five-year sentence for aggravated assault.

Anthony was removed from the home, and not placed until two years later, this time with a family in Harlem. During the next few years he got into minor scrapes with the law, including a number of incidents surrounding fires being set at his grade school. Nothing was ever proven, but the suspicions were enough for Anthony's foster family to petition to have him removed from their home. He was.

Since that time Anthony had bounced around the system, not staying in any one facility more than six months.

Will had also read the summary of Anthony's recent arrest

for shoplifting. When apprehended on the sidewalk outside the video store, Anthony had four items in his possession; DVDs for which he had not paid. The movies were *Backdraft, Ladder 49,* and *Frequency,* as well as a boxed set of the first season of the Denis Leary TV series, *Rescue Me.*

All stories of firefighters.

All stories of fire.

5

They met at the McDonald's on West Third. Will knew that Anthony Torres, who had been released pending his court case, was currently in Non-Secure Detention. An NSD facility was a supportive, home-like environment housing about a dozen kids, with close supervision. Anthony had to return to the facility by five-thirty.

At just after two o'clock Will noticed a shadow to his right, near the entrance.

Even though Will had the boy's particulars in the file, had a pair of recent photographs, he was bigger than Will expected.

Anthony was about two inches shorter than Will's six-foot-one, but more muscular. As Will watched him enter the restaurant, looking around for the man he was supposed to meet, Will noticed a slow, deliberate grace.

Will stood, got the boy's attention.

'Anthony,' he said.

The boy looked over. 'Yes, sir.'

'Will Hardy.'

*

'So, let me get this straight, you say the '61 Yankees would've taken the '69 Mets in four straight?' Anthony asked.

They'd begun their small talk with the weather. It was Will's idea, and not a good one. It never was with a teenager. They quickly moved on to sports.

'If they let the series go, say, seventy games, the Mets might've scored three runs total,' Will said. 'It would've been a bloodbath.'

Anthony shook his head. 'No way. The Amazins had Tom Seaver and Cleon Jones and Donn Clendenon. Nolan *Ryan*, man.'

In the lore of the city, and the sport, the 1969 Mets – the first expansion team to ever win the World Series – had been dubbed the Amazing Mets, instantly shortened to the Amazins.

'All honorable men,' Will said. 'Fine baseball players who rose to the challenge. They're just not Yankees.'

It was an argument as old as the Mets franchise. That said, Anthony Torres wasn't yet old enough to know the true heartbreak of being a Mets fan.

'Maybe you're right.' Anthony nodded as he drained his Coke. 'Mantle and Maris,' he said. 'That would've been the bomb, man. I was born too late.'

Will wanted to add that he, too, was born too late to see the 1961 Yankees, but kept it to himself.

It did not go unnoticed to Will that Anthony had called him man. This was good. It implied a level of camaraderie and kinship.

At that moment an FDNY ladder truck siren rose in the near distance. Will tried not to look at Anthony; Anthony looked anywhere but at Will. After a few moments the truck passed, turning the corner onto Avenue of the Americas.

The shrill sound brought them to the reason they were meeting in the first place, and how their time was moving quickly along.

Before Will could attempt a segue, his cell phone chirped.

He usually turned his phone off during a session, but today was different. He was waiting to hear from Amanda. He glanced at the screen. She had texted him.

'Let me guess,' Anthony said. 'You gotta get that.'

'I do.'

Anthony shook his head. 'Shrinks.'

'Gotta represent,' Will said. 'I'll be right back.'

'I'll be right here.'

Will stepped out of the restaurant for a moment, tapped his Messages icon. He read his wife's text.

We on for Friday?

Will texted back, hoping it wasn't too soon, therefore revealing the excitement and desperation he felt.

Friday is good.

Seconds later:

OK. Let me know where.

While the text itself was the best news he could imagine, the postscript sent his heart soaring. After the word *where* she had typed:

xo

Will put his phone away, floated back into the McDonald's.

'All good?' Anthony asked.

'Golden.' Will pointed at the counter. 'You want anything else?'

Anthony shook his head. 'Stuffed. Thanks.'

Will looked at his watch. Of the three mistakes he would

make this day – the first being meeting with the boy in the first place – this would be the second.

'We still have a little time,' Will said. 'Want to come up to my office? It's not too far away.'

Anthony seemed to weigh it all for a few moments.

'Yeah,' Anthony said. 'Okay.'

Will's office was on the fourth floor. It was small and overcrowded and piled high with papers and textbooks, but it had two windows, one of which offered a view of Washington Square, and a corner of the famous arch.

Anthony stood, his hands half in and half out of his pockets, clearly apprehensive and uncertain in this new space. He looked at the photos on the wall.

'That's my wife and daughter,' Will said of a photograph of Amanda and Detta in front of the Schoenfeld Theater on 45th Street. It was taken on the night that Will's good friend and savior Brian Zoldessy – it was on Brian's couch Will had been camping the last three months – had just appeared in a starring role in *The Normal Heart*.

Anthony gave each photograph on the wall a few seconds of his attention. He then turned to Will and said, 'I guess it's about that time, isn't it?'

'Not sure what you mean.'

'It's about that time when you say "our time is almost up".'

Of course, Will thought. Anthony Torres had seen many therapists in his short life.

Will sat down, opened the file. He kept it tilted toward himself, out of Anthony's line of sight. Anthony sat down on a chair in front of Will's desk.

'Tell me what happened,' Will said. 'On the day in question, as they say.'

'I told them. Like, a million times. Two million times.'

'I know what it says here. I'd just like to hear your side. Your words.'

'It was that pregnant lady.'

'What about her?'

'She had two little kids. I opened the door for her when she was leaving the store.'

'And then what?'

'I was on the sidewalk, right? I was holding the door because the lady had her hands full. I was trying to be a gentleman, you know? Trying to do a nice thing. Next thing I know the dude in the Hawaiian shirt comes running out and goes all RoboCop on me. Talkin' about me robbing him. Laid *hands* on me, man.'

'So you say you weren't stealing the items?'

'The DVDs were under my arm. I was going to walk back into the store. I wasn't stealing. I don't steal.'

'What about this report stating that you assaulted the man?'

'I put my hands up. I was defending myself and I accidentally hit him. What would *you* have done?'

'So you didn't strike him.'

'I made contact, but I didn't throw a punch. Didn't even slap him, although I should have. *Man.*'

There were so many reasons not to believe the boy. Will had heard every excuse, every dodge, every maneuver.

'What about this other stuff?' Will asked. 'These incidents at PS 206?'

'All of that was bullshit.'

Anthony did not raise his voice, did not say this with any heat or malice or anger. 'There's bullshit and there's bullshit,' Will said. 'What flavor is this?'

Anthony shook his head, as if to say it was all the same flavor, and maybe it was. He remained silent. Will moved on.

'There were four separate incidents at that school,' Will said. 'Let's talk about the last one.'

31

'What do you want to know?'

'It says when the fire broke out in the teachers' lounge, no one could put you in that room.'

'That's right.'

'But based on your history, when they brought you down to the office, they searched you. You had twenty disposable lighters in your pockets.'

'Twenty?'

'That's what it says.'

'See? Right there. That's straight *up* bullshit.'

'How so?'

'I had twenty-two.'

Will tried to stifle his laugh. Laughing would be unprofessional. He laughed anyway.

'Okay,' he said. 'Fair enough.'

At this they were interrupted. At the door was Janelle Hirsch, an assistant to four profs in the department. Janelle was in her mid-forties, as efficient as she was discreet.

She glanced at Anthony, back at Will. Her face registered that Anthony was not a student. 'Oh, I'm sorry.'

'Not a problem,' Will said. 'What's up?'

'I just need you to sign something. I can come back.'

Will glanced at Anthony. 'Do you mind? It will only take a minute.'

'All good.'

Will stepped out, closed the door behind him. In fact there were three things for him to sign. All were related to the upcoming budget brawls over funding the department. Will dutifully signed, shot off two text messages. When he was done he re-entered his office.

'Sorry about that,' Will said.

'No problem.' Anthony gestured at the family photos. 'You really got it going on, man.'

'What do you mean?'

'Living the life.'

If you only knew, Will thought.

Anthony walked over to the window, looked down at the street below. He seemed to be collecting his thoughts. Will gave him the time.

'I know we're not here to talk about those DVDs,' Anthony finally said. 'Not really.'

'Okay. What would you like to talk about?'

Anthony rocked back on his heels, lowered his shoulders.

'I like looking at it,' he said. 'That's all I can say.'

The statement caught Will off guard. The kid was opening up. It was a moment therapists live for, and Will suddenly felt conscious of every muscle, every nerve, every movement. He knew the answer to his question, but he asked anyway.

'You're talking about fire?'

Anthony took a deep breath. On the exhale he said, softly: 'Yeah.'

'Okay.'

'They say it's about damage, you know? About *causing* damage. About destroying things. Sometimes they say it's about money, too. I don't understand that. Burning things down for the insurance money. That's just stealing, isn't it?'

'Yes,' Will said. 'It is.'

'I don't get that part. For me, when I look at it, I see ... I don't know ... *things*.'

'What sorts of things?'

Another long, collecting pause.

'I see faces. Faces of people I don't even know. People I never *met*.'

'Who do you see, Anthony?'

The boy glanced up. This was clearly difficult for him. 'My father,' he said. 'I've never met him, never even seen a picture of him, but sometimes, in the fire, I see my father's face. He looks like me.'

For a brief moment, Will felt all the air leave the room. He had not expected this boy's wall to come down so soon, if at all.

At that moment, a door slammed in the outer office. Anthony looked back at Will, the spell broken, and in that instant Will knew the boy was done talking.

Will shuffled some papers on his desk, then brought the conversation back around to the moment. There were realities on the table here, and Will felt obligated to discuss them before they were done.

'I'll be honest with you, Anthony. It doesn't look good, you know? The incidents at PS 206 and now this. All these movies about fire. Like you said, we're not just talking about a misdemeanor shoplifting charge. We both know you'll walk on that, pick up another program, maybe go upstate for a while. We're talking big picture. This stuff goes into a jacket, and it sticks with you for a long time. For the duration, if you want to know the truth. And I think you know the truth. I think you know how it all works.'

'What about you? What are you gonna put in that jacket about me?'

Will had not committed to releasing his notes on this session in any official capacity. In fact, he was nowhere on paper as having seen Anthony in any legal or formal sense.

Against his better judgment, against every tenet of proper therapeutic conduct, Will made his third mistake of the day.

'I want you to have this,' he said. He reached into his messenger bag, took out a small package, unwrapped it.

For a few seconds Anthony did not move. He looked at the cell phone in Will's hand, then back at Will. Will understood the reticence. Here was a kid who'd had things given to him and taken away his whole life.

'That's for me?'

'It's yours,' Will said.

'For real?'

'For real.'

Will handed the phone to Anthony.

'It's topped up for three months or so,' Will said. 'The minute count will be up on that screen.'

Anthony flipped open the phone. Will continued.

'You press and hold down the number 1 to retrieve your voicemail. You press and hold down the number 2 to call me. I programmed in my cell number.'

Anthony did not put the phone into his pocket. 'I gotta ask.'

'You want to know why.'

'Yeah. I mean, it's really cool and all, but I don't really—'

Will held up a hand, stopping him. 'You know what a life preserver is, Anthony?'

'That's the thing in those boats, right? The little boats hanging off the side of the big boats?'

'Yes.'

'They named that candy after it.'

Will smiled. Somehow, this had never occurred to him. 'I guess they did,' he said. 'Think of this phone as a life saver. You don't ever have to use it, but if you need it, it's there.'

'So, I can keep this?'

'Absolutely,' Will said. 'It's yours.'

Anthony put the phone in his jacket pocket.

'Tell you what,' Will said. 'I'd like to continue our work together, but only if you want to. You don't have to decide now. Even if you and I don't continue, I think you should move forward with therapy.'

'What's it going to cost me?'

'It won't cost you a dime.'

Will could see that the young man was trying to process it

all. Free phone, free therapy. There had to be a catch. There always was.

'You have my number,' Will said. 'If you want to have another session, you call me and we'll work it out.'

Will extended his hand. Anthony took a moment, then shook hands with him. Anthony's grip was hesitant at first, but firmed up.

'Thanks for, you know,' Anthony said, trailing off. He glanced out the window, back. 'Thanks.'

'You're welcome.'

As Will prepared to leave, putting the papers he needed for the night into his briefcase, he could not find his Day-Timer. In it were all his important contact numbers, as well as his schedule for the next few months. Although he had all the data on his phone, and his desktop, he still liked to use a paperbound book. It was a holdover from his mother. Sarah Hardy was a meticulous planner and note-taker.

He gave the search a few extra minutes, then relented.

He must have left it at home.

6

The man was taller than she remembered, but this was not as surprising as it might have been to some. He was nearing sixty, with dyed black hair and jumpy, little dog eyes. He wore a tan duffel coat, frayed at the cuffs.

His name was Elton T Matthews, but she expected him to lie about this, if they got to that stage, just as he lied to the world about his height.

This Rivertown Buffet had nearly fifty steam pans split between three lines: roast beef to Gulf shrimp to bread pudding to creamed spinach, even an omelet station. The management put up their all-you-can-shovel shingle on Route 44 around 4 p.m., and the place was starting to get mobbed.

Elton Matthews was bringing up the rear of a group heading to the main entrée line. She edged up behind the man, stepped to the side, gave her hair a quick toss, then cleared her throat. When he glanced at her, she made eye contact. *Deep* eye contact.

'Hey there,' she said.

The man looked her over, as if she were a Holstein, not the least bit shy in his appraisal. 'Hey, yourself.'

'Something smells *really* good.' She made some high drama of sniffing the air.

The man smiled. Yellowed uppers with a gold cap on the right. 'Must be my Old Spice.'

She wondered if they still made Old Spice. She'd long ago figured it went the way of English Leather, Brut and Hai Karate, but you never knew.

'Name's June,' she said.

Elton Matthews hesitated a telling second. 'Arthur.'

She was right. He lied about his name. Then again, so did she. June was her mother's middle name.

After picking up plastic trays, they each grabbed a dinner plate and a pre-rolled silverware package.

'I've seen you around, you know,' she said, seasoning the words with a little extra spice.

'Have you now?'

'I have. Good-looking man such as yourself gets noticed. Especially by an old bird like me.'

'*Old*? I've got cardigan sweaters older than you, darlin'.'

She laughed. She was supposed to blush, too, but it had been a while. Too long, in fact. She made a mental note to work on this.

'I'll tell you how old I am,' she said. 'You know how they say people start shrinking with age?'

'I've heard that very thing.'

'Well, I believe I'm getting smaller by the day.' She picked up a pair of tongs, put some pulled pork on her plate. Then a little more. 'Was a time when I was heading the other way, if the truth be known. Mama used to call me Dandy when I was a little girl. Short for dandelion because I grew like a weed in summer.'

38

As they moved down the line, she checked the day's date on her watch. 'You were here last Tuesday, am I right about that?'

Elton Matthews pretended to think about this for a long moment. 'As a matter of fact I was.'

'I was here with my sister, see, and we came up to this barbecue bar for seconds. You were bellied up right about where you're standing now.'

'You *do* have a good memory.'

'For some things.'

'I like that in a woman.'

He moved a little too close to her. It was a violation of her personal space, as they say in the big city, but she had expected this, too. Hell, she'd asked for it.

'So, either I'm shrinking, or you've gotten a bit taller in the past week or so,' she said.

His expression slot-machined from trust to suspicion then back. In the end, he went with trust. It was a mistake.

'You got me,' he said.

'I do?'

Matthews looked around the restaurant with a conspirator's eye, leaned in, and whispered, 'Can you keep a secret?'

'I'd like to tell you I can, but I simply cannot,' she said. 'Proceed with caution, sir.'

He looked down, lifted a pant leg, revealing a gaudy red sock, and one of his cheap loafers. He said, even more softly now, 'I'm wearing the lifts. Got them mail order a few years back. Secret Tall is the brand.'

'You don't say.'

'I do so.'

Plates piled high, they walked over to an empty booth. With a glance at the table he asked her to join him. With a nod she agreed. They put down their trays. Before they sat she said, 'Got a question for you, Arthur.'

'Shoot.'

'If you were to slip off those shoes and lifts, and I were to measure from the floor to the tip of your nose, what do think I would find?'

'What?'

'I'm thinking it would be precisely sixty-two and one-quarter inches. Give or take nothing at all.'

Suddenly, Elton Matthews – who also went by the names Arthur Kendrick, William Pastor, and Findlay Grimes – was no longer interested in invading her personal space. In fact, it appeared as if he wanted nothing better than to be out of her orbit all together. 'What kind of question is *that*?'

She reached into her bag, pulled out a five by seven color photograph. The picture was a racked-focus shot of a double hung window. She pointed at the top pane. 'See that smudge right there? That smudge was made by a man's nose.'

It was clear that Matthews recognized the location, and the window. He said nothing. His hands began to tremble.

'They tell me that the tip of a man's nose is as unique as his fingerprints,' she said. 'No two alike in the entirety of the world. Ain't that something?'

She had no idea if this were true or not, but sweet *Jesus* in a gold Corvette it sounded good.

'Of course, it would be higher up on the window if you were wearing your lifts, but you weren't wearing them on the night in question. No, sir. You were wearing your running shoes. A pair of size nine Asics purchased from the Shoe Barn in Eastlake.'

Matthews opened his mouth but, for a few seconds, nothing came out. 'How did you—'

'Running shoes for a man running afoul of the law. What you did was, you stood on the back porch – this one right here, at 5665 Cheshire Lane – and you peeked in the window. You always peek for awhile, don't you? Then you broke down the back door and you attacked Miss Wanda Chester.'

As Elton Matthews made a slow move for his weapon, a Buck knife he kept in a sheath at the small of his back, she edged over the hem on her suit coat to reveal the SIG-Sauer holstered on her hip. Right next to that was her badge. She'd considered packing her Beretta, but that was a more elegant weapon, as firearms go, and she reserved it for formal affairs.

When Elton Matthews saw the firearm his eyes got appropriately wide. His hand stopped halfway to the sheath. Moments later two mammoth shadows drew across the table.

For so many reasons, she had requested the Reese twins for this detail. Deputies Dale and Donald Reese – Dale had the sideburns, Donnie had the mustache, it was the only way to keep them straight, seeing as their nametags both read D REESE – clocked in at somewhere north of six-foot-two each, and close to five-hundred pounds total. They weren't too good in a sprint, but they were all-state when it came to grappling.

Chief of Police Ivy Lee Holgrave was hoping Elton Matthews would insist on a grapple. He did not disappoint.

After Dale Reese carefully slipped the knife from the man's waistband, Donnie Reese took the suspect to the ground. Hard. During the process, Elton's pulled pork went flying, as the story would be told later that night. Ivy stepped back, checked the front of her suit. It was her working best, purchased at the Calvin Klein outlet store at Aurora Farms. There was not a drop of barbecue sauce on her. This day was getting better and better.

Donnie cuffed the man, then he and Dale lifted Elton Matthews to his feet like an empty bag of Doritos.

'Elton Thomas Matthews, I am arresting you for the aggravated sexual battery of Wanda Marie Chester,' Ivy said. 'You have the right to remain silent.'

41

Matthews remained so, to Ivy's delight. She leaned close to the man's right ear.

'Not sure if they'll let you bring your Secret Tall lifts with you to state prison,' she said. 'Not to worry, though. I'm thinking you're going to have your dance card pretty full. Good looking man such as yourself.'

Elton Matthews just stared at the middle distance. Apparently, he'd had the sass punched out of him.

'Boys?' Ivy asked.

'Yes, ma'am?' Dale and Donnie answered in unison.

God she loved the Reese brothers. She'd hire them away from the Sheriff's office if she had the budget.

'Please take out the trash.'

The Abbeville Police Department was located in six rooms behind the village library on the east side of the town square. A marked door off the parking lot gave way to a short hallway, and a bulletproof Plexiglas window and security drawer to the left. At least, *bulletproof* was the prevailing theory. In all the time since it had been installed – forty-six years next spring – it had never been tested.

The steel door at the end of the hallway opened with a keypad entry code, and led to a small meeting area. To the right was a battered desk for the duty officer; a hard right led to the village's only holding cell.

To the left of the entryway was a cramped coffee room which served as a storage area for the detritus of police work. Ivy had petitioned six years running at the town council meetings for either the funds to put an addition on the station, or funds to rent a secure storage facility. Not a penny so far.

At the back of the station, in what was no more than a large windowless cubicle, was the chief's office, such as it was. Being a bit claustrophobic, upon getting the job, Ivy had immediately bought some framed posters of sunny settings, travel placards for Bermuda, Fiji, and Cancun.

Since buying the posters at a flea market Ivy had not set toe number one on tropical sand. Maybe she'd go this winter, she thought, or perhaps the ghost of Paul Newman would walk into this dreary place, sweep her off her feet, and take her to Ibiza.

Neither scenario seemed likely.

When Ivy returned to her office it was just after 7 p.m. She made herself a pot of coffee, her stomach rebelling at having been exposed to the bounty at the Rivertown Buffet and not eating a bite of it.

She finished her report on the arrest of Elton Matthews and checked the day's activity. With a population of just over two thousand, Abbeville supported three full-time officers, and three part-timers. The two patrol officers on duty this day had responded to seven calls ranging from a domestic disturbance on Martinsville Road, and a break-in at the Culpepper farm on Route 87. Ivy made note of this call, as there had been a few more break-ins at remote farmhouses of late.

There had been a grand total of thirteen citations written that day. Seven moving violations, six parking tickets.

The only other call was one for backup – a mutual aid request in police bureaucratic jargon – from the Middlefield Police Department, regarding a loose horse. According to the summary the horse, a one-year-old colt named Falstaff, and its mother, were safely reunited.

As Ivy did each night before handing over her watch to the night duty officer, she opened the file cabinet and removed a file. She first let her fingers riffle across the tops of the folders, felt each name and case number drawing her into the past, into the bellowing darkness.

She had long ago reconciled the fact that she could, of course, make copies of the documents, and keep these copies at home.

But that would have felt too much like failure, she thought. That would have felt like she was relegating the open cases to history, to the secret, whispered lore of her village.

This would never happen on her watch, Ivy Lee Holgrave had long ago decided.

She owed the dead girls more than that.

7

When Will arrived at Washington Square Park, twenty minutes late, he saw her sitting on a bench – the bench, as he had come to refer to it – and his heart skipped a beat. He was suddenly transported twenty years into the past.

It was where he had first set eyes on Amanda.

Like her mother, Detta Hardy was petite and graceful, a natural athlete. In school her sports were lacrosse and soccer. As a December baby, and thus always younger than her class-mates, Detta was, in theory, a little too small to excel in these sports, but a fierce determination and a commitment to the repetition of practice had secured her a spot on the A-teams for the three years she'd played. Over the past few years Will had tried to get her interested in cycling, and they had taken a few day trips together, but she didn't seem to take to it as he had hoped.

She had her mother's emerald eyes and flawless cameo skin. Where many of her friends had jumped on the fashion juggernaut that was long, flowing hair – Will was pretty sure Detta called it the News-Barbie style – Detta had cut her hair short the previous summer, and kept it so. It framed her pretty face in a way that made her look even younger.

Her one vice, the one accessory to which she had taken, was eyewear. She had, at last count, nearly a dozen pairs of glasses. Some were inexpensive readers, purchased at Duane Reade, but most were top of the line designer frames. Will often wished cycling had taken hold. It was cheaper.

Today, looking so much like her mother, Detta wore a very studious-looking pair of tortoiseshell frames by Kate Spade.

She looked up, saw Will crossing the square, pulled out her earbuds.

'Hi, honey,' Will said.

Detta Hardy tapped her watch, reminding him, as always, that he was late.

The Film Forum was opened in the 1970s as a minimalist space, a haven for small and independent film, with only fifty folding chairs and a single projector. Now located on West Houston, the complex had grown to a three-screen cinema showing a mix of first run, classic, and independent features, and was the only autonomous non-profit theater in the city.

Today they were showing a film in Will's pantheon of classics: Alfred Hitchcock's *Notorious.*

They settled in their seats, perfect locations for the wonderful sound system, about a third of the way back, near the center. Detta knew Will was a little OCD about these things, and she never resisted or rushed him when he was in film fanboy mode.

The print was pristine. Ingrid Bergman never looked more luminous; Cary Grant had never looked more debonair.

After the film they walked in silence to the Starbucks on

46

Sheridan Square. While Will ordered, Detta fired up her phone. With blurred fingers she shot off texts to her friends.

As he waited for their coffees, Will noticed that the kid filling the order, the boy barista in the Rasta Life T-shirt and dirty blond hair tucked up into a slouchy rainbow cap, was smiling at Detta. Will gave the kid a frosty look as he picked up the cups and stepped over to the table.

Detta glanced up from her phone, read her father's vibe. 'What?'

Will nodded toward the counter. 'Do you know him?'

'Who?'

'Justin Babyface over there.'

'No,' she said. 'He's just being nice.'

'Let him be nice somewhere else.'

'He works here.'

'Oh yeah.'

Will made a ceremony of adding milk and sugar. Detta fired off another text, put away her phone.

'What did you think of the film?' Will asked.

Detta gave the question its due. 'I love the way Hitchcock did that shot from the balcony, the one where Alicia gave the key to Devlin so he could get into the wine cellar. That was great.'

Like her father, Detta always referred to actors by their character names.

Detta sipped her latte, slipped effortlessly into therapist mode. 'It's this Friday, right?'

'Is what this Friday?'

'Your date with Mom.'

Will knew that his daughter knew *exactly* when the date was. And the time. 'Yeah.'

'Where are you guys going?'

'I thought we'd meet at Boris.'

Detta pulled a face. 'The place on Bleecker?'

'No good?'

'Dad. You don't want a bunch of slobbering millennials in Aeropostale hoodies.'

'I don't?'

'My God, are you serious? It would be like spending two hours in an Apple Care queue. You want romance, don't you?'

'I want romance.'

'You want piano music and warm lighting, preferably in the 2,700 K range. Do you remember your Kelvin as it applies to the romance axiom?'

'Kinda.'

'Lower is better,' Detta said. 'Especially when you're over thirty. Five thousand Kelvin is in the light-box therapy range. Nobody wants to get frisky in a Walgreens. Well, that's not true, but you know what I mean.'

'Yuck.'

'Plus a million,' she said. 'Most importantly, at the end of the date, you want boozy, outer space kisses in a doorway.'

The image of his daughter making out suddenly lurched across Will's mind. It was scarier than Robert Mitchum in *The Night of the Hunter*.

'What, and I mean *exactly* what, do you know about boozy, outer space kisses?'

Detta ignored the question. She sneaked another peek at boy barista.

'What are you going to wear?' she asked.

Will had only thought about what he might wear Friday non-stop for the past week or so. He had nothing. He was thinking about hitting Barney's on Wednesday, spending money he really didn't have.

'I'm not sure.'

'It's important, Dad. You've got to go for suave, not desperate. Desperate is not a good look for you. It's not a good look for anybody. You sweat when you're desperate.'

'I do not.'

Detta lifted her iPhone, snapped a picture of him. She tapped the screen, turned it to face him. He was sweating.

'It's hot in here,' Will said.

Detta put her phone away.

'But to answer your question, I was thinking about wearing a blazer and slacks,' Will said. 'Not a suit.'

'That works. Wear your navy Zegna, the two-button one Mom got you. It picks up the blue in your eyes.'

'Okay.'

'Mom will notice that you're wearing something she picked out for you. This is brilliant subtext.'

'You don't think your mother will see through such a lame attempt at manipulation?'

'Of course she will. She's been doing it with you for years. Wear it anyway.'

'Okay.'

As they got ready to leave Detta added, 'I won't be able to chaperone, you know.'

On Friday Detta was going to the theater to see *School of Rock*, still a golden ticket. She would be spending the night with her friend Maddie's family in Chelsea.

Ten minutes later they stood on the corner of Barrow and Seventh. Detta lifted a hand, hailed a cab. Before long, a taxi pulled to the curb.

'I forgot to ask,' Detta said. 'How was your first day of school?'

'You know how psych majors are. They parse every syllable.'

'Gee. I never noticed that.'

'I also caught some flak from a know-it-all grad student,' Will said. 'A transfer from Princeton, of all places.'

'Fire at Will.'

Will laughed. It was an old joke of theirs. He opened the taxi door.

Detta kissed him on the cheek, slipped into the cab, rolled down the window.

'So, how often are you checking the Amazon sales rankings?' Detta asked.

'Hardly ever.'

'*Dad.*'

His daughter read him like the back of a cereal box. 'Maybe every ten minutes or so.'

'That's progress. I'm so proud of you.'

'Thanks.'

'I love you.'

'Love you, too.'

As the cab pulled away, Detta glanced out the back window. She waved. In that moment she looked exactly like her mother, right down to the half-smile that had stolen Will's heart so many years ago.

Friday, Will Hardy thought.

He would do this.

He had to.

8

Ivy Holgrave lived in a white frame house a mile north of the village square, at the end of a cul-de-sac off Platteville Road. The house was nearly ninety years old, with a one-bedroom cottage at the rear of the wooded property, as well as a barn, equipment shed, and two acres of what was once a working chicken farm.

When she was growing up, less than two miles away, this had been the Rademaker spread. Jens Rademaker, the patriarch of the clan at the time, had been a crackpot inventor of sorts. From time to time Ivy still found strange items bolted or screwed or welded together as she tilled the back and side yards of her gardens. She could never quite throw them away, keeping them all in a pair of large wooden crates in the barn, just in case she had the inclination to take one of them onto *Shark Tank* one day.

When Ivy flipped on the kitchen light her eye was caught by the glint of stainless steel on the floor near the sink. Out of reflex and memory she reached down to pick up the bowl in order to fill it with water. She caught herself, and for perhaps the hundredth time felt a pang of sorrow.

Amos no longer needed water.

Amos had been her two-year-old Cairn. Over the years, Ivy had had any number of dogs, almost all of them terriers – Jack Russells, Bostons, Westies, Wire Fox, even a pair of Kerry Blues, littermates named Checker and Domino.

Of all the dogs with whom she'd shared her life, none had been half the ratter that Amos was.

In the end it was a critter that was Amos's undoing. Even though he knew better, had been lectured on the subject many times, he chased a raccoon out onto Bluestone Road and was struck and killed by a car.

Ivy knew she should put his bowls in a cupboard, that she should move on, but she couldn't quite bring herself to do it. Not yet.

She flipped through the day's mail, made herself a sandwich, looked out the back door. The lights were on in the small house at the rear of the property.

All was as it should be.

She took her sandwich, and the files, and walked down to the basement.

The photograph was dog-eared, color-leached by time. In it, the girl – no more than twelve or so – stood on the beach at Edgewater Park, the sun overhead casting a thin shadow at her feet. Her eyes sparkled like the lake behind her. She wore the smile of a young girl at the precipice of adolescence on a perfect summer day.

The photograph next to it on Ivy's desk was of the same girl, three short years later. In this photograph her face had all but been destroyed.

Her name was Charlotte Foster.

Charlotte had been found twenty-five years earlier, almost to the day. She was fifteen at that time. No cause or manner of death was ever determined.

That same year three other girls went missing; never found, never returned to their homes.

Ivy turned in her chair, glanced at the tableau behind her. The calendars filled one entire wall, corner to corner, floor to ceiling. There were now more than one hundred, in all different shapes and sizes and paper stock.

The collection had been curated from garage sales and flea markets and house sales throughout the state of Ohio, and had taken Ivy as far as Allentown, Pennsylvania. From across the room the calendars looked bright and colorful and festive, many given away free as premiums for various products and enterprises. *Dr Morse's Indian Root Pills, The Centaur Almanac, Lustrolite Cleveland.*

Ivy had once created the timelines as a spreadsheet, but found it too impersonal and clinical, as if the days and dates did not belong to people, to the girls who had lived them.

When you looked more closely at the calendars you could see what Ivy Holgrave saw: a diary of terrible secrets.

On the wall opposite the calendars was Ivy's collage of photographs. These, too, were a pastiche of images taken and collected over many years. All the subjects were Ohio girls between the ages of twelve and sixteen. All had vanished without a trace. Some of the photographs were more than a century old.

The questions Ivy asked herself on this night were the questions she'd always asked:

Had they willingly gone with their captors? Had they been enticed into a car or a truck or a van by promises of fortune? Of love? Of simple human kindness?

Almost all of the girls were from hamlets and villages. Ivy knew well the thoughts and dreams and desires of small-town girls, the allure of the road.

53

Wherever these girls were headed, they did not arrive. But until that time when the earth returned their bodies, Ivy would keep them on this wall.

Ivy took the bottle of bourbon, switched off the lights, climbed the stairs to the attic. She stepped out of the dormer, sat on the roof, something she had done since she was a little girl.

Beneath the cloudless night sky Ivy looked out over Abbeville, the village of her birth. Death knew the back roads here, she thought. Death knew the girls from poor families, girls who never wore a piece of clothing unstained by another, girls who sang their own lullabies.

Somewhere out there, in the hills and valleys and forests of Holland County, they walked.

They each had a plea for Chief Ivy Lee Holgrave in this year of dark remembrance, this time of harvest.

It was the silent prayer of the vanished.

Find us.

9

If the week rushed by in a blur, Friday dragged on and on. Will had two lectures that morning, bookended around a meeting of the department sub-heads.

At one o'clock he grabbed a takeout lunch and ate in his office, multitasking between reading papers, answering email, making notes on both his rather anemic ideas for a follow-up book to *A Flicker of Madness*, and a syllabus for the next semester.

He managed to sneak away after his last class of the day, just after 3 p.m. As a fast rule, if a professor was on the tenure track, he or she could not have a rigid door, that being unavailable to drop-by students.

Will left anyway. He'd deal with the fallout on Monday.

On the way off campus he played back the voicemail messages on his phone. One was from Anthony Torres:

'Hey. It's Anthony again. This phone is the bomb, man. Don't get me wrong, it's not a Galaxy or an iPhone or anything, but it's cool. I'm kidding! Just so you know, I had to move your speed dial number

to 9 so I could make room for the ladies. Not kidding about that one. Okay. Well. I'll talk to you later. Give me a call, okay?'

Will made another mental note to call the boy back.

Amelie was a small bistro on West 8th Street between Fifth and MacDougall. The restaurant was recommended by a colleague of Will's, a handsome and athletic thirty-year-old bachelor who knew his food and wine, as well as economy of scale when it came to romance.

When Will arrived, ten minutes early, he saw Amanda sitting at the crowded bar. It was, and had always been, her modus. No matter how early Will was, she was there first. Even Bernadette was born two days early.

Tonight, Will took it as a good sign.

Amanda looked stunning in an emerald green dress. Her deep auburn hair was down to her shoulders. She had never looked better to him. He'd thought for a fleeting moment it might have been her absence from his life, but he was wrong. She was, and would always remain, the most beautiful woman he had ever met.

And, as always, men were swarming around her.

Will had gotten much better with his feelings of jealousy of late, more out of the necessity than any kind of personal growth or maturity.

He took a deep breath, crossed the room. When Amanda looked up, she smiled, and Will's heart danced.

Detta was right. He was sweating.

'Sorry I'm so early,' he said.

Amanda turned to the man next to her, the now disappointed junior executive in the gray Brooks Brothers suit.

'This is my husband, Dr William Hardy,' she said.

Husband and *doctor* in the same sentence, Will thought. This was also good.

Without introducing himself, the man shook hands with Will

and, perhaps thinking better of leaving his business card on the bar in front of Amanda, scooped it up and made a hasty retreat.

After they were seated they made menu small talk, weather small talk, political small talk. Everything but Will and Amanda small talk. Finally, when Will ran out of words, he said:

'You look . . .'

Amanda raised an eyebrow, waiting.

'Spectacular?' she asked.

'Yeah,' Will said. 'That.'

'You too,' she said, winking. '*Love* the jacket.'

Will had taken his daughter's advice and worn his blue Zegna. Detta was also right that Amanda would see right through it.

'It was a gift.'

The waiter brought their salads. Will made elaborate work of cutting his kale and chicken into much smaller bites than needed. He'd talked to hundreds of patients in therapy, maybe a thousand students about their grades, had more than a dozen times visited the Clinton Correction facility and counseled low-risk inmates about their problems, but had never once in his life found conversation so daunting.

When the moment drew out into a minute of silence, he just started talking. He told Amanda about Anthony Torres. He gave her the basics regarding the boy's most recent infraction and interaction with the law.

'How old is he?' Amanda asked.

'He just turned fifteen.'

As a social worker, Amanda knew it meant that there was virtually no chance that Anthony Torres would find a permanent home and a loving family. He would scratch and claw his way to eighteen and then become part of the adult system in some way or another. The time for shaping and forming a productive life was rapidly slipping by. It probably already had.

'Are you going to see him again?' Amanda asked.

Will had not told Amanda about giving Anthony a cell phone, or the boy's unanswered voicemail messages. He knew that his wife would give him The Look, the one she reserved for his monumental therapeutic blunders.

'I don't know,' Will said. 'If he calls me and wants to continue, I'll consider it.'

Amanda smiled. 'There's that marshmallow center again.' She raised a wine glass. '"Let us go forth with fear and courage".'

'"And rage to save the world",' Will finished. It was the Grace Paley quote they'd used on each other since the day they'd chosen their respective professions, always at moments when they questioned the wisdom of their selections.

They stopped a few doors down from the steps of their building. It was a moment Will had been dreading, one for which he had been hoping. The next thing he said, or didn't say, could impact the rest of his life.

Amanda said it for him.

'I miss you, Dr Hardy.'

Will wondered if it was the wine talking. He hoped it wasn't. 'You do?'

Amanda nodded.

'I miss you, too.'

She wrapped her arms around his waist, brought her face to within a few inches of his.

'Come home, Will.'

Will felt the world fall away.

'Do I have to?'

'You do.'

'I don't know, I'm pretty booked. After all, I do have the number thirteen hardcover in the *Times*.'

'The new list is out,' Amanda said. 'It's at fifteen.'

'It is?'

'Just saying.'

'Then I might have an opening. When are we talking?'

'Tonight.'

'Okay.'

His wife kissed him. Will remembered what outer space kisses were all about.

Amanda reached into her bag, removed the key fob with the two keys on it, the very one Will had left on the hall table ninety-three days earlier. She handed him the keys.

'I've got to get a few things for the morning,' Will said.

'Don't keep me waiting, sailor.'

Will watched her walk up the steps, and disappear into the lobby. He thought about jogging back to Brian's loft, but it would have taken too long.

He hailed a taxi.

As the cab eased into traffic Will wondered if it would ever be the same for them. If it *could* be the same for them. He wanted it to be the way it was those first, giddy years when Detta was a toddler, when money was tight, when they'd just moved into their first real apartment: lamps on the floor, books in stacked milk crates, frozen microwave meals for dinner.

Will turned on his phone, put in his earbuds. Within seconds he heard the tone that signaled new voicemail. He scrolled through the calls. Five messages total.

It was the most recent one, from just an hour earlier, that caught his attention.

'Ah, shit.'

The call was from Anthony Torres. His sixth of the week, his second of the day. Will had not returned a single one. He hit the button to play the message. This time, Anthony didn't bother to announce who he was.

'They call it Pride. I never knew what it meant. I always thought it

was a good thing, you know? Like when you do something, and you're proud of it. But it isn't a good thing at all.'

Anthony sounded manic, unsteady. Will glanced at his watch. It was almost ten-thirty. He knew that the curfew at the group home was nine o'clock; lights out at ten.

'But it's all good, you know?' Anthony continued. *'In the end, it's all good. I know you're busy, Dr Hardy.'*

Dr Hardy, Will thought. He had gone from *man* and *bro* back to Dr Hardy. Anthony was distancing himself, putting back in place the boundaries. And who could blame him? Will suddenly felt as if he had failed the young man, another grown-up in a long line of adults who had made and broken a promise. More than one.

'I read something today. From Marcus Aurelius. "Do every act of your life as though it were the very last act of your life." How about that, huh? Makes you think about whatever it is you're going to do. Pride. If you want to counter it, you feel hope. Hope, man. Her name was Eva. You'll see. After tonight you'll understand everything.'

Without really knowing why, Will pressed the button to save the voicemail. He then hit the call back button. A few moments later he got the generic voice of the robot woman telling him that the user was currently unavailable. Anthony had never programmed his own greeting.

If you'd called him back after the first voicemail, you'd know that, Will.

He clicked off, redialed. He listened to the choices, hit the number to leave a message.

'Yeah, Anthony, this is Will. Dr Hardy. I got your messages. Sorry I haven't gotten back to you sooner. Crazy week. I'll tell you all about it when we see each other next. Anyway, I know it's late, and you're probably asleep with your phone off. In case you're still up, give me a call. I'll be up for a while. Got my phone in hand. If not, I'll talk to you tomorrow. Thanks.'

Will hesitated, finding no other words to say, none that would right the ship he had all but scuttled. He ended the call.

He got out of the cab about five blocks early, made a search on his phone for the number of the group home where Anthony lived. He dialed it. After navigating the menu, he reached the supervisor on duty, made his inquiry.

'Anthony isn't here,' the woman said.

'What do you mean?'

'I mean he didn't make curfew. He's not here.'

Will felt his heart plummet. He knew that, with the misdemeanor assault charge hanging over Anthony's head, every infraction was going to weigh heavily on the disposition. 'Any idea where he might be?'

'Are you his case worker?' she asked.

It was going to be too complicated to explain. 'Yes,' Will said. 'Dr William Hardy.'

'To answer your question, we have no idea where he might be. I'm sorry to say that Anthony took a car belonging to a woman who is on the dietary staff here.'

'What do you mean *took*?'

'I mean her car is gone. Video from the parking lot shows Anthony taking it. It appears that he stole the keys from her purse.'

Will closed his eyes and asked the question. 'Did you call the police?'

'I'm afraid we had no choice. The staff member did not give Anthony permission to borrow her car. I'm afraid it's now been reported as stolen.'

Will used his best therapist voice, calm and reassuring. 'I'm sure it's all a big misunderstanding. When Anthony returns, and I'm sure he will, could you have him call me? It doesn't matter what time.'

'Of course,' she said, sounding anything but convinced.

Will gave the woman his number, made as graceful an exit from the conversation as he could. A few seconds later he called Trevor Butler, got his voicemail, left a message.

Will walked quickly down Fifth, through Washington Square, something he had done thousands of times before, but not with this sick sense of foreboding building inside him.

As he rounded the corner onto Prince Street he looked up, saw that the lights were on in the living room and the bathroom. Amanda's room, and Detta's room, were dark. It seemed to take forever to get the keys out of his pocket, and the key into the front door.

When he got to the top of the stairs, it all came to him in a blinding fury. He recalled the smell as if it were yesterday, the harsh redolence of accelerant at his father's workbench.

Gasoline.

10

There was no sound coming from the front room; no television, no radio, no music. Just a still and deathly silence.

In that instant Will flashed on the hundreds of times he had walked through this door, how he would often hear his wife's voice singing along to one of her Broadway CDs.

'Amanda?'

Nothing.

Will fully opened the door. What he saw was horrifying beyond measure. He took it all in within one numbing second.

The living room furniture had been pushed to the walls. Anthony Torres was sitting on a dining room chair in the center of the room. On either side of him were five-gallon gas cans.

Amanda sat in a chair next to him, unmoving, slumped forward, her skin pallid, her eyes closed.

Around the room were small puddles of gasoline. The couch looked to be soaked in it. At Amanda's feet was a propane tank.

Will glanced at Anthony. The boy's eyes were red. His feet were moving up and down with frenzied energy.

'Dr Hardy,' Anthony said. 'It looks like our time is almost up.'

Will opened his mouth, but no words came out. Fear had parched his ability to speak. He swallowed hard.

'You don't have to do this, Anthony,' he managed. 'It's not too late to walk away.'

The boy said nothing.

'Please talk to me. We can—'

'Talk? I don't think so, Dr Hardy. I called you.'

Will tried to make sense of it all. How did this boy know where he lived? How did he know anything about his life?

He knows where you live because you let him into your life, Dr Hardy. He stole your Day-Timer that day in the office, and now he is here to settle his bill.

'I know, Anthony. It's just that—'

'Did you get my messages? Of course you did. It's a stupid question, isn't it? Like when you're texting someone back and forth, and in the last text you tell them that you're going to call them. Then you call them *one second later* and they don't answer the phone. What flavor of bullshit is *that*?'

As he said this, Anthony opened his right hand. In it was a lighter. He tapped it on his palm.

No, Will thought. *God no.*

'Want to know the funny part? I did all of it. Can you believe that? Every single thing. All the shit they said I did, and a lot more. A *lot* more.'

Another tap of the lighter.

'I was living with this family up in Dutchess County this one time,' Anthony said. 'The daddy was a big fat guy, worked for some insurance company. He owned it, I think. Nice house, nice furniture, lots of flat screens. They had this aquarium, too, this huge thing that cost over two thousand dollars, if you can believe

64

that. The daddy he *loved* his fish. Some of them cost more than a hundred dollars each. Think about that. A hundred dollars for a *fish*.' Anthony shook his head. 'Never understood it. Give me a dog all day, you know? Some breed with belly fire. Pit, maybe.

'One day when they were all out, I scooped all those fancy fish out of that aquarium, and put them in a saucepan with some water. I put the pan on the stove, and turned up the heat. Perfect blue flame, man, just kissing the bottom of the pan like a lover. It wasn't high heat, you know? Just enough.

'As the water warmed up, as it got hotter, the little bubbles came up, and I saw it in their eyes. The *panic*. They started swimming faster and faster and faster. They knew they were trapped, just like me. Nowhere to go.' Anthony looked up. Will was chilled by the calm he now saw in the boy's eyes.

'To them it was all about the water. The *hot* water. They understood that. But to me it was about the fire. Just like you.

'Maybe you all let me get away with it, all of you, because you have something to hide.'

Will took a full step forward. 'Anthony, I can—'

Anthony turned the wheel on the lighter, three times in quick succession. Will could see the sparks jumping ever further into the air, seeking the accelerant.

Will froze.

'Ever think about that? You people always do, but you never admit it.' Another three turns of the wheel. A flash of flame jumped through the air, then vanished. 'I've met a lot of shrinks, bro. Probably more than you. You all think you're smarter than everybody, but maybe not, right? I mean, if you're so smart, what am I doing here?'

'Stop, Anthony.'

'What did *you* do, Dr Hardy? What is *your* crime?'

Will had to move, to do something. As he took another step forward, it brought him that much closer to the kitchen.

His horror deepened. In addition to the stench of gasoline, he smelled the gas from the range. He saw that all four knobs on the stove were turned to full.

Will looked at Amanda. She stirred.

She was alive.

Anthony held up a lighter, again flicked the wheel. Will instinctively brought his hands to his face. Nothing caught fire. Not this time.

'He told me you wouldn't call,' Anthony said. 'He knew.'

'Who told you this, Anthony? What are you talking about?'

Instead of answering, the boy reached into his pockets, took out more lighters. They were not all disposable lighters. Some were vintage, old school Zippos. He put them around the chair. There were seven in all.

Will sensed movement to his right. It was Detta. She was standing in the doorway that led to the hall.

She saw Will first.

'Dad? What's that smell?'

His daughter rubbed the sleep from her eyes, and moments later took in the scene. Will saw the growing confusion on his daughter's face. Then the fear.

'Dad?'

Will held out his right hand. 'Come over here, honey,' he said. 'Come to me. Right now.'

Detta did not move. Will saw her eyes flick between Amanda and himself, then to Anthony Torres. She glanced down, saw the gas cans at Anthony's feet.

Within moments she grasped the full horror of what was happening. She took a half-step toward her mother.

'No!' Will screamed. '*Stop!*'

Anthony slowly stood up. He seemed to fill the entire room, as if his shoulders spanned wall to wall. He looked monstrous. He glanced at Detta.

'You can't be here.'

Detta began to cry.

'You have to go,' Anthony said. 'You weren't supposed to be here. Neither of you.'

'Don't do this,' Will said. 'Please.'

'Me? I didn't do this. *You* did this. Just like your mother.'

'What's he talking about, Dad?'

'She is Hope,' Anthony said.

And then Will heard it. It was a tiny sound, the sort of noise that passes in the background of daily tedium, unnoticed, unremarkable. A small click. It was the demarcation point between what Will's life had been up to this moment, and whatever it would become in its aftershock.

As both lighters sparked to life, igniting the world, Amanda leaped to her feet and pushed Bernadette toward Will. The power of the monstrous blast propelled Amanda backward, through the glass doors, onto the balcony, over the edge, and out into the night sky.

Will and Detta were slammed into the hallway. Will felt the drywall shatter at his back, felt the searing heat on his face, saw the interior of the apartment explode in a barrage of scorched, shimmering air.

The last thing Will Hardy thought, in the moment before his world went black, was that his father had been right.

Fire has a voice.

Winter – Ravens

Being the true diary and journal of Eva Claire Larssen

December 11, 1868

There is so much to do! Christmas is coming in two weeks and we are busy making everything ready. Godwin Hall is full of visitors, and they are from all points on the compass. One man is an actor from England! He left a silver dollar for Deirdre under his pillow, as she attends his room. He is very handsome, and when Deirdre talks of him she does not stammer.

December 15, 1868

The people who own Godwin Hall – the Schuyler family – are warm and decent people. Mr Schuyler is tall and strong, always easy with a smile. He often smells of woodsmoke and resin. Mrs Schuyler is rotund, like Mama was. She snorts when she laughs sometimes.

The clientele here is often quite elegant, much like you would imagine. It is another world to me, though, a world in which I feel like a stranger.

December 16, 1868

In the ballroom there have been many entertainments, such as chorales and dances and raffles. This morning we made cakes and trimmed the tree. But the gaiety of Godwin Hall is not what makes my heart beat faster. There is something else about the Hall that makes me swoon. The son of the owners is a tall, shy boy of seventeen years. His eyes are an ocean blue, and he walks with great poise, even when doing the most menial chores. For the longest time I thought he might have been mute, as I never heard him say a word.

Today he talked to me. He asked me if I was looking forward to Christmas. I said I was, very much.

His name is Willem.

December 18, 1868

Zeven Farms, where Veldhoeve is located, is decorated like a fairy tale kingdom. People come from miles around to look at the displays. I think it might actually be enchanted. I am told that, during the war, many orphaned children came to stay here. My room is in the attic, by the back. I am an orphan of the war, too.

December 19, 1868

We spent the morning straining pumpkins for the pies. The owner of Zeven Farms, Dr Rinus van Laar, brought them over to the Hall for us himself. He is a kindly old man. He lost his wife many years ago. I think he is quite lonesome. It seems he has taken a shine to me as his granddaughter.

December 20, 1868

I've had the most unusual day. It began ordinary enough with the morning chores of baking the breads, grinding the coffee, collecting the eggs for the guests of Godwin Hall. Then, after service, I returned to my room. On the way up the back stairs, Dr van Laar met me, and said he had something to show me. He led me back to the main house, and down a long corridor. At the end was a small room called *camera lucida*, and it is wondrous. If you sit in a chair, in the center, you can see for miles and miles, as if you were flying through the treetops. You can even see people who are no longer here. Dr van Laar says it is all done with daguerreotypes and special glass lenses, but he has a twinkle in his eyes, so I am not sure. I think there is magic here. Dr van Laar told me I could come up here anytime, and I think I will.

He says it will be our secret.

December 21, 1868

The Winter Solstice Dance was at Godwin Hall tonight. Folks from as far away as Cleveland came in their finery. It was a lot of work for us preparing the food, but it was all so festive. It lifted my spirits. As Willem danced with a rich girl named Darcy he kept looking at me.

December 22, 1868

Someone told Willem that today is my birthday. I found the most beautiful locket on the pillow of my bed. It looks to be yellow gold with a seed pearl embellishment in the shape of a white bird. I will cherish it always.

December 24, 1868

It is Christmas Eve. Most of the girls who work at Godwin Hall are with their families today. I am by myself in the back attic room at Veldhoeve, crying myself to sleep over Mama and Papa, and my home so far away.

Willem came to me at midnight and we loved.

11

In *camera lucida* the past was ever present. In this secret and silent place, this many-roomed mansion where light collects the soul, the four walls held centuries of memory.

The man standing in the center of the room was tall and elegantly slender, soft spoken and direct in his eye contact, precise in his chosen words.

His name was Jakob van Laar.

Jakob's hands were large but, unlike his fathers before him, they were not a crofter's hands, those of a man who tilled the earth for his food and wage. Instead they were nimble, the hands of an artist or a master tailor. As often as he took a charcoal pencil in hand he played the Steinway in the parlor of Veldhoeve, favoring the études of Chopin and the fugues of Jan Pieterszoon Sweelinck.

He'd done the day's work of a nurseryman in his youth, of course, had saddle grafted hundreds of trees, tilled and irrigated and spaded, had spent many a cold fall night covering young saplings to shield them from frost.

But as Zeven Farms, founded by Dr Rinus van Laar, prospered in his care, Jakob stepped into the shadows, preparing for this time.

In *camera lucida* Jakob walked among the dead, the long buried, and it was through them, and the bounty of his orchards, that he lived.

On this day, as snow gently fell on Holland County, Ohio, he thought:

I am the last of my kind.

It all ends with me.

As he prepared to leave *camera lucida* Jakob felt a presence in the room.

He turned slowly, and saw Sébastien van Laar standing behind him. His father, dead at fifty, wore a brown hunting vest and a pair of Irish Setter Rutmasters. Behind him, on the large table draped with oilcloth, sat his beloved Remington 870, and the defleshed skull and antlers of an eight-point buck.

The sight of the man filled Jakob with a primitive longing, the hunger of a boy for the sound and strength of his father, the safety of his nearness.

What do you see?

Jakob spun slowly in place. The images on the walls had somehow returned, and now showed the four fields that awaited him in the coming weeks and months.

Each meadow held objects he had collected over many years, meticulously placed and replaced, some having grown over with grass and clover, each a layer of a final composite.

It was in Maryland he'd found the brass wine goblet. In eastern Maine he located the silver and ebony gavel. Two days earlier, at an estate sale outside Toledo, he bought the pewter tea urn.

'I see the seasons,' Jakob said.

It will soon be the first day of winter.

'Yes. The solstice.'

Do you remember?

Jakob recalled with clarity the Latin textbook, its corners creased and bent with use, the very smell of it important. He remembered how he stayed up late into the night to learn the language. Decline the noun; conjugate the verb.

'*Iucundissima est spei persuadio et vite imprimis.*'

Very good, son.

Son.

How Jakob missed hearing the word.

Jakob drew on his overcoat, buttoned it, pulled onto his hands supple Italian leather gloves.

He would now return to his living quarters, change his clothing, gather the boy from the barn, and together they would head south, to a small town called Chambersburg.

They watched her enter the store. It was a fueling station with six pumps, three of them diesel. Attached was a small grocery, a convenience store that sold country staples – beer, cigarettes, sugary baked goods, jerky.

Jakob pulled to the side of the road, checked his mirrors. Traffic was very light. He and the boy were in one of the older unmarked service vans, shorn of any reference to the farm or store. The inside was spotless, as new.

Jakob handed the boy a disposable cell phone.

'Call the moment she leaves.'

'Okay.'

The boy got out of the van, hiked the collar of his jacket to the chill, and crossed the road. Jakob watched him, thought of all the children over the years. There was never a shortage of them; wounded birds who had alighted in Holland County from far-flung nests.

As Jakob headed to the secluded spot a half-mile away, he recalled the first time he had seen the girl. She had been about twelve years old and, when he'd first set his eyes on her, he knew so much.

She was a cautious little one, given to blushing when complimented, choosing silence instead of bluster. In her heart, Jakob was certain, there was virtue.

He'd once observed the girl, about a year earlier, as she talked with two of her friends at the fast food court in the Belden Village Mall. The least outgoing of her small group, she had mostly listened, jumping into the conversation only as necessary to keep these acquaintances engaged.

Near them sat a man at a table. He wore tattered clothing, damp-rinsed and wrung dry in some filthy gas station men's room, the soles of his worn boots beginning to waffle.

The girl noticed the man watching her, perhaps saw the desperation in his eyes. While her friends deposited their trash into the nearby trash cans, the girl quite deliberately left her half-eaten sandwich on the table. When she reached the exit door, Jakob saw her turn around to see the man wrapping the sandwich in its paper, and putting it in his pocket.

Each day, after school, she would stop along the two-mile route to her home, a gaunt frame house at the end of a dirt lane off Poinciana Road. Her stop was a welfare check of an unofficial sort with an older woman whom Jakob had observed coming to her door in a wheelchair, an oxygen canister strapped to the side.

Today, as forecast, the snow had begun to fall at noon. Jakob parked the van in a turnoff on a heavily wooded bend in the road. He pulled his wool cap low on his forehead, selected a pair of tinted glasses from the box on the seat next to him.

At just after two o'clock the boy called and told him the girl had left the store. She was coming toward him. It was now a matter of minutes.

When Jakob saw her come around the bend, her shoulders raised to the cold, his heart began to race.

Are you certain of her heart?

'I am,' Jakob said.

He turned to look at the shadow standing next to the driver's door of the van.

Zoals het klokje thuis tikt, tikt het nergens.

Rinus van Laar, who had been scholarly in the works of Erasmus and Rabelais, often spoke to Jakob in proverbs.

The clock ticks at home, as it ticks nowhere else.

Jakob glanced at the side mirror on the passenger door. The girl, whose name was Paulette Graham, was less than one hundred feet away. Jakob stepped out of the van.

The girl looked at him, at the scattered mess on the side of the road. 'What happened?' she asked.

'I'm afraid I took that curve a little too quickly.'

'Oh no.'

'I'd forgotten that the latch on this back door was broken. I've been meaning to get it fixed but, alas, money is tight.'

Paulette smiled. Jakob felt something untoward fuss within him. He pushed it back.

'I can help you with that if you like,' she said. 'Help you put everything back in your truck.'

'Not to bother,' Jakob said. 'It's cold and wet. I couldn't ask you to do that.'

The girl looked down, at her already soaked jacket and jeans. When she looked up, she didn't respond.

'You are most kind,' Jakob said.

They worked in silence for a few minutes. Every so often Jakob would steal a glance at the girl. She could have easily been Charity. The virtues entwine like roots, he thought.

Before long, the van was reloaded, the back door secured with string. As they'd worked not a single car passed. This would not be the case for long.

'I must pay you for your time,' Jakob said.

'*Pay* me? I didn't do all that much.'

Jakob glanced both ways up and down the lane. 'Where are you headed?'

A slight pause, then she pointed over her shoulder, toward Aquila Road. Jakob knew exactly where she was headed. He'd known for a long time.

'Up to Aquila Road.'

'I can drop you off. It's the least I can do for your kindness.'

In that moment she looked away, toward the village square, now laced with gently falling snow. She glanced back at Jakob. Perhaps she was weighing the transaction, balancing the work she had done, the wage offered, considering the wisdom and folly of getting into a vehicle with a complete stranger.

To Jakob she was not a stranger at all. He knew as much about the girl as he had ever known about anyone. He knew that she would now curl her hair behind her right ear, look at the ground for a moment, then look into his eyes. He knew that she would either say *no thank you* or *okay, thanks*.

'Okay,' she said. 'Thanks.'

She slipped into the van, closed the door, and buckled her seat-belt. Jakob stole another glance at the mirrors. They were alone.

And thus, in the way of his fathers before him, he made the first girl his own.

There would be three more.

12

It was somewhere around seven hundred that Bernadette Hardy lost track.

She'd fallen asleep in the chair, her mind still racing out of control, still scrambling up and down the slopes of reason and understanding. That's how exhausted she was. She rarely fell asleep right away, even in her own bed; her comfortable, soft, expensive bed. Even as a child, sleep had been elusive to her, like trying to net a butterfly in the dark.

For more than two weeks, even the Ambien (with which she'd begun overmedicating, but not by that much) had not worked. Today the fatigue finally pulled rank, and she'd lost count of how many times the machines had beeped, something she'd vowed she would never do.

In the closing of an eye her mother was Here.

In the opening of an eye she was Gone.

In one moment her mother had been Amanda Kyle Hardy: swimmer, painter, rooftop gardener, social worker. Amanda Kyle

Hardy, wife to William, mother to Bernadette, daughter of the late James and Sylvia Kyle. Amanda who never cursed anyone, but swore like a longshoreman. Amanda who was always an easy mark for whoever would show up on her doorstep, hands out for some cause or another.

On the afternoon of the day it all ended they'd sat at the small table in the kitchen. Detta made her mom's favorite herbal tea. It was the last conversation they would ever have.

'What are you going to do?' Detta asked.

Her mother took a few seconds before answering. 'I don't know, honey. I thought I had it all figured out this morning, but I don't.'

'Is Dad moving back in?'

Her mother didn't answer. Instead she reached out and touched Detta's hand.

Detta knew a lot of kids from her school whose parents were divorced. Most of them, in fact. Divorce always sounded like a foreign country to her and, because of it, she often felt like a member of a select society, an elite tribe whose parents had a perfect marriage. Her father was a professor and a bestselling author; her mother was a social worker who helped disadvantaged and troubled people.

Seconds after the machines flat-lined a pair of nurses rushed into the room, followed by a doctor, an older man with muddy brown eyes and a calm, measured delivery when it came to bad news. Detta had noticed that this doctor didn't really look at you, but rather looked near you. Perhaps he had delivered so much bad news while looking directly at people that their eyes had begun to reduce him, to take away parts of his soul.

The nurses and doctor touched and scanned and listened and pumped, scurried and scratched things on their charts, checked the machines. They mumbled to each other as the doctor put a stethoscope to Amanda Hardy's chest.

Suddenly their actions took on less urgency. The nurses shut down the machines, one by one; the doctor took the ends of the stethoscope from his ears, and grimly consulted his watch.

Of course, Detta thought. He's noting Mom's time of death. It's the lottery everybody wins. You only have to buy the one ticket.

They would soon explain that it was an aneurysm, this final assault, an anomaly of a burst blood vessel in her mother's brain. Caused, of course, by severe head trauma. Caused, of course, by the fall from the balcony.

Caused, of course, by her father.

Detta glanced over at the chair where her father was supposed to be. He had gone for coffee, or whatever it was he did when he found he could no longer sit in this room. Maybe it was the rigid plastic chair that hurt him, or the reheated and recycled air, or the smell of sickness and repair.

Maybe it was the guilt. No one knew more about guilt than Dr William Hardy.

As the death dance began around her, Detta put on her head-phones. She scanned her playlists, wondering what music might be appropriate for these moments. Over the past two-and-a half months she had amassed a few dozen songs for this very purpose.

Now, when the pain was red and fresh and scorching, she needed loud, an IRT train coming straight at her in a tunnel. In a few seconds, she had it.

'Heart of Fire' by Black Veil Brides.

Detta wandered in the music as the last person left the room. On the way out, they each said something to her. To each of them she mumbled, 'I'm okay.'

Can I get you anything?

I'm okay.

Do you need to talk?

I'm okay.

Your dad brought a monster into your life and that monster killed your mother. How does that make you feel?

I'm okay.

Something caught the edge of Detta's attention, a silhouette in the doorway. She looked over.

It was her father.

He seemed to absorb the totality of the moment all at once, his family suddenly and everlastingly diminished by one third; his beautiful wife, the mother of his only child, the love of his life, now a jagged outline beneath a powder blue sheet.

Detta glanced at her father's hands. They hung limply at his sides. He had nowhere to put them.

When she looked back at his face, she saw that Will Hardy was screaming.

Bernadette Hardy could not hear him.

13

The Corley & Sons Stone Company had been a fixture in Trumbull County, Ohio since 1921. The company supplied shot rock used in the construction of driveways, parking lots, landfills, and logging roads, as well as Indiana limestone, Rustic Buff, and Gray Gorge.

For Lonnie Combs it was so much dust and bullshit. He'd been a driver for old man Corley for the past six years. Today the load was five finished pieces of granite.

Lonnie picked up the stone and got on the road a few minutes ahead of schedule. On the way he stopped at the Gas 'N Go and picked up some chips and some chewing tobacco. They called it smokeless tobacco these days, but Lonnie never would. To him it would always be chaw, just as it was for his daddy. Beech Nut was his brand. He even kept it in his daddy's old Flying Dutchman tin.

Twenty minutes later Lonnie delivered the granite to the Celestial Meadow Cemetery outside Abbeville. Lonnie did some part-time grave digging for the old man, and he had some back-filling jobs today.

When he got the keys to the equipment shed he crossed the gravel lot. A few years earlier, at Lonnie's suggestion, old man Corley had sprung for a used Semco Rotary II. It wasn't the newest or the best, but it got the job done.

On this day there were three separate funeral services under-way. Before long a big white SUV pulled up, and a middle-aged woman exited the driver's side. The back doors opened and a boy and a girl emerged. The boy was all but invisible, but the girl was not. She was about twelve.

Lonnie tried not to look at her. She was way too young, he knew that, just as he had always known, but that didn't stop him from looking. Looking didn't cost anything, did it?

He just didn't want to be caught looking.

Every time something happened with a kid, anywhere in the county, every time some teenaged girl scraped a knee or woke up with the willies after watching some shitty horror movie on Netflix, they came and talked to him. Fucking cops.

He'd done his time, four years total, and there was no way he was going back.

The sound jerked him out of a dream. A good dream, too.

'Who's there?'

Lonnie sat up in his desk chair, sleep-addled, suddenly freezing cold. The only light in his shabby front room was coming from his computer screen.

'I ain't fucking with you,' he said. 'I got a Louisville Slugger in my hand.'

Silence.

Lonnie raked the sleep from his eyes, stood up, his heart hammering in his chest. The truth was he didn't have a bat. He stumbled across the small living room to the kitchen, felt his way along the counter, knocking more than a few dishes into the sink.

He closed his hand around the handle of a crusty steak knife. Emboldened by his weapon, he called out one more time.

'Last chance, asshole.'

No response.

He glanced around the corner, down the short hallway that led to the back door. He now knew why he was so cold. The damned door was wide open.

When Lonnie looked back into the kitchen he saw a long shadow creep across the floor. Someone was behind him. Whoever it was had been in the bathroom.

The next thing Lonnie knew he was face down on the dusty runner carpet, bright orange fireworks behind his eyes. His head pounded.

As the world began to spin out of orbit Lonnie felt moist breath at his right ear, smelled a distinct odor; sour and sweet at the same time.

Then came the voice.

'You bury the dead,' the voice whispered. 'Take heed you are not soon among them, Mr Combs.'

Lonnie Combs lay on the carpet for a long time, eyes tightly closed, waiting for the death blow; the rack of the shotgun, the trill of the knife removed from a sheath.

It did not come.

Take heed you are not soon among them, Mr Combs.

At dawn, as Lonnie picked himself up, swearing off the mash forever, he felt a dampness in his crotch. He'd goddamned wet himself.

Like he always did when he needed to calm down he reached for his tin of chewing tobacco. It wasn't in his pocket or on the table with the computer.

He grabbed the bottle of mash from the table, emptied it down his throat.

87

As he staggered to the bathroom he realized what the other smell was, the one on the warm breath of the stranger – thick and sugary and pungent.

It was apples.

14

In the months since Amanda's death – Will had yet to call her passing what it was, *murder*, knowing full well he could not begin to heal until he did so – he had measured out the lives of himself and his daughter in confections.

Each time he walked by the chocolatier on Bond Street, a place he had frequented as many times in trouble as in celebration to buy the glacé lemon peels, Amanda's favorite, he marked the passing of each uncelebrated day by the theme of the elaborate window displays.

Will had drifted through the wake and the funeral and the burial like a man untethered, rallied around by friends and acquaintances from the university, as well as Amanda's co-workers.

A week after the fire one of Will's colleagues found them a sublet, a one bedroom on East Seventeenth. It was small, but it was safe and held nothing of their former lives.

During the ceremonies Trevor Butler had stood no more

than ten paces from both Will and Detta Hardy. He appeared fallen, as if what happened on that night in some way occurred on his watch.

They'd spent the afternoon of Thanksgiving Day in the parking lot of a restaurant in Yonkers. The restaurant had advertised an 'old-fashioned family Thanksgiving dinner, complete with homemade cranberry chutney and mincemeat pie' and Will naively thought he could engage his daughter in the holiday and the meal if they took the trip.

He was wrong.

In their rented Ford Focus they pulled into the parking lot at just after one o'clock and sat, wordlessly, as snow swirled around the car, heater on full, Christmas standards playing softly on the radio. At two-thirty, without having eaten or said a word, they headed back to the city.

They passed Christmas Eve and Christmas Day in separate rooms in the apartment, each to their own books. New Year's Eve found Will in bed at ten o'clock. At dawn he entered the living room, found Detta sleeping on the sofa, wrapped in an afghan, a repeat of the previous night's Times Square event on the TV. On the coffee table next to her were her prescriptions for Lexapro and Lunesta. Will sneaked the vials into the kitchen, counted the remaining pills, checked and rechecked the fill dates. As he suspected, she was overmedicating, splitting pills, but not yet at a rate that would concern him.

Will used all his sick days and vacation days for the year by the end of January, and met twice with the board about a leave of absence. While he found abundant sympathy and understanding in the board members, he knew that their patience would only stretch so far.

In the time since the fire Will and Detta had seen a therapist, a midtown psychiatrist named Catherine Levinsohn. Her practice specialized in grief counseling, as well as adolescent issues.

She had started Detta on 5 mg of Lexapro, then increased the dosage to 10 mg after six weeks of no improvement. The side effects could be debilitating, and Will had tried to monitor his daughter's reaction carefully. Not easy when she could barely stand to be in the same room with him for long.

How many people had he counseled, people enduring the pain and sorrow of grief? How many times had he moved a box of tissues across an inexpensive laminate table?

He now knew that his words were all empty.

Every one.

He'd found her there a dozen times, sitting at the bus stop on Prince Street, through the rainiest fall days, the most frigid early winter afternoons, watching as the trucks arrived, watching as the scaffolding went up, watching as the tradesman came and left.

By mid-November they had sandblasted the exterior. By the first day of the new year it looked as if nothing had ever happened there, as if a woman's life had not been taken in a tempest of fire and glass and stone.

Each time, without approaching his daughter, Will turned on his heels, and went home.

He began riding at just after 2 a.m. He'd begun the habit in February when his medications would not grant him sleep. He'd gotten on his Cervélo and begun to ride without caution, without any sense of safety or concern or direction. It was not a state of physical fitness he was seeking, as he had his whole life, but rather an atonement for his health and well-being.

On this night he headed west, toward the river. When he reached the Greenway he knew he would head south. He had the note in his pocket, the letter that explained what happened when he was thirteen, as he remembered it, the day flames split the sky and sirens filled his world, as well as the letter that apologized to Detta, the only person on earth who mattered.

The revised last will and testament, written in his hand, was under the pillow on his bed.

As he rode his bike toward the park he wondered what the person would look like, the cop or the FDNY responder. He wondered if this person would be young or old, male or female. You don't get to just die in this world, Will knew all too well. Someone has to find you dead, and then you become part of *their* story.

Once in the park, Will dismounted, leaned the bike against the iron fence, sat on the cold ground, catching his wind.

It didn't take long. Within twenty minutes Will glanced up to see two boys crossing the park, coming toward him. They were both mid-teens, hanging tough and hard. One big, one smaller. They wore dark hoodies, newer Jordans.

When they neared Will, the big one nudged the smaller one. They stood and considered him for a long moment.

'Nice bike, yo,' the smaller one finally said. He was clearly the alpha. He made an elaborate show of lifting the hem of his hoodie to show the grip of a black handgun.

Will said nothing.

'You fuckin' *deaf*?' the smaller one asked.

Will made eye contact. 'I heard you.'

'Then why'n you *say* nothing?'

'You're going to have to take it,' Will said. 'The bike is worth four thousand dollars. If you're really going to use that gun, you have to pull it out now, put the barrel to my forehead, then pull the trigger.'

'You think I won't do it, motherfucker?'

'I don't know,' Will said. 'I don't know anything about you.'

The kid once again looked at his partner, back at Will. 'Fuck's a matter with you, man?'

To Will, in this darkened end of the park, the boy was Anthony Torres. He was all the troubled kids that Will had thought he was helping, kids he thought he could fix. It had all been for nothing, and now it would end.

Will slowly stood up. 'Do it.'

The kid looked away for a second. It was a tell. He had lifted the hem of his hoodie with his left hand, and Will knew that he was going to throw his right. When he did, Will was ready. He leaned away, transferred the weight to his back foot, and struck a clean, hard blow to the kid's solar plexus. The sound echoed in the night.

The kid staggered back, his hands at his throat, gasping for air. Will stepped forward, took the gun from the boy's waistband, a cheap Hi-Point C9. As the kid sagged to the ground, Will leveled the weapon at the other boy.

'You had your chance,' Will said. 'Now go home.'

No one moved. Will's hand was steady.

The tall kid helped his friend to his feet. Without taking their eyes from Will, they slowly backed across the park.

Will stood in the darkness, in the cold rain, his heart pounding.

He lost track of time.

Heading back home he blew right through intersections, faster and faster, not looking for cross traffic, not slowing for stop signs or red lights, just as he had done that day riding home from Gould Park. The night dissolved into long streaks of muddy neon, the staccato brass of car horns and distant sirens.

Street by street, corner by corner, Will implored the city to finish what was started in Canal Park.

The city did not oblige.

When Will returned to the apartment, and walked down the hallway to his room, he saw Detta's door closing. She knew he'd left the apartment in the middle of the night.

Will tried to calm himself, to reconcile what he had done with what he had almost done. He peeled off his sweat-soaked clothes, sat on the edge of his bed, motionless, lost in thought, for almost an hour.

At dawn he stepped out on the balcony, burned the note, along with the hastily drawn will, along with his *mea culpa* to Trevor. In it he'd asked Trevor to watch over Detta.

The ashes scattered on a breeze.

Will walked back into the apartment, into the bathroom. He closed the door, and vomited in the sink.

15

New Dawn Villa was a twenty-bed, long-term care facility in Windsor, a small township in Ashtabula County. It was a state-run center for indigent patients.

Jakob had stolen into the woman's room long after the evening's dinner had been served, after the tray tables were rolled away, the medications administered, after the meager night shift had taken up their books and sodas.

Once inside he'd stood by the window and looked at the woman for more than a few minutes. Before long the woman sensed a presence, opened her eyes.

'You look beautiful, Camilla,' he said.

The woman tried to focus on him, his face illuminated only by a pair of dim nightlights. 'I do not look beautiful.'

Camilla Strathaven was in her eighties. She had once been a stout and vigorous farm girl, pretty enough with her hazel eyes, straw-colored hair and sifting of freckles. Camilla had been a patient at New Dawn Villa for nearly six months.

Jakob brought a chair silently to the edge of the bed, and sat down. 'I remember when I was just a boy, not even old enough to shave, I would cut the grass behind Godwin Hall. You would bring me cold apple cider on hot summer days, cider from my family's orchards. I had, of course, grown up with the nectar, but it somehow seemed sweeter and colder in your glass.'

Camilla blushed. There was still some of the village girl left in her.

'Do you recall what we talked about on my last visit?' Jakob asked.

Camilla just stared at him, as if there were a wall of glass between them. Earlier in the month he had looked at the woman's chart. Camilla Strathaven had an aggressive and in-operable brain tumor. She had three months at the outside, one turn of season. What he needed from her was now a matter of great urgency.

'On my last visit, we discussed something,' he said. 'You made a phone call. I dialed the number for you, but you talked on the telephone. Do you remember that?'

'I talked to my brother.'

'Yes.'

It was not her brother, who had passed away more than forty years ago. It was an attorney. 'I have the papers with me,' Jakob said. He reached into his pocket, removed the envelope.

'Papers?'

'I don't want to burden you with the details until you are recovered and back home again,' he said. 'Your brother looked them over and he said everything is in order.'

It took nearly a full minute, but in the end the woman managed to scrawl her signature.

'I'll be getting the newspaper now,' Camilla said. 'Delivered.'

'Right to your door.'

'How much will it cost?'

'It won't cost you anything. It will be my treat.'

Another smile. 'My precious Theodore.'

Theodore Edmunds had once run the town's bakery. The story, as everybody of an age in the village knew it, was that Camilla, widowed at twenty-two, had fallen hard for the man – a married man with three daughters – and had never given up hope that he would leave his wife and children for her.

He never did.

Theodore Edmunds, too, had been in the ground for decades.

'Yes, my love,' Jakob said. 'Theodore is here.'

16

The small house sat a hundred feet from the main house, just at the edge of the tree line that bordered Zeven Farms. Originally the dwelling had been built to house summer and harvest workers for the orchards. In the 1940s, the van Laars built a barracks-style compound closer to their barns.

Ivy Holgrave knew that the current resident of the cottage, the sole resident, was heavily armed. Of the firearms Ivy knew about, the Charter Arms Bulldog and the Desert Eagle were the deadliest of the arsenal. She also knew of a Mauser .380 and a Remington 770.

And yet Ivy never went in armed.

At just after 7 a.m. Ivy slipped her key in the lock, turned it, slowly opened the door.

'I'm coming in.'

Ivy knew that her presence had been announced, more than once, by the dated but still quite capable security system, tracking her from the driveway, across the expanse of the yard, onto the porch, even in the small foyer.

Ivy peered around the corner into the parlor.

The woman napping in the La-Z-Boy recliner across from the large Vizio flat screen, was in her seventies, thin and surly from a lifetime of spent anger. On the TV tray was the remote, along with that Bulldog.

Ivy made some noise before stepping into the room. She knew her mother was never more than one footfall away from awakening. It was one of the reasons Ivy was never able to sneak into the house as a teenager.

Her mother opened her eyes. 'Delia?'

'I'm not Delia, Mama,' she said. 'You know that. I know you know that. We do this every time, don't we?'

Her mother held the crazy-woman look as long as she could. She then waved a dismissive hand, calling an official end to the charade. She picked up the remote, muted the talking head on the *Today Show*.

Not only was Ivy Lee third-generation Ivy – her grandmother was Ivy Belle, her mother was Ivy June – she was also third-generation law enforcement. *Woman* law enforcement. Ivy June had retired from her job as a deputy sheriff for Holland County two decades earlier.

Ivy's mother had raised Ivy and her sister alone at a time when being a single mother carried a lot more baggage and innuendo than it did today.

When her father had walked out, in Ivy Lee's sixth year, everyone and anyone who had an opinion knew the reason, or thought they did, and did not hesitate discussing it over the wash line.

The truth was that Frank Holgrave was a weak-willed man who could not stand the fact that his wife was a strong-willed woman, a woman who had ticketed and arrested a number of his tavern and union buddies.

Ivy set out the coffee and fresh crullers, as she did every morning. She sat on the couch, tucked in.

They sat in silence, Ivy June turning her attention to the newspaper, Ivy Lee watching the news, keeping an eye on her cell phone. She was officially on duty.

At eight o'clock, as every morning, Ivy got up and cleared away the clutter. She stepped into the small kitchen, filled her mother's water glass with orange juice, set a fresh straw in it, put it on the TV table next to her mother's chair.

She took a moment, considered the woman.

Here was a lady who at one time could knock back four fingers of Jack Daniels, then cut a bull's-eye with her Smith and Wesson six out of six times.

She was getting smaller, Ivy thought, ever closer to her place in the earth. Ivy wished she knew a way to stop time.

'I'll pick up some takeout tonight,' Ivy said. 'What do you want?'

Whatever you want is fine with me.

'Whatever you want is fine with me,' her mother said.

'Chinese okay?'

Not Chinese.

'Not Chinese.'

'Love you, Mama.'

'Love you back, baby girl. You stay safe.'

'Always.'

Before she stepped out the back door Ivy glanced at the calendar on the kitchen wall. She felt her heart flutter when she saw that the day's date had been outlined in red. Nothing was penciled inside the square, but Ivy saw that her mother had drawn a small flower with red petals and green leaves.

She *did* remember.

Holy Cross was the largest Catholic cemetery in Cuyahoga County, located in Brookpark, Ohio, just a few miles from Hopkins International Airport.

Ivy parked her SUV, cut the engine. She took her service weapon from her hip, locked it in the glove compartment, then exited the vehicle, crossed to the back, and opened the rear gate. She took out a pair of gloves and a small pair of clippers.

The grave she was visiting was at the top of a small incline, in the shade of two large sycamore trees. She knelt next to the grave marker, put on her gloves, began to trim the grass around the stone.

James D Benedict.

It was the way he introduced himself, always with his middle initial. The first time they'd met, shaking hands in the rear parking lot of the Fourth District headquarters on Kinsman Road, she'd thought it an affectation, an icing that this strikingly handsome and charming young man did not need. Within a few months she'd come to learn that the D stood for Denton. It was his grandmother's maiden name.

Jimmy was twenty-eight on his final day. It had felt old enough at the time to Ivy, but it seemed like a child's age now.

She touched a hand to his headstone, closed her eyes, remembered the day as if it were yesterday, heard the monstrous blast of the rifle, still echoing these many years later.

Terrance Duncan was the killer's name. He was sixteen. He was distraught because his girlfriend had left him for another boy. The crack helped put the rifle in his hands.

Ivy said her piece, gathered her tools, and walked back to her vehicle.

Ivy sat in the parking lot of the Airport Marriott. She thought about heading east, getting onto St Clair Avenue, over to 152nd Street, down to Holmes Avenue. Five houses on the left. The tidy double, painted powder blue the last time she'd seen it.

She wondered if the Terrance Duncan's grandmother, Arcella

Richards, was still alive. It was a ritual Ivy had kept up for more than a decade but had now passed into memory.

Perhaps it was better if it stayed there.

Ivy settled into the chair in her basement, opened the file on her desk.

The dead girl's name was Paulette Graham.

The scene was a remote clearing in the forest, near the intersection of Route 44 and Jennings Road, just east of the Holland County line. In the long shot photograph, the dead girl's body was a smudge of chalk white against the bark of the box elder.

According to the coroner's report, the girl had been dead more than three weeks when she had been discovered by a pair of teenaged boys. In the time between the girl's last breath and her body's discovery, it had snowed and melted twice. The remaining snow was arrayed in the field in large white patches.

The close-up of the victim showed the bloated and darkened flesh, nearly unrecognizable as having once been human.

Ivy sometimes envied those who worked in urban settings – she'd done so herself – for the simple reason that they often arrived at a crime scene minutes after the crime was committed, and therefore walked into an all but pristine setting. Blood, fingerprints, hair and fiber, all in a fully preserved state.

In the country, especially with homicides, there were many more hazards to investigations. When nature is disturbed, it immediately tries to heal itself, to keep to its heart its secrets.

Paulette was, by all accounts, a shy and respectful girl, abandoned by her mother when she was only two, raised by her grandparents. An average student, she kept to herself, volunteering at a food shelter in southern Holland County on holidays.

She was last seen at the Gas 'N Go on Route 40 at just before 2 p.m. on December 14. Video surveillance from the store showed her enter the property alone, walking into the lot from the northern entrance. Once inside the store, she picked up a loaf of sandwich bread and a tin of potted meat. She paid cash at the register, passing a few words with the clerk.

Video showed her exiting the property, alone, at just after 2 p.m.

She was never again seen alive.

Ivy slipped the USB flash drive into her laptop. She clicked open the program.

She'd seen the video dozens of times, but each time she watched it anew she saw something else. At the 1:57:20 mark Paulette is seen entering the frame from the right. There is only one other person in the frame, an elderly man filling his Toyota truck.

At the 2:00:02 mark a subject enters the frame at the upper left part of the screen. The person appears to be male, but age and race are undetermined, as the subject's upper body is not visible. The subject is wearing heavy boots, denim jeans, a heavy coat and gloves.

As always, Ivy stopped the video when the subject turned toward the camera.

Something was in the subject's gloved right hand. At first, Ivy had thought it might be a small handgun, and it might have been just that. The cause of death determined by the coroner was inconclusive, but there was no evidence that Paulette Graham had suffered a gunshot wound.

Because Ivy had already printed out this frame, as well as having saved it as a digital image, she let the video play. The subject lingers for a few moments, then exits the frame, heading in the direction of the store. He does not enter.

At the 2:01:16 mark Paulette Graham is seen crossing the parking lot with her small bag of groceries, and exiting the frame heading north.

Her body was found in a field, precisely 8.7 miles northeast of the Gas 'N Go, twenty days later.

Ivy poured herself a few inches of Jim Beam. She crossed the room, stepped into the small alcove that housed her washer and dryer. She opened the dryer, took out a clean sweatshirt and pair of yoga pants; pants designated *yoga* in name only.

She returned to her computer.

As she did every night she scanned the databases and wires. There had been no Amber Alerts in the tri-county area on this day. The two missing persons reports were males.

She sat down in front of her iMac, and opened Photoshop. It brought her to her current project, a photograph she had been restoring, on and off, for more than a year, one pixel at a time.

She had just about every book she could find and afford on the early days of photography, including a signed copy of *Paul Strand in Mexico*, and Eve Arnold's *All About Eve*. She also had many books on the pioneers of photography, including works by Julia Margaret Cameron, James Mudd and, of course, Mathew Brady.

In the photograph, Delia stood on the Fairgrounds, near the center, right by the huge sugar maple. She wore faded jeans and her favorite white cardigan, one that Ivy had purchased as a birthday present for her from the O'Neils at Rolling Acres Mall.

This picture was the last photograph ever taken of Delia, at least as far as Ivy Holgrave knew. It was taken in the late afternoon, seven days before the beginning of fall, just hours before Delia Holgrave disappeared into the mist.

17

It had gotten to where Will didn't know where the dream stopped and the waking started, what was real and what was the dark vestige of sorrow.

His days were wind sprints from Xanax to Wellbutrin to Valium to Ambien. The four medications were a toxic cocktail keeping him numb to his loss.

His was a hollowed-out life, a feeling that he was existing in white, featureless time. Each morning, an hour before the alarm sounded, he lay in darkness and tried to think of a single reason to get out of bed.

In March he found one.

On a late Saturday morning in mid-March Will and Detta walked back from the Whole Foods at Union Square. Winter was still clinging to the city, but there was something in the air that day, a scent of spring that delivered Will Hardy to a moment in the past, an incident when Detta had been about six years old. Will had been teaching part time at Hunter College.

On that day they had just gotten off the IRT at 68th Street. While they'd been on the train Will had been approached by a homeless man. The man asked Will for money, but Will denied him. The man, too beaten down by circumstance and weather, had moved on without asking a second time, or pressing his luck, as some in his position were wont to do.

Later, while waiting to cross at 69th and Lexington, Detta furrowed her brow.

'Dad?' she asked.

'Yeah, honey?'

'That man on the train?'

In that moment, Will expected his daughter to ask about the man's plight, about why he was dressed the way he was dressed, why he was unshaven, or why he smelled the way he smelled, which was not pleasant. Will geared up his best explanation – at least the one that might fly in the mind of a six-year-old – regarding homelessness, and society's role in both the many causes and the many possible solutions.

'What about him?' Will asked.

'How come you didn't give him any money?'

Oh, boy, Will thought. He did not have a back-pocket answer for this one.

'It's kind of complicated, sweetie.'

The light changed. They joined hands, walked across 69th Street.

'Right now that man doesn't have anywhere to live, you see,' Will said. 'And I feel for him, I really do. It's just that—'

'He doesn't have a house?'

'No honey. He doesn't.'

'But we have a house.'

Technically a co-op, Will thought, but close enough for a

six-year-old. 'Yes,' he said. 'We do. But sometimes life can be really unfair, and he—'

'Does that man know where our house is?'

Will was more than a little surprised by the question. 'Do you mean does he know where we live?'

Detta just nodded.

'No, honey. Why would you ask that?'

'Because,' she said. 'If you gave that man money, how was he going to pay us back?'

Will almost laughed, but checked himself. 'Well, that's a really good question.'

Will then went into an overly long explanation of the difference between loaning someone money and giving someone money. He didn't do a very good job. By the time they got to the Ukrainian bakery at 71st, with its bounty of treats in the window, Detta had moved on.

Does that man know where our house is?

Anthony Torres had known where they lived.

After fumbling with the keys and the bags of groceries, Will managed to get the door opened. Detta brushed right by him, heading to the steps, knocking a bag from his hands.

She didn't stop to help him, didn't even acknowledge what she had done. She just kept walking. Will was getting used to this, but it did not make it better.

While gathering the oranges scattered across the lobby, Will's cell phone rang. He fished the phone out of his pocket, looked at the screen. It was Patrick Richmond. As much as Will liked the man, had needed his counsel and legal expertise over the past months, he hoped this was not another welfare check-in. He took the call anyway.

'Hey, Patrick.'

'How are you, Will?' he asked.

There were probably a hundred answers to that question. Each time someone asked, Will considered all possible responses. If he had learned anything in his many years in his chosen profession, it was that it was better to wear the mask of your own choosing.

'One day at a time still,' Will said. 'Just getting home from the grocery store.'

'And Bernadette?'

Will now knew that this would not be a drive-by. He sat down on the step. 'Not great,' he said. 'She's still not talking much.'

'She'll come around. She's a tough kid.'

Just like her mother, was the line that usually came next. Patrick was too smart, and too sensitive, to say it.

'I'd like you to come by my office today, if you can,' Patrick said. 'Tomorrow at the latest.'

At first, Will thought he had heard incorrectly. He thought he was done with the legal aspects of murder and the virus of its aftermath.

'What's this about?'

'It's probably best that we talk face to face at my office. Or, I could come to your place. Or we could meet for coffee. Whatever's most convenient for you.'

Will could not go to the man's office. He'd signed too many papers there. Amanda was a folder in a steel cabinet there.

'Can you meet me at my place?' Will asked.

'Of course. I can be there in an hour,' he said. 'Will that work?'

'Sure.'

'See you then.'

Will did not touch his coffee, coffee he didn't want to make in the first place. Patrick had taken only one or two polite sips from his mug. Will knew he made the worst coffee on earth. Somehow he managed to mess up K-Cups.

'Not sure how to begin with this,' Patrick said. 'I received a

FedEx delivery yesterday from a man named Charles Bristow. Are you familiar with that name?'

Will thought about it. The name didn't ring a bell. 'I don't think so.'

'Mr Bristow is an attorney in Ohio.'

Patrick reached into his briefcase, took out a large envelope, opened it. He extracted a single document.

'Mr Bristow is the attorney of record for Camilla Strathaven's estate.'

'I'm at a loss here, Patrick.'

'Mrs Strathaven was a stepsister to Janna Schuyler.'

Will thought he had surely misheard the man. Janna Schuyler was his mother's mother, whom he'd never met. There were no Strathavens in his family. Then it hit him. He was talking about Aunt Millie. His mother's great-aunt's name was Camilla, not Millicent, as Will had assumed. He never knew her married name. In fact, he didn't know anything about her. Sarah Hardy had spoken of her estranged family in Ohio only a handful of times, and even then it had been a bit cryptic.

'I thought she died years ago,' Will said. This was more of an assumption than anything based in fact.

'Not years ago,' Patrick said. 'Just recently, in fact. She was in a state-run hospice in Ohio. I'm sorry for your loss, Will.'

Will didn't know what to say. He said: 'Thank you.'

'Because she was indigent, she didn't have many possessions. In fact, she just had one.'

Patrick placed a photograph on the coffee table. Will glanced at it. It was a large, ornate house, with two wings and a rather expansive field behind it.

'I have to say, I've been practicing estate law for twenty-six years, and this is a first for me.'

Will pointed at the photo. 'What is this?'

Patrick was silent for a moment, then said, 'It's yours, Will.'

'I don't get it. How could this be mine?'

'I should say, it will be yours if you want it.'

It was as if Patrick was speaking another language. His attorney moved ahead. More envelopes, more pictures.

'The property itself is just over three acres in an incorporated village called Abbeville. The town is located about forty-five miles east of Cleveland in Holland County.'

Patrick pushed a few photographs across the coffee table. They were reprints of old black and white pictures of a county fair, complete with a midway, food stalls and a Ferris wheel in the background. One of the pictures appeared to be from the 1920s or 1930s, with women in high-collared blouses and long skirts.

Quoting Denzel Washington's character in *Philadelphia*, Will said what he felt. 'Talk to me like I'm eight years old, Patrick.'

'I understand.' Patrick consulted his notes. 'Well, it looks like Camilla took over the property from her parents – your great-grandparents – when they died in the 1960s. She ran the property as a general manager of sorts until the early 1990s. It was listed as a boarding house, but I believe it has served as a hotel, as well, back in the 1800s.'

'Why didn't I know anything about this?'

Patrick looked up. His eyes answered most of the question, the part about parents and children and communication. And secrets.

'I'm afraid I can't answer that, Will.'

'You're right. It was an unfair question. I'm sorry.'

'Not at all, my friend,' Patrick continued. 'As I was about to say, in addition to the real estate, there is quite a substantial trust attached.'

'What kind of trust?'

'In the event that you decide to keep and renovate the estate, and subsequently operate the property as a boarding house or a bed and breakfast, or any sort of rental property, the trust allows for a twenty-five-thousand-dollar sum for repairs and bringing the property up to code, as well as a ten-thousand dollar a year stipend to help defray basic operating costs.'

The numbers were all jamming into each other. 'For how long?'

'There is one hundred thousand dollars in an account in a Chardon, Ohio bank. Chardon is the county seat of Geauga County, the next county east of Holland. It is a money market account. But you can only draw ten thousand a year for the next ten years. The final payment will include any interest accrued.' Patrick tapped his briefcase. 'I have a certified check for twenty-five thousand dollars with me.'

'Camilla set this up?'

'Her lawyer did,' he said. 'But yes. It was Camilla's wish. I have a copy of the signed document.'

'If she was indigent, why did she have these assets?'

'I'm afraid I can't answer that one either. I do know that this provision kicked in upon Camilla's death. The money was not available to her by the provisions of the trust. Perhaps her parents thought she was incapable of running the property on her own. It happens quite a lot. Mental illness, physical limitations, criminal record.'

Will's mother had never talked much about Millie. What she had told him made it seem as if the woman was a bit scattered. As Will understood it, Camilla lost her husband at a very young age and never remarried. Will had no idea she owned property. She was just the dotty, mysterious aunt from somewhere in Ohio.

'Believe it or not, the property has a name,' Patrick said.

'A name?'

'Yes,' Patrick said. 'Godwin Hall.'

After Patrick left, Will went cycling to clear his head. It did not help.

Godwin Hall.

The two words moved something inside him, something obscure and indefinable. Had his mother said something about it? Had something bad happened there?

After an hour or so of riding in somewhat of a spell, Will Hardy pointed himself toward the apartment.

How do I begin? he thought.

It had been five days since his meeting with Patrick. Will had spent an hour or so before each night's bedtime looking at the photos, researching the scant history of the property online.

He did not discover much. He learned that the area around Abbeville had a long history, having been settled in the late 1700s by Dutch settlers. Indeed, this is where the name Holland County had its origin.

None of this would matter to his daughter.

18

Detta sat on the sofa, the blanket over her legs, her phone in her hand. Will brought a chair from the dining room. He put the large envelope on the coffee table.

'I met with Patrick Richmond last week. Do you remember Patrick?'

Will did not expect a response. He did not get one.

'Patrick is my lawyer. *Our* lawyer. I think you met him once or twice. Anyway, he called me last week, said there was something we needed to talk about. He got a package from an attorney in Ohio.'

On the word *Ohio* Detta looked up. She remained silent.

'Well, as you know, my mother's family was from Ohio. My grandmother Janna had a stepsister. Her name was Camilla. Camilla Strathaven.' Will decided to just keep talking. To him it sounded like he was reading from a book, telling a story about other people.

'They lived in this town called Abbeville. Aunt Millie died a few months ago, and it turns out that she owned some property there. A big house called Godwin Hall. According to her will, she wanted us to have the house and the land.'

Detta looked up at him again. There was a world of fear and hurt and betrayal in her eyes.

'As you know, things have not been good with my work. To tell you the truth, my tenure is pretty well finished.'

Will had never said these words before. Even to himself.

'And this place, this city,' he said. 'I just don't know what is here for us anymore, do you know what I mean?'

Detta eyes began to fill with tears.

'The property in Ohio is ours if we want it,' Will said. 'We don't have to make any decisions right now, but I thought we could take a trip to Ohio and see what it's like. If we like it, if we feel comfortable there, maybe we could stay for a while. It would be a fresh start, for you and me. For us.'

Detta began to chew her fingernails. Sometimes this was a good thing. It meant she was thinking about something. Perhaps she was considering the idea.

'I did a little research on the area,' Will said, forging ahead with his pitch. 'There's a campus of Kent State University right near there. I can send my résumé and see if they're interested.'

Nothing.

'It wouldn't be like before. I wouldn't be on the tenure track. In fact, I would be teaching part time to start, if they'll have me. Just to see if we like it there.'

He reached over to the envelope on the coffee table, opened it. He took out the large photograph of Godwin Hall. Once again, the sight of it fluttered something within him, something at once unsettling and secretive. He put the photograph down on the sofa next to his daughter.

After a few moments Detta glanced down at it, but only for a second. She went back to chewing her nails.

Although they had three months leeway on the sublet, every-thing went quickly. Will contacted a former student who worked for a Mercedes dealership in Newark. He closed the deal on a pre-owned Mercedes Sprinter in just a few hours.

There was not much to pack. Everything in the apartment had been destroyed in the fire. What they had in storage – winter clothes, some sporting equipment, and three bicycles – fit neatly into the back of the Mercedes, with a great deal of room to spare. The smaller pieces of furniture in storage were donated.

Through it all Detta remained silent. Will had many times wished she would lash out in anger, or refuse to take part in this new tablet of terrible mistakes, or tear into him with the fury of her anguish and grief and pain.

She did not.

Will watched the man's face, searching for a sign. Dr Gerald Marsh was a world-renowned neurologist, currently the head of the department at New York Presbyterian.

Will had suffered his first serious head trauma at thirteen. It happened on the day of the fire in Dobb's Ferry. When he returned to find his house engulfed in flames, he did what he knew his father would have done. He ran into the structure, his T-shirt over his mouth. He did not take more than two steps into the back door when the building began to fall under its weight. Will was struck in the back of the head by a falling ceiling joist.

The official diagnosis was head trauma and concussion, and Will spent more than a week in the hospital's ICU. He had no clear recollection of the day his mother perished in the fire. In fact, it would be months before he could remember much of anything of his life before the tragedy. There had been a number of black holes in the years since.

Dr Marsh made a few entries on Will's chart. He took off his glasses, turned in his chair. Will found that he was holding his breath.

'Everything looks good,' he said.

Will felt a wave of relief wash over him. He had hoped for the best, prepared for the worst.

'That's great.'

'I still want you to have an MRI every six months or so. At least for the next two years. If you decide to stay in Ohio I can give you any number of referrals. You're going to be close to Cleveland Clinic, and they are top flight.'

'What about complications?' Will asked. 'My memory?'

'Too soon to tell, I'm afraid. Your short-term memory seems to be fine. As to regaining long-term memory, we're going to have to wait and see.'

As Will prepared to leave, he stole a glance at the computer screen, at the image of his brain. Will had studied the human mind for nearly two decades, and knew that most of it was still unknown. What was memory? Where did it live? How is it formed, catalogued, stored?

Somewhere in there, Will thought, in that mass of gray tissue, was the memory of Amanda's face.

As long as he didn't lose that, he would survive.

On March 21, the day of the spring equinox, Will pulled over on a marginal road next to the expressway. He got out of the truck.

He looked at the New York skyline. How different it was now. How foreign and strange. He hadn't grown up in the city, but he'd met Amanda there, had asked her to marry him there, had spent his professional life there. His daughter was born in the city. Each celebration of their lives had been marked by an intersection, a block, a neighborhood, a scent, a sound. All of it New York.

But now it no longer was home.

Without a word, Will got back into the vehicle, and together he and his daughter headed west.

Spring – Abbeville

Being the true diary and journal of Eva Claire Larssen

March 22, 1869

It is springtime. Abbeville is beautiful, with the snow all melted and the grass turning green!

April 2, 1869

This morning Mr Schuyler gathered the girls at Godwin Hall and told us about all the festivals that will take place in and around the village over the coming months. He said folks come from everywhere and that there would be much to do. Especially the grandest festival of all, Appleville, which is held every twenty-five years to celebrate the return of the white raven.

As he talks I touch the gold locket at my neck. It is my own white raven.

April 5, 1869

Of all the rebirth in Abbeville this spring, the biggest change is in Dr van Laar. He suddenly seems younger, I guess I would say. Before the first day of spring, he had been listless, an old man slipping into the darkness. Now there seems to be a lilt in his step, and grand purpose in his day.

April 12, 1869

I am so exhausted. We didn't finish cleaning until after midnight. When I left the Hall I could hear something, some sort of commotion coming from down near the river beneath Veldhoeve. I stole to the edge of the forest and saw Dr van Laar working in the moonlight. He was clearing an area near the river bank, tearing out brush and hedges. He seemed to be a man possessed.

April 14, 1869

Each night, from my window, I watch Dr van Laar clear the groves. I watch as he measures, takes elevations, tills the soil by hand. There are many day-laborers at Zeven Farms who could surely do this work. This must be something special. Perhaps it has to do with his departed wife.

May 2, 1869

It is becoming known in the village that Willem and I are a pair. Willem has gone to Cleveland to attend school and I see him only rarely when he comes home to visit. When he is gone he writes me almost daily. At night, when I miss him so, I touch the gold locket at my breast and I feel as if he is here with me.

May 21, 1869

With the van Laars on a trip to the city, I let curiosity get the best of me. I let myself wander to the river behind Veldhoeve, and there I saw what Dr van Laar had been working on these many weeks. He had cleared a large number of groves – seven in all. At the entryway to each grove was a small bronze plaque with words written in Dutch. I do not know what they say.

19

Ivy pulled into the parking lot at the Abbeville station house at just after noon. Coffee in hand, she was just about to unlock the back door when the call came over police radio from County Dispatch. She keyed the rover.

It was a burglary call.

'Show me responding,' Ivy said.

The two-story house was set back from the road about one hundred feet on a semi-wooded lot. There were two outbuildings along with the three-car garage. The house and two sheds were painted a lemon yellow. The garage was a shade or two darker. To Ivy's eyes it looked like an attempt to match the colors that fell just a bit short.

Ivy exited her vehicle, walked across the driveway and around to the side door. Before ringing the doorbell she examined the lock, the doorjamb, and the windowpanes. All intact.

A few seconds later Peggy came to the door. Peggy Martin was

Ivy's age, a part-time Realtor in and around Abbeville. She invited Ivy in. Once in the kitchen, Peggy poured Ivy a cup of coffee without asking. They caught up briefly on town and personal chatter.

'How are the kids?' Ivy asked.

'Mark is doing fine. He works for Merit Brass now. Dating a nice girl. She's Methodist, but still.'

Mark Martin had always been a painfully shy young man, into ham radio and video games, anything to keep him from socializing face to face. Ivy had pegged him for a loner the rest of his life. She was glad to hear this.

'So what happened here, Peggy?'

'Well, let's see. I dropped Tammy off at her job, then did some grocery shopping. Stopped to talk a little bit too long with Cass Kellogg. You remember Cass?'

'Sure do,' Ivy said.

'Anyway, she can and does go on a bit. When I left the store I was running late, so I just came home to take a quick shower. When I walked up on the back door I saw the glass broken out.'

'The door was locked?'

'Always.'

'Can you show me?'

'Sure.'

They walked across the kitchen, down a short hallway, to a small entry room that served as a mud room. Ivy noticed the glass on the floor. A broom with a dustpan leaned against the wall.

'It was like this?' Ivy asked. 'All the glass on the inside?'

'Yes.'

Ivy examined the door jamb. It appeared that whoever had staged the burglary had shattered the glass, reached inside, and turned the deadbolt lock.

'What was taken?' Ivy asked.

'Well, the only thing missing, as far as I can tell, is my mom's vase.'

'What kind of vase?'

123

She thought about it. 'I have no idea, really.'

'Is it expensive?'

'I can't imagine it would be worth anything to anyone except me and my brother. It was just Mom's vase.'

'Did you ever have it appraised?'

'Gosh, no.'

'Can you describe it for me?'

She did. Yay high, yay wide, blue, with a gold rim.

'Anything else missing?'

'To be honest, I just don't know, Ivy. I haven't really looked everywhere.'

'Any drawers pulled out, closets emptied?'

'Nothing like that.'

Ivy made the note. 'How long were you gone this morning?'

'No more than an hour, give or take.'

'I have to ask,' Ivy said. 'Is Tammy dating anyone?'

'No one special,' she said. 'Why do you ask?'

'Just wondering if she has a boyfriend who comes over, spends time in the house.'

'No one lately. She's going through a phase.'

'Has anyone else, outside of family, been in the house lately? Tradesmen, cable TV installers, like that?'

'No,' she said. 'Not that I know of. I'll ask Don when he gets home.'

'Do you have any pictures of the vase?'

'Not *per se*, but I might have some pictures where it's in the background. That kind of thing.'

'That will work.'

Ivy spent the next ten minutes checking out the rooms in the house. In the master bedroom the drawers in the dresser did not look rifled, the closets looked orderly. A jewelry box on top of the nightstand was closed. Ivy opened it to see a collection of inexpensive earrings and bracelets. A pair of watches. Nothing luxurious, but still worth stealing, if money was the reason for the burglary.

So, if it wasn't money, she thought, what were they looking for?

A blue vase?

The only place in Abbeville that might be in the mix as far as selling a stolen antique was a curio shop at the eastern edge of the village called Time Past. The owner was a woman named Angel Harrow.

Ivy stopped in and spoke to Angel, who had not had anyone visit the shop trying to sell a blue vase recently. The woman said she would keep an eye out and give a call if someone did.

Ivy lingered in the small parking lot, collecting her thoughts. Before long she heard the police radio crackle in the SUV. She opened the door, picked up the handset, responded.

'This is Ivy, go ahead.'

Garbled speech. It sounded like Melissa Kohl. Missy Kohl was one of the two Abbeville Police officers on duty for today's day shift.

'Missy?'

There were more than a few long moments of silence, followed by equal time of radio static. Ivy was just at the outside signal range of the tower. New radios with wider reach were also on the long list of things she intended to pitch for at the next budget free for all.

'Can you say again, Missy?'

More muddled speech.

'I don't know if you can hear me,' Ivy began. 'But I'm just entering the county now. If it can wait, I'll raise you on the radio when I'm in signal range. If it can't, call me on my cell.'

Ivy listened for a response. For a few moments there was only radio silence. Then, clear as a bell, for only the second time in her life as a law enforcement officer, Ivy heard these two words over a police radio:

'It's bad.'

20

As they passed through western New York and eastern Pennsylvania, Will had done his best to be upbeat. Detta was more sullen than ever. She seemed to be pulling further away from Will, from life.

In the days and weeks that led up to the move, Will had tried to include Detta in every decision he made, decisions that were going to deeply impact their lives, both short and long term. He printed off the details on the move, the route, the general map of their new location, the details on the school system, the libraries, the town's history, the stores. He'd even bound it all into a book. In the end, though, he'd made all the decisions himself, and probably all of them for selfish reasons.

As to their destination, he'd done due diligence. Abbeville, Ohio was equidistant between Cleveland and Akron. While neither place was New York, these two cities were urban centers and had large populations. Will was certain that, in time, he could engage Detta in what these cities had to offer in terms of theater and culture and the arts.

The Abbeville school system was highly ranked in the state. For a while Will had considered the move in terms of where Detta might choose for college, but he soon realized that this was a very long time away. Just six months earlier it had felt like it was rushing towards them, but now Will thought in terms of days and weeks, certainly not years.

Even as he was doing these things, he knew in his heart that there was no long term. He had no idea if this move was a good idea or not, this total destruction of their lives in an attempt to rebuild.

They exited I-271 at Mayfield, Ohio, and stopped at a small café and bakery called Casa Dolce. Will ordered for Detta, even though he knew it wouldn't matter.

The food was delicious but, as expected, Detta didn't touch hers. Before leaving the café Will carefully rewrapped the sandwich and put it into his messenger bag.

They got back on the road and headed east on Route 322. The suburban sprawl of newer colonials and ranches and townhome clusters soon gave way to the country, and the four-lane highway became a two-lane highway, with steep hills and broad winding curves. The road took them through towns and villages called Gates Mills, Chesterland, Chagrin Falls. Will wondered what these roads would be like in the dead of winter.

The signs announcing villages appeared every few miles or so, the center of the hamlets often nothing more than an intersection, with a church and a small cemetery.

As they neared their destination the silence became unbearable.

'What do you think, honey?' Will asked. 'It's beautiful, isn't it?'

Detta stared out the passenger side window, chewed on a fingernail.

When they passed the sign that announced they were entering

127

Holland County Will felt as if he recognized the road, the trees, the landscape, as if he knew what would be around the bend in the road.

But that was not possible, was it?

They entered Abbeville from the south, at just the opposite side of the town square and the small commercial strip of stores and offices. Will had booked rooms at the town's only bed and breakfast, a newer establishment built in the 1990s called Red Oak Inn.

The inn had a large center hall, flanked by a pair of two-story wings. There were only a handful of cars in the parking lot.

Without a word, Will exited the vehicle, walked to the back, opened the rear door. He took out both of their suitcases and a shoulder bag containing their toiletries.

They walked beneath the *porte-cochère*, entered the building. Will's first impression of Red Oak Inn was a good one: polished wood, brass fittings, sparkling glass.

'Hello there,' came the voice from the other side of the lobby. The woman was in her fifties. She wore a red flannel shirt with a black vest, black jeans. 'Welcome to Red Oak.'

'Hi,' Will said. 'Will Hardy. This is my daughter, Bernadette.'

'Nice to meet you, Will and Bernadette,' she said.

She stepped behind the counter, touched a few keys on a computer keyboard. 'Any trouble finding us?'

'None at all.'

She continued to work on the computer for a few moments. She then hit the return key, and a printer behind her came to life. She reached into a drawer, took out a pair of electronic key cards.

'You are in rooms 304 and 306, two of our Valley View guest rooms. They are usually booked far in advance for this time of year, but we had a cancellation. I think you'll like them.'

'I'm sure we will,' Will said.

She handed the key cards to Will. 'Name's Reina. If you need anything, just pick up the phone and touch 8. Day or night.'

She pointed to the far end of the lobby, where Will could see into the dining room and, through the floor to ceiling windows, out on to a vast green field and a tree line beyond. 'Breakfast is buffet style, six to nine-thirty.'

Reina glanced at Detta, then back at Will. Will sensed that the woman had a daughter or two that had once been Detta's age. It was a look of compassion and understanding and empathy.

Will handed one of the cards to Detta. She took it from him and glanced around the lobby.

'Elevators are right through there,' Reina said. 'Stairs are right next to the elevators.'

Without a word, without acknowledging the woman in any way, Detta crossed the lobby and disappeared down the hallway. For a moment Will was ashamed of his daughter, a feeling that instantly morphed into his own shame. It was his way of late, and the feeling neither surprised or upset him. He looked back at Reina, a sheepish grin on his face. She winked at him. She'd been through this.

'Can I get you something?' she asked. 'Coffee or tea?'

'Coffee would be great.'

Reina pointed to the dining room. 'I'll put on a fresh pot.'

Will grabbed his bag, walked to the dining room. He was surprised at how large it was. There were thirty or so tables, with a pair of buffet tables with gleaming steam pans on one side. He looked out the large windows.

The rear of the property gave way to a gentle slope that fell to a line of trees and a forest that stretched for many miles. It was a panorama of soft and peaceful green. Will was suddenly aware of how quiet it was here.

To the left of the field was Centennial Village. The grounds were dotted with rectangular white structures, as well as circular white tents. It was surrounded with apple trees.

A few minutes later Reina approached him, in each hand a steaming mug. She handed one to Will.

'Cream and sugar is just over there.'

'Black is fine. Thanks.' Will turned back to the view. 'This is so beautiful.'

'Isn't it? Every time I start taking it for granted the season changes and I am wowed anew.'

Will sipped his coffee. It was strong and flavorful.

'I had no intention of ever being in the hospitality business,' she said. 'My husband and I stayed here twenty years ago, right when it opened, and we fell in love with the place. Five years later we heard it was for sale.'

'May I ask what you did before this?'

'My husband was an executive with Lincoln Electric in Cleveland for thirty years. I was a library administrator. We have a nice little library here, by the way. Just off the square.'

'My daughter is a big reader,' Will said. He suddenly felt as if he had to sell this woman on the notion that Detta was not some kind of brat.

'What brings you to Abbeville?' she asked. She had a manner about her that did not make the question sound as if she were prying. Will suddenly was at a loss for the words to describe the move. He couldn't figure out how to put it all into a sentence or two.

'Just visiting, really,' he said. 'We're looking into moving to the country. Thought this might be a good place to start.'

Not a lie, really. Just a thin slice of the truth.

At this Will heard the sound of the front door to the inn open and close.

'I think you're going to be seduced by the many charms

of Holland County,' Reina said. 'I think you're going to find this home.'

'Thanks.'

'If you'll excuse me.'

'Of course.'

As Reina took her leave, Will looked out the windows. The forest at the far end of the field was thick with old growth trees. Pin oak, maple, ash, sycamore. The inn was on a rise, and he could just see the canopy of the woods as it stretched out for miles.

How was Detta going to adapt to not only the next few weeks, but also the possibility of living somewhere like this? When they left the city it was with the proviso that they might one day move back. Will knew he had to keep open that option, but in his heart he hoped and planned to never return.

But it isn't just about you. Is it, Dr Hardy?

No, Will thought as he finished his coffee and headed back to the lobby and the elevators.

It is not.

If the first floor of Red Oak Inn had been welcoming, the guest rooms were even more so. The walls were a soft cream, with a deep green Berber carpet. The room boasted a king-size bed, two wing-back chairs and a secretary's desk. A pair of French doors gave way to a small balcony, which offered an even greater view of the forest. In addition was an armoire with a decent sized flat screen TV and DVD player.

After putting everything in the drawers and closets, toiletries in the bathroom, Will stepped into the hallway, walked down to Detta's room. He put his ear to the door, heard nothing. He knocked.

'Detta?'

No response.

'Are you okay?'

Will heard the TV volume get louder.

'I'm going to go for a walk,' Will said.

He thought about asking if she wanted to accompany him, but knew it would be pointless.

'I'll be back in a while.'

Nothing.

Will waited a few moments, then walked down the hall, the silence a hot, dry wind at his back.

21

Tucked between the winding paths behind Veldhoeve, just north of the seven sacred groves, was a small, private solarium. This structure was not open to the public. Indeed, no one not named van Laar had ever entered.

While seedlings for Zeven Farms were cultivated and refined in a large greenhouse at the north end of the orchards, in this hothouse was grown many secret and delicate plants, among them *belladonna, brugmansia, datura, henbane*. Stubborn germinators all, over the centuries the van Laar family had developed exotic hybrids of these forbidden plants.

Jakob stepped into the greenhouse, slipped on a pair of gloves. In the cool light thrown from the T5 fluorescents, he examined the plants. There was one in particular with which he was most interested on this day.

Rinus van Laar had originally brought the *mangradora officinarum* to Holland County from the coast of Yugoslavia as a homeopathic preparation. With it came many legends and folkloric myths, one of which included the belief that digging up the plant would cause it to shriek, thereby scaring the digger to death.

A distant cousin to the deadly nightshade, the plant had been used as an aphrodisiac and sedative. Its hallucinogenic properties, when administered in precise amounts, made it mythical, used in magic rituals and ancient witchcraft.

To know its full effect, Sébastien van Laar, Jakob's father, had brewed it into a strong decoction made from the roots of the plant. Jakob recalled that night, the evening of the summer solstice, as if it were yesterday.

Ten-year-old Jakob had sipped the tea until it was cooled, then drank it all in one gulp. At first he'd thought it was not going to have any effect. He'd thought himself too young. But before long there was suddenly a depth and breadth to his vision, a dimension he had never experienced before.

He saw so many things that moved his heart. He saw the roots beneath the soil. He saw Eva Larssen waiting beneath the octagonal roof of the gazebo in the town square.

On this day, as Jakob prepared the root of the plant, he thought about this extraordinary strain, the first and last of its kind. Over the centuries it had been called many names: Silver Vine, Angel's Trumpet, Four o'Clock Plant, Mexican Tarragon.

It was also known as Satan's Apple.

22

Will walked the short distance to the town center, a leafy green square marked by a huge water tower, and a large painted ox.

He saw an inviting bench, standing in a wedge of warm sunlight.

He sat down, closed his eyes, and saw the studious-looking redhead who sat alone that day on Washington Square, her headphones connected to her Sony Discman, a half-eaten apple in one hand, a worn paperback copy of *Madame Bovary* in the other.

Washington Square had been busy that day, bustling with students fresh to the new academic year. Will sat down at the other end of the bench, searching for something clever and witty to say as a sort of *amuse-bouche* to a conversation. Someone nearby had a radio playing Lisa Loeb's 'I Do'.

Over the years Will tried mightily to recall how their conversation began, but could not. It seems as if he'd just found himself talking to Amanda Kyle, as if he had known her forever.

They talked until the sun began to go down, the conversation ricocheting from topic to topic, each one a revelation to Will.

As the day turned into early evening, they both knew they had things to do, books to pore over, a full semester of classes to prepare for.

'Tell you what. I'll make you a bargain,' Will said.

'I *love* bargains.'

'You do?'

'Absolutely,' she said. 'Despite my elegant appearance, I do most of my shopping on Seventh Avenue on Saturday.'

'I would never have guessed. I pegged you for a trunk show junkie.'

'Stop stalling,' she said. 'What's my deal?'

'Okay. Four years from now, on this very day, assuming we're both still here, and I haven't been kicked out, I'll meet you right here.'

'Right here as in right here?'

'Right here as in right on this very *bench*.'

Amanda nodded, looked away for a few moments, then back. 'I'm not seeing the value, my friend. I mean, I like you and all, and you're kind of cute in a mismatched pair of socks sort of way, but I need a prospectus of some sort.'

'I'm getting to that.'

'Okay.'

'All things being equal, if you can still stand to look at me, and I haven't yet blown what is clearly a wonderful relationship up to this point, I'm going to propose to you.'

Amanda opened her mouth, surely to reply with some sort of clever rejoinder, but said nothing. He had caught her off guard.

'You don't have to say yes now,' he added.

'See, that's a huge relief right there. I was starting to feel the pressure.'

'So, what do you think?'

Amanda made dramatic business of counting off the years on her fingers.

'Okay then,' she said. 'You have a deal.'

They dated other people during those next four years, none of their relationships lasting more than a month or two, each time returning to each other. They had a terrible sense of timing for awhile, each involved with someone while the other was free.

Will knew that he had hardened his heart after his father's death, and the fire in Dobb's Ferry, as well as in all the cloistered corners of his boarding schools. He had steeled himself to relationships with any measure of intimacy. As he got to know Amanda he learned that this was also true for her. She'd lost both her parents at a young age.

In his junior year Will had the crazy notion that he might have found someone about whom he could be serious, but soon realized that most of that was based on the fact that Amanda had been unavailable, at the time dating a Sarah Lawrence transfer who ate his pizza with a knife and fork.

Will spent much of his senior year abroad, communicating with Amanda mostly by letter, save for a pair of ill-advised and ill-timed phone calls, calls during which he was certain Mr Prissy was nearby.

He returned to the states with Trevor Butler's idea floating in his mind, a prospect that sat high in his thoughts. The notion of getting to ply his clinical skills in an exotic but dangerous place like the Middle East, experience he knew would serve him well in grad school. He knew that his father had been a man who had run toward the fire, not away, and knew that this was something he needed to prove about himself.

At long last the day arrived. Will changed his clothes a dozen times, shaved more closely than he ever had in his life. Because they had not specified a time of day, he got to Washington Square around 8 a.m., a dozen roses in hand. By noon he was beginning to feel stupid. When she didn't show by 5 p.m., he was certain of it.

That night he got drunk, and faxed the signed papers. In that order. He was going to the Middle East.

The next day he wandered around the NYU campus, mostly considering how he'd screwed up any chance with Amanda with his fear of commitment.

Before heading back he stood behind the bench, watching the students walking quickly across the square, feeling really old.

'You're here.'

Will spun around. Amanda was standing right behind him.

She looked more beautiful than ever.

'You didn't show yesterday, so I just figured . . . '

'You figured what?'

'I figured you weren't coming.'

'Wrong day, buster.'

'What?'

'You forgot Leap Year.'

'I did?'

Amanda nodded, put her arms around him. 'So, about that deal.'

Will told her about his upcoming year in the Middle East. For a long time she just stood there, looked off into the distance. He'd blown it. He was sure of it.

'Well, then,' Amanda said. 'There's only one option.'

'What's that?'

Forty-eight hours later, they were married at city hall.

On the way down the steps, Amanda said: 'So, about that Leap Year thing?'

'What about it?'

'When you tell this story to our grandchildren, you better get that part straight.'

A battered red Frisbee sailed across the Abbeville town square, and landed at Will's feet. He saw a shadow approaching rapidly from his left; a really small shadow. He turned to look. Apple cheeks, the brightest blue eyes, wispy blond hair sneaking out of a knit cap. Will picked up the Frisbee, handed it to the girl, who was no more than four years old.

Our grandchildren.

Will got off the bench and was across the street before his emotions betrayed him.

23

When Ivy had heard those two words, she knew.

It's bad.

'You have your cell phone with you, Missy?'

'Yes,' she said. 'Yes, Chief.'

'I'm going to call you right now.'

Nothing. Just radio static.

'Missy, you have to tell me that you hear me, and that you understand. Can you hear me?'

'Yes, Chief.'

'I'm going to call you right now on your cell phone. Do you copy?'

'Yes.'

When Ivy called Missy Kohl, she answered in one ring. Usually, cell communication was inferior to radio communication in this part of the county. Not today. At least Ivy could understand what her officer was saying now.

'What's going on, Missy?'

'There's ... there's a dead body.'

'Where are you?'

Missy gave her the location. It was about ten miles south of the village square, down a two-lane road that was mostly county-owned land, sparsely populated overgrown farm land, near the Abbeville Wetlands. The Wetlands was a seven-hundred-acre preserve located within the upper Cuyahoga River watershed.

'Male, female?'

'Female,' Missy said. 'Young.'

'A juvenile?'

'Teenager, I think.'

Ivy felt a cold finger on her spine. She glanced south, toward the crime scene location, and in the darkening clouds saw the face of Paulette Graham.

'I'll be there in about fifteen minutes,' Ivy had said. 'I need you to secure the scene.'

No response. It was infuriating.

'Missy?'

'Hurry, Chief.'

What do you see, Ivy Lee?

It was her mother's voice, her mother's question.

Ivy's first recollection of the riddle was when she'd once accompanied her mother to a minor disturbance on a Saturday afternoon, just a few days after school let out for that year. Ivy had been about ten years old at the time.

The 'disturbance' was a domestic dispute, but in those days it was called wife beating. Bill Rogers had taken a hand to his wife again, it seemed.

When Ivy June emerged from the Rogers house with a disheveled, unshaven Bill Rogers in handcuffs, he wore only one corduroy slipper. There was blood on his ripped T-shirt.

Her mother leaned in the window of the patrol car and asked the question.

What do you see, Ivy Lee?

141

In that moment Ivy saw past the obvious, saw the beetles beneath the sod. She saw the nature of some men, and the way they treat their women. She saw that these men – her father was one of them – were just bottom shelf bullies, and even in defeat could not stand up to what they truly were. Bill Rogers had taken a few licks from his wife, but he'd rather go to jail than admit it.

It was one of the reasons Ivy first picked up a camera, a Kodak Instamatic she found at a barn sale in Huntsburg. She wanted to document the things she saw, print them out, and compare the photograph to her memory.

More than once she found that her memory, and what really happened, were two different things.

The scene was an isolated clearing a half-mile north of a dying parcel of land that had one time been a small but thriving dairy farm. Pell Gardner's place. As Ivy approached she saw that there was still a main house with a swaybacked roof, a large barn and a pair of small outbuildings, all but owned by time and neglect and nature.

What do you see, Ivy Lee?

She could see the north side of the main house, the curled paint chips on the siding. The roof was in deep desire of repair, patched and tarred in a dozen spots, the gutters on the west side of the house dangled. The side yard was overgrown with knee-high grass. A pair of truck fenders marked the entrance to the access road that disappeared into the tree line about a quarter mile behind the barn.

Officer Melissa Kohl was twenty-eight, a petite brunette in just her second year on the force. As a rule Missy was quiet and reserved and exceedingly well-mannered, a blusher of the first order. Today, Ivy noted, her complexion was paper white.

Missy was deployed at the end of the driveway, halfway

between the house and the main barn. She was nervously drumming the fingers of her right hand on her right thigh. Ivy knew that this was her officer's first suspicious death.

'Hey, Chief.'

Ivy nodded. 'Where's the scene?'

Missy pointed to the path that led to the woods. 'Back there. Maybe a half-mile.'

'This was a 911?'

'It was.' Missy had her notebook in hand. She flipped a page back. 'Call came at 8.21 this morning. Man named Dallas Lange.'

Ivy knew Dallas. 'Did he say what brought him back here?'

'Not that I heard.'

Ivy had a good idea what it was. Dallas Lange was a four-season hunter. These few weeks, in Holland and surrounding counties, were designated for bearded turkey shoots. There was a good chance that Dallas was on the hunt or clearing the area of bait. It was unlawful to hunt bearded turkey with bait.

'Is Mr Lange still here somewhere?'

'No, Chief. I met him here, he showed me the spot, then he said he had to take his wife to the doctor. Said he'd be right back.'

'Okay.'

'Where do you want me?'

'Right by my side, Missy.'

Officer Kohl blanched.

'Tell you what,' Ivy said. 'I'll get Walt on his cell phone, have him come out and help us secure the scene.' Officer Walt Barnstable was off duty today, or at least that's how his day began. He was on duty now. 'Then I'll call BCI and get that started. Meanwhile let's get out the tape and cordon this area off.' Ivy pointed at the four corners she meant, boxing in the house and outbuildings, as well as the path. 'If you don't have enough tape, check the backseat of my SUV. You'll need some stakes, too. But first I need you to walk me back.'

Officer Kohl nodded, stole a quick glance at the path, still looking a little shaky. A *lot* shaky.

'You okay?' Ivy asked.

'I believe I might be sick.'

Ivy put a hand on the young woman's shoulder.

'I believe you will not,' Ivy said. 'I believe you are going to take a few deep breaths, and remember in full color your training. We are hewn from the same tree, Missy Kohl.'

On the tail of a deep breath she said, 'Okay.'

'Plan B,' Ivy said. 'You raise Walt, I'll string the tape. Then I'll walk myself back.' Ivy patted her belt. 'Need to work off Sandy's fry pies.'

'I'm on it.'

In short order Ivy had the yellow tape staked and strung. Before walking into the woods, Ivy returned to her SUV, took out her Nikon D60.

She then approached the overgrown path. At the foot of it were two wooden posts that were not buried deep enough into their post holes, and were canted at sharp angles. A rusted chain lay half buried in the ground, as was a rusted NO TRESPASSING sign.

But someone *had* trespassed.

As Ivy walked toward the woods she did not notice any recent tire tracks of either the two-wheel or four-wheel variety. The weather had been on a routine of rain and shine every day for the past week or so, sometimes every few hours.

Every ten yards or so Ivy would turn and glance back at the receding homestead, as well as the road. If the victim had taken this route into the woods, and something was gaining on her, Ivy wanted to see it the way she saw it.

About five minutes later she emerged into a clearing, approximately fifty yards square. In the center was a charred circle of earth and burned logs. The logs had moss on them. It had been a long time since someone had built a campfire here. Dotted around the clearing were rusted objects, broken things.

When Ivy stepped from the trees, and saw the victim, she knew. The forensics might prove her wrong, the circumstances surrounding the death of this girl might demonstrate something wholly other, but Ivy felt something awaken in her at that moment, something that began its life twenty-five years earlier, and now, with the still-unsolved death of Paulette Graham, and the sight of this girl, it roused to great and terrible life.

Mindful of where she was stepping, Ivy drew closer. The girl was indeed a teenager. She was white, no more than fifteen or sixteen. She had long, nearly ink-black hair, pulled into a single braid that wrapped around her throat. She was lying on her right side.

Ivy stepped to the victim to look more closely, to confirm she saw what she was seeing.

'My God.'

Just a few inches from the victim's head was a crown made of bird wings. The pair of wings seemed to be attached to a circle of thin branches, bent and lacquered and secured by a wire. The wire was not rusted. Whatever this was, it had not been out here long.

And neither had the victim. Although Ivy would wait for the coroner, she believed the girl had been exposed to the elements fewer than three days. Anything longer would surely have invited the attention of any number of wildlife, as had the body of Paulette Graham, which made the cause and manner of death inconclusive in that case, just as it had with Charlotte Foster.

Ivy closed her eyes for a moment, saw Paulette Graham's body in that other field, located about twenty miles south, saw all the girls, and wondered if it was the same for them, if they had taken darkness by the hand and willingly walked a winding path into the forest, into the beyond.

24

Will had thought he would give himself a day to settle at Red Oak, but he was restless. There was still one document to sign, not to mention getting the keys to Godwin Hall.

He decided to get it all out of the way.

The law offices of Charles Bristow, Esquire were located above an independent shoe store on Melville Street, just off the town square.

Will called and made an appointment.

As it turned out, Mr Bristow had an opening, and within an hour Will signed the necessary documents, and was told he could have the keys that afternoon, as soon as the notary returned from his morning fishing trip.

At no extra charge, Will learned that the Bullfinch Tavern had a tasty lunch special available until 2.30, and that Centennial Village would be worth the visit, even though the main attractions were not yet open for the season.

*

Centennial Village was a two-acre site that, according to the bronze plaques near the entrance, was laid out to resemble Abbeville as it was plotted and built in the early nineteenth century. To the east was the banks of the Cuyahoga River. To the west were a few hundred trees of the orchard that bounded the Fairgrounds between Godwin Hall and something called Veldhoeve.

The attraction was comprised of a dozen or so buildings that had been built around Holland County in the past two hundred years, many of which were transplanted to the site and set up to create the village writ small. And all of it overlooked a breathtaking view of the valley and the river as it wound its way through the countryside.

In addition to the first house built, there was a saw mill, a tin shop, a blacksmith and a tannery.

Will imagined what it would be like in summer, and he could see how Godwin Hall could be a viable business, even if it only attracted guests for the spring, summer and fall months. The attraction was a bit shopworn, but was still quaint and carried enough history to be a destination of sorts. At the north end, near the town square was a two-story yellow clapboard building.

At street level a small sign announced that the Abbeville Historical Society was housed on the second floor, above the barber shop. The entrance, on the side of the building facing the school, was an exterior stairwell.

Will glanced at his watch.

He had time.

The main room was small and carefully cluttered, with a glass counter to the left. On the counter were a number of wooden boxes and wire racks in which were displayed vintage and current postcards for sale.

Under the glass were older items; a top hat, a pottery pitcher, a pair of antique ice cream scoops, a whale oil lamp. On the bottom row were cast iron bookends, cupboard jars, and a tin shaving mug, each with a small card detailing their year and significance. Over the door was a crest bearing two beautifully carved ravens. One black, one white.

Feeling a bit like an intruder, Will closed the door behind him, and stepped fully into the room. Straight ahead was a display of antique household machines, corn shellers, washing tubs.

To the right there were three other rooms. A glance into the room on the right showed that it was a small area dedicated to vintage and antique clothing. Will could see that there were a pair of glass cases that held jewelry and women's accessories like hats and scarves and mufflers.

'Hello.'

Will spun around. Before him stood a man of indefinable old age, perhaps in his eighties. He wore a powder blue cotton shirt, buttoned to the top, loose around his thin neck. Over this he wore a navy blue suit coat, shiny from many a Sunday's wear, a four button style that Will had not seen in years.

'Didn't mean to startle you, young man,' the man said.

'I guess I was just . . .'

'Lost in time?'

'I think you're right,' Will said. 'This is a really interesting collection you have here.'

'I will say thank you on behalf of the Abbeville Historical Society,' he said. 'They were around long before I was born, and they will be around long after I'm gone, I expect.' The man straightened a few brochures on the counter. 'What brings you up here today, young man?'

'Curiosity, I guess.'

'Are you just visiting Abbeville, or have you fallen under the spell of Holland County and decided to pound your stakes?'

'I guess you could say the latter. I just moved here. Just this week.'

The old man slowly made his way around the counter.

'Name is Eleazar Johnson,' he said. 'Folks call me Eli. Welcome to Abbeville.'

'Will Hardy.'

The moment drew out. 'You're here for Godwin Hall.'

'I am.'

Eli continued to hold his hand for a while.

'I have something to show you,' he finally said.

Eli returned to the area behind the counter. It took everything Will had not to help him, but the man made slow, steady progress. Once behind the counter Eli reached over, opened a drawer, retrieved a single key on an old leather fob. He made his way back around into the main part of the room, this time a little more spryly, a man on a mission.

They passed through the room with all the household displays. Eli pushed open the drapery, revealing an old door with a skeleton key lock.

Eli opened the door. He reached inside, fumbled for a few moments, then found the light switch. Will could see that the lighting in the room was provided by a pair of large, globe fixtures. Above the door was a legend. It read:

Godwin Hall.

Nearly all of one wall in the small room was dedicated to photographs of Godwin Hall over the years. On another wall there were nearly three dozen posters and photographs. The Apple Butter Festival, the Maple Syrup Festival, the River Fest, Ice Festival, various pancake breakfasts, wine fests, ice cream socials.

The largest poster was for something called *Appleville.*

Will pointed at it. 'Is that a typo?'

Eli laughed. 'You're not the first person to think so. Fact is, the Appleville Festival is a pretty big deal around these parts. It's only held every twenty-five years.'

'Why twenty-five?'

'That's when the white raven returns. People come from all around just to get a glimpse.'

'Kind of like the cicadas?'

Eli winked. 'Or Brigadoon.'

'Have you ever seen it?'

'The white bird? Oh yeah. First time when I was eight. Next time wasn't until fifty years later.'

'And you say the festival is a big draw?'

'It is. If you get the Hall spruced and fit in time you'll make out all right.'

'Wait – you're saying the festival is *this* year?'

'This very one. The gala is put on by the van Laar family, which has been bankrolling it since 1869.' Eli pointed at the largest photo, a beautiful portrait of Godwin Hall in its glory years. 'The Hall has a history, as does any building of its age. More than most, seeing as it was a hotel and rooming house for many years. People come and go, and leave their stories behind, don't they?'

'Yes they do,' Will said.

'Are you a family man, Will Hardy?'

The question caught Will off guard. Even when he anticipated such a query, it was an arrow. He said, simply: 'Yes.'

'Any children?'

'I have a daughter. Her name is Bernadette. She's fifteen.'

'Is she taken by stories of ghosts and lingering evil?'

Will didn't have to think about this too long. 'No,' he said. 'Not particularly.'

It was true. Detta was always the level-headed one, the realist. Just like her mother. If anyone was 'taken by ghosts and lingering evil' it was Will. He'd grown up reading Shirley Jackson, H.P. Lovecraft, and Richard Matheson, books his father had read between calls.

Eli pointed to a photograph, a small sepia print. 'Can you hand me that one there?'

'Of course,' Will said. He crossed the room, took the framed print from the wall. The area behind the photograph was a much lighter shade of yellow. The picture had not been moved for many years, it seemed. He handed the photograph to Eli.

Eli sat in the padded folding chair next to the door, adjusted his glasses, stared at the image for a few moments. Will could see that it was a picture of eight young women, teenagers by appearance. They wore white cotton dresses with aprons, uniforms used by scullery maids and housekeepers. They each wore a floppy white hat.

Eli touched the glass, brushed away some of the dust. 'This was taken just outside the back door at Godwin Hall. These young ladies worked there.'

'They all worked there at the same time?'

'Yes. They worked in the kitchen.'

'It seems like a pretty big kitchen staff.'

'Oh, it's my understanding that there were more people working there than this,' he said. 'You've got to understand, in its early days, Godwin Hall was quite the place to be. Especially in the 1800s. Back then it was known as the only hotel of taste and elegance in this part of Holland County. Anyone who was anyone stayed there.'

The girls' names were written along the bottom in faded blue ink. The last girl on the right, the smallest of them, had much of her face obscured by scratches. Beneath her image was a name written in blue ink.

Eva Larssen.

Eli pointed at her. 'There is a story told that this girl came to a tragic end,' he said. 'More than a story, really. It is part of the dark lore of Abbeville.'

'What happened to her?'

Eli thought for a few seconds.

'Let me put a few things together for you,' Eli said. 'I'll have it by the next time I see you. I think you'll find it all pretty interesting.'

'Okay,' Will said. 'That would be great.'

Eli pointed to the row of photographs near the crown molding of the high ceiling. 'There's some better pictures up there. We'll get those down next time.'

Will took a step back. 'This is great stuff,' he said. 'I could spend all day here.'

'You are welcome to do just that.'

Will glanced at his watch. 'I've got to be somewhere. What days are you open?'

Eli reached into his inside coat pocket, took out a three by five card. It was printed in old-style fonts. The museum was open three days a week. Seven days a week in July and August.

'You're at Red Oak?' Eli asked.

'I am.'

The man reached behind the counter, brought up a small stack of folded newspapers. Will noted that it was a local publication called *The Villager*.

'Help yourself to a copy,' Eli said. 'It's all about the comings and goings and doings in Abbeville.'

Will took one of them. 'Thanks.'

'I've got a granddaughter does some writing for them. She's still in high school. Just an intern, I guess they call it.'

'Okay.'

'Think you might have a minute or two to talk to her? Tell her about your plans for the Hall?'

He didn't really have any plans yet.

'Uh, sure,' Will said. 'No problem.'

'She'll be thrilled. Her name's Cassie Mills. Cassandra is her byline name. I'll give her a call right now.'

'I look forward to it.'

The old man once again offered his hand. 'Welcome home, Will Hardy.'

25

Dallas Lange leaned against the fender of his truck, a perfectly maintained Silverado. Dallas was in his seventies, but stood hickory straight. He wore his hair a little long, but it was always trimmed, as was his handlebar mustache. He was often seen in the village during the summer months on his classic Indian Scout motorcycle.

Ivy had known Dallas Lange as long as she'd known any adult, except her mother and her grade school teachers. Before Dallas began doing welfare checks for the county, he had owned Abbeville's only picture frame shop.

As long as Ivy could remember, she would take her film to the shop to get her pictures developed. It was just a little more expensive than it was at the Rexall in those days – back when there was a Rexall – but the drugstore didn't have all the items that Town Frame had. Mr Lange's shelves were stocked with glassware, custom jewelry, imported stationery, and greeting cards. Now everything was digital and you could buy a color printer for $29.00.

'Dallas,' Ivy said.

'Chief Holgrave. Been awhile.'

Ivy wasn't sure what he meant by this. She'd seen him just a few days earlier at Sundae in the Park, the ice cream wagon parked at the edge of the Fairgrounds in the spring and summer months. 'What do you mean, Dallas?'

Dallas looked out over the field. 'The last time was Thad Morrison. Did you know Thad?'

Ivy had never met the man, but she knew the story. At least, the version kicked around the tables at the Bullfinch. 'Never had the pleasure.'

'We were tracking deer that time. North of Cumberland. Me, Thad, his two brothers. George's Remington misfired. Found Thad bleeding at the bottom of the quarry. That was the last time. Until today.'

Ivy now knew what he meant. He was talking about the last he had seen a dead body.

'Saw my share in Vietnam, of course. More than my share.' He looked back at Ivy. His eyes were rimmed with red. 'Never a young one like this. Lots of young boys tore up. Never a girl.'

'You okay to talk now, Dallas?' Ivy asked. 'If you want I can meet you back at the station. Give you some time.'

'No time like now, Chief.'

'Okay.' Ivy took out her notebook, flipped to a fresh page. 'Tell me how you came to be back here today.'

Dallas gave her a brief recount of his morning, how he'd taken his breakfast at Kate's Kitchen before waiting in line at the BMV in Jenkintown. He then told her that he had come out to the area north of the Gardner place in order to clear bait before turkey hunting season kicked off the next week.

'I was just getting ready to head back when I thought I saw something in the clearing. Didn't even know the clearing was back there, truth told.'

There were any number of glades in the wooded lands of Holland County, thousands of acres that contained small areas cleared of timber years ago when logging was the main industry of the area. Mostly, the areas were cleared to make way for a cabin or logging station, structures that never got built.

'What did you think you saw?'

'Wasn't sure. It just looked like it didn't belong.'

'Did you see anybody else?'

'No one. Not today, anyway.'

'What do you mean?'

'I was out early yesterday morning. Needed to check where the bait needed to be cleared.'

'And you saw someone?'

Dallas nodded. 'I saw somebody turn off Cavender.'

Cavender Road was an east-west two-lane, another quarter mile north of their position.

'Which way did they turn?' Ivy asked.

'North.'

'Was it a car? Truck? Van?'

'Pickup. White in color.'

'Have you seen it before?'

'I think I have. The only reason I know the truck is that set of bar lights across the top. You know how some have the red and white lights in it?'

'I do.'

'It was like that. Don't see that too much.'

'Are you saying it was a county truck? Some kind of official vehicle maybe?'

'No,' Dallas said. 'I think it belongs to the Deacons.'

Ivy's pulse picked up. The Deacon family had a long and checkered history of interaction with the police, as well as the courts and correction facilities in Holland County, going back two generations.

155

'You're saying it was one of the Deacon boys?'

'Can't say that for sure. Couldn't see who was driving. I just remember that rack of lights up top, and how some of those bulbs were red.'

'And what time was this?'

'Early. Sun was up, but just.'

Ivy made the note. 'Just a few more questions for now, Dallas, if you're okay with that.'

'All the time you need, Chief.'

'Did you move anything?'

'What do you mean?'

'Back in the field. Other than clearing the bait, did you move anything?'

'No. The moment I saw what it was I just froze, to be honest with you. I kept thinking she was going to sit up, like she was just sleeping or something.'

'How long did you watch?'

'Maybe a minute or so. It kind of felt like I was snooping for a while there. Like I came up on something private. When she didn't move I called out a few times. When she didn't respond, I knew.'

'Do you know this girl, Dallas?'

Dallas shook his head. He was getting visibly upset. Ivy knew she should wrap up this phase of her questioning soon.

'No,' he said. 'I don't think I've ever seen her before.'

A car crested the road just to the south of them, and for no apparent reason, Ivy Holgrave and Dallas Lange fell silent as it approached, perhaps in unspoken respect to the gravity of their conversation.

'What happened to this girl, Ivy?' Dallas finally asked.

Ivy had her ideas, but she'd keep them close for the time being. 'We're looking into it. Early days.'

Dallas reached into his back pocket, pulled out a pair of

driving gloves. He made a short ceremony of putting them on, fitting the fingers.

'It's not supposed to be girls, Ivy,' Dallas continued. 'Boys rough it up, get into dangerous games. Some live that hard life. But girls? It's not supposed to be girls.' He looked over at Ivy, a sheen glossing his eyes. 'That makes me pretty old-fashioned, I guess.'

'Not at all.'

In the distance, Ivy could hear faint thunder. She had to move.

'You've got my number,' she said. 'Give me a ring if you think of anything else. If not, I'll be in touch to get a formal statement in the next day or so.'

Dallas nodded again. He crossed the road, got into his truck, started it. A few moments later he pulled off the berm, and headed south on Route 44.

Ivy watched until his truck vanished over the crest of the hill. Then, for the moment, Holland County was once again silent.

26

The boy was in the south barn. The smell of the hay and ordure always returned Jakob to his childhood.

He crossed the main area and pushed open the door to the large box-stall. There, in the center of the space, was a table constructed of a pair of six by twelve sheets of laminated plywood on saw horses. Drying on top of the table, propped on sixteen-penny nails, were items of bedroom furniture. This part of the barn smelled of mineral spirits.

The furniture was older, perhaps even antique if one were to stretch the accepted definition of the word – which was far more common in the trade than people were wont to admit, there being a thin line between junk and collectible.

Before long, the boy came around the corner, tack cloths in hand.

'Did you follow the inscription?' Jakob asked.

'Yeah,' he said. 'It's just like it was written.'

The boy picked up a microfiber cloth. He touched one of the

items with a wrapped forefinger. 'It goes from here to here,' he said, moving his finger across the breadth.

Jakob leaned close. He could not discern anything that might raise a doubt or suspicion.

'What about the photograph?' Jakob asked.

The boy crossed the barn, returned with a pair of printed documents. He handed them to Jakob. Jakob angled the paper to the light streaming through the barn door. It was perfect. The color photograph was just faded enough to give the viewer an idea of the color and quality of the item, without looking too professional. The text beneath the image was concise and to the point, and even contained a typographical error.

'How much more time do you need?' Jakob asked.

The boy glanced at the items. 'Maybe a day or two.'

'Fine,' Jakob said.

Jakob again looked at the document.

'Do you remember where to put this?'

'Yeah,' the boy said. 'And not to do it until you say so.'

Jakob reached into his pocket, removed a single one-hundred-dollar bill. The boy's eyes lit up.

'When you place it, do not be seen.'

27

The Deacon spread was a throwback to an earlier time in Holland County, but not a good one. To Ivy it looked like one of those Depression-era small farms where the grass is browned out, the trees are dead or dying, with a half-dozen vehicles in some state of decay and disassembly, perched on blocks.

Then again, this wasn't a surprise. If the Deacons loved anything, it was cars. So much so that the three boys, of this generation anyway, were named Dodge, Ford and Chevy.

There was a main house, along with two outbuildings. One was a two-car garage, from which one of the doors had been removed, and not with a tool. The roof was caved on the south side.

As Ivy approached she saw no movement on the property, nor did she see a white pickup truck; red and white bar lights above or otherwise. She made her way to the porch, gave a glance through the windows. Nothing stirring. The screen door was closed, but the inside door was open.

A few seconds later Ivy saw Theresa Deacon walk out of the kitchen, wiping her hands on a dishtowel.

'Afternoon, Theresa.'

Terry Deacon had been a beauty in high school, a tall athletic girl who'd had her pick of the boys. She was once a Miss Something-Or-Other. Ivy could never keep the small-town beauty queen titles straight, having never been in the running. Holland County had no shortage of festivals, and there was always a girl to lead the parade with a plastic tiara on her head.

But that was a long time ago. Now Terry Deacon looked depleted in a way that only women of an age who'd made bad choice after bad choice in their men and their lives could look. Her hair was up in bright yellow hot rollers.

'What brings you out here, Ivy?'

Take your pick, Ivy thought. *They're your boys.*

'Any of your sons around?'

'Chevy's working,' she said. 'He's got them two ex-wives now and y'all gonna jail him up if he don't pay his alimony.'

'All due respect, Terry, he was the one who married them. Wasn't like a village ordinance or anything.'

She flicked a hand, meaning, *whatever.* 'Youngest is off doing whatever the hell it is he does during the day.'

Ivy knew exactly what he was doing. Ford Deacon had been arrested twice for possession of meth, more than a half-dozen times for burglaries to pay for his habit. No hard stretch in prison yet. Matter of time.

'Where's Chevy working these days?' Ivy asked.

'He's over to Aqualine.'

Aqualine Water Quality Systems was a small manufacturing plant in Geauga County.

'What shift is he working again?'

'First,' Terry said. 'Got a side job, too. Making deliveries. Why you asking?'

161

'All part of a broader investigation,' Ivy said. 'Nothing to worry about.'

This was her stock answer, and had been for years. She learned it from a lifer in the Cleveland PD.

'What about Dodge? Is he around?' Ivy asked.

Terry looked over Ivy's shoulder, nodded in the general direction of the outbuilding. 'He's been sleeping in the shack since it's warm enough. Comes and goes. Got his music and his trashy girlfriend. He's been seeing that Warburton girl.'

'Do you know his whereabouts over the last few days?'

Terry Deacon laughed, but there was no joy in it. 'Might have been on Mars with that shit he smokes.'

'Fair enough,' Ivy said. 'That's not my business today.' She pointed at the shack. 'I'll just go give him a quick knock, see if I can have a word or two with him.'

'Suit yourself.'

'Meant to ask,' Ivy began. 'One of the boys has those bar lights on top of his truck. The kind with the red and white lights?'

'What about it?'

'I want to get some for my personal truck, but I can't seem to find them at Wal-Mart or Target. Any idea where they got them?'

'I have no idea. But every time one of the boys turns them on it looks like a goddamn tornado coming through here.'

'Okay,' Ivy said. 'Thanks.'

Ivy put away her notepad, looked at the outbuilding. In an attempt to make the decaying building look more like a dwelling there was a blue and white gingham tablecloth stapled over the window as a curtain. As Ivy approached the structure she saw someone walk around the far corner, a black plastic Hefty bag in hand.

It was Dodge Deacon.

A rangy young man in his late twenties, Dodge wore filthy

black Levi's, mud-caked to the knees, camo cap, and a ratty OSU hoodie with more cigarette holes than thread. When he saw Ivy come around the corner of the shack he dropped the sack in his hands and turned to run.

'Hold up there, Dodge.'

Dodge Deacon stopped, but didn't turn to face Ivy. If there was anything she had learned in two-plus decades of law enforcement, especially on patrol, it was how to read body language. In her time she'd had people run, jump, swim, shimmy, scurry, lope, and stumble away from her. Or try to. Dodge was in what she called the shotgun-shell mode, ready to blast himself across the field in any number of directions, as long as it wasn't anywhere near Chief Ivy Holgrave.

'I'm too old to chase you,' Ivy said. 'I think you're counting on that.'

'But I didn't *do* nothing.'

'Never said you did. Now, are you going talk to me or are we going to have to ratchet this up a notch or two?'

Dodge relaxed his shoulders, his legs. He turned to face Ivy, hands at his sides, a little away from his body.

Ivy took out her notebook, clicked her ballpoint, flipped a page.

'Need to know your whereabouts over the past few days, starting with yesterday.'

'This past yesterday?'

'That's the one,' Ivy said. 'The one that came before today.'

'Yesterday?'

'Still yesterday.'

Dodge wiggled the fingers on both hands. 'I think I was home all day.'

'Should I take a peek at your iCal?'

'My what?'

'Let's start with the morning part,' Ivy said. 'What time did you wake up?'

More finger calisthenics. 'Yesterday?'

'I'm going to put in a request that you never again say that word in my presence. Ever. Can you oblige me on that?'

He nodded.

'I appreciate it,' Ivy said. 'Let's start with geography. Did you wake up in this house?'

'Yeah.'

'What time?'

He shrugged twice. 'I don't know.'

'Before noon?'

'What time does *Price is Right* come on?' he asked. 'The new one. The one with that funny guy from Cleveland. Not the old one.'

Ivy hadn't watched the show in years. She had no idea what time it came on. She'd look it up. 'Eleven o'clock.'

'Right around there, then.'

Finally. A note. She wrote this down. 'Were you alone?'

'I was with Maggie.'

'She can confirm this?'

'I don't know. I guess so.'

'Who is this Maggie?'

Dodge pointed at the back door of the shack. It took Ivy a few moments, but she finally saw what he meant. It was a grimy plastic salad bowl, dotted with dead flies. Next to it lay a rusted chain.

'Maggie's a dog?'

'Yeah.'

This raised a quill. 'What kind of dog is Maggie, Dodge?'

'A mutt. Got some hound in her, but mostly a Rott.'

'A Rottweiler?'

'Yeah.'

Ivy moved her hand closer to the grip on her weapon, glanced around the yard, toward the tree line. The truth was she'd rather hurt some humans she knew than hurt any dog. Unless that dog was trying to eat her. 'Where is she right now?'

Dodge glanced at the sky, as if Maggie might be flying overhead. 'Can't say for certain about where she is this very minute, but my brother took her with him to the Home Depot this morning.'

Ivy relaxed a little.

'Don't know what, if anything, you've heard about this bad business that happened out at the Gardner farm,' Ivy said. 'My inquiries at this point are just routine, but I still have to make them. Do you understand what I'm saying?'

Dodge Deacon shifted his weight onto his left foot, slightly away from her.

'Look, you and I don't really have a history, Dodge. I had a few run-ins with your daddy, that's true, but you and I both know that was Ray's doing. You ask for something hard enough and long enough in this life, you get it. I didn't put him in Lucasville. He put himself there. I was sorry to hear of his passing.'

'Thank you, ma'am.'

'I need to know what you know about this business, Dodge.'

Dodge Deacon just stared at his boots.

'Were you out by Cavender Road recently?'

'Cavender Road?'

'That's right.'

'No,' he said. 'I don't go out there.'

'But your truck has the bar lights on top, doesn't it?'

'No.'

Ivy retrieved her notepad. 'It's registered to you. A 2014 F-150, white in color.'

'See, now, that's Chevy's truck.'

'Then why is it in your name?'

Dodge again looked at the sky. Ivy had a good idea why.

'There's isn't anything you can say that's gonna make me clutch my pearls, Dodge. We're just two folks talking.'

'It's because of the credit.'

'The credit?'

'Chevy don't have none. He had to buy the truck on time, see, but he couldn't get the credit. Mine is still good.'

'So you're saying Chevy drives that 150?'

'Yes, ma'am.'

At this Ivy's cell phone rang. She looked at the caller ID. It was from someone at BCI. This was good. She answered.

'Can you hold a minute?'

On the phone, a man's voice said that he could. Ivy turned back to Dodge Deacon.

'Don't go anywhere.'

Ivy stepped away, took the call. It was Special Agent Gary Baudette from BCI. He told her he was en route to the scene with his mobile crime lab, and estimated his time of arrival at around forty-five minutes. Ivy thanked him, signed off, looked at the angry clouds to the west. She hoped the rain would hold off. She stepped back to where Dodge Deacon stood.

'I'd like to continue our discussion, but I have to be somewhere,' Ivy said. 'Can we talk later today?'

Dodge said nothing.

'I know you know full well where the police station is, but I'm going to give you my card so there's no misunderstanding.'

Dodge held out a hand, Ivy handed him a card.

'You won't make me come looking for you, right?'

'No, ma'am.'

'I aim to straighten this out, and you can help me, Dodge.'

'Yes, ma'am.'

As Ivy climbed into her vehicle, she glanced back to where Dodge Deacon stood. His shoulders were shaking.

He was crying.

*

166

When Ivy returned to the Gardner farm the scene was buzzing with activity. Baudette and two of his BCI agents were setting up.

The Bureau of Criminal Investigation was a part of the Ohio Attorney General's office, with more than four hundred employees, covering the three divisions – Laboratory, Investigation, and Identification. The laboratory section handled evidence processing, firearms, documents, anything a full-service laboratory might process.

Agent Gary Baudette was in his mid-forties, a lifer. He was from a small town in Franklin County, near Columbus. Ivy had never seen him without a tie. He was a trim man, on the shorter side, but solid. Today he wore a navy blue BCI windbreaker.

'Afternoon, Ivy,' Baudette said.

'Good to see you, Gary.' This was a common enough greeting, even though the circumstances that put them in the same place were rarely good.

'Coroner's come and gone,' Baudette said. 'He's pronounced her.'

'He say anything about cause or manner?'

Baudette shook his head. 'Not yet.'

'What about time?'

'Nothing official yet.'

When Ivy stepped away Baudette and his two investigators began to process the immediate scene. A good deal of the lab work took place in one of BCI's labs – the nearest one in Richfield, Ohio – but there were many parts of the investigation that began at the crime scene, including blood samples, touch DNA, and footwear.

Baudette directed the agents to collect a few of the items near the body, specifically the 'crown' found nearby the victim's head.

At the side of the field, Ivy took out her knife, cut open a large paper evidence bag, spread it out on the grass. She placed the crown on the paper.

The circle of wire was about seven or eight inches in diameter. It looked to be made of a long, green twig, wrapped in galvanized wire, the sort you might use to hang a heavy picture frame. It might have been a thin wire coat hanger. On either side was a fixed bird's wing.

The wings were spread, and were attached to the base with thin wires wrapped around narrow bone.

Baudette stated the obvious. 'That is definitely man-made.'

Ivy pointed to the area where the wing was attached to the wire. It looked like short pieces of plastic or wood, with an oval shaped hole in the center. 'What is this right here?'

'That's the radius and ulna,' Baudette said.

Ivy looked up at him. 'I'm sorry?'

'A crow's wing is not all that different from the human arm,' Baudette said. He pointed to parts of his own arm. 'Humerus, ulna, radius.' He wiggled a few fingers. 'Even digits.'

'You just happen to know this?'

Baudette smiled. 'You live, you look, you learn.'

'So, you've run across this before?'

'Nothing exactly like this. But whoever did this has some knowledge about these birds, of bird anatomy in general.' He pointed to the area through which the wires looped onto the crown. 'There was a lot of care in removing this wing from the bird without damaging the bone structure.'

'Let's get some more close-up photographs of the victim's head,' Ivy said. 'I want to know if she has any scratches that might be consistent with this.'

Ivy took out a tin of Altoids. Baudette took one. Ivy took three. They were probably going to be her lunch.

'Did we find anything like this crown at the Paulette Graham scene?' Ivy asked.

'Didn't see anything like it,' Baudette said. 'But the victim's body and the scene itself were pretty well compromised by the elements. A lot of animal activity and a pair of snowfalls between time of death and discovery of her body.'

Ivy had taken a lot of photographs of that scene, and she knew that BCI took an extensive array of their own, plus a video. She had copies. She made a mental note to go over them all again, this time under magnification. If there was something she missed, if there was anything resembling this crown of wings, it would open the investigation up in many ways.

Unless and until they had an ID on this victim, they could not begin to piece together these two lives, where and if they crossed paths, if they knew each other from school, social media, church, sports, hobbies. At this moment the only thing that tied them together was that they were white teenaged girls found dead in remote clearings in Holland County, Ohio.

That was the official line. Ivy knew in her heart it was more than that. She looked at her watch.

Chevy Deacon was about to get off shift.

28

The house stood in silence.

Will had walked the neighboring blocks for an hour, putting off this moment. He told himself that it was merely an excursion to learn the neighboring streets, perhaps to meet some of the neighbors, or to get a general lay of the land. He'd learned that the nearby homes were neat and trimmed Cape Cods with small front yards, each defined by a pastel shade and contrasting shutters. He learned that mail was delivered into a postal box at the street. He'd learned that these side streets did not have sidewalks or bike paths.

With each turn of a corner he glanced toward Platteville Road, looking for the finial that he knew graced the roofline on the large gabled end of Godwin Hall, more than once seeing it rising into the clotting gray clouds.

Will walked in ever tightening circles until he found himself standing in front of the structure. Before him, on a weathered gray sign, was the house's name.

He had not known what to expect at this moment, whether he would feel mere curiosity or something else, something deeper, something entwined among the roots of his heritage. Godwin Hall was the reason he was in this place at this time.

He was, of course, giving the structure too much power.

It did not live and breathe. It did not know the story of William Hardy, Amanda Hardy, and Bernadette Hardy. It did not care about the millstone of grief on his shoulders, or the life they had left behind. It was brick and stone and mortar and wood. Nothing more.

He opened the notebook he had prepared. In it were a dozen or so photographs. Three of them he had gotten from Patrick Richmond on the day he had learned of his inheritance. The rest he had downloaded from the internet. Each showed a moment in the history of Godwin Hall.

But now that he was standing in front of the house it was different. Could this be a home to Detta and himself? Would she ever come to *think* of it as a home?

Will had expected the yards surrounding the house to be wild and unbound, tall grass, untended shrubs. Instead the grounds were neatly kept: azaleas, spirea, boxwoods.

Will turned his attention back to the porch. To the right was a huge flagstone on the ground. It was just a few feet from the bay window on the one-story wing of the house.

The warning arrived fully formed in his mind. When it landed, it felt like a damp hand around his heart.

You don't want to end up like Daniel Troyer.

His first sensation, upon entering Godwin Hall, was the smell. Beneath the layers of mildew and neglect, beneath the furniture polish and pine-based cleaning solutions, Will smelled pipe tobacco and gardenias and fermenting apples. He smelled old plaster and dry firewood.

Ahead and to the right was the steep staircase leading to the second floor. The treads were covered in sun-faded cocoa brown carpeting with small, cream-colored fleur-de-lis. The center of the treads were worn bare to the ticking. Dust bunnies lurked in each corner.

To the left, tucked beneath the railing in the entry hall, was an old oak sideboard, cluttered with items. There was a teapot and two cups with saucers, gold and white; a wooden antique yarn pull; a basket full of carefully folded burgundy linen napkins. He looked more closely at the teacups. In each was a dried red rose.

Next to the sideboard was a stack of baskets, the uppermost packed with pine cones. Next to it, an old steamer trunk in front of a half-door that led to the area beneath the steps.

The muddy boots go here.

The second thought also came to him unbidden. For an instant it raised the hairs on his arms.

He moved through the first floor, into the parlor to the left of the entry hall. In the center of the room was a large brocade sofa, piled with cardboard boxes. The sofa was a mauve silk, worn through at the arm rests. The mantel of the fireplace held more teapots, as well as ceramic and metal figurines, mostly birds, sitting as silent adjudicators overlooking the empty room.

The dining room held no table, but there was a three-section mahogany breakfront that appeared to be in good condition. On each of its shelves were crystal plates and glassware, and yet more figurines. In the center of the piece was a drop front secretary. The top had a beautiful molded cornice.

There was one large drawer that spanned the width of the cabinet.

No silverware. Needles and thread.

Again, this thought came to him uninvited. Just a casual thought, really. A speculation of sorts. Wasn't it? He decided not to look inside the drawer.

172

The small kitchen was empty, void of any appliances. In one corner was a square table with a single chair. On the surface of the table was an old pad and a pen. Nothing was written on the paper.

In a room off the dining room was a single bedroom with a small bathroom attached. There was no bed or furniture in this room, save for a pair of nightstands pushed to the wall. On the floor was a rolled-up area rug with a tag attached.

Upstairs were the six guest rooms, three on either side of the long hallway. Will poked his head into each. All were empty, dust-laden. A few had old metal bed frames with no mattresses on them. One had a stack of ceramic wash basins in the corner.

At the end of the hall was a large guest room with a balcony.

Will crossed the room, opened the doors, strode onto the terrace, which seemed firm and solid. He looked out onto the immense green field lined with trees on either side, again struck by the quiet. He saw a large house on the other side of the Fairgrounds, its gabled end facing him. This was Veldhoeve. It seemed to grow from the mist, having no foundation or footing, but rather offering the illusion of floating.

Will imagined, for a moment, this scene as it might have been when Godwin Hall opened, the huge sycamores and birch trees mere saplings at the time, the winding river visible for miles into the surrounding hills of Holland County.

He wondered who it might have been, which tradesman had stood in this very spot, proclaiming Godwin Hall straight and plumb and level and true. Again, his waking dream engaged, and he heard the sounds of children running across the bright and festive midway below, the trill of the calliope, the rich aromas of fry cakes and birch beer.

Welcome home, Will Hardy.

Will walked down the stairs, looked for the door leading to the basement. When he strode into the dining room he found his fingers upon the handle attached to the drawer in the breakfront. Before he could give it any further thought he opened the drawer to find that, indeed, there was no silverware in the drawer. Instead there were three small spools of brightly colored thread, and dusty pin cushions stuck with tarnished silver needles.

'Now how did I—'

Before he could finish the question to himself he saw a long shadow falling across the floor in the late afternoon light. It seemed to move toward him.

Will spun around.

There was a man standing behind him.

29

Judge Judy became Dr Phil, who became Ellen. Show after show, channel after channel.

Detta glanced at her watch. It was now four minutes since the last time she'd looked. Now there was another judge.

She turned off the TV, took out her phone, scrolled through her playlists. There was absolutely nothing she wanted to hear, no soundtrack for this day.

How did this all happen? she wondered. How did her life become this other girl's life, this Lifetime Channel movie about a girl who loses her mother, and then she and her father move to some godforsaken place in the country?

She knew how it happened. She just didn't want to *accept* how it happened.

When her father had mentioned the possibility of leaving New York, leaving his job and their life, Detta had thought it was something that would pass, that it was one of his therapy friends who had suggested it to him to help get through his grief. She didn't think he was serious.

Then one day, when she was sitting in the kitchen of the sublet, he just announced that they were going to do it. Just like that. As if he were telling her what was for dinner.

In the end, there was not much to pack. The fire had all but wiped out everything they'd ever had. The only pictures Detta had of her mother were the four pictures she had uploaded to Facebook. One was of Mom and Dad sitting at a table of a café on Houston Street, Da Tommy Osteria. In the picture her mother and father are sitting next to each other in the garden section of the restaurant. It was her mother's thirtieth birthday party, and it had been a surprise.

As a rule, her mom did not like surprises, but she had quickly gotten over her faux-rage at this one. She had let her daughter take more than a few sips from her sparkling wine. Detta had paid dearly with a kid-size hangover the next morning, but at the restaurant she had been flying high. It was why, of the ten or twelve pictures Detta had taken, all but this one were out of focus.

In the one good photograph her mother was leaning slightly forward, her emerald eyes sparkling in the candlelight, a sly smile on her lips, a secret knowledge passing between herself and her daughter.

On the day they left New York, as they crossed the bridge, Detta looked into the side mirror, saw the buildings recede in the distance like a faded postcard, and wondered then, as now, if she'd ever see the city again. She doubted it. It wasn't as if Mom was in a cemetery there, a place they were abandoning. Her mother was, at that moment, in a small copper urn in her father's room.

Dr Levinsohn had told her all about grief, grown-up grief, about how it doesn't ever really leave, doesn't dissolve or disappear, how it just sits there waiting for you to deal with it. Dr Levinsohn made a lot of suggestions about how to begin the process, but Detta had taken none of them.

One of the ideas was to make a collage of photographs. Anthony Torres had checked that one off the list.

The second one was to write a letter to her mother. Detta had started a few of them, then given them up. As it had always been since she was small, whenever faced with the task or the desire to do something creative, her first and only instinct was to draw. She couldn't paint or write or sculpt or compose music. She drew. Maybe again one day, but not today.

For now she had her pills. And right now, that's all that mattered. She had her Xanax and Lexapro and Lunesta, and she had forty-one Valium she had managed to score before leaving the city. She dreaded the day when she ran out of Valium, but for now, the comforting rattle of the amber vial was good.

She took a Xanax and a Valium, washed them down with a warm Diet Coke, closed her eyes and waited for the feeling. She then split a second Valium, hesitated for a few moments, then took it. She rattled the pill vial. Still had plenty left. It was amazing how comforting that sound was, how terrible was the sound when there was only one left, the tiny click of a single little pill bouncing around a plastic cylinder.

She sat up in bed, looked out over the balcony, at the thick woods behind the inn. The trees were almost filled with leaves. She could only see a little ways into the forest. There were parts of Central Park that were pretty heavily wooded, but this was different. In the city you knew that if you just went a few blocks in any direction you would be back among the buildings, back to civilization. Here it looked as if the forest could swallow you whole, that there was nothing on the other side of it.

As the Valium kicked in, the view took on a soft focus. It suddenly looked like all the forests of all the stories: *Hansel and Gretel, Little Red Riding Hood, Beauty and the Beast.*

As she took the second half of her second Valium she thought about walking down the hallway, taking the elevator to the first floor, out of the building and across the field. She thought about walking into the forest and never again walking out.

She wondered what was hiding out there.

30

The man standing just outside the back door was Will's height, but much broader through the chest. He had a chin beard of deep walnut, flecked with gray. Will made him to be in his late thirties or early forties, but he might have been older. He was stout, but not overweight. He wore a black broad-brimmed hat, silvered with dust.

'Hello,' the man said. He stepped off the porch. Will followed him outside.

'Hello to you.'

'Seems I alarmed you some. My apologies for that.'

'Not at all.'

'Reuben Yoder,' the man said, extending a hand.

'Will Hardy.'

'I heard that someone might be reopening the Hall. The idea filled me with delight. Might that someone be you?'

'I'm not sure about that,' Will said. He glanced at his watch. 'But about two hours ago the place became officially mine.'

'Quite the news around here.'

Will hadn't thought about this, but he imagined that the man was right. It was a small town, and something like Godwin Hall was a significant part of its history.

Reuben took a few steps back, looked up. 'The roof still looks good to these eyes.'

Will joined him on the walk. It occurred to him that he hadn't even looked at the roof.

'Does it?'

'When we put up the new, the old roof was in bad shape. Maybe not repaired since the 1960s. There were a few patches, but they were tar paper.'

'You put on this roof?'

'My brothers and I. I think my father might have had a hand or two in that one.'

'I have to say that the exterior doesn't look too bad, considering that it's been unoccupied for twenty-five years.'

'It has not gone completely untended.'

'How so?' Will asked.

'There's a local group here, part of the Abbeville Historical Society. They've provided a small yearly fund for basic maintenance and repair and such. For the exterior only, mind you. Helps to keep the place presentable for the folks who come to town for the festivals.'

'Do you do work for them?'

'I do.' He pointed to the brickwork. 'Did some tuck pointing here a few years ago. If I say so myself, you can't tell the new from the old.'

It was true. Will couldn't see any difference. Then again, he wouldn't know a tuck point from a toast point. If he had any intentions of living here, and working here, that would have to change.

Back at the front of the house, Will again noticed the

flagstone on the right side of the porch. 'Do you know what that is?' he asked.

'That was the original well. It used to be open, but a long time ago a boy fell down there and drowned.'

'Oh my.'

'He was an Amish boy. Daniel Troyer.'

You don't want to end up like Daniel Troyer.

Will thought: *Had he read about this?* He made a mental note to look at the material he'd downloaded from the internet on Godwin Hall.

'Want to come inside?' Will asked.

'If you'll have me.'

As they walked around to the back Will noticed Reuben giving the place the careful once over. He nodded a few times, apparently in approval.

'I haven't been inside for a few years,' Reuben said. 'More than a few now.'

Just a few feet inside the door Reuben bounced lightly on his feet.

'These floors are still beautiful.'

'What kind of wood is it?' Will asked.

'Chestnut,' Reuben said. 'At one time it was the most plentiful material available in these parts.' He pointed at the breakfront with his pipe stem. 'If you're ever of a mind to sell that, I know a few people who would give you a price. Dates to the early 1800s if I'm not mistaken.'

'I'll keep that in mind.'

After a quick tour of the first and second floors, they once again stood in the dining room.

'I'd say you have yourself a pretty solid building,' Reuben said.

'Good to know.'

'Needs some work, of course, if you're thinking of moving in. More so if you're going to go for an occupancy permit for guests.

If you get to that point, I've got a hard-working crew. We have worked by the hour, but it's mostly by the job, and then most of the time it's barter.'

'Barter as in trade?'

'The very kind.'

Will had no idea what he might have to trade. He imagined that the calls for a clinical psychologist in this town were few and far between.

'I'll keep you in mind if and when,' Will said.

'That's all I can ask.'

They walked across the front porch, down the steps. There was a woman standing on the sidewalk, just in front of an older model, idling Ford. She was Amish, and wore a plain blue dress, fastened at the waist with safety pins, a long gray apron and a dark bonnet.

'Will Hardy, this is my fair wife, Miriam.'

'Nice to meet you,' Will said.

'And you,' she said. 'Are you going to reopen the Hall?'

'I'm not sure,' Will said.

'If you do, will you be offering food?'

Will had never considered this for a moment. It suddenly occurred to him that bed and breakfast meant just that – breakfast.

'I'm not sure about that either.'

'Do you cook?'

'Does a microwave count as cooking?'

'It does not.'

'Then the answer is no. I wouldn't know where to start.'

Miriam smiled. 'There will be no shortage of offers from this village. Mine among them.'

At this moment the car idling at the curb backfired. Will realized there was a man behind the wheel. The car was a late nineties Taurus, its fenders dented, its exhaust brewing smoke like a coal plant.

Behind the car was hitched a utility trailer, itself having seen much better days. If the vehicle and trailer were banged up, the man behind the wheel was the original model.

More than a few pounds above his fighting weight, sorely in need of a shave, he was himself smoking a rather foul-smelling cigar. He was reading what looked like an old science fiction pulp paperback.

'That's Rascal,' Reuben said. He lowered his voice. 'His real name is Bertram Shames, but apparently he was quite the ladies' man in his earlier years. Personally, I'm not seeing that, but we humor him nonetheless.'

'So, he's a friend of yours?'

'Give or take some. Mostly give. He drives us around sometime, hauls things with that hitch. There's a lot of folks in his business around here.'

Now it made sense. Will had seen notices for Amish cabs and taxis at the Historical Society.

'What sort of vehicle do you drive?' Reuben asked.

Will pointed to the Sprinter at the back of the driveway.

'Very nice.'

Miriam, perhaps sensing a long conversation of men talk, crossed the sidewalk, slid into the back seat.

'I think I'm going to need a good bit of help here, Reuben. But I'm not sure what I would have to barter with.'

Reuben nodded at the Sprinter. 'I'm thinking you could fit quite a bit in the back of that truck on our behalf. I'm also thinking it's a lot more comfortable than Rascal's jalopy.'

Will was starting to get it. 'Okay, then.'

Reuben reached into the pocket of his jacket, produced a business card. It read *Hale Hardware*.

'Hale is just up the street, right on the town square,' Reuben said. 'Been there more than a hundred years.'

'This is your store?'

'No, sir. I just work there now and again. If we don't have it we can get it. If we can't get it, you might not need it.'

'Sounds like a slogan.'

Reuben smiled. 'As you'll see, there's no room on the sign for it. It's a small store.'

Will put the card in his shirt pocket. He extended his hand. Reuben Yoder followed suit.

'I think we can conduct some commerce, Reuben.'

'God has a plan.'

Will waved at Miriam. She smiled and waved, then went right back to her knitting.

As Will was preparing to leave for the day, there was a knock at the front door. When he answered he found a teenage girl standing on the porch. She identified herself as Cassie. It took a moment, but Will remembered. She was the cub reporter for *The Villager*. Eli's granddaughter.

Cassandra Mills was no older than seventeen, a smiley redhead with green eyes and a mouthful of braces.

After getting the details out of the way – Will's age, profession, brief history, current status – she asked a few questions about Godwin Hall, and his plans for it. He noticed that Cassandra repeatedly called it 'The Hall', which Will had begun to notice was common practice in Abbeville, although Cassandra Mills was by far the youngest person to do so.

At the end of the interview she held up her phone and asked if she could take a few pictures. Will had not been prepared for a photo shoot, but he did a quick reconnaissance of his hair and clothing, stood on the entrance steps to Godwin Hall and let the cub reporter have at it.

Thirty minutes after she'd arrived, she was gone, story and photos in hand.

*

Will locked the back door at Godwin Hall, walked toward the town square. He stopped in front of Hale Hardware, but did not go inside. The storefront was a throwback, as were most of the businesses on the square.

When he returned to Red Oak the lobby was bustling. A tour bus was idling in the parking lot.

Will took the steps to the second floor. As he fished out his electronic door key he noticed the room service tray on the floor just outside Detta's room. Her door was ajar. Will stepped down the hallway, gently knocked on the door jamb. No response.

Will eased open the door. His daughter was under the covers, fast asleep, the blackout curtains closed.

He wanted to wake her up, to share his day with her. He wanted to tell her about Godwin Hall, its many rooms and its fascinating clutter, about how he'd felt walking around this living chapter of their family's past. He wanted to tell her about his new friends, Reuben and Miriam Yoder, about Eli. He wanted to tell her about a rather slovenly character named Bertram 'Rascal' Shames, and his Amish taxi service, about how they might be on the brink of entering that very business.

He did not.

He stood there for a long time.

31

Chevy Deacon emerged from the main building at Aqualine. A medium-size manufacturing plant on Route 87, Aqualine made water filtration and desalination equipment, as well as flood water and waste water systems.

Chevy crossed the lot, talking to one of his co-workers. He got into his vehicle, started it, pulled onto the access road heading north.

Ivy had decided to put eyes on him for a while to see his after-work habits, but especially to see if there was any behavior consistent with someone who had just committed a serious crime.

Chevy got onto Route 87 and drove east for a few miles, passing through Burton and the La Due Public Hunting area. Ivy kept a safe distance, holding three or four cars behind him.

He was driving a white F-150 with the red and white bar lights on the cab. Ivy knew him well enough to know that he was not going to talk to her voluntarily, so she had a Plan B.

She made the call on the way.

*

When Chevy reached Middlefield, he headed south a few blocks on 608, and turned into the parking lot at a freestanding hovel of a building tucked into a mostly industrial and light commercial district. The place was Yellen's Crab Shack, a shot and beer emporium that had not offered anything resembling a crab in more than twenty years.

Chevy Deacon parked, exited his truck, crossed the lot, entered the establishment. Forty minutes later he emerged.

Ivy Holgrave got out of her vehicle and crossed the parking lot to meet him.

Chevy Deacon was in his mid-thirties. On this day he wore a dirty ball cap, scuffed Red Wing boots, and the dark blue overall uniform of Aqualine employees. His oily brown hair hung to his shoulders.

As Chevy dug for his car keys in one of the pockets he noticed Ivy approaching him.

'Jesus Christ. Now what?'

'Just want to talk to you for a few minutes,' Ivy said.

'About what?'

'I'm getting to that, Chevy. Could you take your hand out of your pocket for me, please?'

Chevy took the keys from his pocket, slipped the thick key ring over the middle knuckle of his right hand. It was a classic lowlife bar fight move, a sucker punch tactic.

'Thanks,' Ivy said 'What I'd like to—'

'I don't have to tell you a fucking thing.'

He was slurring his words, and had the false bravado of a midday drunk. A few people walking to their cars heard the F-word and decided to watch the goings-on.

'That's absolutely true right there,' Ivy said. 'But it will be in your best interest to do so. It would help me mightily.'

'Why the *fuck* would I want to do that?'

'Let's just call it civic duty.'

Chevy Deacon snorted. 'I look civic-minded to you?'

'Appearances can be deceiving. Just need to ask a few—'

'I know where you live.'

And there it was. A direct threat. Whatever happened from here on in, in any legal sense, would be predicated by that statement.

'And I know an old woman who would cut you a third asshole with a steel .44 if you set one foot there. Stop by anytime. Monday is meat loaf.'

The man looked at her, trying to process this. Instead he smiled a nervous smile, trying to hang onto some tough-guy cool in front of the onlookers. He shook his head, started walking across the lot, toward his vehicle.

'Need you to stop right there, Chevy.'

He did not stop. When he rounded the back end of the Yukon parked next to him, he saw that there was a man sitting in the back of his truck.

'Well, well. Who do we have here?' Ivy asked.

'What the fuck is this? Get the fuck off my truck.'

'Step on out of there, please, sir,' Ivy said.

The man kept his hands in plain sight, slid off the truck bed. He was in his forties, small and round and bald. He wore a grimy quilted vest over an equally dirty blue chambray shirt.

'Let me see some ID,' Ivy said.

The man slowly reached for his wallet. He took it out, opened it, handed Ivy his license.

Ivy scanned it. 'Casper G. Walls. I know you.'

'Yes, ma'am.'

'Refresh my memory. Where from?'

'Two years ago. Over in Carlton.'

'That's right. You were part of Junior Luton's crew.'

Casper shifted his weight from one foot to the other. 'I don't run with that bunch anymore.'

'Good to hear,' Ivy said. 'How do you know Mr Deacon?'

'I know him from around. From places.'

'Why are you sitting in his truck today?'

Casper hesitated for a moment, then said: 'Not going to lie to you. He told me he could score some meth for me.'

Chevy Deacon exploded. 'That's fucking *bullshit*. I don't know this guy.'

'This surely violates your probation, Chevy,' Ivy said. 'You know that, right? Consorting with felons?'

In that moment Chevy Deacon put his weight on his left foot, pivoted, and launched his right fist toward Ivy's face. Ivy side-stepped the blow with ease, got behind the man and took him to the asphalt hard. Within a few seconds, she had Chevy Deacon secured by handcuffs.

Ivy worked Chevy to his feet, gave the man some time to decelerate. He was breathing heavily, blowing air in short bursts, his face bright red, scraped by the rough pavement.

'Bad move, Chevy,' Ivy finally said. 'Your day just got a whole lot worse.'

Ivy contacted Walt Barnstable on her rover. She turned back to her suspect.

'Chevy Deacon, you are under arrest for public intoxication and assault on a police officer,' Ivy said. 'I'll put in a call to the county on the violation.'

Ivy could see the knot starting to grow on the right side of Chevy Deacon's face. She waved a hand in front of his eyes to get his attention. He looked up.

'And I haven't even gotten to the part about why I wanted to talk to you in the first place.'

When the patrol car pulled out of the parking lot, with Chevy Deacon in the back, Ivy turned her attention back to Casper Walls.

'You ever take any acting classes, Casper?'

'No classes, ma'am. But I was in *Grease* when I was in junior high.'

'You were Danny Zuko?'

'Nothing like that. I was just one of the guys.'

'You might have missed your calling.'

Casper smiled. 'Did you know he was gonna take a poke at you like that?'

'No,' Ivy said. 'That was just icing on a cake I was going to eat anyway.'

She reached into her pocket, took out a fold of bills, peeled off a twenty. 'You have to promise me you'll spend this on drugs or alcohol.'

Casper snapped the bill from her hand.

'You have my word.'

Before returning to the station house, Ivy collected some items from the rear bed of Chevy's truck. Specifically, a half-dozen large burlap bags.

Inside the bags were dead leaves and twigs. She did not find any overt evidence that was consistent with a human being having been inside any of the bags, no clothing or personal items. Ivy put them into paper evidence bags, and marked them to be sent to BCI to check for blood, hair and fiber.

Ivy picked up a can of Mountain Dew, and the small bag of sour cream chips, and opened the door to the interview room.

'How we doing, Chevy?'

As expected, Chevy Deacon said nothing. Ivy sat down, put the Mountain Dew and bag of chips on the table. Chevy Deacon didn't acknowledge the gesture.

'Do you know why you got the invite, Chevy?'

'You set me up is why.'

'I set you up? How'd I do that?'

'Putting that fat little fuck in my truck.'

'So it is your truck, then?'

'You know it is. Just like you know it's in my brother's name.'

Ivy took a moment, opened a folder. On top was Chevy Deacon's sheet. He glanced down at it.

'Now, I'm not looking to jam you up, Chevy. I haven't yet called your PO, and I don't have to do that.'

'I think maybe I should talk to my lawyer.'

'We can play it that way if you want to. But we both know you don't have a lawyer. I'm going to have to call the public defender's office in the county seat and they are not going to get here until, maybe, noon tomorrow. When they get here we're going to present them with all the evidence we have on your consorting with known felons, not to mention the assault charge which, in and of itself, is going to rob you of some serious daylight.'

Chevy Deacon said nothing. Ivy continued.

'You work with me a little bit, and I'll see what I can do for you,' Ivy said.

'What do you want?'

'I just need a play-by-play of your whereabouts starting Sunday night, right up to this afternoon. Don't leave anything out.'

Chevy Deacon took a while to line up his thoughts. He told a brief tale of how he got up late on Sunday, drove to Mantua to pick up some parts for a Mustang he was trying to restore, met some people at a bar there, put on a major drunk, slept it off in the parking lot. At dawn he drove back to Holland County, stopped at the McDonald's on Lambert Road, got home and flopped into bed, where he stayed until his alarm went off. Then he went to work.

'How did you come to be on Cavender Road?' Ivy asked.

'Cavender Road?'

'Yes, sir.'

'Who says I was there?'

'We have an eyewitness puts you on the corner of Cavender and 44.'

'They're mistaken. Wasn't there. I was home sleeping.'

Ivy held the man's gaze until he was forced to look away. He was lying.

'Ever do any bird hunting, Chevy?'

'What?'

'Bird hunting,' Ivy said. 'Pheasant, duck, quail. The occasional chukar. Lots of great preserves in this part of the state. Ever hunt birds?'

Chevy looked suitably confused by this change of tack. Ivy had just introduced firearms to the conversation, which caused him to tense.

'No.'

'What about the nuisance birds. Ever pick off a few blue jays on your spread?'

'No.'

'Starlings? Pigeons?'

'No.'

'Crows?'

Ivy watched the man carefully when she said the word crow. There was no tell or tic.

'Why are you asking me this?'

'All part of a broader investigation.'

'Why are you asking me about hunting? Did somebody get shot?'

'Do you have knowledge of a shooting, Chevy?'

The man just stared at her, the wheels, such as they were, beginning to spin out of control. Whatever put him on Cavender Road was something criminal. Whether it had something to do with the death of that girl was yet to be determined.

'Get me that lawyer.'

Ivy gave this a few moments.

'Okay,' she said. 'I'll get right on that.'

Ivy gathered together her papers, exited the room. She saw that Walt Barnstable had been observing the questioning.

They entered Ivy's office, closed the door.

'I don't think he's our boy,' Walt said.

'I think you're right about that.' Ivy looked at her watch. 'Let's let him marinate for an hour, then cut him loose.'

Ivy reached into the file cabinet, took out the keys to the holding cell. 'Box him up for me?'

'Be my pleasure,' Walt said.

While Walt bundled Chevy Deacon to the holding cell, Ivy did a little housekeeping on her desk. Chevy's possessions were loose on the blotter, next to an empty plastic evidence bag. She began to put the items in the bag. On the sheet next to the bag she had written down what he'd had on his person at the time they brought him in and frisked him: an almost empty pack of Newports, a yellow Bic lighter, a few twenties, a pair of empty dime zip bags that smelled of pretty good weed, a cash receipt from a Taco Bell.

Ivy picked up the cash, slid one of the bills to the side, and found that it was really five bills.

Walt returned, put the cell keys on a hook by the door.

'Is Slim Shady in there always this belt-fed?'

'Oh, yeah,' Ivy said. 'Today was about average. His old man was worse.' She held the small stack of bills in the light. 'Look at this.'

'Brand new bills.'

'Yeah,' Ivy said.

'None of them look circulated at all. All clean.'

'Chevy Deacon is a lot of things,' Ivy said. 'Clean isn't one of them.'

'So why would someone like him have brand new bills in his pocket?'

Ivy considered the question. 'Maybe it has something to do with why he was out on Cavender Road. Maybe they're from some kind of transaction he's trying to keep secret.'

'And whatever the reason is, he's willing to get violated for it?'

'Let's see what we get out of his truck. I'll see if I can red line that search.'

As if anticipating her call, the desk phone rang. It was her direct line, not the police station number. Ivy answered. It was Gary Baudette.

'Hey Gary,' she said. 'What's up?'

'I have something.'

'That was fast.'

'Not the new case,' he said. 'My team is still on scene there. I'm back at the Richfield lab. This is about the Paulette Graham case.'

Ivy sat straighter, got Walt's attention. He crossed the room. Ivy wrote *Graham* on the legal pad on the desk in front of her, turned the pad so Walt could read it.

'I'm here with Walt Barnstable,' Ivy said. 'Okay to put this on speaker?'

'Sure.'

Ivy did so. 'What do we have?'

'I went back to the evidence collected at the Graham scene. Something had been nagging me since we hit the wall with the forensics.'

Ivy heard some papers rustling on the other end.

'As you know, there wasn't a lot, and what we have is pretty compromised. Much of the material found in that field was soggy, wet, rusted, or rotting. A lot of it was refuse, dumped around the field over many years.'

'Right.'

'Remember that tin box we found about five feet from the victim?'

194

'I do,' Ivy said. 'It was covered in ice.'

'Found a thumbprint on the underneath side of the top part of the tin. On the *inside*.'

'What made you revisit?'

'Craziest thing. When you offered me that tin of Altoids, you held the box between your thumb and forefinger, opened it, and as you did this your thumb slid inside.I didn't think to process the inside of our tobacco box, because the box had been out in the elements and rust had begun to corrode the surface. The inside was still pristine. We've got a perfect sample.'

Ivy's heart picked up a beat. Gary Baudette wouldn't be calling if he hadn't run the print through AFIS and the other databases available to BCI.

'You have a name,' Ivy said.

'I have a name.' Baudette gave it to her.

'Got it.'

'You know him?' Baudette asked.

Ivy reached into her desk drawer, removed her service weapon, holstered it.

'Yes,' she said. 'I do.'

32

The smell was overpowering, a foul stew of rotting food, feces, and human decomposition.

The scene was a two-room apartment on the second floor over a long-shuttered commercial establishment at the far end of Jenkintown Road, a run-down section of the village that had once served, in the 1950s and 1960s, as a secondary commercial district.

In the 1990s an attempt was made to bring the structures up to code for occupancy as office space and living quarters. Ivy was sure that none of the buildings actually met that code, just as she was certain that people were renting the spaces for cash. As long as there were no fires, and people behaved themselves, it was not a concern for the Abbeville Police Department.

Until today.

Today, in this stifling hovel on the second floor of the building at the southeast corner of Blake Street and Jenkintown Road, the swollen corpse of Alonzo 'Lonnie' Combs was hanging from a beam.

*

Ivy knew Lonnie Combs from a few bar fights, and had seen him around the village when he was on deliveries. Lonnie Combs was a registered sex offender, and every one of his kind was on Ivy's radar. She had never arrested him, but felt it was only a matter of time. In her experience it always was.

Missy Kohl was on her way to Corley and Sons, the place of Lonnie Combs's employment. Ivy was standing just inside the front door at Lonnie's apartment with Walt Barnstable.

Before joining the police force Walt worked as an insurance investigator for a large national company.

A lifelong bachelor, Walt had lived with his elderly father for years in a small bungalow on the north of the village. When his father passed away Walt took it hard. He went for a Caribbean cruise and came back with a new outlook and a new purpose to change his life. He applied to the police academy at the age of thirty-two and was accepted. When he applied for a job as a part-time officer with the Abbeville Police Department there wasn't really an opening. But Ivy had known Walt a long time and believed that she could find a place for him on the small force.

What do you see, Ivy Lee?

The dead man was all but naked, wearing only a pair of stained white briefs. The nylon rope around his neck was looped through a large iron ring that was screwed into the beam in the ceiling.

Beneath the body, on the floor, amid all the filthy clutter, was a pair of dice. They were oversized, foam rubber, the kind that were popular to hang from a rearview mirror in the 1970s. They were a lot cleaner than everything else in the room.

'What are we looking for, Chief?' Walt asked.

'We're looking for anything linking Lonnie Combs to Paulette Graham. Photographs, personal items, notes or letters, jewelry, clothes. Start in his bedroom in the closets and drawers. I'll handle his computer.'

Walt took a deep breath, blew it out. 'I'm on it.'

He slipped on a pair of latex gloves and stepped into Lonnie Combs's cluttered bedroom.

Ivy turned her attention to the sitting room.

Every square inch of the space was stacked with debris. In one corner was a grimy Formica table with a hotplate, as well as an old-style CRT monitor. Beneath the table was a dust-choked tower computer. Ivy saw the green light glowing.

As she poked through the bookshelves that were jammed with jigsaw puzzles and smudged and torn *Penthouse* and *Playboy* magazines, her eyes and attention kept returning to the bloated body hanging in the middle of the room.

She noted the position of the overturned chair near the body. It was close enough to have been what he'd stood on.

Ivy took a number of photographs, then righted the chair, sat down at the dinette table in front of the monitor. She turned on the monitor, and with a gloved hand clicked a mouse button. When the computer warmed up she saw a screensaver, a photograph of a 1970s era Dodge Charger. The text box in the window called for a password.

Ivy began typing. Everything she tried came up as an error. She looked around, spotted a pair of grease-streaked jeans folded on the counter. She crossed the room, took Lonnie's wallet out of his jeans, returned to the computer. She tried inputting his birthday, his address, his driver's license number, his name forwards and backwards. She tried his social security number. She tried Paulette Graham's name. No luck.

Beneath the flap she found a weathered and smudged laminated card. It was Lonnie Combs's probation card from the Department of Corrections. Ivy input the number.

She heard the hard drive begin to turn. Within a few seconds an image began to display across the screen.

It was a photograph of Paulette Graham.

'Chief?'

Ivy turned in the chair to see Walt standing in the doorway.
'What is it?'

Walt was colorless. 'I think you should see this.'

Ivy took off her gloves, pocketed them, put on a fresh pair. She walked near the wall, entered the bedroom. From the doorway she took it all in. Three laundry baskets full of soiled clothes, an overturned plastic bucket for a nightstand, a lamp with no shade. In one corner was a pile of car parts – air filters, carburetors, radiator hoses. Against one wall was a filthy single mattress on the floor.

Walt pointed at the stained pillow on the bed. 'Underneath.'

Ivy crossed the room. She kneeled next to the bed, lifted the pillow.

There, beneath the pillow, was a dead crow.

It had no wings.

33

The Bullfinch Tavern was almost empty. Ivy needed it that way.

As she turned the shot glass in her hand her thoughts drifted to Lonnie Combs. Creepy Lonnie Combs.

What was the direct line between Lonnie Combs and Paulette Graham? When had Lonnie put eyes on the girl? Had he been at the Gas 'N Go on that day in December? Had he followed her down the road and taken her?

So why didn't she buy it?

She'd watched the video of Paulette Graham at the Gas 'N Go for the hundredth time. Could the figure at the upper left of the screen have been Lonnie Combs? It could have been. The compression and poor quality of the video itself, combined with the fact that the upper half of the subject's body was not visible, meant it could have been just about anyone. When she stopped at the Gas 'N Go before coming home, and talked to the manager, he confirmed that Lonnie Combs had been a gas customer, occasionally coming inside for snacks and beer.

Ivy took out her phone, looked at the photographs she had taken. Had Lonnie Combs really taken apart a dead black bird and fashioned that crown?

If so, where was the other one?

It was with these thoughts rumbling through her mind that Ivy caught a shadow to her left, someone sliding onto the barstool a few doors down.

It was Johnny Paulson. Johnny was in his late forties, a recently retired mail carrier.

'Did you hear about Godwin Hall?' Johnny asked.

As always, the mere mention of Godwin Hall started a spider web spinning inside Ivy. Sometimes the web grew; sometimes the slightest breeze took it down.

'What's happening with it?'

Johnny set himself to deliver the goods. It was standard Abbeville conveyance.

'I heard someone bought it,' Johnny said. 'Someone from out of town.'

'An individual or a motel chain?'

'Haven't heard that part. I heard the news from Libby Thomas, and she heard it from Colleen Clausen.'

Libby was a busybody who worked for the town's one and only Realtor; Colleen was a busybody who worked for the town's one and only insurance agent. Nobody gossiped more, or with greater gusto, than these two. Odds were fifty-fifty on the truth.

Ivy remembered the first time she had climbed the stairs onto the porch of Godwin Hall as a child, the way the cold air seemed to come from inside. It seemed like yesterday.

'Are they going to reopen it?' she asked.

'No idea,' Johnny said. 'But if that's the case, I hope they've got some deep pockets. Can't imagine what it looks like inside now. Betcha the wiring is a bonfire in the brewing.'

Ivy looked at her empty glass.

Did you hear about Godwin Hall?
She ordered a nightcap.

The evening was warm, the sky clear and cloudless, the stars abundant.

As Ivy crossed the Fairgrounds to the center of the field, to the area near the gazebo, her thoughts, as always, turned to Delia.

Partially deaf since birth, Delia Holgrave had been thought to be developmentally challenged in her early school years. Because she could not hear what her teachers were saying, or the incidental conversations around her, Delia's grades were consistently poor.

When the problem was diagnosed at age ten, a lot of the psychological damage had already been done. Delia had acquired feelings of inadequacy and failure. Her mother scraped together the money to see specialists in both Akron and Cleveland, and had purchased her any number of hearing aids, which Delia could not wait to throw into the river, or stomp beneath her feet in a tantrum.

When Delia was thirteen she picked up a cheap drum kit at a garage sale, purchased with her babysitting money, and began to practice out in the field behind the house. Many a spring, summer, or fall day would find Delia Holgrave banging away, her huge headphones in place, plugged into her Sony Walkman. Ivy recalled seeing her sister out there in a downpour, oblivious to the elements. More than one Walkman shorted out because of this practice.

By the time she was fourteen Delia formed a rock band with three other area kids who were also hard of hearing. They called themselves Deaf Penalty, and gained quite a reputation in the area, mostly for playing their music bone-jarringly loud. It drove the neighbors crazy, but brought Delia Holgrave a cult status of sorts, at least as much as could be culled in a small town in a mostly rural county. The band played county and village fairs and even had one memorable gig at Newbury Junior High School, hosted by a DJ from Cleveland.

Although it was supposed to be the other way around, it was Ivy who ended up looking up to her younger sister. Delia was everything Ivy wanted to be. Delia was bold. Delia had flair and a style that set her apart from the other kids her age, calling attention to, instead of trying to hide from, her disability.

More than once Delia had stepped into the fray on Ivy's behalf. Ivy was more than capable of taking care of herself when it came to schoolyard and town square bullies – education in the fistic arts come early to the daughters of a police officer – but it seemed that Delia saw it as a calling.

With this new-found rock star celebrity came a change of attitude in Delia. She began to find ways to interact socially, and even gained a sense of responsibility, a sense of acceptance of her lot in life. She started to volunteer her time to work with deaf and hearing-impaired children, learning American Sign Language, and passing along her knowledge to the community.

She also picked up part-time work as a housekeeper in order to keep herself in Marlboros and drum sticks. Three days a week she worked with the room attendants at Godwin Hall, which was in its last throes of life as a boarding house.

One fall day Delia Holgrave finished her shift, walked out the back door of Godwin Hall, and was never seen again.

Plenty of small town gossip had ultimately distilled into folk-lore, mostly told as cautionary bedtime stories by parents trying to scare their kids from both Godwin Hall and the forests of Holland County.

Ivy June never recovered from her daughter going missing. She continued on the job as deputy for a few years after, sleeping three hours a night, spending much of her off-duty time driving every back road in the county, rousting all the fringe players – small time drug dealers, petty thieves, tomcats, tavern bullies, kiddie watchers – hoping for some sort of clue, or answer, or direction.

She never found it. Two years after Delia disappeared came a mild stroke from the stress, and Ivy June turned in her deputy badge and uniform.

Ivy's last memory of her sister was from the day she went missing, standing in the middle of the Fairgrounds, striking a hip-shot, bad girl pose. They had talked about taking the picture to Dallas Lange and Town Frame and having it blown up to poster size. They never did.

On this night, these twenty-five years later, with Paulette Graham's violated body long in the ground, and another girl's body in a cold room at the county morgue, Ivy found herself standing directly behind Godwin Hall.

I heard someone bought it.

Someone from out of town.

Ivy wondered what the new owners knew of Godwin Hall's prime, of its elegance and decadence, of its shadows and light. She wondered if they heard the rumors about what had taken place in the Fairgrounds behind the house, under the cover of clouds, under the shroud of ritual.

Something drew Ivy's gaze to the top floor of Godwin Hall. When she looked over she saw a light wink once from a window in the dormer, on the northernmost of its gables.

Then, just as quickly as it appeared, it was gone.

Summer – Godwin Hall

Being the true diary and journal of Eva Claire Larssen

June 8, 1869

For the past week I have felt sickly each morning. Yesterday, as we were preparing egg breads for the guests at Godwin Hall, I felt so dizzy I had to sit on the floor. In the afternoon Mrs Samuelsson took me to see the doctor in Chardon and he confirmed what I felt to be true.

I am going to be a mother.

June 16, 1869

Willem has returned home from school for the summer and he is very attentive. More than once his mother, who has been very kind throughout, has broomed him from the kitchen. We do not sleep together – there is scandal enough in this village already, I can see it in the eyes of all the gossipy wives at the market each week – but he comes to me every night before I sleep and tells me of our future together.

June 22, 1869

This morning, before my chores, Dr van Laar told me he wanted to show me some things. He had dressed in his finest and I could see where he'd nicked himself while shaving. He smelled of lavender. He led me through the grand hallways on the upper floors at Veldhoeve, hallways I had never seen. On the third floor he showed me what looks to be an art gallery. In it there are fourteen drawings on the walls.

Seven pictures of sin. Seven pictures of virtue.

The drawings of vices are the things of nightmares. Dr van Laar whispers when he talks of these drawings. He says that I bear a strong resemblance to the girl in one of the virtue drawings, though I do not see it.

June 30, 1869

Tonight, long after I had snuffed the candles, I heard a beautiful song from just below the window. It was a mandolin. I stole from the bed, and went to the window to look and listen.

But it was not Willem below my window.

It was Dr van Laar.

34

With a lot of help, in just a few weeks, Will was able to make a serious dent in the task of getting Godwin Hall tidied up, aired out, and in some kind of presentable shape. During the first week Reuben and his brothers Lemuel and Samuel had gone through all the rooms and separated the usable from the unusable, a process Will had come to think of as Amish triage.

The larger items of furniture were grouped into the center of the room that was once used as a ballroom: a pair of armoires, five or six accent tables, a roll-top desk, two love seats, a green velvet fainting couch.

When all of these items, and many others, were gathered together, Reuben and his brothers did a silent assessment of their worth. Before long they decided on which items could be refinished, screwed, dowelled, glued, fitted, repurposed, leveled, and glazed. Will soon learned that if a group of Amish men could not fix something, it was basically kindling. There was not much furniture in the entire house worth salvaging.

If his relationship with Detta had not deteriorated, it had evened out into a routine of silence and tolerance. They ate most of their meals in their rooms at Red Oak; did much of their communicating, such as it was, by phone or text.

As Will was getting ready to leave Godwin Hall for the day he saw that there was a flyer in the handle of the back door. Will removed it, unfolded the single page. It was a notice for a barn auction, including a list of the items that would be auctioned off. Among them were household goods such as dinnerware, flatware, glassware. There were three color photographs at the bottom. One of the photos showed a trio of bedroom sets; headboards, side rails, and footboards.

But it was the tag line at the bottom, beneath the bedroom sets, that caught Will's eye, typo and all.

These special items were once part of the splender that was Godwin Hall.

The auction started in an hour.

Will made a shopping list, and was just about out the door when he heard a tone on his laptop, the ringing sound when he received a Skype call.

Will answered. Within seconds, the Skype window opened and Will saw Trevor Butler. Trevor was at his desk in the den of his house.

'Have you been working out?' Will asked.

Trevor sat a little straighter. 'Do I look better?'

In truth he looked exactly the same. Will would never tell him this.

'You do.'

'Even for a shrink you're a pretty good liar.'

'It's a blessing and a curse.'

They caught up on their families. It sounded as if Trevor was finally coming to terms with his divorce. He told Will that he had spent the previous weekend with his girls, and that his oldest, fourteen-year-old Gemma, had casually (or so she thought) left hints about signing up for match.com on his cell phone.

Will gave Trevor a quick rundown on Abbeville, its people, and the progress at Godwin Hall.

'So, to what do I owe this rude intrusion?' Will asked.

'I can't just call an old friend?'

'Not in my experience, no.'

'Okay. I ran across a couple of things. First off, we recovered Anthony Torres's phone.'

Will felt a sudden chill. He remembered handing the boy the phone as if it were yesterday. 'Where was it?'

'Turns out it was in the trunk of the car he stole. The owners of the car found it, turned it over to the administrator of the NSD home where Anthony was staying, and he called us.'

'What did you find on the phone?'

'Nothing yet,' Trevor said. 'It's password protected, but we're working on it.'

Will was all but certain he didn't really want to know what was on the phone.

'You said a couple of things,' Will said, anxious to move on.

'Right. Well. I know you told me this before, but tell me again. How did you first run across Anthony Torres?'

'I got an email from an associate.'

'An associate from where? A colleague at NYU?'

'No,' Will said. 'He was from NYBTA.'

'And you knew this guy?'

'No. But it was not all that unusual. It's not that big of a club and all my contact information – everybody's contact information – is in the registry.'

'And he contacted you through your NYU account, or your personal email?'

'I'm sure it was my NYU account.'

'Did you print off the email?'

'No,' Will said. 'I don't think I've ever done that, to be honest with you. Amanda would've killed me. Saving trees and all that.'

'Do you still have access to your NYU account?'

'I have no idea,' he said. 'I have the feeling that all of it's been deleted. I can check.'

'Can you check right now?'

'I guess. If I do will you tell me what this is all about?'

'I promise,' Trevor said. 'Just humor me, mate.'

Will opened his mail application. He had deleted his NYU account folder not long after the fire in an inebriated rage. He'd regretted doing it a few times, but the feeling passed. He created a new folder, put in his username and password, and clicked on the get new mail icon.

Account not found. He tried again. Same result.

'No,' Will said. 'It's gone.'

'Okay. Last question for now. Do you remember the guy's name? The guy who sent you the email?'

'Not really. I think it was something like Kessel. Maybe Kessler.'

'And you're sure it came from someone at this organization?'

'I was until this very second, buddy. This is freaking me out a little bit.'

'That's the last thing I want to do. I'm casting a wide net here. I'm just doing it out loud.'

'I understand.' Will knew that his dear friend had all the best intentions.

'Maybe, and there's no rush on this, you could go into the registry on that organization and see if you could pin down who sent that email. If you can't, no problem. If you do I'll just put it in the file and probably leave it there forever.'

'I'll do it today,' Will said.

Twenty minutes later Will was looking at the NYBTA list.

There was no one named Kessel or Kessler.

35

Will had never been to an auction. His only notions came from *North by Northwest*, where Cary Grant uses an odd bidding technique in an attempt to elude the clutches of James Mason and Martin Landau.

He was hoping for less intrigue.

The items were displayed in a huge semicircle, maybe thirty setups in all. Many of the pieces were on folding tables; some of the larger items were on the ground.

There were cast iron pans, boxes of drapery, towels and sheets, hand tools of every type, bottles and collectible tins, bowls, dishes and flatware. There was one table devoted to old postcards and magazines, one table held box after box of 78 rpm records.

Behind the tables, where the larger items were arrayed at the edge of the field, he found the items he was looking for, the three bedroom sets that were shown in the flyer; furniture that was originally in Godwin Hall.

The largest of the three was a queen-size set, a headboard

and footboard that, according to the description, was Carolina Drexel Heritage. Will knelt down to get a closer look. The finish looked to be in decent shape, with just a few nicks and dings. It was painted white, and Will could see the original finish beneath it, a light brown stain.

'Nice furniture.'

The voice came from behind him. He turned around.

The woman was in her forties, wore a rust-colored barn coat and jeans, Ecco boots. Her white-blond hair was pulled back into a ponytail, fixed with a leather butterfly clip. Her eyes were cerulean blue.

She pointed at the printout in his hand.

'Bidding today?'

'Not sure,' Will said. 'I'm thinking about it.'

'I'm afraid a lot of these household good auctions are folks buying and selling the same things back and forth to each other.'

'Really?'

She pointed at a nearby table. On it was an older style Kitchen Aid with a pair of mixing bowls. 'I sold that to Carrie Rigden six years ago. She sold it to Betty Gest. Now it's here. Funny thing is, I could use one of those, but I'll be damned if I'll buy it back.'

'Do you go to a lot of these?'

'Some,' she said. 'When you're older in these parts this is kind of a social thing.' She nodded at the printout in his hand, the photographs of the bedroom sets. 'How much were you thinking about spending?'

Will had three hundred in cash. He was hoping to spend less.

'Maybe two hundred?'

She smiled. 'Is that a question?'

'Not a good strategy?'

'No. You should always have a set amount in mind. Like when you walk up to a blackjack table. This much, not a penny more.'

'Okay.'

'You're thinking about picking up all three sets?'

'Yes.'

She lowered her voice even more, stepped closer. 'I think we can bring this home for a lot less than two hundred.'

Will matched her volume. 'How are we going to do that?'

'I'm going to bid against you.'

'How does that work again?'

She explained it to him. It was good.

'So, do you think you have it?' she asked.

'I think so.'

'Good,' she said. 'When I do this, you bid one more time.' She smoothed the right arm of her coat, put her left hand in her pocket. 'No matter what the increase was on the previous bid, you bid only two dollars more.'

'Two dollars.'

'No more, no less. If the auctioneer pretends that he's suddenly gone hard of hearing, and throws the bid out at five or ten dollars more, you set him straight.'

'How do I do that?'

'By not saying another word.'

'And that will shut it down?'

'It will.'

Will could see that the auctioneer was getting ready to start. He glanced at the woman, who touched a finger to the side of her nose – a la *The Sting* – and stepped away, engrossed now in her own auction printout.

The auctioneer was a man in his sixties, an unassuming local dressed in jeans and a red plaid flannel shirt. When he opened his mouth, auctioning the first table, it was like every auction Will had ever seen in the movies: a rapid fire, triple-speak that sounded like it was coming from a Mars probe.

Some of the older Amish men seemed to be bidding without moving anything but their thumbs. One man was bidding with his pipe. Will watched him carefully. When the auctioneer looked to him for the next bid the man just let the bowl of his pipe drop a quarter-inch or so.

When they took a short break, Will called Detta just to check in on her. As expected, as always, it went to her voicemail.

The next item was the Drexel Heritage bedroom set. Will made the first bid at ten dollars. A man on the other side of the group immediately bid twenty dollars. Will looked at the woman. He did not see the high sign. Will bid thirty dollars. The woman, his confederate, bid forty.

At this, the woman smoothed the sleeve on her coat, put her hand in her pocket.

Will bid forty-two dollars.

'Can I get fifty?' The auctioneer looked around the crowd, at the woman, at the man, who had already dropped out, it seemed. 'Do I hear fifty?' He asked this five more times. It might have been ten more times. Will had never heard anyone talk as fast as this guy. 'Do I hear forty-five?'

No one said a word. The auctioneer seemed to meet the gaze of everyone in attendance. When no one spoke up he pointed at Will and said:

'Sold.'

Will looked back at his compatriot. She winked at him. Apparently, he had just bought something at an auction.

A few minutes later they did this same routine again, this time bidding on the pair of maple bedroom sets. Will got these items for sixty-five dollars.

He was starting to like Holland County.

As Will prepared to leave, he found the woman in the rust-colored coat, his partner in auction intrigue, standing at the table where they were selling coffee. He walked over.

'Get you a cup?' she asked.

'No, thanks,' Will said. 'I just wanted to stop by and say how much I appreciate this. It was very kind of you.'

The woman paid for her coffee. 'It was my pleasure.'

'I'm still not sure what happened.'

'Just a bit of country commerce. You took right to it. I think you have a knack.'

'I don't know about that,' he said. 'Name's Will Hardy, by the way.'

The woman extended a hand. Will took it.

'Ivy,' she said. 'Ivy Holgrave.'

With a little bit of wrestling, Will got the headboards, footboards and side rails out of the Sprinter, and down into the basement at Godwin Hall. He made a note to get some high lumen LED bulbs. If he was going to do any kind of work down here, it would have to be a lot brighter. After making himself some coffee, he got on his laptop and tried to find some websites devoted to furniture refinishing. There were just over ten million hits.

He decided to visit Hale Hardware.

If visiting the Historical Society museum was a glance back in time, stepping into Hale Hardware was setting foot into the way Abbeville looked and smelled a hundred years ago. By the door there were racks of seed packets and for sale signs, aluminum buckets and wash basins. Along the first aisle were hacksaw blades, wood and cold chisels, to the left were nuts, bolts, screws, nails and bolts.

The floor was a well-worn and stained wood planking. Overhead were strung pet beds, leashes, leather harnesses.

'Can I help you find something?'

Will turned to see a robust and ruddy man in his forties. He wore a blue work shirt, red braces. He had a full beard, just going gray. His nametag identified him as Dave.

'Well, I just picked up some old bedroom sets, and I'm thinking about refinishing them.'

'Okay, I think we can steer you in the right direction on this. May I ask you a question first?'

'Sure.'

'How serious are you about refinishing?'

Will did not expect this. 'I've never done it before.'

'Are you looking to do a good job?'

That was two odd questions in a row. He was starting to think it was Dave's way. 'I guess I am.'

'Are you a patient sort?'

'I'm from New York.'

'So, all due respect, not in abundant supply.'

Will laughed. 'I would say no.'

'I'd use something called Zip Strip.'

'Sounds good to me.'

'Do you need all the trimmings?'

'I do.'

Dave put it all together in a big basket, and walked Will to the back counter.

'This is a great store, by the way,' Will said.

'I thank you.' He pointed to the small nook at the back of the store where an older man and an even older man sat. They were gray and grayer versions of Dave. 'My dad and grandfather thank you.'

The men turned from their game of checkers, nodded their pipes. Will waved. He'd have to work on his Abbeville Meerschaum Pipe Nod.

'I saw a photograph of this place,' Will said. 'I think it was from right around when you opened.'

'That would have been 1881.'

'Wow.'

'Whereabouts did you see this?'

Will pointed over his shoulder, not really knowing if he was pointing in the right direction. 'At the Historical Society. I stopped in the other day. Great little museum.'

'It is that.'

'Eli gave me a brief history of the area.'

'Ah, Eli. He was the real deal.'

The word jumped out. 'I'm sorry. Was?'

Dave handed Will his credit card receipt. He scanned Will's expression.

'I guess you haven't heard, then.'

'Heard what?'

'Hate to be the bearer of sad tidings, but Eli passed away.'

Will felt gut punched. 'What happened?'

'Can't say I know all the facts, but I heard tell that he was found at the bottom of those steep steps leading up to the museum. Had a broke neck.'

'When was this?'

Dave glanced at the back of the store. 'Dad, when did they find Eli?'

The man took his pipe out of his mouth, thought for a moment. 'Early yesterday morning, it was.' He reached for the lighter on the table. 'It was the Benchley girl found him.'

'Lita Benchley does some of the cleaning for the village buildings,' Dave said. 'And she's no girl, by the way. Sunset of fifty, I think.'

Dave bagged Will's purchases.

'Eli was one of the old guard,' Dave added. 'He and my grand-dad were in the same outfit in Korea. Granddad is still going strong. I had the notion that Eli would outlive us all.'

As Will walked back to Godwin Hall, he considered how fleeting his relationship had been with Eli Johnson, how the man had lived so many years, only to lose his life to something as awful and tragic as a fall down the steps.

36

Ivy did a search on the internet for Dr William Hardy. What she found was heartbreaking. At first it was her interest and curiosity about who was moving into Godwin Hall. She figured that whoever would do so had a history in hospitality, or perhaps a retiree couple chasing that dream of opening a bed and breakfast in the country, like Reina and her husband at Red Oak.

The articles detailed the man's life as a professor of forensic psychology at New York University. Included in the background of these articles was how Will had written a book about the movies called *A Flicker of Madness*, a *New York Times* bestseller.

But it was the reason the articles were written in the first place that broke her heart. Dr Hardy had taken on a patient, a troubled young man named Anthony Torres, who had ultimately started a fire that killed Hardy's wife, Amanda. According to the articles Torres had a history of arson.

In all she'd found dozens of reports about the incident. Anthony Torres had perished in the fire, which happened at

Will Hardy's home in Greenwich Village. The follow-up articles continued for a week or so, mostly focusing on the state system through which the young man had passed, the shortcomings of foster care and child service agencies.

The accompanying photographs showed the badly burned façade of the brownstone where the murder had occurred. There were also photographs of Hardy, one of him taken at the university; another in desert camouflage, taken in Iraq.

The article stated that Will Hardy had one daughter, Bernadette. There were no photos of the girl.

Before Ivy closed her laptop she again looked at the photo of Will Hardy at his desk at NYU, and the caption.

Forensic psychologist.

Ivy knew that she could have had the information sent by fax or email, but she decided to take the drive to Richfield, as much to clear her head as anything. After meeting with Gary Baudette, she took with her the reports, which included the fingerprint and hair and fiber analysis, as well as the initial toxicology report from the body of the still unidentified girl.

Ivy stopped at a small diner on Granger Pike and scanned the documents, her pulse beginning to race. She knew that the coroner's ruling was inside this folder.

In the eyes of the law there was murder, manslaughter, and justifiable homicide. There was also felony murder, in which a person dies while the defendant was involved in the commission of a crime.

Ivy quickly skipped through the documents to find the one that would make all the difference. In moments, she had it.

The coroner ruled that the cause of death was exsanguination. And because there was no weapon found on the scene, the manner of death, in his opinion, was homicide.

The girl had bled to death, and it was no accident. It was what

Ivy believed to be true all along. The photos showed deep puncture wounds to the girl's brachial arteries.

This was a murder.

She could now build a case.

Carl Tomlinson owned a sod farm in North Bloomfield. Now in his seventies, Carl had been the Abbeville police chief for twenty years before Ivy's tenure. He had been circling retirement for a few years when Ivy's mother had her stroke, and when Ivy returned to Holland County from the Cleveland Police Department, Carl had lobbied the then mayor and city council hard for Ivy to get the job.

Although they had never been family-close, Ivy had looked up to Carl in a way that some might consider to be a father figure. He had given Ivy her first job on patrol, and had been instrumental in her transition to what would surely be her last job as a law enforcement officer.

Carl was chief when Delia went missing, and he stood at Ivy June's side in those crucial, terrible first months. Ivy had never forgotten the kindness the man showed, far beyond the call of his duty. Ivy had always wondered if it had been more than a kindness, if Carl had felt in some way responsible that Delia's disappearance had happened on his watch.

She missed Carl, and had too many times put off calling him and stopping out to see him, especially now that he was widowed. She always felt good and comfortable and safe here, not the least of the reasons being that Carl was a pushover for rescue dogs. He never had fewer than six or seven.

On her way from the SUV to the house she was greeted by a Sheltie wearing a green bandana, a pair of older pugs, a one-eyed black Lab who'd been rolling in something ripe, and Carl's oldest dog, a Corgi named Jemima, slowly bringing up the rear.

222

Ivy greeted the dogs, glanced up to see Carl stepping down the front steps.

Carl looked good. A little heavier, maybe, a little grayer, but retirement, and the life of a country squire – such as it was when you ran a sod farm – was agreeing with him.

They sat on the sunny enclosed porch, a French press on the wicker table between them. They got their personal small talk out of the way first.

'How's Ivy June?' Carl asked.

'She's good.' Ivy told him about her mother's hip replacements and current rehab status.

'I can't see her sitting around for too long,' Carl said. 'She was never a house cat.'

'She's getting stronger every day.'

They sat in silence for a while. There was news about Abbeville that Ivy remembered to share.

'Eli Johnson passed away.'

'I heard that,' Carl said. 'He was a good man. A veteran.'

Ivy reminded herself that there was now one more flag to put on a grave this Veteran's Day. One more so far.

'Millie Strathaven passed, too.'

Carl shook his head. 'Seems like the whole village is under siege. Millie couldn't have been more than a few years older than I am.'

'And the Hall has new owners,' Ivy said. 'There's talk of it reopening.'

'Now that's some *good* news.'

Ivy wasn't sure about that. She did not share particularly warm feelings about Godwin Hall.

Like all cops, in the life or out, the talk made its way to the job. Ivy told Carl about her current cases. He took it all in, studied his coffee cup.

'It's a different world now, Ivy,' Carl said. 'I'm not sure I would be a cop now, if I was a young man. Not sure if I'd be cut out for it.'

'Sure you would.'

'When I was coming up, and you had differences with another man, you put up your hands. Now you pick up a knife or a gun.'

Ivy could not argue with this.

She told him basic details about Paulette Graham and Lonnie Combs. She also told him about the latest victim.

'This new case,' he said. 'This girl. You say it was by the Gardner farm?'

'Yes. Right close by.'

'And it's a homicide?'

'Just got the ruling.'

'How was she discovered?'

'You remember Dallas Lange?'

'Sure, I remember Dallas.'

Ivy told him how Dallas had seen someone driving what looked like Chevy Deacon's truck right around the time.

'The Deacons,' Carl said without a hint of nostalgia or wistfulness. 'I think I arrested Ray Deacon a dozen times. I told him he should just start getting his mail down at the station.'

'Apples and trees, right?'

Carl nodded.

'You think Chevy Deacon did this thing?' he asked.

'He's a lowlife and an abuser, but I just don't know about this. All we have is Dallas Lange's possible sighting of the truck.'

Ivy decided to take a chance and bring Carl more fully into the fold. She'd more or less decided to do this on the way over. It might have been the real reason for her visit.

'Can I show you something?'

'Of course.'

Ivy didn't even bother to say that what she was about to

show him was confidential. He was the one who taught her all about it.

Ivy took out her phone, scrolled through a few photographs, found the one she wanted. She turned the screen to face Carl. He put on his glasses, took the phone from her.

'My goodness,' he said.

'Did you ever run across anything like this in your time on the job?'

Carl looked even more closely at the screen. 'Those are crow's wings.'

'Yes.'

'They're affixed to something.'

'They are,' Ivy said. 'Swipe to the next photograph. It's a close-up.'

Carl did so. 'Will you look at that.'

Carl studied the photographs for a while. Ivy sensed that he recognized something in them, but perhaps could not quite pin it down. She was right.

'I want to say I've seen this before,' Carl said.

'As part of a case?'

Carl stared off into the woods for a moment. 'I don't know. My memory isn't quite what it used to be, Ivy. Time was when I knew half the license plates in Abbeville.' He looked at the photo. 'Then again, this might just be something I saw in a movie or a book. But I'll be doggone if it isn't familiar.'

'I can get you a copy of these photographs if you think that might help.'

'I think it might.'

'Email okay?'

'Young 'un,' he said with a smile. 'Email's fine.'

As Carl handed back her phone, a shadow caught the edge of Ivy's field of vision, something entering the porch through the doorway into the house. She looked over to see that it was a dog she had not seen earlier, a young female German Shepherd. When Ivy leaned forward the dog made eye contact, then looked away, lowering her head. No aggression, but she wasn't backing up, either. This was her room.

'Who's this movie star?' Ivy asked.

'That's Francesca Lindor.'

'Seriously?'

'Yep.'

'She's named after the baseball player?'

Francisco Lindor was the young All-Star shortstop for the Cleveland Indians.

'Apparently so,' Carl said. 'The breeder is a fan.'

'That's a lot of name for a dog to carry around.'

'She's a big dog. Retired bomb squad. Cadaver training, too.'

Ivy again looked at the dog. She was beautiful. A lustrous black and tan coat, almond shaped eyes, good shoulder definition.

'She was on the job only a few months,' Carl said. 'Word is she was the best they ever had.'

The dog made a few passes in front of Ivy, getting a sense of her threat level.

'What happened to her?' Ivy asked.

'The way I hear it, she and her partner were working a house when some kind of IED went off in the next room. She never got over it. My back door slams and she runs for cover.'

Ivy watched the dog check and recheck the corners of the room. No invading hordes.

'She's still ready and willing, but you know how it is,' Carl said.

Ivy did. She'd been through the same process, the same heart-break, the same long road back.

Carl sipped his coffee. 'Too big for me to handle, I'm afraid. She's only on a pit stop here.'

Francesca Lindor made another pass behind Ivy, then curled

twice near Carl's feet and lay down. Ivy took one more look at her baby browns. Something passed between them.

'No,' Ivy said. She hadn't meant to say this out loud. It just came out.

The dog got up, padded over to Ivy, suddenly full of energy and canine bonhomie.

'I'm sorry?' Carl asked. 'No what?'

'I can't take this dog.'

Carl looked at Francesca Lindor, back at Ivy. 'Did I miss something?'

Yes, you did, Ivy thought. You missed the look. Once that look happened between Ivy and any dog, the bond was forged. Ivy tried to glance anywhere but the dog's big, sad, soulful eyes.

Ivy made a show of staring at her watch. 'Wow,' she said. 'Look at the time.'

She was usually a pretty good liar – she'd always thought that this was one of the hallmarks of a good cop, another arrow in the quiver – but this time the line sounded as phony as a drug suspect saying he didn't know how the crack got into the front pocket of his jeans.

Ivy stood. She hugged Carl. Francesca Lindor seemed to sense an opportunity slipping away, and did her best little-dog act to get in between them.

'Great to see you, Carl.'

'Let's not make it so long next time.'

Francesca Lindor nuzzled Ivy's leg.

'I won't.'

'Give my best to your mother.'

'I will.'

'And if you get me those pictures I'll put a mind to it,' he said. 'When you get old the memories take a little more excavating.'

'I appreciate it, Chief.'

Before the dog could start singing spirituals Ivy made her

way quickly across the porch, out the door, and all the way to her SUV.

She opened the driver door, looked back at the house. The dog was now sitting in the front window.

Ivy looked at the silhouette of those perfectly peaked ears, and thought about this dog at a shelter, knowing full well that a big skittish dog was never going to find a forever home. An eighty-pound former police dog, at that.

Damn it.

Why did you look into those eyes, Ivy Lee?

It was over. She closed the door, walked back to the house.

Francesca Lindor was officially her dog.

They were still a quarter mile from the house when Francesca Lindor began to pace in the back of the SUV.

When Ivy pulled into the drive and opened the hatch the dog bolted from the vehicle and began to conduct a perimeter search, sensing and sense-logging all the animals on the property, including the half-dozen dogs who had once lived there, marking the property as her own every few minutes.

Estate fully claimed, Ivy opened the back door to her house. Francesca Lindor hesitated until Ivy entered. The dog soon followed.

As always, the sight of Amos's empty water bowl caught Ivy's eye. Francesca Lindor was on it in a flash.

'You know what?'

Francesca Lindor barked once.

'Exactly,' Ivy said. 'We're going to need a bigger bowl.'

She sat at her computer late into the night, working on the photo of Delia. She knew she would have to stop one day but she wasn't quite ready. She still felt that the answer to what happened to her sister could be found in the photograph.

Before shutting it all down for the night she glanced again at the autopsy report of the latest victim.

Dr William Hardy, she thought.

Forensic psychologist.

She would make the call.

37

The girl sat on the settee near the window, a book in her lap. She looked small and frail.

'Good morning,' Jakob said. He crossed the room, put down the tray with the tea and the fresh rolls. 'Did you sleep well?'

She shook her head.

'What's wrong?'

'I don't want to be here anymore.'

Jakob sat down next to her.

'May I ask why?'

She shrugged, said nothing.

'You can leave at any time, my dear.'

'I can?'

'Of course.'

She glanced across the room, at the door that led to the hallway. 'But the door is always locked.'

'I'm afraid you are mistaken.'

The girl got up from the settee, crossed the room, tried the door. It pulled open with ease.

She stood in the doorway, perhaps unsure what to do now that the path was available to her. She closed the door, returned to her seat by the window.

Jakob pointed across the field.

'Do you see that square of land? The one with the young saplings?'

'Yes.'

'That is yours. And it will be for all eternity.'

Jakob could see a sheen come to her eyes. She was an emotional sort. He'd known this since seeing her for the first time at the food bank where she had given her time. It was one of the reasons she was who she was, and did the things she was compelled, by her heart, to do. It was why he had chosen her. It was why, ultimately, she had come to him.

'Nothing has changed,' he said.

Jakob stood, crossed the room. Near the door was a table and a brocade satchel. He returned with the bag, undid the clasps.

Inside were neatly banded stacks of currency. He watched the girl as she peered into the bag, saw her eyes widen. He heard a slight catch in her breath. Considering her heritage, her life as it had been lived to this moment, he understood.

'The bag has always been in your room, and the door has always been open. You can leave whenever you want, and you can take this with you.'

'This is a promise?'

'On my honor.'

She took a deep breath, slowly exhaled. 'I'm afraid.'

'There is no need to be afraid.'

'Can I see it again?'

She was not talking about the money. She was talking about her grove. 'Of course.'

They rose, crossed the room to the large windows overlooking the property behind Veldhoeve.

'Tell me about her.'

Jakob knew what she meant. He asked anyway. 'Who, my dear?'

'The first girl,' she said softly. 'Tell me her story.'

'Of course,' Jakob said. He sat down next to her on the settee, extended his arms. She nestled against his chest.

'Her name was Eva,' he began.

Jakob told her the tale, as it had been told since the beginning. He told her about Eva's journey, about her family, about the first time she fell in love.

'Would you like to see the drawings again?'

The girl nodded.

They took the back stairs up to the gallery. As always, the girl sat in front of the Virtues, rapt, her eyes glistening.

Sometime later, Jakob walked her back down to her room, and held her until she fell asleep.

When he left, he locked the door.

38

Will had most of his hardware store purchases arranged on the dining room floor. If he had the energy, he would get started on the refinishing later in the day. He just needed a few more things before he could do that.

The closest big box stores – Target, Wal-Mart, Home Depot – were in neighboring Geauga County.

He locked the doors at Godwin Hall, walked back to Red Oak, up to the second floor.

Even though he knew the answer, by rote, he would ask Detta if she wanted to accompany him. He left his room, walked down the hall, knocked. The door was ajar.

'Detta?'

Silence.

He pushed open the door. Detta was on the bed, her ever-present earbuds in place. She acknowledged him, but did not take out her headphones.

'I need to get a few things,' Will said, louder than he had

to. 'There's a Wal-Mart not too far away. Do you want to go?'

Maybe it was just cabin fever, maybe it was out of boredom, but for whatever reason, Detta grabbed her shoulder bag, slid off the bed, and marched out of the room.

Will followed.

As Will walked the aisles at Wal-Mart, picking up some inexpensive sheets to use as drop cloths, among other things, he found that he couldn't get his mind off Eli. He wondered what the man's life had been like, what he had been like as a young soldier, what he had done for a living after the service.

He wondered if the man had been at the bottom of those steps a long time, if he had suffered at all.

'Miss?'

The word brought Will back to the moment. There was some sort of commotion in the next aisle. As Will walked around the end cap he saw two older people, a man and a woman, looking down the aisle. Their expressions seemed to hover between interest and fear.

Will looked.

Detta was at the far end of the aisle, standing next to a shopping cart. In the cart were five or six bottles of wine, potato chips, a few packages of Oreos. As Will took a few steps closer he noticed that one of the wine bottles in the cart was on its side, and had no cap. It looked to be empty.

When Will looked at his daughter's right hand he understood. Detta had another bottle in hand, and it, too, was well on its way to being empty. He could smell the alcohol from ten feet away.

'Detta?'

She glanced over, her eyes unfocused. She brought the bottle to her lips, took a long drink.

One of the Wal-Mart employees, a rather stout young woman in a blue smock, was rapidly approaching Detta from the other end of the aisle. Will could see by the employee's body language that this was not going to go well.

Will managed to get between the young woman and his daughter just in time. He put a hand on the employee's shoulder.

'It's okay,' he said. 'I'm her father.'

The young woman backed off a little, but did not leave. She brought her walkie-talkie to her lips and said something in retail employee code. You did not have to be in the business to know that she was calling security.

Will stepped closer to Detta. As he approached, Detta took yet another long drink from the bottle. A quick glance at the shopping cart showed that one of the bottles was indeed empty. It meant she had consumed an entire bottle of wine, and then some, in less than fifteen minutes.

'Honey.'

His daughter pulled away from him.

'Don't you *touch* me.'

'Detta, we can talk about this. You don't have to—'

'Leave me *alone*.' Detta wiped at the tears that were gathering in her eyes. 'I fucking hate this place, this town, these people with their pancake breakfasts.'

Will glanced over his daughter's shoulder. There was a small crowd collecting at the end of the aisle.

'Detta, we don't have to do this. It's not your fault. None of it.'

'*My* fault? Of course it's not *my* fault. How could any of it be my fault?'

At this, his daughter began to knock items off the shelf. Luckily, they were mostly plastic dishes and other picnic items. Her face began to redden even more deeply. As she waved her arms, wine came flying out of the bottle.

Behind her was now a large young man. Will was sure he was security for the store.

'Are you her father?' the man asked.

'Yes.'

'Sir, you're going to have to get control of her, or I will.'

Will took out his wallet, handed his Visa to the stout female employee. She looked at her boss, who nodded, then took the card. She backed up to the end of the aisle.

'It's *your* fault,' Detta said. 'All of it. It's *your* fault for meeting that boy, that psycho boy. It's *your* fault that you let him know where we lived. It's *your* fault that he came to our house and started that fire. *You* killed Mom. *You* killed my mother.'

'Let me help, Detta.'

'What, like you helped that boy? With your behavioral therapy? Do you want me to do some yoga breathing?'

Will opened his mouth to speak, but no words came out.

There were no words to say.

They spent less than an hour in the store's loss prevention office.

The damage came to only forty-six dollars. The officer declined to call the local police, even though Detta's consumption of alcohol was a violation of the law.

When they returned to Red Oak Detta walked to her room and slammed the door.

39

He was a big man.

His dead father spoke to him from the shadows, latticed by the soft gray moonlight streaming in the mobile home's front windows. In his lap was a package, wrapped in brown butcher's paper. It was closed with strong twine.

He came home from the war in June of that year. Had a dishonorable discharge.

'What did he do to merit the discharge?' Jakob asked. His voice sounded small, like a child's.

As I understand it, he was a thief. He was caught trying to steal from a commissary. He continued to ply that dark trade around Holland County.

'Did he steal from us?'

He never got the chance. He came looking for employment, but we knew of his past, his misdeeds. When he was denied, he took to threats.

He came to his end in September of that year. When they found him in two pieces on the railroad tracks he had near him the spiked oaken barrel and silver coins.

'Avarice.'

Yes.

Avarice was one of Jakob's favorite drawings.

'What came of his passing?'

It was wartime, and the man was seen by many to be a traitor. He was quickly forgotten. To the good people of Abbeville his passing was considered to be the harvest of black seed.

'Where is the man now?'

Do you know the path from the main barn to the river's edge?

Jakob had walked it many times. Just that morning in fact. The path was laid with huge flagstones. In between the stones there was never a problem with weeds and grass.

Jakob understood. He'd heard this story many times as a boy, but never tired of it.

He sat in silence, and readied the pistol.

When the man awakened in the chair he glanced around, disoriented, then looked down to see two open bottles of whiskey at his feet. He tried to focus on the man sitting across from him. When he saw Jakob in the dim light he perhaps thought of standing to confront this intruder. Then he saw the firearm.

'Who the fuck are you?'

Jakob lifted the pistol. 'Drink.'

With a trembling hand the man reached down, picked up one of the bottles. He brought it to his lips, tilted it upwards.

'More.'

The man tried to drink more. He spit much of it back. He was moments from passing out again.

'You can no longer live with yourself.'

'What are you *talking* about?'

'You and the girl,' Jakob said.

The man's small eyes darted back and forth between Jakob

and the two items on the table in front of him. He weaved in the chair.

'You're fucking crazy.'

'A very fine line,' Jakob said.

Jakob pointed again at the bottle, this time with the barrel of the pistol.

The man once more tilted the bottle to his lips. Half the whiskey poured down his chin.

Jakob stood, walked behind the man.

In front of him, on the coffee table, was the classified section of the day's newspaper and a magic marker. Jakob put the magic marker in the man's hand. When the man dropped it Jakob put the pistol to the side of the man's head. The man picked up the marker.

'You will write her name.'

'Whose name?'

Jakob told him. With great effort, the man repeated the name on the newsprint until he could no longer write.

Jakob folded the paper, sat down. It was time.

'You and Mr Combs.'

'Who?'

'*Soort zoekt sort,*' Jakob said.

The man tried to focus his eyes, to make sense of something he could not understand. Jakob translated.

'Kind seeks kind.'

Jakob continued. He felt the presence of his fathers behind him, smelled the sweat of their labors. It was important that this man knew what was happening to him. It had always been important.

'You have lived a useless life. You have grown nothing, and you will leave nothing behind. There are some people who say – many people, to be fair, and I would not presume to judge them regarding this – that God makes no mistakes. Would you agree with this assessment?'

Silence.

'I do not agree. I believe God has made many mistakes, but has done so on purpose. They are puzzles for us to figure out. Complex equations.

'Think of the many who have not had the opportunities you've had. Your general health and luck of the draw to be born in such a place as this.'

The man began to cry.

'No. You've chosen to live a life of larceny and degradation. A life of vice.'

Jakob was moved by the symmetry and beauty of it. He did not need the flesh, just the blood. He uncapped the *flacon*, set it on the table.

With his gloved hand he placed the fearsome device in the man's left hand.

Moments later, the razor-sharp steel began to whir.

40

What had she done?

She didn't even remember what she'd said. All she could recall was that she was shouting, and that people were staring at her.

And she remembered the devastated look on her father's face. She'd hurt him badly.

They hadn't said a word when they got home.

She hadn't slept at all.

The morning after the Wal-Mart incident Detta got dressed before 8 a.m. and left Red Oak. She walked idly past the small stores – a gun store, an old hardware store, a coffee shop, a Realtor – and wondered if this little town was going to be the rest of her life. She wanted to talk to her mother. She wanted to crawl into a hole.

She wanted to die.

*

Uncle Joe's Sweet Shoppe was a small cedar-shingled storefront, second last of the stores on the north side of the square.

The window display at Uncle Joe's boasted leftover decorations from Easter, with baskets full of green hay and a three-foot stuffed bunny who had seen better days. Its left eye was missing.

As Detta entered the store she heard a bell tinkle overhead, and was greeted by the aromas of chocolate and spun sugar. Beneath it were the sharp fragrances of cherry and raspberry and orange and mint.

Standing at the back of the shop, next to the four-stool fountain, were five teenagers; three girls and two boys. Two of the girls looked like identical twins, pale and faux-Goth. They both had smudgy eyes, like extras in *The Walking Dead*.

The third girl was short and stocky, her head shaved on one side, the other side swept up into a purple Mohawk. She wore mauve lipstick and a magenta midriff T-shirt, at least two sizes too small. It exposed a cantilevered roll of pasty white flesh over her spangled belt.

Standing next to the girls were two boys, doing the standard routines when boys are trying to impress girls – laughing a bit too hard, pushing each other, high-fiving and fist-bumping. A pair of banged-up skateboards leaned against the wall at their feet.

Within seconds of noticing Detta walk into the store, all five of them drilled holes in her.

Detta was bored to tears. These girls were bargain-basement versions of the kids who had annoyed the hell out of her in the city. They were so 2012.

Detta stuck near the front of the store. She cruised the shelves and was pleasantly surprised to see some pretty cool items. They even had a small section of artisanal root beers.

'Hey.'

Detta turned around. It was the taller of the two boys. He was okay looking, but dressed like a slob.

'My name's Cody. How you doin'?'

Detta gave him a non-committal half smile, cold as January.

'What's your name?' he asked.

Deeper chill. The boy slouched back. More high fives.

'What can I getcha?'

The man behind the counter was older, in his sixties, mostly bald, with tassels of silver hair over his ears. It suited him. His eyes sparkled, and it made him look younger. She'd wondered if he was Uncle Joe, and his name tag confirmed it.

'I'm just kind of looking.'

As she said this, she heard the kids at the back mimic her and laugh. Uncle Joe shot a glance to the rear of the store, then looked back at Detta. 'Don't mind them,' he said. 'I was dealing with their mommies and daddies thirty years ago. They were pretty much standing in the same spot.'

Detta smiled. Uncle Joe gestured to the barrels of wrapped candies. 'Samples are always free here. If you want to try anything under the counter let me know. I make my own gelato and ice cream.'

'Thanks.'

In the end Detta bought two chocolate turtle tartlets. She wanted to buy a dozen, but she knew they would never make it home.

The day had warmed a little more, so Detta took off her hoodie, rolled it into her backpack. She walked her bike to the corner facing the square, leaned it against a bench, sat down.

The tartlets were to die for. Maybe this town wasn't such a bad place after all.

She turned her face to the sun.

'Hey, girlie.'

Detta spun around. The three girls were now standing on the corner just outside the entrance to the Subway. The two boys were leaning against an older model, rusted car on the other side of the street, smoking and looking at their cell phones.

Detta said nothing.

'I'm *talking* to you,' Mohawk said. In one hand she had a half-eaten éclair. Like she needed it.

Detta stood up and turned to face the girl fully, but still said nothing.

'You deaf or something?'

'I'm not deaf.'

'Where you from?'

Detta stood up and took the opportunity to look more closely at Mohawk. Her skin was greasy, uncared for. Her hair looked brittle, as if pieces of it had broken off.

'I am so tired of hearing myself talk,' Mohawk said.

That makes two of us.

'I asked where you're from.'

'The city,' Detta finally said.

'*The* city. Which one is that?'

It looked like Detta would have to dignify this skank with a conversation, or they weren't going to let her go.

'New York.'

'New *York*? Damn, girl. Here I always thought that New York was a fancy place. I thought girls knew how to dress there.'

Detta squared herself in front of the girl. 'Why do you *talk* like that?'

The girl looked slapped. Apparently, kids around here didn't talk to her this way, if they talked to her at all.

'Excuse me?'

'You talk like you think you're some kind of thug. Are you a gangster or something?'

The girl tried to stand tall, but Detta could see the embarrassment growing in her eyes. It was a moment all bullies dread; whether to step up or step back.

244

'What did you say to me?' the girl asked without any aggression or heat. It was as hollow a threat as Detta had ever heard.

'Are we back to the deaf thing? I mean, isn't this where we started? With you asking me if *I* was deaf? Want me to talk louder?'

At this the three girls glanced over to the other side of the square, saw a police car waiting for the light. Mohawk looked back at Detta.

'We're not done,' she said.

'Bring it,' Detta said.

'Oh, I'll bring it, bitch. You just watch your ass.'

Detta stood up and gave her the once over, taking a long moment to scrutinize the considerable fat roll spilling over the top of the girl's jeans.

'Maybe I'll watch *your* ass. It's certainly big enough.'

One of the zombie twins laughed, then quickly zipped it. They all walked quickly away.

It was over.

For now.

The library was a small red brick building with a legend over the front door that read 1859.

The lobby had that old-building smell. At least it was a clean smell. So many of the really old buildings in New York smelled like some kind of body function. This one smelled like leaves.

The main room was straight ahead. At the center was a U-shaped checkout desk, staffed by a girl about Detta's age.

Detta looked for a while at the paperbacks, then turned to the large room to the left of the lobby. In there were tall stacks for Sociology, History, Accounting, Marketing, Economics.

As she turned toward the lobby and the front door she saw a shadow on the carpeting. Someone was standing at the end of the aisle. Because the aisles were so narrow, her natural instinct was to choose another aisle to walk down. She didn't really feel like playing the 'excuse me' game. But when she looked up her heart nearly stopped.

There, at the end of the aisle, was a boy.

He was staring at her.

And he was beautiful.

Detta found herself frozen in place. Her legs felt like concrete pillars.

When she was able to move she turned to give a quick look behind her, just to be sure that the boy was still there.

There was no one behind her.

She walked up and down the aisles, a little too quickly to be checking out the titles, a little too slowly to be looking for someone. When she was certain the boy had left, or had been a mirage, she turned the corner in the YA section and saw him.

He was thumbing through a book near the front doors to the library, his back to her. He was tall, maybe even six feet. His hair was a little long and shaggy. He had broad shoulders.

Suddenly he turned around, looked right at her, and put the book on the table. He then went down the three steps, pushed open the door to the lobby, and was gone.

When he disappeared from view Detta turned her attention to the table near the door, and the single book sitting among the neatly stacked flyers and brochures. Even from this far away she could see it was not a new book. There was no dust jacket.

She had to know what it was.

As nonchalantly as possible she glanced around the area, approached the table, took one of the flyers in hand, pretended to read it. It was something about a home repair resource center.

She then picked up the book, and saw that there was something stuck in it, a bookmark of some sort. It was a white feather pressed between two pieces of waxed paper.

When she fully opened the book her gaze went immediately to the top of the right-hand page.

Handwritten there were three words – words she didn't recognize – followed by a fourth, a proper name. The words were written in a beautiful script, in a very light pencil.

Somehow, this beautiful stranger had been holding this book, and inside, on one of the pages, were written three foreign, exotic words.

Mijn eeuwige liefde.

Then there was that fourth word.

Bernadette.

41

Detta spent the afternoon in her room at Red Oak, thinking about the boy, the library, the book.

Had she imagined it? Had she imagined that the boy looked right at her? Had he wanted her to pick up the book and look inside on the page that had the white feather as a bookmark? The page where he had written her name?

By four o'clock she was climbing the walls.

She walked up the main street, window shopping but not really seeing things.

She stopped in front of the Subway, caught her reflection in the window. She looked like a major frump. For her, orange was certainly not the new black. She looked like a tangelo with two chopsticks for legs.

Before she could think about it, she turned her body toward the corner, toward the crosswalk, toward the other side of the street, toward the library.

*

She walked into the building on eggshells, ready to dash to the door if she had to. She rounded the corner where the books on Psychology were shelved, glanced at the table where the boy had put the old book.

It was gone.

Why hadn't she looked at the title?

'Can I help you find something?'

Detta spun around. The woman had a nametag that identified her as Jennifer. She was in her twenties, and wore a peach cardigan and beige slacks.

'I'm not sure.'

'Are you looking for a particular book? A particular section?'

'It's an old book.'

'How old are we talking about here? Harry Potter old?'

'No,' Detta said. 'I've read those. Older than that even.'

'Do you have a title? The author's name, perhaps?'

'No,' she said. 'It's one of those books that's so old it doesn't even have a dust jacket. Like the Bible or something.'

Jennifer laughed. 'That would be one of the oldest. But I know what you mean. We have a section of classic fiction. We can start there. I'll show you.'

The classic fiction section of the library was four tall stacks of clothbound books.

'Like the regular fiction section, these are shelved by "main entry", that being the author's last name,' Jennifer said.

'I know the title of the book has the word "house" in it. That's about all I can remember.'

Jennifer ran her fingers over the spines of the books, moving to the shelf with authors whose last name began with D. She pulled a book. 'Might it have been this?'

The book was called *Bleak House* by Charles Dickens. It was all wrong. This book was blue. The book she wanted was brown.

'No,' Detta said. 'I don't think this is the one.' She handed the book back. Jennifer returned it to the shelf, continued to look.

'This, perhaps?'

House of Mirth by Edith Wharton. Although the book was brown, it didn't seem right.

'No,' she said. 'The one I'm looking for had a longer title.'

Jennifer took a step back, thought for a moment. 'This might be it,' she said.

When she removed the book from the shelf Detta's heart began to race. While she didn't know the title or the author, she knew the book itself had a long scratch on the front cover, a dented bottom right corner.

The book was called *The House of the Seven Gables* by Nathaniel Hawthorne.

'This is the one,' Detta said,

'Hawthorne is one of my favorites. Is this a school assignment?'

'No. A friend of mine recommended it.'

'It's a wonderful book. Our only copy. It has some interesting twists, and even somewhat of a surprise ending. Quite modern in that respect.'

'I like surprise endings,' Detta said. This wasn't entirely true. She liked surprise endings in movies and books, but not in life.

After completing the process to get a library card, Detta checked out the book. When she left the library she rushed down the steps, her valuable cargo clutched tightly to her breast.

There was an old stone wishing well in the town square with a bench next to it. When she reached the bench, she sat down, opened the book to the title page.

The House of the Seven Gables: a Romance by Nathaniel Hawthorne.

She felt a chill flutter up her back. Firstly because he had read this. The second reason was because of that word: romance.

You're losing your data, Detta. Serious meltdown, girl.

She knew what page the boy's inscription to her was on. It was on page seventeen, on the left-hand side, facing page eighteen.

She opened the book to the page.

It was gone. The inscription was no longer there.

Had she imagined it? Was she so whacked out on her meds that she was starting to hallucinate, to create boys who weren't really there, and cryptic messages left for her in old library books?

Then, before she closed the book she saw it.

There were eraser crumbs in the crevice.

She wasn't crazy after all.

Her name had been written in this book, then someone had erased it.

'Hi,' Detta said.

'Hello again,' Jennifer said.

'I was wondering something.'

'Sure.'

'About that sign you have on the corkboard over there. The one by the door.'

'Which sign?'

'The one that says you're looking for part-time help.'

'What about it?'

'I'd like to apply for the job.'

42

All three of the bedroom sets Will had purchased at auction needed refinishing. The oldest among them needed some repair as well, the mortise and tenon joints having worked themselves loose over the years. Will had conducted a Google search on how to repair such things and bookmarked it for later, hoping that somehow he would acquire some modicum of skill in this area before the furniture fell apart.

He read and reread the instructions on the Zip Strip. It seemed easy enough. Dave was right.

After it was all dry Will noticed a few areas that had not been completely stripped. He did a second coat, spot stripping these areas, specifically along the face of the footboard.

An hour later he took a few steps back, checked on his work.

It was coming together.

The day had taken more out of him than he had thought. He'd taken a long, hot shower, his thoughts never far from what had happened at Wal-Mart.

Will knew in his heart that Detta had not meant the things she said. In some ways the episode was a good thing. He would certainly counsel this to a patient, telling them that Bernadette was relinquishing her grief in the guise of anger. He had wanted and hoped for her to take steps like this, but he had not expected it to hurt so much.

He sat at the small secretary desk in his room at Red Oak, the French doors open to the warm evening. He opened his laptop, navigated over to the Word document he'd started for notes on what was supposed to be his next book. He hadn't a single idea. He thought about a follow-up to *A Flicker of Madness*, another book examining criminal psychosis in film, but he couldn't seem to muster sufficient enthusiasm for the project.

'Dad?'

At first, Will thought the voice was coming from his laptop, that it was a streaming video ad that just started on a website.

When he heard nothing after it – no music, no other voices – he turned around. Detta was standing in the doorway leading to her room. She wore the new robe he had bought for her. In her hands were two cups of cocoa.

Will felt his breath catch in his throat.

'Detta? What's wrong?'

She looked at the floor for a moment, then put the two cups down on the desk. She stood there, hands at her sides, looking small and lost and broken.

'I'm so sorry, Dad.'

Then came the tears.

Will stepped forward, unsure of what to do, afraid that if he made the wrong move they would lose this moment. He reached out his arms. Detta stepped into them.

They held each other for a long time.

*

Neither of them knew how to say goodnight, how to go to bed, how to end this moment.

Will told Detta about Reuben and Miriam Yoder, about Eli and the Historical Society, about Hale Hardware, about the auction. He told her about the bedroom sets, about how he had picked out their rooms at Godwin Hall. She seemed to come alive as he revealed all these things, to take a genuine interest.

Detta shared with him that she had been to the square a few times, that she was starting to get a feel for the layout of Abbeville.

They sat in silence for a while.

'Do we get Amazon here?' Detta asked.

'Do you mean deliveries from UPS and FedEx?'

'Yeah.'

'Of course. No problem. They come here. I've seen the trucks. We're getting mattresses delivered via UPS on Friday. For sure they come here.'

'I'd like to order some stuff,' she said.

'Of course. We can just—'

'But you don't have to pay for it.'

'I don't understand,' Will said. 'What do you mean?'

'I'm going to get a job.'

'That's great, honey. Where?'

'The library.'

'The little library? The one on the square?'

'Yeah,' she said. 'It's just part time, and I'm a volunteer to start, but they said that if it works out I'll get paid. It won't be much, but it will be something.'

'That is so cool.'

'I'd like to buy some art supplies on Amazon. Some pads and pencils.'

Will had to look away for a moment. He chose to look at his laptop, where he clicked over to the Amazon site. When he looked back he was, more or less, under control.

He decided to just say it out loud.

'I'm thinking we might move into Godwin Hall this week.'

He waited for the worst news possible, news that his daughter didn't want to make the move. She hadn't even been inside yet.

'This week?'

'Yeah. Unless you want to stay here for a while. We could do that if you want to. We don't have to move in. Whatever you want to do is okay with me.'

'This week is good,' Detta said. 'I'll be ready.'

'Great,' Will said. 'That's just, well, *great*.'

'Dad?'

'Yeah, honey?'

'You're sweating.'

'No I'm not.'

Detta crossed the room, sat down in front of the laptop.

'Now, if you'll excuse me,' she said. 'I have some shopping to do.'

43

Ivy decided on a full breakfast at Coffee Nook. She bought a newspaper, but left it unread. Her mind was filled with the new developments on what was now a homicide.

As she finished her meal, she sensed someone standing to the left of her table. She looked up. It was Will Hardy. She was going to find a way to call him today. Fate had intervened.

Ivy decided to take it as a sign.

'Dr Hardy,' she said. 'Good morning.'

'Will, please,' he said. 'Good morning to you.'

Ivy gestured to the chair. 'Join me.'

'Thanks.'

'How is the furniture working out?'

'Really well,' he said. 'I can't believe I got it so cheaply. Thanks again for the help.'

'I love working a room like that.'

They talked weather, the change of the seasons, the progress being made at Godwin Hall, the upcoming festivals. When the conversation slowed, Ivy said:

'I have to confess I looked you up on the internet. Occupational hazard.'

Will smiled. 'I understand.'

'So, you're a criminal psychologist?'

'A forensic psychologist, really. The sexy Hollywood term is profiler, but I haven't really done much of that. Not for a while, anyway. I taught at NYU right up until the move here.'

'I saw that you worked with NYPD.'

'I did. Many times. I've also done a lot of work with correctional facilities, jury selection, competency evaluations.'

Ivy had wrestled with the idea since the man sat down at her table. In truth, she'd thought about it since she'd read about his *bona fides*.

She told Will the basics of the new case. She left out her theories. For the moment.

'I saw that on the news,' Will said. 'I didn't realize it was so close. I'm not yet too familiar with the geography here.'

'The girl was no more than fifteen or sixteen,' Ivy said.

'Can I help in any way?'

'With the case, you mean?'

'Yes.'

'I couldn't ask you to do that.'

'I have a good bit of experience in this. I did some work with NYPD helping them draw up interview guidelines.'

'It wouldn't be an imposition?'

'Not at all,' Will said. 'I've got nothing scheduled all morning.'

'It wouldn't be in any official capacity, of course.'

'So, I don't get a badge?'

'I'll see what I can rustle up.'

Ivy gave it one last thought, trying to find a reason not to take the man up on his generous offer, one she'd hoped would be presented.

She found none.

*

They'd taken just a few steps toward the porch when the front door opened. The house was a rambling, ivied colonial set back a hundred feet from the road.

In the doorway stood Bianca Woodruff. Bianca was in her forties, thin and angular. On this day she wore a green kimono and a lavender turban-style hair scarf. Bianca, who began life as Andy Woodruff, lived on the outskirts of Abbeville, just inside the Cuyahoga County line.

Ivy had gone to school with Andy Woodruff, whose father used to beat his son senseless every month or two. For a while it looked like the man waited for Andy's bruises to heal before he tore back into him, like the boy couldn't be seen in the man's presence without looking like he'd paid the price for not being the son he wanted. He put Andy in the hospital more than a few times.

Denny Woodruff got paid back in full when he stepped up to someone his own size at a bar in Richfield. Died face down in the rain.

In the last few years Bianca had begun to take in the runaways, the strays. When they couldn't find shelter, when there was nowhere else to go, Bianca gave them refuge. But they could not stay long, and there were rules. No drugs, no tricks, no drama.

'As I stand and faint,' Bianca said. 'Miss Ivy Lee Holgrave.'

As she got closer Ivy saw that, beneath the housecoat, Bianca wore a New York Dolls *Immaculate Conception* T-shirt.

'Bianca, this is Will Hardy. He's brand new to Abbeville.'

They shook hands. 'Nice to meet you.'

'You as well,' Will said.

'Is this a porch visit or a parlor visit?' Bianca asked Ivy.

'Parlor. Do you have a few moments?'

'For you, always.' Bianca opened the door fully, stepped to the side.

Ivy had not been inside this house in five years or more,

and she was all but certain not a single thing had been moved. The décor was a pastiche of Norma Desmond meets Pee-Wee Herman: rattan furniture, porcelains, Japanese fans.

'How's your mother, Ivy?'

'Still taking names,' Ivy said. 'Thanks for asking.'

'She a good woman, your Ivy June. Always treated me with respect. Even back when I was acting out.'

'She's a rare and precious jewel.'

Bianca straightened her kimono. 'So, what's up, Ivy? You've got that cop look today.'

'I need to know if you've seen a girl. Around sixteen, dark long hair, petite, maybe one hundred pounds.'

Ivy reached into her folder, removed the photograph she had printed at the station. It was a close-up of the victim. The picture revealed the victim's face, but nothing else. She handed it to Bianca.

'Oh, my,' Bianca said.

'Do you recognize her?'

Bianca nodded, tears brimming her eyes. 'I do.'

Ivy took out her notepad. 'What's her name?'

'Josie,' she said. 'Josefina.'

'Do you know her last name?'

'No,' she said. 'We don't press the kids. They have enough problems.'

'How did you come to meet her?'

Bianca grabbed a tissue from the box on the end table, dabbed her eyes. 'One of the girls here, LaChelle, I think, brought her here one night.'

'Is LaChelle here now?'

'Yes,' Bianca said.

'Could we speak with her?'

'Of course. *Chelle?*'

A few seconds later a young girl came around the corner from the kitchen, drying her hands with a dish towel. She was about seventeen, and about seven months pregnant. Bianca made the introductions.

'They want to ask you a few questions about Josie.'

The girl continued to worry the edge of the dish towel. 'Something happened to Josie?'

'I'm afraid so,' Ivy said. 'We're just gathering information at the moment. Is it okay if we ask you a few questions?'

The girl nodded.

Ivy glanced at Will. He picked right up on the idea that the girl would be probably more comfortable talking to someone not in a police uniform.

'How long have you known Josefina?' Will asked.

'A month, maybe. Then some.'

'Do you know her last name?'

The girl shook her head.

'Where did you meet her?'

'Up at the mall. Belden Village.'

'Was she working there, or just hanging out?'

'Hanging out. She was all by herself. She looked pretty sad, so I just talked to her.'

'Talked to her about what?'

'I don't know. Things. Boys and such. She told me she was living with her grandfather because her mom had taken sick, and she couldn't take care of her. Said her mama was on the hospice care.'

'What about her grandfather? Did she ever say who he was or where he lived?'

Another shake of the head. 'No. She said she was living with her aunt and uncle for a while, but she didn't like them.'

'Did she tell you what that was all about?'

'Not really. She said her uncle was always trying to get her alone.'

'Did Josefina say she had ever reported her uncle to the authorities?'

'I don't know. I don't think so. We had some talks and such, but I got the feeling she didn't want to talk too much about that. Her uncle, I mean.'

'How did she come to stay here?' Will asked.

The girl shot a glance at Bianca. Bianca nodded.

'I told her about this place. About Bianca and everything. I don't always do it with the lost kids, but like I said, she was pretty sad.'

Bianca said, 'I told her when she got here, like I tell all the kids, somebody has to know they're here.'

'You mean like a family member or something?' Ivy asked.

'Yeah. I don't need any trouble from higher powers, if you know what I mean. If someone knows that you're staying here, then implicit consent is given. As you know, we are not a safe house. We get no money from the county.'

'And you say that she told family members she was here?' Ivy asked.

'That's what she said. I take the kids at their word.'

'While she was here were there any incidents? Any drama?'

'Nothing that I heard or witnessed,' Bianca said. 'She was pretty quiet. Just a fawn. She took my heart.'

They turned back to the girl. Will continued.

'Did she tell you anything about what might've been going on in her life outside of her home situation? Work or school or anything like that?'

'I remember that she told me that she volunteered at a shelter.'

'Did she say which one?'

'No. But she said she did it because her mama was on food stamps and Medicaid and such. Felt like it was something she could do to help other folks.'

There were five or six shelters in Holland County. As Josefina

261

didn't have a car, and there wasn't a lot of public transportation in the county, the two shelters that were in walking or hitchhiking distance were probably the ones.

'When was the last time you saw Josie?' Ivy asked Bianca.

'A month ago. She just didn't show up for a few days and I figured she had gone back to live with her mother or her grandfather. I keep tabs on the kids when I can, but there's been a lot of kids over the last five years and some just slip into the ether. I just hope and pray for the best for them. As soon as you turn around there's another face in the rain.'

'Did she leave anything here?' Ivy asked. 'Any clothing or personal items?'

'She left some clothes,' LaChelle said.

'Can you show them to me?'

LaChelle again looked to Bianca, who again nodded.

The girl went up the steps to the second floor. A few moments later she returned with a pair of jeans, and two sweaters. She handed them to Ivy.

'Thanks,' Ivy said.

Ivy went through the clothing. In one of the jeans pockets was a still-wrapped cherry cough drop and a red elastic hair band. The other pockets were empty. One of the sweaters was a crew neck pullover. The other was a hoodie with two pockets. Ivy could feel something hard in one of the pockets.

Inside was a heart shaped piece of plastic with writing on it. It said, *Thank You, Volunteers! March 2–4.* Beneath that was a logo with which Ivy was familiar.

Calvary House.

Ivy held up the chip. 'And you're sure this belonged to Josefina?'

'I don't know for sure. I've never seen that before. But that's her hoodie.'

'I'll need to take these things with me,' Ivy said. 'Is that okay?'

262

Bianca nodded.

Ivy reached into her shoulder bag, took out a large paper evidence bag. She put the clothing inside.

As LaChelle returned to the kitchen, Ivy and Will and Bianca walked to the front door.

'If you think of anything else, give me a call,' Ivy said.

'Of course.'

Ivy lingered for a moment. 'Thanks for your help.'

Bianca gathered the top of her kimono together. 'You know you are always welcome here, Ivy,' she said. 'Sorry it had to be like this today.'

'If there's anything I can do.'

'You don't happen to have a few dozen cases of Kleenex, do you? We use a lot of Kleenex around here.'

Ivy smiled. 'I'll see what I can do.'

44

Calvary House was a nine-bed facility run by the Franciscan Sisters of the Poor. It had been in continuous operation for more than thirty years, providing a transitional home for women who were victims of domestic abuse.

Ivy was told by the receptionist that the director of the facility, Sister Della Marie, was not on the grounds. The woman pointed to the dining hall, where they met a woman named Rebecca Taylor. Rebecca was one of the women staying at the shelter, a den mother of sorts.

Rebecca Taylor was in her late thirties, a brunette with cautious brown eyes. Ivy introduced herself and Will, showed the woman her ID. Ivy asked if the woman remembered a girl, a volunteer named Josefina.

'I remember her very well,' she said. As she talked she folded and stacked bed linens on one of the tables. 'I hope she's not in any kind of trouble.'

'We're just gathering some information at this point.'

'I'll be happy to tell you what I know,' she said. She grabbed a stack of sheets and pillowcases off the table. 'If you don't mind me doing some housekeeping while we talk.'

'Not at all,' Ivy said.

She led Ivy and Will to the stairs at the end of the hall. They walked up to the second floor. At the top step Rebecca stopped, called out.

'Man on the floor! Man on the floor!'

After a full minute or so, they continued.

Ahead was a long corridor with bedrooms on the right and left side, a bathroom at each end. They entered the first bedroom on the left. It contained a single bed, a dresser, and a chair. Above the bed was a framed painting of St Francis.

As they talked Rebecca began to strip the bed. Ivy pitched in, and Will interviewed the woman.

'What can you tell us about Josie's time here?' Will asked.

'She wasn't here all that long. Maybe three months total, and then just part time.'

'Is there anyone she was particularly close to here?'

'Not that I know of.'

'What was she like?'

'She was a good kid. Nice and respectful. None of the sass you usually get from kids her age.'

'Did she ever talk about any abuse she may have suffered at home? Altercations or problems she may have had at her school before she left? Anything like that?'

'No,' she said. 'Nothing like that. But I had the feeling she was holding something in. She never said what it was, and I didn't press her.'

'What about the men?'

'What men?'

'Any of the men on staff here,' Will said. 'Counselors, therapists, social workers.'

'The only man who comes here regularly is Dr Chambliss, and he's over seventy. The women here think of him as their father or grandfather. In a kindly way, I might add. There's a special place in heaven for Dr Chambliss. Can't imagine he gets paid much, if anything at all. Might be pro . . . '

'*Pro bono?*'

'Yeah,' she said. 'That.'

'Did Josie ever talk about people outside this facility? Girlfriends, boyfriends, significant others?'

'Now that you mention it, I did see her once.'

'See her do what?'

As they finished making the bed, Rebecca walked over to the window. She pointed. 'Josie was on her break. She always had a cigarette when she was on her break. We all tried to get her to quit. But she would just look at the lot of us – the sorry state of us – more or less telling us we had no room to talk. She was right, of course.'

'What was she doing that day?'

'She was standing down by the gate over there. The one that leads to the walk and the path over to the river. Through those trees.'

'And she was with someone?'

'Yes. She was with a boy.'

'Do you know the boy she was with?'

'No. I don't know him.'

'White kid, black? Tall, short?'

'He was white, tall, had kind of a mop of brown hair. Good posture.'

'Good posture?'

'You know how kids that age are always slouching? This kid was not. He had his shoulders squared. Maybe he was an athlete, or maybe spent some time in military school. Maybe even a dancer.'

266

Ivy made the note. She would check the local school sports teams and their rosters.

'And you're saying he didn't look familiar to you in any way?' Will asked. 'Like someone who has done some work around here? Landscaping, deliveries, something like that?'

'No. I didn't recognize him at all. But then again, they were pretty far away.'

'When did this happen?'

'Not long before she stopped coming around. Maybe a month ago.'

'Did you ever see this boy again?'

'No,' Rebecca said. 'I just saw him one time.'

'Do you think anyone here would know Josefina's last name?' Ivy asked.

'She never told me. Even amongst ourselves we tend to go by our first names. It's a habit, I guess. Some of us are short timers, and a lot of us unfortunately took a man's last name. That's something a lot of us are here to shed.'

Ivy just nodded.

'As to the girl's last name, Sister Della Marie might know.'

Ivy took out her card case, handed a card to the woman. 'Could you ask her to call me as soon as possible? It's important.'

Rebecca took the card, pocketed it. In her eyes Ivy could see that she understood that whatever had led a police officer to her door on this day was bad. She didn't ask, perhaps to shield herself from any more heartache.

They sat in silence in the small parking lot behind the station. Before long, Walt Barnstable pulled into the lot. His shift started in just a few minutes.

'Thanks again for today, Will. It really helped.'

'Any time, Ivy. To be honest, I miss the field work.'

'Any thoughts on what we learned?'

Will took a moment. 'I don't think Josie was abused. She probably would have shared with one of the women at Calvary House, and that would have gotten around quickly. I have the feeling Rebecca Taylor is on top of things. She would have known. I'll be able to tell you a lot more when you ID her, and we can find out about her home life.'

'Is it okay if I call you when I get that?'

'Absolutely.'

Ivy got home at just after ten. She checked on her mother, and barely got undressed and into bed before the exhaustion took over.

As she slipped beneath the covers she thought about Calvary House, and what Rebecca Taylor said.

She was with a boy.

45

Detta left Red Oak around noon. The sky was clear and cloudless, the air sweet with the fragrance of ripening apples. It was a
Rockwell painting of a day.

She took part in the hour-long orientation at the library.
There was one other new part-timer in attendance, a sweet girl
named Renee Billets. Renee was Detta's age, and seemed to be a
bit in awe of Detta when she found out that she was from New
York. Everyone was really nice, and Jennifer patiently walked
them both through all of their duties.

There was no sign of the boy.

After the meeting Detta got on her bike and headed down the
main road, riding against the traffic.

The street went from the few businesses that were on the
south side of the town square to long stretches where there were
only a few houses per mile.

She knew from Google Maps that a winding country road

called Treetop Lane would be coming up soon on her left, a road that led down to the river. In short order she saw it, and curved around to the two-lane road.

She came upon the river quickly. It was beautiful, and this part of it was very secluded. It was as if she were the only girl in the world. She got off her bike, lay it down near the edge.

She found a patch of warm, dry grass, sat down. Across the river, on a low hill, was a shack of some sort. It was the outbuilding of a nearby farm that had surely seen better days.

Detta found a dry branch, snapped it a few times, crafting a makeshift stylus. She made a rudimentary outline of the building in the drying mud.

Not bad. She found a smaller branch and made some cross-hatching, shading the dark side of the shack. She knew that when the level of the water rose, it would wash away her half-hearted drawing, but that was okay.

Detta tossed the small branch into the river, and as it floated away she began to cry. She didn't stop for the longest time. She didn't want to.

Twenty minutes later she stood up her bike and began to walk slowly along the path toward the village. After she'd gone fifty feet or so she saw something near the base of the huge apple tree near the river bank. At first she thought it was a piece of paper, a candy wrapper, perhaps.

When she looked more closely she saw that it wasn't a piece of paper after all. It was an apple peel. A long, carefully carved corkscrew of an apple peel. The part that didn't make sense was how fresh it looked. She'd baked enough apple pies with her mother to know that apple peels, and apples themselves, began to brown within just a few minutes. This was fresh.

But she'd been out here for more than an hour. No one had passed by. It didn't make sense.

'I like your drawing.'

Detta nearly jumped out of her skin. She whipped around to see who had spoken to her but there was no one there. She turned again, and again.

'Up here.'

Detta took a few stumbling steps backward. She looked up into the tree. There was someone there, sitting on the lowest branch of the huge apple tree.

But it wasn't just *someone*.

It was the boy. The beautiful boy from the library.

And he was holding a knife.

46

The boy wore a deep green hooded sweatshirt, a white T-shirt beneath, faded blue jeans and a pair of tan work boots. His sandy hair was a little long, and adorably messed up. He had the bluest eyes she'd ever seen.

Still, even though he was really cute, she wanted to kill him for frightening her.

When he came down from the tree he grabbed the branch beneath his feet and swung himself downward.

'You scared me,' she said.

'I know. I'm sorry.'

Detta tried to fix his age. She imagined he was sixteen or seventeen. Then again, he might have been even older. He seemed to have an older boy's confidence.

'I was sitting up there for a while,' he said. 'Just watching the river go by. Now that it's warm enough I like to do it whenever I can.'

Detta said nothing.

He leaned back, against the tree. 'I saw you come around the bend on your bicycle. I thought you were going to just ride by. I was going to say hello, but I didn't want to bother you. Then you stopped.'

'And you spied on me.'

The boy put up both hands in surrender. 'Guilty as charged, Your Honor. Although I wouldn't really call it spying.'

'What would you call it?'

The boy thought for a few moments.

'Have you ever been to an art museum?'

In truth, Detta had been to just about every art museum in Manhattan. Many times.

'Yes. I have.'

'So, you're walking around the museum, looking at everything, and for the most part it's a bunch of stuff you don't really relate to. I mean, the medieval armor is pretty cool, and the portraits of the old dead English kings are all right, but, for the most part, nothing really speaks to your soul. Do you know what I mean?'

She knew *exactly* what he meant. She couldn't believe he was actually saying these things to her.

'It's a couple of hours later and, just when you're getting ready to leave, you come around the corner and you see something you didn't expect to see. One of those museum pieces that is set aside and given its own special place, its own special lighting, to show it just as the artist intended.'

The boy took a few steps forward.

'That's what I thought when you came around the bend. I thought about saying something but I knew there would never be another moment like this. I would never again have the opportunity to see you in this perfect light. I didn't want to mess up the moment with my idiot blathering. So I just watched you. I hope you'll forgive me. I was being selfish, and I was wrong.'

Detta felt dizzy. Instead of saying anything witty, she took a deep breath, and said:

'It's okay.'

'Am I forgiven?'

'Yeah,' she said. 'Yes.'

He leaned back against the tree. 'I really like your glasses.'

For a fleeting moment Detta could not remember who she was wearing today, which designer. They all looked the same from her side of the frames these days.

'Thanks,' she said. 'I'm blind as a bat without them.'

'When I first saw you I thought you looked a little sad.'

'Yeah, maybe that's because I've been in the dogs'. I'm out now, but it was bad.'

'Uh oh. What did you do?'

She wasn't sure she wanted to tell anyone what happened, least of all this boy. On the other hand, in this town, everyone probably already knew what had happened in that store.

'I went full Chernobyl in Wal-Mart.'

'Wait. That was *you*?'

Detta looked up, horrified. 'What did you hear?'

The boy held her gaze for a few agonizing seconds. Then he smiled. 'I'm just kidding. I didn't hear anything. It isn't *that* small of a town.'

'Yes, it is.'

'So, what did you do?'

'I opened a couple of bottles of wine.'

'In the store?'

'Yeah.'

'Okay. At least you didn't drink them.'

'Yes I did.'

The world suddenly went silent for a few seconds. Then the boy clapped his hands. 'Oh, *no*! That is awesome!'

'It wasn't awesome. It was stupid.'

'It was awesomely stupid,' he said. 'But therein lies the beginning of a legend around here.'

'Great.'

'Were they the screw top kind or the corkscrew kind?'

'Screw top.'

'Well played. How did it all end?'

Detta shrugged. 'No handcuffs. My dad had to pay for the stuff I broke.'

'You broke stuff?'

'I told you it was bad. The worst part is that I said terrible things to my father. I didn't even mean them.'

'Then why did you say them?'

Detta felt the emotions close in on her. 'I was just mad, I guess.'

'At what?'

'I don't really want to talk about it. We made up, but I still feel bad.'

'I understand,' he said. 'My name is Billy, by the way.'

'I'm Bernadette.'

But you already know that, she wanted to add. You know that because you wrote it in *The House of the Seven Gables*.

She didn't say these things because she wasn't quite sure she believed them, and she didn't want him to think she was crazier than he already did.

'Bernadette is a beautiful name,' he said.

Except for her mother and father, no one had ever said this to her. Not once.

'You think so?'

'I do. There is a Saint Bernadette, you know.'

She had never heard this. Trying not to be too obvious about it, Detta stole a glance at her watch. Where had the afternoon gone?

'I should get going,' she said. 'If I'm not home by dinner my dad calls in a SWAT team.'

Billy nodded, picked up his backpack, shouldered it on. 'Come on. I'll walk with you.'

Before she could say anything, he crossed the path, righted her bike and, without a word, headed toward town. She caught up with him in a few seconds. They followed the river all the way to town, came around the bend. They soon arrived at Red Oak.

Detta didn't want to walk up to the inn. She didn't want to be anywhere in the world other than where she was at this moment, in this place.

'I guess I should go.'

'Okay,' Billy said. 'Maybe I'll see you around town.'

'Maybe.'

'I'm doing summer work in the orchards. I'll be around.'

'Okay.'

He reached out, touched the back of her hand. It was just the slightest contact, but it sent a low-level electrical charge through her.

'Abbeville is a pretty cool place,' he said. 'I think you'll like it here.'

Detta took her bike by the handlebars, walked it up to the front entrance of Red Oak, reminding herself that she had been walking for years, that it wasn't that hard to do. Except now, in this place, at this moment, Billy was watching her.

When she reached the door, she decided to spin around slowly, and wave. It would be a cool move. A Lauren Bacall move.

One, two, three. She turned around.

Billy was gone.

47

As Will walked from Red Oak to Godwin Hall there was a spring in his step. He felt as if a weight had been lifted from his shoulders, that in each blade of grass, in every note of birdsong, there was hope for the future.

Life had a pretty fair resemblance to good.

He thought about his work with Ivy Holgrave. She was a good cop. He made a mental note to call her and ask about any progress she might have made in the case.

He stopped at the coffee shop on the square for his daily dose. The owner called him by name, and wished him good luck. He was starting to be known.

As he drank his coffee he picked up a copy of the local weekly, *The Villager*. He saw why people were giving him greetings. On the front page was the short article on Godwin Hall written by Eli's granddaughter. It was odd to see his name in print. He had been written about before, had indeed suffered the barbs of lukewarm book reviews, but to see his name used in connection with something other than his work was strange.

When Cassie had asked him personal details he had been taken off guard, and simply told the truth. Now that he saw the word *widower*, in connection with his own life, he felt as if it were somebody else.

He moved on in the article. The piece ended with an upbeat note, that he and Detta were welcome new additions to Abbeville, and that if Godwin Hall reopened as a bed and breakfast it would be an asset to the village, the county, and the landscape of north-east Ohio as a whole.

At some point during this day Will knew he would receive a visit from the local building inspector. It would be then that Will would learn if all the work he'd done – mostly by Reuben Yoder and his crew – would pay off. It was up to the inspector as to whether or not he received an occupancy permit.

It was with this equal amount of excitement and trepidation that Will walked the final block to Godwin Hall.

When Will rounded the corner to the rear entrance he was surprised to see a number of packages waiting for him. The two largest, by far, were the mattresses he had ordered via Amazon. Next to them was a forty-two-inch LCD television and a few smaller boxes.

The sight of these items, stacked so casually against the red brick façade, made him laugh. He needed no further proof that he was no longer in New York City. The fact that a box containing a flat screen television had not been stolen was all the validation he required.

He got one of the mattresses up the steps and down the hallway to the last bedroom on the left, a sun-splashed room with a window overlooking Platteville Road. It was to be Detta's room.

After a short break he went back downstairs, unboxed the

flat screen, took it into the parlor and set it on top of some milk crates in the corner. He knew that the cable installers had been by a few days earlier when Reuben's crew had been in the house. He hooked up the television, flipped it on, found a news channel. Same as it ever was.

He flipped off the TV, went back into the dining room. He worked the last mattress into his bedroom. He cut off the packing material and flopped it onto the bed.

He was just about to take out the trash when something caught his eye. Something he had not seen before. When he had refinished this bedroom set he'd noticed that the headboard had a number of nicks and grooves in it, something he decided was character, instead of flaws. But now, in this light, he saw that it was something else. It looked like a carving.

He stepped across the room, opened the Venetian blinds fully. He walked back to the headboard and ran his fingers across the nicks and cuts. There were a lot more than he had thought.

He leaned close and saw that, in total, there were seven words. They were definitely not English.

Will walked out to the dining room, grabbed his notepad and pencil. He walked back, sat down on the mattress, and started to transcribe what he saw.

After a few minutes, he had it.

Iucundissima est spei persuadio et vite imprimis.

It was surely Latin, but he had resisted the language mightily in junior high school, and therefore had no idea what it meant.

That, of course, was what the internet was for.

He watched her; her facial expressions, her body language, how she moved through these new spaces. She was tentative at first, but before long she took to Godwin Hall as he had hoped she might.

Will told her about his day with Ivy. Detta listened, asking all the right questions, not the least of which was her concern about the dead girl about her age being found in the nearby woods.

Will assured her that all was safe.

After giving Detta a tour of the house, they stood in the dining room. Will could see the emotion in her eyes. She was probably thinking what he was thinking, that Amanda Hardy would have loved this place.

'It's beautiful, Dad.'

'You really think so?'

'I do. I can't believe how big it is.'

'Try painting it. Which, by the way, you're going to have the chance to discover.' He pointed at the box of brushes, rollers, and drop cloths in the corner. 'Godwin Hall is hiring.'

'Bring it on,' she said. 'I'm an artist. What's a few thousand gallons of latex?'

Will smiled.

Detta glanced at her watch. 'I have to get to the library.'

'Okay,' Will said. 'While you're there, could you look something up for me?'

'Sure.'

They walked across the dining room to Will's bedroom. He showed Detta the engraving on his headboard, the bedroom set he'd bought at auction.

'It came like this?'

'Well, it was painted,' Will said. 'I stripped off the paint and then I saw this underneath.'

He handed her the sheet of paper with the transcription.

'It's Latin, right?' she asked.

'Pretty sure it is. '

'I'm on it,' she said. 'I'll check it out at the library.'

To Will she sounded like the Detta Hardy of old. Inquisitive, bright, helpful, determined.

'Also, I need to ask you something,' Will said.

Detta looked a little nervous. '*Okay.*'

'Have I ever talked about this place?'

'What do you mean? This house?'

'Yes. Godwin Hall. Or even this village.'

'I don't think so. Why?'

'So, you don't remember me ever talking about Abbeville, or Ohio, or Aunt Millie?'

Detta thought for a moment. 'No.'

'I never talked about coming here when I was a kid?'

'Wait. You've *been* here before?'

Will wasn't sure how to respond. If he said he didn't know, it would cause concern. 'No,' he said. 'I'm just trying to remember if we'd planned a trip here when I was a kid. Right around when my mother died.'

Detta thought a few more moments. 'I don't think you ever mentioned anything like that. In fact, the first I ever heard about this place is when you told me right before we moved here.'

'Okay,' Will said. 'Just curious.'

Detta considered him for a few suspicious seconds. She stole another glance at her watch. 'I'm out of here.' She kissed him on the cheek. 'Good luck with the inspector,' she said. 'Try not to sweat.'

Will laughed. 'Thanks, honey.'

As she stepped out the back door, she stopped, poked her head back inside.

'And Dad?'

'Yeah?'

'I love my room.'

While waiting for the inspector, Will paced the first floor. He felt the way he felt when Amanda went into labor a few days early

281

with Detta. Granted, the stakes were a bit higher on that day, but that didn't stop the feeling. The worst that could happen was that the inspector would cite some reasons they couldn't get an occupancy permit, and they would stay at Red Oak a while longer.

A few minutes after noon Will saw someone approaching the front walk. Will tried to fashion a look of honesty and competence, and opened the door.

'Hello,' Will said.

'Good afternoon, sir.'

The first thing Will noticed about the housing inspector was that the man was younger than expected. He was around Will's age. The few inspectors Will had dealt with in the city had been into their fifties and sixties; city-hardened, day-weary men who took in all your connivances and corner cutting in one glance. This man had about him an openness which Will guessed was a small-town thing.

'Please,' Will said. 'Come in.'

The man stepped over the threshold. 'Godwin Hall,' the man said. After a few moments he added, 'You've done a lot of work.'

'I had a lot of help. But yeah. It took some doing.'

'It looks marvelous.'

Instead of poking around the electrical outlets, fuse boxes, plumbing fixtures, and gas lines, the inspector walked through each room taking in the spaces in total.

Will found himself following the man around, which was probably bad form. He excused himself, and tried to make himself busy in the kitchen. Now that they had a new refrigerator and a working stove they would be preparing meals, and Will made out a shopping list. He wanted the first dinner for himself and Detta at Godwin Hall to be special.

He heard the man moving about the attic, the old ceiling joists creaking under his weight.

Before long he heard the sound of footsteps on the stairs. He went out into the parlor to get the bad news.

'I used to come here as a child,' the man said. 'It was a special place to run around and play. So many rooms. I can honestly say that I have the same feeling today. Godwin Hall is in good hands.'

Will didn't know what to say. The possibility of a rather large and expensive 'but' might still be on the way. He said, 'Thanks.'

'On behalf of no one but myself let me extend a warm welcome to Abbeville, Ohio,' he said. 'I know that you and your daughter will be quite happy here, and that Godwin Hall will surely return to its former splendor and prominence.'

Will was taken aback a bit by the warm wishes from this total stranger. But in a good way. It also struck him as a bit odd that the man knew he had a daughter. Perhaps he had read the piece in *The Villager*.

'I'm sorry,' Will said. 'I didn't catch your name.'

The man extended his hand. Will took it.

'I am Jakob van Laar.'

48

Ivy had worked on the photograph of Delia most of the night, and half of the morning. She caught two hours' sleep total, both of them sitting up.

When she stood back from Delia's photo, she found that an image was beginning to take shape in the trees over Delia's left shoulder, a smudge of white near the lowest branch of a maple. It was one of the last areas that Ivy had to restore before she was finished.

At three o'clock she received a call from Dispatch.

When Ivy and Walt Barnstable arrived at the trailer park there was a crowd of a dozen or so people gathered near the entrance. Edson Estates was a small common of a dozen or so single-wide mobile homes, located just outside Abbeville in neighboring Inglewood.

Ivy and Walt both got out of the SUV, held their badges up so the people could see them. The gathering was a mix of older people in their sixties and seventies, with a few smaller children; retirees and kids too young for school.

'Who made the call?' Ivy asked of the crowd in general.

A man standing off to the side lifted a hand. He was hitting a cigarette hard. He seemed to be shivering, even though it was a warm day.

The man was around thirty, with close-cropped brown hair and a long mustache. He wore a clean uniform from Aqualine, identical to the jumpsuit they had seen on Chevy Deacon.

Ivy and Walt approached him.

'Your name, sir?' Ivy asked.

'Bensicker,' he said. 'Tom Bensicker.'

'And you work with Mr Deacon?'

'Yeah.'

'How did you come to be here today?'

'I was supposed to pick Chevy up for work today. We do that sometimes on half-shift days. Carpool like that. Every other time like.'

'When you got here did you see anyone hanging around this house?'

'No.'

'What did you do when you arrived?'

He nodded at his truck. 'I just sat there. Honked the horn a few times. When Chevy didn't come out I went to the door and knocked.'

'Did you hear anything coming from inside the house?'

'Like what?'

'Like a radio, TV? Maybe somebody talking?'

Again the man shook his head. 'No,' he said. 'Nothing like that. It was quiet.'

'What happened next?'

'When he didn't answer the door, I opened it.'

'So the door was closed and latched, but not locked.'

'Right.'

'What did you see when you opened the door?'

Ivy watched the man closely. He began to blanch at this. He raised his hand absently, touched the left side of his head.

'I seen him. I could tell right away something was wrong. He was all bloodied up.'

'This is Mr Deacon we're talking about, correct?'

The man nodded.

Ivy caught Walt's eye. Walt would continue to interview the man, while Ivy entered the mobile home.

Ivy stepped to the SUV, reached into the back seat, took out a fresh pair of latex gloves, put them on. She could see some of the people in the gathering whispering to each other, considering her with some suspicion and distrust.

Ivy braced herself, walked up the two steps to the front door. She stepped into the trailer, a twelve by sixty with a dry-walled front end. The interior walls were painted lime green. To the right was the small kitchen, bathroom and bedroom. To the left was the living room area.

The table in the eating area was a bit grimy, and the tile by the front door was streaked with dried mud, but it wasn't the jumble that she expected, or quite what they'd found at Lonnie Comb's place.

Chevy Deacon sat slumped on a dining room chair in the middle of the living room. At his feet were two empty fifths of whiskey. His arms and hands dangled at his sides. Like Lonnie Combs he was dressed only in white briefs that were now soaked in blood.

Ivy did not need to look too closely for cause of death.

A twelve-inch drill bit was pushed in all the way to the hilt in Chevy Deacon's left temple. The tip of the bit protruded an inch or so from his right temple. The bit was still attached to the small cordless drill, which angled downward from the weight of the tool. The dead man's face was purplish and distended from the trauma. In his lap, and down the front of his bare chest, were gobbets of flesh and bone, along with a thick trail of vomit. His left eye was all but destroyed.

What do you see, Ivy Lee?

Ivy had seen a number of suicides in her time on the job. There were differences between men and women as regards suicide. Women made more attempts than men; men completed the act with higher frequency. Men tended toward carbon monoxide poising, firearms and hanging. Women reached for pills.

Ivy was all but certain that when they completed the search of Chevy Deacon's home they would find a handgun, probably more than one.

So why not use a gun?

Ivy looked down at the coffee table. The newspaper there had the name Josie written on it at least a hundred times in black magic marker.

As EMS paramedics prepared to remove the body from the trailer, Ivy and Walt interviewed some of the people gathered around the entrance to the trailer park. Ivy had not been mistaken. There was indeed an air of hostility in their attitudes. Apparently, the fact that Chevy Deacon had recently been braced by law enforcement didn't sit well with them. Ivy wondered how the man's proclivity for beating up the women in his life sat with them, but didn't ask.

In short order they had what they expected. Nobody saw anything. According to the folks at Edson Estates, this was a tragic suicide.

But Ivy knew better.

As she was just about to step back into the trailer she was hit hard with a fist on the left side of her face. Ivy saw stars for a moment, stumbled a few feet, but kept her balance. She turned.

It was Terry Deacon.

'You fuckin' *bitch!*' Terry screamed.

The woman's eyes were red, her fists tightly clenched. She charged Ivy again, but this time Ivy was ready for her. She stepped to the side and Terry Deacon's forward momentum caused her to fall to the ground. She scrambled to her feet, got ready to charge again.

'Hold it right there, Terry. Just stop.'

The woman hyperventilated. Before she could lunge forward Walt stepped behind her and got her in a tight bear hug. The woman kicked and screamed at the top of her lungs. She tried to slam the back of her head into Walt's face but he was able to lean out her range.

'You fucking killed him!'

Walt held on tight until the woman began to run out of steam. Her face was still inflamed with rage.

'Listen to me, Terry,' Ivy said. 'Just listen to me for a minute.'

The woman spit as far as she could. It did not reach Ivy.

'Walt is going to let you go, but you're going to have to calm down. We'll get to the bottom of this. I promise you.'

Terry Deacon showed no sign of calming down.

'Terry? Do you hear what I'm saying?'

Walt looked over Ivy's shoulder, back into her eyes. Ivy could hear people coming up behind her. She reached down and unsnapped her holster, put her hand on the grip of her weapon, but didn't turn around. She saw in Walt's expression that the people had halted their approach.

'I know you're in hell right now, Terry,' Ivy said. 'I can only imagine what you're feeling. But going to jail is not going to make things better. You've got your family to think of. They need you right now.'

Ivy watched the woman's eyes dart from side to side, considering her next move. Then, in an instant, it was over. Ivy saw the woman's shoulders drop, saw the fury leave her body. She slumped in Walt's grasp. When he did not immediately let her go she said, quietly:

'Get . . . your fucking hands . . . *off* me.'

Walt slowly released the woman, but did not step back.

Ivy stood in front of Theresa Deacon, watched the woman sob, watched as she began to ebb from anger into grief. There was nothing Ivy could do but stand there, ready to catch Theresa Deacon if she fell.

Ivy had tried to reason with herself on the way to this new horror, had advocated on the side of bad luck and odd coincidence and the grim happenstance of fate.

But, in her heart, she knew there was no longer room for debate.

A darkness had descended on her town.

49

'You must come and visit Veldhoeve,' Jakob said.

They sat in the parlor on the only two available chairs. Will suddenly felt self-conscious about the furnishings, or lack thereof, in the presence of this man.

The man was not, of course, the building inspector. He was the owner of Zeven Farms.

'I'd like that.'

'At the risk of sounding falsely modest, the history of Veldhoeve *is* the history of Abbeville. Godwin Hall, as well. These two houses have faced each other for two hundred years. I could not be more pleased to see the Hall returning to its glory.'

As they chatted Will learned that Jakob van Laar's house, Veldhoeve, was even older than Godwin Hall. He learned that it had at one time been an orphanage of sorts. He learned the first apple trees had been planted in the 1800s.

Will also learned that Jakob's ancestors and his own had been neighbors and friends, and that Will's Dutch forebears, his mother's lineage, named the boarding house after a fermented brew made by Jakob's ancestors. They called the drink 'God's *wijn*' and thus: Godwin.

'Although I was very small, I remember the Hall and its grandeur,' Jakob said. 'My father would tell stories of the famous people who stayed here. Some of them infamous.'

Will was intrigued. Jakob went on to give him a brief history of the village, its days as a logging station.

'Tell me how you came to the decision to take up this family tradition,' Jakob said. 'That is, if I'm not being too busy.'

'Not at all.' Will gave Jakob a brief précis of his life, of the events leading to the day Patrick Richmond had called him with the strange news. Jakob seemed to take it all with interest and compassion.

'And you never met Camilla?'

'No,' Will said. 'My mother never really talked much about her family.'

'I remember Camilla well,' Jakob said. 'Even when the Hall had fallen on hard times, she was kind and courteous. I always felt welcome here.'

'I hope you feel the same way now.'

Jakob smiled. 'How has your daughter taken to the move?'

'She's adjusting,' Will said. 'Needless to say, Abbeville is quite a culture shock from New York.'

'I would imagine so. I think she will find the schools here quite rigorous. They are among the top tier in the state.'

'That's what I understand.'

'What does she hope to do?'

'Not really sure,' Will said. 'She is an amazing artist. Mostly charcoal, some watercolors. I can't draw a circle with a compass, but she is really talented.'

'My family has been collecting art for many years. Bernadette would be more than welcome to view the pieces at Veldhoeve. Perhaps she would be inspired.'

'That's very kind of you,' Will said. 'I'm sure she'd be thrilled. When we lived in New York she would be at the museums all the time. The other kids would be at the mall, and she would be at the Whitney or the Guggenheim.'

Jakob glanced at his watch. 'I fear I've kept you from your day.'

He stood up, reached into his pocket and removed a silver card case. He extracted a single card, placed it on the mantel. He then took out a beautiful fountain pen, flipped the card over and wrote on the back. He gently waved the card, drying the ink. He handed the card to Will.

'If you need any assistance with any of the bureaucracies associated with the purveyors and inspectors with whom you will be dealing, please do not hesitate to contact me. I am on just about every board that matters in Holland County.'

'Thanks,' Will said. 'I might take you up on that.'

'Zeven Farms receives many visitors from all over the world. I would be more than happy to include Godwin Hall in all our promotional and business correspondence.'

Will looked at the ivory vellum card. On one side it read, simply, *J van Laar*. No business name, no email or website. On the other side was written a phone number.

'At the risk of imposing on our new acquaintance, would it be all right if I continued to look around for a few more moments?' Jakob asked. 'It has been quite a while since I've been inside and, as I said, I have many fond memories.'

'Take all the time you like.'

'Perhaps I can repay your kindness with a gift basket from Zeven Farms.'

'That would be great.' Will pointed over his shoulder. 'I'll be out back. Just finishing up painting the garage. Give a shout if you need anything.'

'Spoken like a true innkeeper,' Jakob said. 'And not to worry. I will let myself out.'

50

As she prepared to leave Edson Estates Ivy received a call from Sister Della Marie at Calvary House. The nun said that she did not know Josefina's last name. Mostly this was because Josie was a volunteer at the shelter, and there were no W-2 forms to fill out.

She did tell Ivy that Josie had mentioned her home life in a small village in the eastern end of Holland County called Ashdale.

Ivy spent the next hour on the phone with the school administrators from the three schools that Josie might have attended. Before long she received a .jpeg of a student that fit Josie's description.

It was confirmed.

The dead girl's name was Josefina Mollo.

A follow-up call to the girl's school told Ivy that Josie had lived with her grandfather in a remote house near the Iron River.

Her pulse racing, Ivy got back in her SUV.

On the way to make notification she decided to stop by Godwin Hall.

51

As Jakob ascended the stairs to the second floor at Godwin Hall he felt many sensations flower within him. For years – indeed, all his life – he had anticipated and planned for these days.

He approached the doorway with heady anticipation. It was as close as he had ever been to her, having only watched her from afar these many years.

He glanced out the bedroom window to see that Will Hardy had taken up his brush and was painting the side of the garage.

Jakob stood at the foot of the bed. He closed his eyes and let his mind drift to thoughts of his mother, a woman he had never met. As all the women in his family, she was a Dutch farm girl of modest means and religious upbringing. To Jakob's knowledge she had never breached the boundaries of her hometown. Sébastien van Laar, Jakob's father, had returned to Holland when he was of an age, combing the countryside for a girl of good health and sweet nature. Sébastien met a girl in Naarden, a pretty girl named Jeltje, the daughter of a trawler captain.

A year later, Sébastien departed the country with his newborn boy, leaving the family a tidy sum. No woman had ever taken matrimonial residence in Veldhoeve.

Sébastien died at fifty in a ceremony in the special copse at the center of the seven sacred groves,. In his hand was a small silver *flacon* full of apple nectar, infused with belladonna.

Whenever Jakob had asked his father about his mother, about her manner and coloring and deportment, his father had responded the same way each time.

Look to your own eyes for her, Jakob.

Jakob opened the closet door. He touched each piece of the girl's clothing once, felt the shame and recrimination of his thoughts. He quickly shunned them away.

Before leaving, Jakob lingered at the bedroom door, bringing his fingertips to his nose, breathing the girl's essence. It mingled, for just a moment, with all the other perfumes of the season: earth, root, leaf, vine, fruit.

'Eva,' he said softly.

He thought of the harvest.

It would not be long.

52

When Emmett Mollo opened the door to find Ivy and Will on his porch, Ivy could see the anticipation begin to build in the man's eyes. Just the fact that a police officer had made an unannounced visit to his home meant that something might have changed, that something was not as it had been that morning when he'd awakened to another day without his granddaughter Josefina. Maybe it was all a terrible mistake, his look said, that everything he believed to be true, the brutal weight of his granddaughter's disappearance, was somehow being taken back.

Mollo was in his late seventies, and wore a tattered gray suit and black tie with a tarnished silver tie clip. In the middle of the day, in the middle of the woods, he was wearing a suit, Ivy thought.

Without a word he turned and slowly made his way to the kitchen. He walked with a cane. Ivy and Will followed.

In the kitchen Ivy noted that there were printed labels on

everything; the light switches, the stove, the refrigerator, the thermostat. On the counter top were laid out one spoon, one knife, one fork. On the table was a plate and a cup. By the sink a small glen of amber vials stood, each on top of a sheet of paper with printout instructions for dispensing the medications.

Emmett Mollo did not sit down, did not offer a chair to his guests. Instead, he smoothed the front of his suit coat, leaned his cane against the stove, and stood as straight as he could.

'Sir, we're here about your granddaughter,' Ivy said.

The man said nothing.

'Before we begin, do you have any photographs of Josefina?'

The man reached into the chest pocket of his suit jacket. He took out a stack of worn photographs. The first was Josie as a toddler, the second was a school photograph from perhaps second or third grade, the next was Josie as a pre-teen.

The dead girl in that field was Josefina Mollo.

Ivy handed the pictures back. Emmett held them in a trembling hand, but did not put them back in his pocket.

'Is she gone?' he asked.

Ivy opened her mouth but no words came forth. Will sensed this, and stepped up.

'I'm afraid so, sir,' Will said. 'We're so sorry for your loss.'

Mollo took a long moment, then reached into another pocket, removed a single photograph. This one, a Polaroid, was of an older teenage girl, a smiling blonde in what looked like a prom dress. The fashion looked 1990s' vintage.

Will pointed at the photo. 'May I ask who that is, sir?'

'My daughter,' Mollo said softly. 'They're together now.'

Ivy understood. Josie's mother had been in hospice care. It now appeared that she had died. Ivy could not imagine what this man was going through at this moment.

'When was the last time you saw Josie?' Will asked.

Mollo turned to a wall calendar in the kitchen. It was a full year calendar, and Ivy saw that the last forty-eight days had a small red circle around the date. She made note of the first date.

When Mollo looked back, Ivy saw that he was losing his will. She stepped over to him, eased him to a chair. He did not resist. Will pulled out a chair and sat next to him.

'Sir, we're trying to figure out what happened to Josie, and we could use your help. I just have a few more questions, would that be all right?'

Emmett Mollo looked up, nodded.

'Did Josie ever talk about anyone she was having problems with?'

'No, sir.'

'It's our understanding that before Josie came to live with you, she was living with her aunt and uncle. Can you tell us what their relationship to you is?'

'My stepson Jack and his wife.'

'Where do they live?'

Emmett Mollo raised a hand. He pointed in a southerly direction.

'They live nearby?'

He shook his head. 'Florida.'

'Okay,' Will said. 'I'd like to mention a few names to you, see if you recognize them. Would that be okay?'

Silence.

'Alonzo Combs?' Will asked.

'No, sir.'

'Alonzo went by Lonnie. Does Lonnie Combs ring a bell?'

Nothing.

'What about a man named Deacon? Chevy Deacon?'

'Don't know any of them.'

Will took a moment. 'Mr Mollo, Chief Holgrave will need your stepson's name and where he lives in Florida.'

Emmett Mollo gave Ivy the information.

'Would it be okay if I took a look at Josie's room?' Ivy asked.

Mollo pointed again. 'Down there.'

'Thanks.'

Ivy went down the short hallway. The door on the left had bright yellow and orange stickers on it. She stepped inside.

The room was tidy. There was a single maple-frame bed pushed against a wall. On top of the afghan bedspread were a small army of older plush animals. The posters on the wall were from Disney animated movies, none of them recent vintage – *WALL-E*, *Ponyo*, *The Little Mermaid*. Ivy did a quick look through the dresser and found very little. Just a few sweaters and T-shirts, some underwear. Two of the drawers were completely empty. The closet yielded less. There were no skirts or dresses. The top shelf held a large cardboard box. Ivy pulled it down, opened it. Inside was a child's plastic tea service.

Ivy looked under the bed and saw two pairs of slippers. They were much smaller than a girl Josie's age and size would wear. They were silted with dust.

There were no diaries or journals or letters or photographs, no personal mementoes of any kind.

At the door Ivy turned back to the room, to the cold light on the faded pink bedspread. Looking back at her was a little girl's room in an old man's house.

When Ivy returned to the kitchen, Mollo had a glass of water in his hands. Will sat across from him.

'When Josie left that day and didn't come back, what did you do?' Will asked.

'I called Jack,' he said. 'He said he knew what to do.'

'Did he tell you that he called the police?'

Emmett Mollo just shrugged.

'Are you saying that no one from the police or Sheriff's office has come by to see you about this?' Ivy asked.

'No, ma'am.'

Ivy's blood began to seethe.

'Is there anyone we can call for you right now?' Will asked. 'Any family or friends?'

Ivy saw the man reach again for his pocket, the one containing the photos of Josie. She understood. His daughter and granddaughter were his whole family.

'Do you need help with her arrangements?' Ivy asked.

It was clear that Emmett Mollo didn't know what Ivy meant.

'With the funeral,' Ivy said. 'Josie's funeral. We can have someone come out and talk to you about it.'

With some effort Emmett Mollo stood, walked out of the kitchen into the small parlor. Will and Ivy followed him. There, on the couch, was a small duffel-style bag. It was blue nylon, and looked new. Mollo slowly unzipped it, reached inside. Of all the things Ivy anticipated the man removing from the bag – perhaps some clothing, an outfit in which Josefina might be interred – what he took out made the breath catch in her chest.

He handed Ivy a thick, banded stack of twenty-dollar bills.

'I don't understand,' Ivy said. 'Where did you get this?'

'It was here,' Mollo said. 'On the front porch.'

'All this money was on your porch?'

He nodded.

'Do you know who put it there?'

'I figured it was the church,' he said. 'They sent it to help.'

Ivy glanced inside the bag. There had to be ten thousand dollars.

'Mr Mollo, we can drive you over to your bank if you like,' Ivy said. 'The money will be safer there.'

He shook his head. 'I don't need it. Take it for Josie. Make it nice for her.'

'We can't do that, sir, but we can have someone come by to discuss your options. You won't have to go through this alone.'

Emmett Mollo said nothing.

53

They sat in a diner on Route 87. Ivy wasn't hungry but she ordered food anyway.

They had visited the Lutheran church on Route 18, having gotten the information from the calendar in Emmett Mollo's kitchen. The pastor confirmed what they already believed, that the money did not come from the congregation.

'The reason you never got an Amber alert on Josie Mollo was that it was never called in,' Will said.

'The uncle,' Ivy said. 'The one she was having problems with. He figured that if he couldn't have her the world could. He never made the call.'

Ivy had already put in a call to the Holland County Sheriff's office with a request to reach out to the Broward County Sheriff's office. They would visit and interview Josie's uncle. Ivy did not hold out much hope for this. She knew in her heart that the person they were looking for was right here in Holland County.

Still, she took deep comfort that the son of a bitch uncle would get rousted and grilled. He had it coming. And more.

Before they left Emmett Mollo's house Ivy had taken a number of photographs. Among them were pictures of the bag, the money, and a few close-ups of the bills.

In addition, Ivy had asked the man if she could take one of the twenties and replace it with one of her own. He did not object. The twenty now sat on the table between them.

'It's a new bill,' Will said. 'Uncirculated.'

'Just like the ones found on Chevy Deacon.'

Will sipped his coffee. 'I never met the man, but from what you've told me about him, I can't plug him into doing anything like bringing ten thousand dollars to this old man.'

'Me neither,' Ivy said. 'But I'm thinking that wherever Chevy got the money from is the same place Emmett got the money.'

As the waitress topped their coffees, they took to their own thoughts. Ivy had gained a lot of respect for Will Hardy in just a short period of time.

'So what was your path?' he asked.

'You mean why did I become a cop?'

Will smiled. 'You know all about me. It's only right.'

'Fair enough. Do you want the director's cut or the *Reader's Digest* version?'

'I've got time, and they've got lots of coffee here.'

Before she could stop herself, she just started talking.

'Well, to be honest, I really had no intention of being a cop. My idea of going wild, of burning down the world, was going to Cuyahoga Community College, about forty miles from here.

'Near the end of my second year – as a theater major, believe it or not – I came home right before spring break. Turns out my mother was involved in this case, this domestic gone really bad. The daddy had holed up in a shack down in Parkside, holding

302

his wife and two babies hostage. The way I heard it my mother dropped her gun belt, earned her way into the house, and talked the man down without anybody getting hurt. The county gave her a citation for that. I remember sitting in the back of the hall that day, watching this tough little lady who raised me on her own step onto that stage in her pressed uniform. And I knew.'

'Knew what?'

'I knew that there would be no other life for me. When I got back to school I changed my major to criminal justice. By the time I was twenty I was in a CPD uniform.'

The waitress brought their food. It was a good thing, too, Ivy had felt the emotions welling up inside. She didn't need to go all PMS and weepy on this man. By the time she finished half her burger she seemed to have it all under control again.

'CPD threw me right into the Fourth District because I was a female and I was a rookie. Right out of the gate I'm undercover. I got sent to the taverns and the gambling hotspots gathering intel. People talked to me, you see, and I was good at getting inside. Drugs, prostitution, illegal liquor, gambling, stolen cars. I did that for a year and couldn't get enough of it.'

'Is this where your theater training came in?'

'Exactly. I got to dress up. Makeup, hair, wardrobe. I learned to draw from an ankle holster too, although, thank God, I never had to.

'But it was my second year on the job that I discovered the feel of patrol. I asked for nights. Took all the shit details that none of the other boots wanted. The truth was, I loved working nights. Still do.'

'Why is that?'

Ivy didn't have to think too long about it. 'Lots of reasons. But mostly it's because night patrol cuts out the wholesaler, you know? You don't have to go through people, good people, to get to the bad ones. It's all buyer and seller at night. I had a great

FTO, too. I learned a lot from him in that first year. After that, I got partnered up.'

'Are you still in touch with your old partner?'

And there it was. Ivy's first instinct was to shut down. But it had been too long.

'No,' she said.

Will waited. It was clear that he knew there was more.

'Did you know any cop couples in NYPD?' Ivy asked.

'A few,' he said. 'Can't say that any of them made it too long, though.'

It was true. Two-badge households, happy ones, were rare. The stress that brings you together initially is the stress that drives you apart.

'Neither of us meant for it to happen. It just did. He was a few years older than I was and I was on my own in a big city.

'Jimmy and I were on last out on a warm spring night. We picked up a call of shots fired at an apartment complex in Fairfax. When we rolled up it was a war zone. Five sector cars on scene. The shooter was barricaded in an apartment on the second floor and he was blasting away with a long gun.

'When we approached in the cruiser we both saw the muzzle flash, not thirty feet away. We had driven right into the middle of it. When Jimmy saw what he'd done he slammed on the brakes, turned hard to the right, came to a halt directly in the line of fire. We were blocked in. In that moment I knew what he did. He saw the flash and angled the car so he would be between me and the shooter.'

Will said nothing. Ivy steeled herself. She hadn't talked about this in twenty years.

'The suspect got off one more shot before Tactical took him out. Terrance Duncan was the kid's name. Sixteen years old. The shot he fired hit Jimmy in the left side of his face. He was dead before he closed his eyes.'

What Ivy couldn't say was that the round had passed through her partner and caught her just under her vest. The baby growing inside her died the moment her father did.

'When I got out of the hospital, I went to visit the kid's grandmother. Arcella Richards. She looked at me at the door and knew who I was, that I had been there in the last seconds of her grandson's life, that Terrance had taken the life of my partner.'

The waitress approached with the carafe of coffee. Will shook his head. Ivy continued.

'I went to see her after that day.'

'The grandmother?' Will asked. 'Mrs Richards?'

Ivy nodded. 'I went to see her on the anniversary of the shooting. Every year, on the same day. We'd sit over coffee and Pepperidge Farm cookies. We never talked about what happened.'

'For how long did you keep going back?'

'Ten years,' Ivy said. 'Then, one year, I just stopped. I'm not sure why.'

'I'm so sorry, Ivy.'

'Yeah, well. It was a long time ago,' Ivy said. 'I was just a kid.'

Will looked at her. In that moment Ivy could see both the understanding and the pain of loss in his eyes. She also saw the compassion.

'It's never a long time ago,' he said.

54

The next morning Ivy got into the station two hours before her shift.

She had a town council meeting upcoming, and to be prepared for her budget fight she needed to collate all the facts and figures for the first two quarters of the year.

The story of Chevy Deacon's death had run on the local news channels out of Columbus, Akron, and Cleveland. Ivy wondered where the story originated, which one of the hostile crowd had called the media. Thankfully there was no mention of the method Chevy Deacon had used, or any reference to Josefina Mollo.

The BCI team had processed the scene, and the preliminary findings were that Chevy Deacon had put a cordless electric drill to his temple and, with great force, had drilled into his skull. The bit was brand new, available at any hardware store. Because of its razor sharpness, and the force by which it was used, combined with the fact that the drill had been locked into the on position, the tip penetrated all the way through before Chevy Deacon succumbed.

Ivy tried not to think about the fact that the drill had continued to run until it ran out of battery power.

Another preliminary finding was that the handwriting on the newspaper, the name *Josie*, appeared to be in Chevy Deacon's hand, based on examples found in the house.

When Ivy got all the budget numbers entered into her spreadsheet program her desk phone rang.

'Abbeville PD.'

'Ivy, it's Carl Tomlinson.'

'Hey, Carl. Twice in one month. People will talk.'

'Let them,' he said. 'I heard about that bad business with the Deacons.'

'Crazy days, Chief.'

'Anything I can do to help?'

Once a cop, Ivy thought. 'I'll let you know, Carl.'

'Okay. How's Francesca Lindor doing?'

'She's officially Frankie now. I think it's a teenage thing.'

'I like it. She looks like a Frankie.'

'So,' Ivy said. 'What can I do you out of?'

'Well, I've been thinking about what we talked about. About those pictures you showed me.'

'What about them?'

'I knew I'd run across something like this before. But it's a lot of years ago. More than you've been alive.'

Ivy drew a notepad across the desk.

'What do you have?' she asked.

'This happened when I was just a couple years on the job. Even before Abbeville even had a police department. I was working in Middleton. I was a patrol officer then.'

'When are we talking about here, Carl?'

'Don't call me on this, but I have been trying to work that out. I'm thinking it was 1969.'

Ivy made the note. Carl continued.

307

'A call came in one night. It was right around the beginning of summer, just before the Fourth of July. Some kids had gone down to the quarry with fireworks. Raised a big noise as I recall. There's some houses around there and the neighbors complained.'

'Which quarry was this?'

'The one off Route 87. Near the Quilliams farm. Or what used to be the Quilliams place.'

Ivy knew the location.

'A body was found in one of those caves down there,' Carl said.

Ivy felt the hairs on her arm raise. 'A body?'

'Yeah,' Carl said. 'A young girl. A teenager. Do you know the caves I mean?'

Ivy did. She and her friends used to go down there to smoke their pot and drink their Colt 45. 'I know the place.'

'It seems to me that there was something really similar on the ground right near the body. Something to do with crow's wings.'

'And you say it was like the evidence I showed you?'

'It was a while back, but I can see it in my mind's eye so clearly now. Back then I didn't make anything of it. You weren't around, but it was a crazy time, the 1960s, what with acid trips and Woodstock and crazy clothes. The idea of a teenager dressing up with feathers on her head didn't ring any alarms. Seems like all the kids had on Halloween costumes all the time back then. Even in Middleton.'

'Do you remember what happened with the case? Was the case ever closed?'

'I don't know about that.'

'Do you know if there was a ruling on cause or manner of death?'

'Well, we weren't set up to do any kind of investigating or detective work back then. And I was just a boot, of course. I secured the scene, called it in, waited for the fire department

308

to come out and bring the body in. That was pretty much my involvement.'

'And you're saying this was in the summer of '69?'

'I'm going to say for sure it was,' he said. 'But the interesting thing is, when the case got turned over to the county, they continued the investigation.'

This was not unusual, Ivy thought. Back then, when many of the smaller towns and villages were unincorporated, law enforcement was conducted at the county level. If you called the police, or emergency services, you got a county employee. It was still the same way now for many small towns.

'What's interesting about that?' Ivy asked. 'Sounds like SOP for the time.'

'Well, what I mean is, I got relieved that night by two deputies.'

'Holland County deputies?'

'That's right,' Carl said. 'And here's the interesting part.'

'What's that?'

'One of them was your mother.'

55

Before hanging up with Carl Tomlinson Ivy had gotten the rest of the man's thoughts and recollections from that night in 1969. Carl did not know or remember the victim's name, or anything else about the dispensation of the case, whether it was ruled a natural or accidental death, or a death under suspicious circumstances.

When she hung with Carl, Ivy called the Sheriff of Holland County.

'Oh, God,' her mother said. 'Joe McGrath. I haven't thought of him in years. Do you remember him?'

Ivy sort of remembered a man named Joe. If she said she remembered him well, she might not get the story. 'No,' she said. 'Not really.'

Her mother fluffed her hair. It was her way when she was talking about the old days. 'He picked me up at the house for a few months when we didn't have a car.'

'We had a car?'

Her mother smiled. 'Not so you'd notice.'

Ivy recalled they'd had two Buicks for a while; one on blocks, the other on bald tires. One winter they used the comatose car to jump the dead one.

'Was he a really young-looking guy?' Ivy asked.

'That's him. We were understaffed in those days. You went on patrol and had to do the work of detectives. A lot of it was break-ins and such, so we're not talking Holmes and Watson. But still. We didn't get any overtime, but I couldn't get my fill of it.'

Ivy told her mother about the old case, the body near the quarry.

'I do remember a girl being found down there,' her mother said. 'Joe is the one you should talk to about it.'

'Joe McGrath's gone, Mama. It was the cancer. I'm sorry.'

Ivy June looked out the window. 'Joe,' she said softly.

Ivy consulted her notepad. 'His wife's still living out on Baintree Road.'

'I can't remember her name.'

'Michelle. They call her—'

'Mickey. Mickey McGrath,' Ivy June said. 'She had red hair. Probably not anymore, though.'

Ivy took her mother's hand. 'No, Mama. Probably not.'

'Why are you bringing up all this?'

Ivy told her, keeping it all in a broad sense. Many times over the years Ivy had wanted to share with her mother the details and theories she had about her village. She ultimately did not, knowing how painful it would be to consider that Delia's disappearance might have been part of it all.

'Well, in those early days, I didn't have much to do,' her mother said. 'I was just a young one, mind you. Joe took over the scene. My job was trying to keep people from trampling things.'

311

Ivy had made printouts of the crown of wings found at the Gardner farm. She showed them to her mother.

'Do you remember anything like this?' she asked.

Her mother studied the pictures for a while. 'No, baby girl. But it was dark when I was out there. By morning they had removed the body, and collected what they wanted. My next shift I was back on patrol.'

'I checked on the records at the Sheriff's. There's nothing from around that time.'

'Wouldn't imagine there would be. Every time there's a new sheriff things go missing.'

'Do you think Joe kept anything?'

Ivy June considered this. 'Could be. He was a stickler for detail. Neatest car you've ever seen.'

'I'm thinking I might take a ride over to his widow's place. Maybe there's something there.'

'Maybe you should.'

'Can you make the call? I could do it myself, but it might be better if it came from you.'

'No,' her mother said. 'I don't think so.'

'Why not, Mama?'

Her mother stood up. 'Because I'm going with you.'

Mickey McGrath was a slight, animated woman a few years older than Ivy June. It turned out she did still have red hair. A little bright for her age, Ivy thought, but it suited her fair complexion.

The two women kept hugging and crying, hugging and crying. Ivy gave them time and space.

When the conversation settled on the present, Ivy asked Mickey:

'Did Joe keep anything from his time in the department?'

'I don't know what you mean.'

'Mementos or souvenirs,' Ivy said. 'Maybe some photographs or case files.'

'He kept his uniforms,' she said. 'His summer one and his winter one. Still have them in the closet. I get them cleaned every so often, even though.'

'Anything else?'

'He kept a storage shed. God only knows what's in there. A whole lifetime of things, I imagine. I haven't been out there in years.'

'The shed is here?'

She pointed out the back window. There were two outbuildings near the property line. One was a corrugated plastic instant shed you can buy from Home Depot or Lowes; the other a wood shed, quite the bit worse for the seasons.

While Ivy June and Mickey caught up, Ivy set up shop in the shed. From the door she could see that there were a number of banker-style boxes stacked at the rear of the lean-to, but in order to get to them she would have to move a lot of junk.

It took most of a half-hour to move the rusted rotary push mower, the banded stacks of mildewed *National Geographic* magazines, the boxes of rags and nearly empty paint cans, the dozen plastic bags full of Christmas lights, Halloween decorations and plastic Easter eggs.

There were dartboards and lampshades, a pair of clothes hampers, a broken dot-matrix printer with a dead mouse in it.

The banker's boxes at the back contained mostly cash register receipts as well as news clippings about law enforcement and crime in general in the tri-county area.

At the bottom of the stack were two boxes wrapped in yellowed masking tape, each with a scrawled signature along the part that sealed over the lid.

Ivy brought the boxes into the light, took out her penknife, cut the tape on both boxes.

313

The containers were filled to the top with Xerox copies of police files, folders, case summaries, witness statements, court records. Ivy rifled through one stack. There was folder after folder of photocopied crime scene photographs, autopsy protocols, as well as toxicology reports.

If Joe McGrath had kept anything about the old case, it would surely be in these two boxes.

56

In her first full day at the library Detta mostly shelved and re-shelved books. She got a break at three, and took the time to get a sandwich from a food truck on the square. Summer was in full burn, and people were walking their dogs and riding their bikes. Almost every person she passed said hello. It was kind of nice. She was even starting to recognize people.

She stopped at Uncle Joe's and picked up a pair of apple turn-overs for the evening's dessert. She resisted the ganache tartlets.

As she rounded the corner onto the block where Godwin Hall was located she had the oddest feeling she was being followed.

She stopped, looked back over her shoulder.

There, about a block behind her, was Purple Mohawk, suddenly getting really interested in the window at the insurance agent's.

Was she following her?

Detta ate her sandwich on the square, tossed a few bits of bread to the birds. She used to like doing this on Washington Square, and noticed that even the birds were a little bit more laid-back in the country.

No further Mohawk sightings. This was good.

Detta gathered her trash, walked it over to the can by the stone wishing well. When she turned around he was there.

One minute there was an almost empty village square, and in the next minute Billy was right in front of her.

'Hi,' he said.

Everything she'd planned to say to him the next time they met dissipated into thin air.

'Hi.'

'So,' he said. 'Abbeville.'

'What about it?'

'How do you like it so far?'

She shrugged. 'It's okay. Met some nice people. I can't say the same for everybody here, though.'

'What do you mean?'

Detta told him about her run-in with the creepy kids, the leader of the group in particular.

'She has a purple Mohawk,' Detta said. 'Do you know her?'

'Unfortunately, I do,' he said. 'Not well, of course. Not my type. But she is kind of hard to miss.'

'What is her problem?'

'I'd say it's jealousy.'

'Jealousy? Seriously? Why would she be jealous of me?'

'The fact that this is not obvious to you proves my point.'

Detta was confused. Maybe it was just his way of saying that she was pretty.

'What happened between you two?' he asked.

As they walked across the square, toward the library, Detta told him more about the day she met Purple Mohawk and the zombie twins, about their exchange.

'She told me I needed to watch my ass.'

'I see,' he said. 'Is she bothering you?'

'A little, I guess. It was kind of creepy to think she might have been following me. Maybe I got under her skin.'

They walked in silence for a while.

'How do you like working at the library?'

'I like it,' she said. 'I like it a lot, in fact. And do you know what I like the most?'

'Besides the old lady shoes and Ace bandages?'

'Can you be serious for one minute?'

Billy smiled. 'Sorry.'

'I like the fact that it's an old library. I like that people walked into this building more than a hundred years ago to get their books. I like that some of the same books are still on the shelves. I think that's so cool.'

Billy reached out, took each of her hands in his own. She noticed for the first time that he had a tattoo on his right forearm.

'There's a reason you are drawn to the past,' he said.

'There is?'

'Yes. I knew what it was the moment I saw you for the first time.' He looked at her, his eyes bluer than she'd ever seen. 'It's because you're an old soul.'

Before she could respond, it started to rain. Just like that. No warning, just a quick darkening of the sky and rain. More like a downpour.

Billy took off his jacket, put it over their heads as they ran up the steps to the library. He opened the door for her. As Detta stepped inside he drew her close, and kissed her. It was a brief kiss, and it happened so quickly, just like the downpour, that she had not a second to think about it.

He turned to leave, took three or four steps into the rain, then spun around and said:

'I know who you were, Bernadette Hardy.'

She could barely hear him over the thunder. She wasn't quite sure what he'd said.

'Wait,' Detta said. 'What do you mean?'

Billy smiled, but it was sad somehow.

All afternoon she walked in the light of those five words.

I know who you were.

When her shift was over for the day, she sat down at one of the computer terminals, signed on. She took out the piece of paper bearing the odd inscription her father had given her, the one carved into the headboard on the bed he got at the auction.

Iucundissima est spei persuadio et vite imprimis.

It took a few attempts to get the spelling right, but she finally did. When she hit Enter, she was directed to a website called Explore. It was a page dedicated to a Dutch artist named Pieter Bruegel. Detta had heard the name, had run across it in some art books, but did not really know anything about him.

She scrolled down the page, and found a translation of the Latin phrase. Translated, it said:

Sweet is the trust that springs from hope, without which we could not endure life's many and almost unbearable adversities.

She read it twice, then a third time. She liked it. She thought it was a pretty cool thing to have carved into your headboard. She wondered who had done the carving, and how long ago they had done it.

She was just about to write down the translation when she remembered that she was a trusted employee of this establishment.

She hit Print.

Before she left for the day she checked out a huge coffee table book on the complete works of Pieter Bruegel.

57

As Detta approached Godwin Hall, she noticed that the sign out front seemed to be newer, or at least a cleaned-up version of the original. When had her father done this? The letters, embossed in gold, seemed brighter. She was able to read it from almost a block away.

She walked around to the back, took out her keys, stepped inside. She saw a note taped to the refrigerator door.

I have a meeting with KSU. There are sandwiches in the fridge. I'll be back by six. Wish me luck. Love you. Dad.

She walked into the front room, flipped on the TV. Midday stupid shows: people groveling in front of rent-a-judges, political shouting matches, infomercials for rolling toenail clippers.

She turned it off, went upstairs and changed her clothes. Her father had put fresh flowers on the milk crate that was serving as a temporary night stand.

Her chore for the afternoon was cleaning the back door. Or, more accurately, *scraping* the back door.

Specifically, the job was removing the decals from the door, which she imagined was the front entrance when this place had been open for business. There was an old MasterCharge decal (*The Interbank Card*, it read below), as well as one for BankAmericard, whatever that was. There was one for Diners Club and one for Carte Blanche.

Before long she'd gotten most of the decals off the door and the floor swept. She rummaged around the cabinet under the kitchen sink, found the Windex and the paper towels.

She stayed with it until it was crystal clear.

Chore completed, she decided to explore the basement.

The main room in the basement was somewhat tidy, with the boxes stacked along the walls. Along one wall were three old steamer trunks, the kind people used to travel with in the 1930s and 1940s.

She walked over to the trunks, flipped the latches on the top one. She gingerly lifted up the lid, slowly, in case there was some kind of creature inside, some vampire laying dormant for a hundred years, just waiting for some stupid girl from New York to open it and become his blood slave for all eternity.

No such luck.

The top layer was a bunch of newspapers. They were yellowed with age, and had that papery-musty smell. Beneath that smell was one of lavender. She stepped aside from her own shadow, looked at the papers. They were old, as in very old. The date was Monday, July 18, 1917. The headline was: *Number of Holland County Men for Draft*.

She gently placed the newspapers aside, along with a few layers of tissue paper. On top was a small velvet jewelry case. She opened it. Inside was a delicately beautiful gold locket, with what looked to be a pearl embellishment of a bird in flight.

Detta took the necklace from the case, slipped it around her neck. Then, as if the day could get better, she moved the next layer of tissue, and what she found beneath took her breath away.

The trunk was full of clothing. *Women's* clothing.

Beautiful *vintage* women's clothing.

On top was a white cotton chemise. It was trimmed with a beading lace at the top and bottom and had the kind of neckline that could be worn off the shoulder.

After a few more layers of tissue was a headpiece, the kind with lace and small silk flowers. The pink blossoms were sewn onto a metal comb.

Beneath this was a corset cover with shell button and lace trim, a beautiful ivory.

Item after item in the steamer trunk were gorgeous, exquisitely preserved articles of clothing. Scattered throughout the trunk were lavender sachet bags.

At the bottom of the trunk was a thick layer of tissue. Detta found that she was holding her breath as she removed them.

She gently peeled back the final layer of tissue and saw that the last article of clothing was a ball gown. The overdress was a lustrous peach with white lace ruffles at the neck and shoulder. The overskirt had a white netted lining. There was also a white underskirt with matching taffeta ruffle.

Detta took it all out and draped the clothing over the boxes. She crossed the room to the other side and retrieved the full-length mirror leaning against the wall. With a little bit of a struggle she got the mirror to the center of the room, leaned it against a support beam.

She held up the ball gown, fitting it to her shoulders. Whoever this dress was made for was just about her size. The gown looked almost like custom fit for her. As was the locket.

She couldn't wait to get all this upstairs in some decent light. She would—

Before she could finish the thought a shadow skittered across the floor. She jumped. She turned 360, expecting to see someone in the basement with her.

'Dad?'

No answer.

'*Dad?*' This time louder. Still no answer.

Another shadow, this time on the other side of the basement room.

Was someone looking in the windows?

Was it that skanky bitch who had followed her?

Detta stepped behind the brick pillar, took a deep breath. She looked at the beam of light on the basement floor.

Nothing moved.

She made a decision. If there *was* someone, she was not going to get trapped down here. She put the dress back on top of the steamer trunk, took a deep breath, and sprinted back up the stairs, across the dining room.

By the time she opened the back door, whoever was looking in the window – if there *had* been someone looking in the window – was gone.

58

With the exception of Walt Barnstable, Ivy had never seen anyone eat quite as much as Will Hardy. The man was bottomless. He was about as fit as a teenager, tall and athletic, without an ounce of fat on him. Ivy hated him.

She'd called him, absolutely certain he would tell her to leave him alone. Either that or put him on the village payroll.

He did neither. When she told him about the boxes at Joe McGrath's, and her mother, he came right over.

When Will finally pushed his plate back he said, 'I have a confession to make, Mrs Holgrave.'

Ivy June looked at her daughter, then back at her guest.

'Will I be scandalized by this knowledge?' she asked.

'I don't believe you will.'

'All right,' she said. 'Shoot.'

'That is the best fried chicken I've ever had.'

Ivy June blushed. It didn't happen that often.

'Learned at the apron bow of my mother, also named Ivy.' She pointed at the stove. 'That's the same cast iron skillet she used. I think maybe it's the pan.'

Will shook his head. 'It's the hand that turns the drumstick.'

'Thank you for the kind words.' Ivy June got to her feet. 'Now, I know you two want to get to what's in those boxes we got from Joe McGrath,' she said. 'You go on and get to it. I'll clean up.'

'Might need your help on this, Deputy Holgrave,' Will said.

Her mother blushed again.

She was going for the record.

When Ivy opened the door to her house, she held the door for Will, who shuttled inside the two boxes of files.

'Where do we want these?' Will asked.

'Anywhere is good.'

Will put the boxes on the dining room table. When he turned around, Frankie was standing right behind him. He almost jumped.

'Oh, *hello.*'

Frankie gave him the twice over. Will apparently had enough experience and dog-wisdom to let her. When Frankie began to wag her tail, he relaxed.

'That is one big girl dog,' he said.

'That's Frankie.'

'Okay to pet her?'

'Oh yeah.'

Will petted Frankie. Frankie lapped up the attention.

As Frankie gave her new guest one final assessment, and lay down in the corner, Ivy took off her jacket and holster.

'Coffee?'

Will looked at the boxes. 'Make it a double.'

Ivy June showed up with a plate of her coconut cookies. They split up the files. Ivy took the photographs and the autopsies and court records. Will took the witness statements and summaries. Ivy June took the newspaper clippings.

They all read and in silence for a while, making notes.

'Good cookies,' Will said absently.

Ivy June beamed.

As Ivy sifted through her pile, she soon found the case from 1969. Although it was a photocopy of the photograph, and maybe a second generation one at that, there was no doubt that Carl Tomlinson had been right.

A crown made of crow's wings had been found at the scene.

She showed the picture to her mother.

'Oh, my,' Ivy June said. 'That's the girl. The girl we found by the quarry.'

'Her name was—'

'Elizabeth,' Ivy June said. 'Elizabeth Hollis.'

'Yes, Mama.'

Ivy read the summary aloud.

An honor student and a member of the Carver High drama club, Elizabeth Hollis was sixteen when she was found. Elizabeth's father was a long-haul trucker who was killed on an icy road in Summit County when Elizabeth was only five years old. Elizabeth and her two younger sisters were being raised by their single mother, who worked two jobs as a waitress and a house cleaner.

When Elizabeth did not return home from school one day, her mother called the Sheriff's office. Elizabeth's decomposing body was found on June 30.

'Joe made one visit to Carver,' Ivy June said. 'Something about one of her teachers, I think.'

Ivy found a summary of the visit. Joe McGrath had made a few notes regarding Elizabeth's drama teacher, a twenty-seven-year-old man who did not supply an alibi on which Joe was particularly sold. But there was not enough suspicion for Joe to have followed up on the matter.

According to the report, on the morning of June 30, three boys, all around the age of twelve, walked across the vast field and over to the edge of the quarry, perhaps anticipating unearthing some limestone with their explosives.

The oldest of the boys, Tommy Reardon, was the leader of the gang, and therefore the director of the festivities, and the deployer of the more powerful ordnance.

As the three boys spread out in the field Tommy came first upon an item which he recalled as being a large wicker basket. In front of the basket was a short four-legged stepstool. Although, according to his statement, he could not be positive, he seemed to recall that on the stepstool was a pair of old shoes. Grown-up shoes, a pair in size ten or eleven or twelve.

None of this would have been much worth noting – Holland County was famous for many things, not the least of which was the propensity for people from outside the county to dump their unwanted goods and pets – but for the fact that the only access path to the field, and that end of the quarry, was cordoned off by a chain, which had not been breached. Whoever had dumped these items had walked them back.

'All these objects,' Will said. 'Weren't there a lot of things placed around the clearing where Paulette Graham was found?'

The word leaped at Ivy. But only because she knew it echoed her own, private thoughts.

'Placed?' she asked.

Will thought for a second. 'I *did* say placed, didn't I?'

They held each other's gaze for a moment. Something – something like understanding – passed between them.

When they finished with the files, Ivy went into the garage and came back with a large erasable whiteboard. Will helped her tack it to the wall. When Ivy picked up a black marker, her mother said:

'Let me do it,' she said. 'Nobody can read your writing.'

Ivy June crossed the room to the whiteboard, took the marker from her daughter, and made two columns. In one she wrote:

Victim profile:

Female. Mid-teens. Caucasian. Slight build.

Poor/Working class.

Troubled home life.

Volunteer.

She underlined the last word three times.

'I'd look there,' Ivy June said. 'The papers said that the Graham girl was a volunteer, also.'

Ivy and Will exchanged a glance. Will smiled.

'If you ever want to come out of retirement, I have a contact at NYPD,' Will said. 'They'd be thrilled to get you.'

'Never been to New York,' Ivy June said. 'Might just take you up on that when my hips get better.'

After walking her mother back to the cottage, Ivy returned to find Will lost in thought in front of the whiteboard. He had circled the word volunteer.

'Sort of cries out, doesn't it?' Will said.

'It does. All these girls did volunteer work.'

'But not at the same places.'

'No,' Ivy said. 'But it can't be coincidence.'

'Are these places part of a larger network?'

'They might be now, maybe linked at a county or state website, or one belonging to an advocacy group.'

'But not in 1969.'

'No,' Ivy said.

'Which means that back then—'

'Someone put eyes on Elizabeth Hollis.'

'Yes.'

Ivy made a second column. She wrote:

Suspects:

Mid-thirties/early forties

Criminal record

History of violence

'You've got physical evidence at the Graham scene in Lonnie Comb's tobacco tin,' Will said. 'Nothing so far at the Mollo scene. The rest is circumstantial.'

He was right. The photograph on Lonnie's computer, and Dallas Lange's sighting of what might have been Chevy Deacon's truck on Cavender Road was not enough. Even including the page of the newspaper bearing the name Josie in Chevy Deacon's handwriting at his house.

There was no DNA evidence on either victim, no blood or tissue beneath their fingernails, nothing left behind by the perpetrator. There was no evidence of sexual assault in any of the cases, therefore no transference or semen. There were no fingerprints.

'Have you ever run a ViCAP?' Will asked.

Maintained by the FBI, the Violent Criminal Apprehension Program was the largest investigative repository of major violent crime cases in the US designed to collect and analyze information about homicides, sexual assaults, missing persons, and other violent crimes. If the signature of a crow's wings had been used before, and was collected as evidence, it would be in there.

'I have,' Ivy said.

'I did a little work on it with NYPD and a joint FBI task force. Setting up keywords, databases. Maybe you should plug this in.'

'Good idea,' Ivy said. In the ten years or so ViCAP had been available through a secure internet website, Ivy had only used it a handful of times.

Will pointed at her laptop on the dining room table. 'Is this hooked up?'

'It is.'

'Okay to use it?'

'Absolutely.' Ivy sat down, navigated to the site, entered the login information. 'All yours.'

Will sat down at the table, picked up his coffee cup, drained it. He looked at Ivy. 'I'm going to need something a little stronger than this.'

'I'm on the case, Doc.'

59

The lights were still on in her mother's house. Ivy walked across the yard. Frankie took off for the woods.

When Ivy stepped inside her mother's house she saw that Ivy June was on the couch, wired, still wide awake, the TV on low volume.

'How is it going?' her mother asked.

'Ongoing,' Ivy said.

Ivy reached into the dining room hutch, retrieved a bottle of Maker's Mark. Her mother nodded at the bottle. 'Where do you think you're going with that?'

Ivy grabbed a pair of glasses from the kitchen, poured them each a few inches.

Her mother took the glass. 'Thanks.'

They clinked.

'Lots of memories today,' Ivy June said.

'Any good ones?'

Her mother sipped her drink.

'I don't know. I guess what I'm trying to say is that today was ...'

'What, Mama?'

Her mother took a few moments, organizing her thoughts. 'It's just too bad it all had to be over these little girls.'

Ivy had an idea about where this was going. She said nothing.

'But being out there today? Looking at those old case files? Talking to Mickey McGrath again? Working with you and Will?' She glanced up at Ivy. Her mother looked more alive and vibrant and engaged by life than she had in months. 'It felt good, you know? Like I was making a difference.'

'You did make a difference.'

'It felt like I was important again.'

'You *are* important, Mama.'

Ivy June waved a hand. 'You're just trying to humor an old mare.'

'Who elected you mare?'

Her mother laughed. This was an old joke of theirs, rooted in how some people in Ohio and Pennsylvania said the word 'mayor'. It often was attached to someone bitching about getting a speeding ticket and announcing how they were best friends with the mare.

'I'm going to get back to it,' Ivy said.

'You have to get some rest.'

'I will,' Ivy said. 'You got everything you need?'

'I do, baby girl. I do.'

'All right then.'

'And Ivy Lee?'

'Yeah?'

'That Will,' she said. 'He's a good man.'

'You're just saying that because he likes your fried chicken.'

Ivy June smiled. 'Maybe so. Love you.'

'Love you, too.'

Ivy stepped onto the porch. She glanced toward the river, and the Fairgrounds. The night was still and warm and silent, dotted with fireflies. It was every summer night of her youth.

But she knew better.

Before Ivy crossed the yard she called in to the station house for a status report. Missy Kohl was on duty.

'Not too much happening,' Missy said. 'Pretty quiet, really. A bar fight up at the Riverside, of course.'

'I'm shocked.' Every Friday was fight night at the Riverside Tavern.

Missy went on to say that the Claytons were at it again. Mitch and Holly Clayton held the record for the longest running marital cage match in Holland County history, going on thirty-seven years of wedded misery. Missy said this time there were broken plates and cups, but no bones. No arrests, either.

'Also, one of the kids from Carver got into some kind of dustup behind the school tonight,' Missy added. 'Got beat up pretty good.'

'Do we know what happened?'

'The girl said she was smoking a cigarette behind the gym and she got jumped from behind. She's up at the emergency room at Hillsdale.'

'*Hillsdale*? How badly is she hurt?'

'The ER doc says she'll make it just fine, but she's darn well busted up. Black eyes, fat lip, scraped knees. She says her arm is broken, but the doc says no.'

'Do we know her?'

Ivy heard some notebook pages turning. 'Her name is Audrey Lawson.'

The name didn't ring a bell. Ivy said so.

'You've seen her around,' Missy said. 'She's kind of on the chunky side, lots of hardware on her face and ears. Usually sporting a purple Mohawk.'

Now Ivy remembered the girl. She'd had a few run-ins with her, mostly loitering. Bad attitude, but nothing violent. Until tonight. Maybe the kid mouthed off to the wrong person.

'Let me know if her condition changes or you hear anymore about what happened,' Ivy said. 'I'll be up for a while.'

'Will do, Chief.'

When Ivy returned to her house Frankie was waiting on the porch. The dog was covered in leaves and dirt.

'You're not coming in like that,' Ivy said. 'I just vacuumed.'

Frankie seemed to understand. She tried to shake it all off.

As Ivy stepped into the front room Will was still on the laptop.

'Any hits?' she asked.

'Nothing promising yet. There are a few hits regarding signatures with animals, mostly of the Son of Sam variety. Nothing specific to crows and serial murder. Not yet.'

For the next hour they tried inputting as many variables as the cases called for. Nothing jumped off the screen. Ivy tapped the photograph of the Lonnie Combs scene.

'The dice on the floor beneath the body. One of them is a three. One of them is a one. Does this mean anything or am I just reaching?'

'Everything is within reach,' Will said.

For the next half-hour they tried to apply this aspect to the lives of all concerned, thinking maybe a birthday was March 1, or 1931, or perhaps an address or phone number. No luck. There was no point in plugging in 13. The results would have overwhelmed them.

At midnight they took a break. Ivy held up the bottle of Maker's Mark. Will nodded.

Ivy retrieved a glass from the kitchen, poured Will a double. He took the glass from her, sipped the bourbon, savored it.

'Wow.'

'Good, isn't it?'

A few minutes later Ivy's phone rang. She answered. It was Gary Baudette. Ivy made a few notes, signed off.

'BCI found something in Chevy Deacon's place,' Ivy said.

She sat down at the laptop, opened the mail app, clicked on the email message from Gary Baudette.

It was a high-resolution photograph, and took a few seconds to load, revealing itself top to bottom.

The picture was of a dead black bird in a dusty shoebox. As with the crow at Lonnie Combs's place, it had no wings.

'Where was this?' Will asked.

'Under the bed.'

'Anything tying him to Josie Mollo?'

'No,' Ivy said. 'Not yet.'

Ivy looked at the dead crow, and considered when it had happened for her. She concluded that she'd made the decision somewhere between her mother's house and her house, a decision to let go of thoughts and ideas and hopes and fears she'd kept inside for twenty-five years, things so private and close to her heart that, until this moment, she'd believed she would take them all to her grave.

Will Hardy was the right person.

Now was the right time.

For two full minutes Will did not say a word. Perhaps he was speechless. Then he said again, simply:

'Wow.'

They were standing in the basement in front of the walls of calendars and photographs. Above the computer monitor was the corkboard bearing the photographs of Josefina Mollo, Paulette Graham, Charlotte Foster, and others. Ivy pinned a grainy picture of Elizabeth Hollis next to them.

Will pointed at the corkboard. 'And these are the known dead?'

'Yes,' Ivy said. 'I never had a solid link until today.' She held up the photocopy of the crime scene photograph taken in 1969. 'This is the link.'

Will tapped the picture of Charlotte Foster on the corkboard. 'Who is this?'

Ivy told him the story of the discovery of the girl's body.

'She was found in a remote field in Summit County. Like Paulette, the animals had gotten to her. Manner of death was ruled undetermined.'

Ivy pointed to the column of photographs. 'These are also girls who went missing that year. None of them ever turned up, as far as I know. I've tried to follow up as quietly and discreetly as possible, without disturbing the families. Mostly internet searches, Facebook and Twitter searches, and the like. There is no trace. Even after twenty-five years.'

'And these?'

He was pointing at the other columns, each of them with four photographs.

'Same scenario, different years. All four girls disappeared within thirty miles of where we're standing.'

'And you feel these are all connected?'

It wasn't a feeling, Ivy thought. Still, she needed to make her case. 'I'm working on it.'

'What are we looking at?' Will asked. 'Some kind of ritual?'

'Yes.'

'A religious ritual?'

'I don't know.'

Will looked at the newest pictures, photographs Ivy had taken of the Josefina Mollo crime scene. He compared them to the pictures taken of Elizabeth Hollis. The crown of wings was almost identical.

'What's the link between Lonnie Combs and Chevy Deacon?' Will asked.

'In a small town like this, I wouldn't be surprised that they knew each other. But this kind of relationship would have to go deeper than two lowlife creeps doing bottom-shelf shots at a roadhouse.'

Will remained silent.

'These were ordinary men,' Ivy said. 'Less so than that. Lonnie Combs couldn't even wash the dishes in his sink, or do a load of laundry. He was a cheap drunk and a kiddie freak. Chevy Deacon beat up his wives, and couldn't even conceal the fact. How on earth could they hide the depth of darkness this would require, the level of secrecy? I don't see it.'

'So you believe that there is something going on at a deeper level.'

'Yes.'

'That these men were used.'

'Yes.'

'Which would mean that they were murdered.'

'Yes.'

Ivy walked over to her file cabinet, returned with a thick folder.

'Look at these.'

Ivy spread out the files on the table.

She put out newspaper clippings from long ago, decades. Stories of accidental deaths under suspicious circumstances, deaths ruled to be suicides. Suicides from 1994, 1969, 1944, 1919. There were even two from the *Abbeville Ledger* dated 1894.

'All these men. All ruled suicide,' Ivy said. 'All in Holland County, or right near the Holland County line.'

Ivy watched Will. She saw the wheels turning.

'The dates.'

'Yes, sir. The dates.'

'Missing girls, men found dead by their own hand, all within twelve months of each other.'

'Notice anything about the years?' Ivy asked.

336

'They're all twenty-five years apart.'

'Yes.'

Will tapped his finger on the pile of photos and news clippings.

'This just became something else, didn't it?'

Ivy wanted to say that it became that for her a long time ago, in the time it took to snap that picture of her sister. The image of Delia on that day was how her sister remained in her mind, her whole life forever captured in a fraction of a second.

'Every twenty-five years a new rash of killings and disappearances,' Will said.

'Yes.'

'And it coincides with the Appleville Festival. And the return of the white raven.'

'Yes.'

'But if Elizabeth Hollis's killer was even twenty years old back then, he'd be seventy now. It doesn't compute, does it?'

'No, it doesn't.'

'Maybe he has a protégé. Someone younger.'

'Maybe,' Ivy said. 'It's crossed my mind.'

The two of them stared at the mountain of information in front of them.

'Of all the things I know about this, there is at least one thing I believe to be true,' Ivy said.

'What is it?'

'All these girls? Going back to just after the Civil War?'

'What about them?'

'It's all the same case.'

Autumn – Harvest

Being the true diary and journal of Eva Claire Larssen

September 16, 1869

This coming week is the Appleville Festival. I feel that little May will arrive just as the festivities get under way. I have twice been to see the doctor in Chardon this month and he assures me that all is well. Mrs Schuyler has been so kind to me. She has kept my duties light, and has even commissioned her son to make me a special stool on which I can sit in the kitchen.

September 21, 1869

Little May is born! Six pounds ten ounces. She has sparkling blue eyes like her father. I am blessed.

October 9, 1869

I am back on my feet again. Little May is beautiful but so very fussy. Mrs Schuyler is helping me with all the things I do not know about being a mother, which is almost everything.

October 18, 1869

Willem came to the kitchen today. He brought his camera and took a photograph of all the girls just outside the back door. Before he left he took me aside and pressed something into my hand. It is a beautiful gold ring. He said we will go to the county seat and be wed, if I will have him.

I am soon to be Mrs Willem Schuyler, Mama.

October 30, 1869

Willem left for school today. He will be gone for two weeks, then we will be married.

November 5, 1869

Dr van Laar has become a ghost in the village. He seems to spend all his time on the third floor of Veldhoeve. Or down at the seven groves – counting, ciphering, proclaiming things to the heavens, raising his fists. Of the few times I have seen him up close he has been pale and drawn.

I fear that he has an illness.

November 11, 1869

He stands beneath the sugar maple in the Fairgrounds, watching, waiting. Night after night. His figure is slight, but tightly coiled, like a serpent. I am afraid for myself and Little May. Willem will be back this Friday, a day that cannot come too soon.

This will be my final entry, dear journal. Tonight I will hide this journal well in Godwin Hall. If something terrible befalls me, or little May, I want you to know what happened.

It was Dr Rinus van Laar.

60

Will looked at the certificate. It hardly seemed real. At the top of the official document it read:

VILLAGE OF ABBEVILLE

CERTIFICATE OF OCCUPANCY

At the bottom were various codes and permit numbers regarding plumbing and electrical and HVAC and smoke detectors. But the two things that mattered, the two things that Will understood, were the signature at the bottom, right beneath the word *Approved*.

The night they received the certificate Will and Detta celebrated with a takeout meal from Bullfinch Tavern (Carl Bristow had been right, the food was great), and Will even opened a bottle of Moët.

He was at first a little hesitant about pouring his daughter a glass of sparkling wine, but Detta promised not to start swearing and breaking things. Will found it funny, to Detta's obvious relief.

On the table that night were a number of books Detta had ordered at the library. To Will's surprise there existed a *Complete Idiot's Guide* as well as a *For Dummies* book on running a bed and breakfast. There were also a few more professional tomes on the subject, which Will decided to order for purchase. He had always been one to write in the margins of his textbooks, and had the feeling that Detta's boss would not appreciate this practice.

Godwin Hall was beginning to fill up with furniture, and every time Will turned a corner, and saw a room almost fully fitted, he was amazed how well it was coming along.

Will also purchased a few different software subscriptions, most notably a web authoring package. Detta was getting quite proficient at it, and had come up with three different ideas for a Godwin Hall website; had already established an email relationship with all the main travel and lodging sites.

As a trial balloon she had mentioned Godwin Hall on a Facebook page and they'd gotten a handful of inquiries about rates and availabilities.

At just after noon, on a late September day, Will heard someone knocking on the front door. He opened the door to find a young man on the porch. He was tall and lanky, collegiate looking in ivory chinos and dark blue vest sweater over a white Oxford shirt. He had a large manila envelope in his hands. Will's first thought was that Detta would love his tortoiseshell frames.

'Hi,' Will said.

'Are you Mr Hardy?'

'I am.'

'My name is Zach Johnson,' he said. 'Eli Johnson was my grandfather.'

'Nice to meet you,' Will said. 'You're Cassie's brother?'

'She's my cousin.'

'Ah, okay,' Will said. 'Please. Come on in.'

'I can't really stay too long. But thanks.'

Zach walked inside, looked around the foyer, the parlor.

'Wow,' he said. 'This is really nice.'

Will had earlier in the day finished tacking in a new carpet runner on the stairs. The brass grommets gleamed.

'Thanks,' Will said. 'It's a process.'

Will found that he had been saying this a lot lately. He imagined he would for a long time to come.

'My grandfather used to talk about this place now and then, about its heyday. He told me he never came here without a jacket and tie.'

Somehow, even with his limited acquaintance with the old man, this sounded like Eli.

'I was sorry to hear of your grandfather's passing,' Will said. 'I only met him the one time, but he was a kind man. He welcomed me to Abbeville, in fact. He was among the first.'

'Thank you,' Zach said. 'We moved away when I was small, so I only saw him when we came here for the fairs. I wished I had known him better.'

'Are you here for one of the festivals?'

'Yes and no,' he said. 'I'm here to wrap up a few loose ends from Eli's estate. We might stay the weekend.'

The young man glanced out the door, toward the street, then back at Will.

'To be honest, I had no idea who you were,' he said. He pointed at the handwriting on the package. The inscription stated, simply: *For Will Hardy*. 'That's all I had to go on, just the name. I put it aside for a while, then forgot about it. We still get *The Villager* mailed to us, but I don't really read it any-more. About a week ago I picked it up and saw that article about you and Godwin Hall. I then realized that the package was meant for you.'

He handed Will the parcel. It was not that heavy.

'Eli wanted me to have this?'

'Yes.'

'Do you know what's in it?'

'No,' Zach said. 'I figured that was between you and my grandfather.'

Of course, Will thought. He hoped he hadn't offended the young man. He held up the package. 'Thanks for bringing this by. I hope it wasn't too much out of your way.'

'Not at all.'

'Are you sure I can't get you a cup of coffee or tea?'

'I'm sure,' he said. He glanced at his watch. 'I'm running late already.'

The young man moved toward the door. Before leaving he hesitated a moment.

'I'm pretty sure Eli said he met my grandmother here. Right before he shipped out for the service. He said they had dances here back then.'

'Yes, they did.'

'He used to say that he was sorry that this place closed down, that it was part of what made Abbeville special for him.'

Will opened the door. The young man stepped through.

'Thanks again for this,' Will said.

Zach Johnson walked down the front walk, turned once at the street, waved. In that moment, in that light, Will could see the resemblance to the old man.

61

As summer turned the corner to fall, the challenges facing the Abbeville Police Department evolved with the colors of the leaves. The months of August and September were when the festival seasons kicked into high gear in Holland County.

Especially this year.

An increase in the number of visitors to the area, along with all the trials they brought with them, were considerable. Parking, crowd control, littering, vandalism, the myriad problems associated with alcohol consumption. Whenever more people gathered, the number of petty criminals increased proportionally.

The investigations into the deaths of Paulette Graham and Josefina Mollo had all but stalled. The two girls, along with their alleged killers Lonnie Combs and Chevy Deacon, had been interred, and the discussion of the cases had moved from the coffee shops to the taverns.

Ivy had twice revisited the field where Paulette Graham had been discovered and, because it had been months, there was nothing to be found. If there had been a crown made of crow's wings, the organic material had fully disintegrated. The field was full of dead grass and low shrubs. She'd found some rusted wire, but BCI could not make a definitive match to what was found more recently.

Ivy had contacted Paulette's extended family and paid a visit to their home. She kept the true purpose of her visit close to the vest, telling Paulette's family that she was merely conducting a follow-up. What she wanted to know was whether the Graham family had suddenly come into a great deal of cash, as had Emmett Mollo.

When Ivy broached the subject she immediately saw that they became furtive, avoiding eye contact, having to suddenly be elsewhere. In the end they denied receiving any unexpected windfall. But Ivy made note of the new sixty-five-inch television in the family room, and the presence of at least ten new storm windows installed on the rather dilapidated house.

Walt Barnstable had followed up on the currency they had found on Chevy Deacon. Anything regarding banks and banking was federal, and Walt, who still had contacts from his days as an insurance investigator, had put in a request to follow up on all this through the proper channels, that being the FBI and, subsequently, the Treasury Department.

Nothing from them yet.

Ivy had returned to restoring the photographs they had gotten from Mickey McGrath, and continued with her magnum opus, the full restoration of the picture of Delia on the Fairgrounds behind Godwin Hall.

Ivy June had begun getting around without the aid of her cane and her walker. In the past two weeks she had been seen a few times at the Bullfinch, regaling the regulars with her stories of skullduggery from Holland County's past.

Frankie was beginning to settle down, to adjust to her forever home. Where at first the dog would react to every loud noise by bolting under the dining room table, she now was beginning to take it in stride. More or less. Ivy had rented the Blu-ray edition of *Black Hawk Down* and Frankie had toughed out what was one of the loudest movies ever.

Ivy soon learned the difference between leash-walking a terrier and leash-walking a Shepherd. At least she was getting an upper body workout every morning and evening.

On the day before the opening festivities of Appleville, Ivy got a call from Gary Baudette.

'I ran across something I think you might be interested in, Ivy,' he said. 'I did some further tests on the contents of Chevy Deacon's vehicle. Do you remember those six burlap bags in the back?'

'I do,' she said. 'Big bags. They were all folded.'

'My initial tests didn't yield too much. Organic material mostly, some fibers and hair. None belonging to the victim. But when I revisited this yesterday I found trace of two different materials I hadn't detected before.'

'What is it?'

'In four of the bags there was something called *Symphytum uplandicum*. Also known as Comfrey tea. Have you ever heard of it?'

'Can't say that I have,' Ivy said. 'Not much of a tea connoisseur, to be honest. I can't imagine that Chevy Deacon was either.'

'Well, I'd never heard of it either. I got as far as the Wikipedia entry for it, but no further yet. I'll keep digging. There's a reason it was in those bags, though. Just not sure what that reason is yet.'

'What else did you find?'

'On each of the six bags was trace evidence of horse manure.'

'No shortage of horses or their output in Holland County, Gary.'

'That's for sure,' he said. 'There wasn't very much of it, but what I found interesting is how it was deployed.'

'How is that?'

'I only found trace on the *outside* of the bags, and then only along the bottom seam, end to end. Which would mean—'

'The bag was placed on the ground, in or around horse manure. Placed, but not laying down on its side.'

'This is what I'm thinking. What might be even more telling is that this particular organic material is spread along the first four or five inches towards the top of the bag on all sides.'

'Which would mean that whatever was in the bag when it was placed on the ground was heavy. It spread out.'

'That's the consensus around here,' he said. 'Have you ever considered a career change, Ivy? Maybe moving over to BCI?'

'I do look good in a lab coat,' she said. 'Can you put this all in a memo and fax or email it to me?'

'Already in the works, Chief. And I'll let you know what I find when I dig deeper into the Comfrey tea.'

'Can you also give me that technical name one more time?'

Baudette spelled it for her.

'Thanks, Gary. Keep me posted.'

Ivy knew that the Deacons didn't keep horses, but that did not mean that someone had not crossed their spread recently on horseback. She knew that horses were not all that discriminating about where and when they did their business.

On the way to making her rounds she stopped at The Tea Cup on Parkwood Road and talked to the owner. Ivy often got her morning coffee here, and knew that the shop carried a lot of exotic and foreign teas. She learned that Comfrey tea was a herbal tea not commonly found in tea shops and pantries, but rather used as a healing compound for minor skin wounds, bedsores and insect bites.

Ivy bought a large coffee and took it over to one of the benches at the northern end of the Fairgrounds. The area was alive with vendors setting up for the next day's festivities. It reminded Ivy that she was pretty much on duty for the next forty-eight hours, and that this case might have to wait.

Still, she could not bring herself to put this new information aside. She took out her iPad, tapped the browser icon, drilled down to her Google Maps app.

She had placed push pins at the sites where the bodies had been found, going all the way back to the 1940s. She zoomed in to the area where Josefina Mollo had been found. There were only a few roads in the area. Her eye traced the route from the Deacon spread over to Cavender Road. There were any number of horse trails in that area, so the manure could have come from any of these.

But why all six bags, and why only on the bottom?

As she scanned the area one last time she saw the dirt access road snaking into the woods just north of Route 44 and Cavender Road.

Of course, she thought.

Why hadn't she seen it before?

Heritage Equestrian Center was a multidiscipline training facility located on a one-hundred-acre parcel of land at the easternmost section of Holland County.

As the crow flies it was less than two miles from where Josefina Mollo's body was found. In order to get to Route 44 from the entrance you had to drive along Cavender Road.

Ivy had called ahead and when she pulled into the driveway she was met by the company's owner.

Stella Eames was in her forties, a fit and vigorous woman with close-cropped silver hair. They met in the reception area of the main building. Ivy told the woman the bare basics of her inquiry, specifically about the Comfrey tea.

'I've never heard of it,' Eames said.

'It's herbal tea.'

Eames thought for a moment. 'I'm a pretty big tea drinker, but I've never really been adventurous. Earl Grey, chamomile, peppermint.'

Ivy asked if she knew Chevy Deacon. She did not. Ivy took out her notebook, scanned the timeline. She told her the date in question.

'Do you know if you got any deliveries that day?' Ivy asked.

'It's surely possible. We buy almost everything we use here.'

'Can you check your log?'

'Of course,' she said. 'Come on into the office.'

The offices were on the second floor of the main building, and overlooked the training track. Eames sat down at her desk, opened her laptop, tapped a few keys.

'We got a few deliveries that day, but only from UPS and FedEx.'

'No local concerns or independent haulers?'

She looked again. 'No,' she said. 'Sorry.'

'And all deliveries would be on your schedule?'

'They're supposed to be. There's five of us here, though,' she said. 'It's possible that an independent delivered something I don't know about. I can ask the other employees.'

'Would you do that for me?'

'Of course.'

Ivy handed her a card.

'Can you call me as soon as you talk to them?'

'Sure thing.'

As Ivy headed back to the village she drove the same route that someone leaving the center would take to bring them to the intersection of Cavender Road and Route 44. It was as thickly wooded as any area of Holland County.

Perfect cover, she thought, for someone to transport the body of a dead girl.

352

62

Will had a final meeting with the HR department at Kent State at two o'clock. He took a shower, put on slacks and a blazer, made himself a sandwich. When he sat down at the dining room table he opened the package he had gotten from Eli's grandson, Zach.

He carefully opened the large envelope, gently shook out the contents onto the table. Inside were three smaller envelopes, perhaps six by nine, all sealed with a metal clasp. One of them contained an old leather notebook, as in *very* old. Its cover worn and creased, rutted with use. Will could see that the pages were yellowed and brittle.

Etched on the cover was:

Daily Pocket Remembrancer

He set it aside, opened the second envelope. This one contained a stack of photographs, similar to the ones that had been on the wall at the Historical Society. These seemed even more brittle than the notebook. He put them back in the envelope.

The third package was a children's book. The binding on the book, titled *The Eclectic Reader*, was all but disintegrated, the pages loose. Will gently flipped through it. The contents were a mix of stories and fables and poems, all illustrated.

Let me put a few things together for you.

Why had Eli Johnson wanted him to have these things? While they looked like collectible items, memorabilia for history buffs in Abbeville, nothing looked like anything one might put on display.

He set aside the book and the photographs for later in the day.

He then opened the journal. Inside the front cover, on the left-hand side, in deep blue ink, was written in a beautiful cursive hand:

Being the true diary and journal of Eva Claire Larssen.

On the right side was printed:

For the recording of events, sums and sundries.

Will again looked at the inscription. He remembered the name Eva Larssen from the old photograph of the eight girls standing behind Godwin Hall, the scullery maids and room attendants, taken not ten feet from where he now sat. The thought gave him a chill.

Will wondered if she'd sat on this very spot, in this very room, and wrote in this diary.

As he was about to begin reading, he suddenly had the feeling that he was prying. Whenever he was with a patient, and the person began to open up about their most private feelings, it was different. He was not prying at those times, but rather listening, helping the patients to understand.

Not so with a diary.

A century and a half after this young woman wrote down her innermost thoughts, Will felt that reading her words might not be right.

There was little chance that Eva Larssen had written this

journal for eyes other than her own, surely not for a man one hundred fifty years in the future to read.

Detta was another story. She would *love* to read it.

He took the book into the kitchen and wrote a note for her.

Thirty minutes later he locked Godwin Hall, and cycled the two miles to the campus.

63

Jakob stood at one end of the long, narrow gallery on the third floor of Veldhoeve. The corridor ran the entire length of the structure, north to south, end to end, gable to gable. On the east wall of the gallery there were seven peaked dormers, each aligned with a section of the whitewashed wall that stood opposite.

The corridor itself was a mere forty-six inches wide, room enough to walk shoulder to shoulder. It was carpeted in a rich burgundy wool. The hardwood floor beneath was a burnished chestnut, highly glossed with a polyurethane finish.

Jakob sipped his tea, breathed deeply the air, the sweet *tisane* of apple blossoms, the grace note of every memory he'd ever had.

Tremble at this day, came the voice from Charity.

Jakob closed his mind to the voices.

The only furniture in this part of the house was a small white table at one end of the gallery, upon which Jakob preferred a crystal vase with white irises. On either side of the table were two fine mahogany chairs in the Queen Anne style. Each chair was upholstered in black silk.

In the morning, Jakob's cherished time of day to come here, he would watch as the sunlight gently ascended the wall. As a child he had many times spirited himself away from the orchards to watch the chalky, luminous light slowly reveal each of the drawings.

If the world knew what he had in his possession it would beat a frenzied path to his door. He had known this just as his fathers had known. It would shake the art world to the extent that books would surely be rewritten, histories revised. Scholars from all over the world would rethink what they had generations ago thought to be true, knew to be true.

Pieter Bruegel had produced fourteen preliminary sketches of his seven virtues and seven vices.

Upon Bruegel's death in 1569 the rough sketches were thought to be lost. In truth, an apprentice in Bruegel's studio had spirited the drawings away in a secret compartment in an exquisite oak cupboard with ebony inlay.

Rinus van Laar purchased at auction the *kolommenkest* in West-Friesland. Three days after the night of his wife's murder, Rinus, in the hallucinatory grip of the *mandragora*, saw the future.

He would create a legacy to Bruegel's virtues in the seven sacred groves at Zeven Farms. Four virtues to each grove, each representing one season.

Jakob knew as a young man, as had his fathers, that what he would create would be a meager impression of the master work. Even with the years of planning and arranging, the care with which they had all curated the objects, the final result could only be an approximation of Bruegel's vision.

Jakob had once tried to log the miles, the total distance, that all the objects had traveled, and had forsaken the exercise some-where in the tens of thousands.

On this day Jakob came to a halt in front of the final two drawings, as he had every day for the past twenty-five years, except for those days when he had been collecting.

This is the day that the Lord hath made, came the voice of his father.

Jakob opened the small drawer in the table, retrieved his magnifier, a fine Edgar Berebi with a burnished silver handle.

He stepped closer to the drawing, brought the glass to his eye. There had been renderings before and after, by many gifted artists, but for Jakob, and his fathers, this was where it all began and ended, the faultless center between the light and the dark, between equinox and solstice.

He looked at the inscription at the bottom.

Sweet is the trust that springs from hope, without which we could not endure life's many and almost unbearable adversities.

Hope, he thought as he glanced out the window, across the Fairgrounds, at Godwin Hall. He reached into his pocket, retrieved the two photos. Eva Larssen and Bernadette Hardy. The two handmaidens of his legacy.

The last girl is the first girl, he thought.

The last girl is Hope.

64

Walt Barnstable walked into the station at three o'clock, flushed with purpose. He had two documents in hand.

'I was just at the Sheriff's to pick up some posters,' he said. 'They asked me to bring these back. I think we're going to want to follow up on them.'

The documents were two missing-person case summaries. Two teenage girls; one fourteen, one fifteen. Both had been missing for a month. Neither of them were from Holland County, but were from the tri-county area.

Ivy's eyes scanned the pages. She saw what Walt wanted her to see. While it was not that rare for teenage girls to run away, or go missing, these two girls made them potentially special to this case.

One of the girls, the younger of the two, was last seen near her home in Auburn Valley. She was a volunteer at the Red Cross clothing drop-off center in nearby Hazelton. The other girl, missing from Waite Hill, volunteered at the Lake County food bank.

As Ivy read the documents she felt her heart clock a little faster. 'They volunteer,' she said.

'Yes.'

Ivy looked at the full reports. Both were light on details. One of the family interviews was conducted by a rookie county deputy; the other was by a village police officer, a part-timer.

'Have you spoken to both families?' Ivy asked.

Walt nodded. 'I called them on the way over.'

'Have they had any contact with the missing girls?'

'None.'

Before leaving the station Ivy decided who would get which file. Ivy took the fourteen-year-old girl. Her name was Julie Hansen.

The Hansen house was in a sub-development called Auburn Valley Greens. Built in the 1970s and 1980s, the zip code was now home to middle income families with children, as the schools were among the better funded in the county.

On the way out to Auburn Valley Ivy stopped by the Pooch Pawlor in Kimmel Junction to pick up Frankie. Ivy had sprung for the works. Frankie's coat gleamed.

Meredith Hansen was in her mid-thirties. She was willowy and fair, and moved in a way that suggested she had at one time been a good athlete, a tennis player, perhaps. To Ivy she seemed tightly wrapped, ready to uncoil at any moment.

The front room was full of lighted votive candles in red glass holders.

While they talked, Meredith Hansen sat on the very edge of the couch. In deference, Ivy did the same thing, matching the woman's posture. Ivy had seen it many times. Women in Meredith Hansen's dire circumstance wanted to be ready to move. She kept her cell phone firmly clutched in her right hand.

Ivy got the basics out of the way first. Then she moved on to what had, for her, become the beating heart of the case.

'Julie is a volunteer?' Ivy asked.

'Yes,' Meredith said. 'She's always doing something. She works with the Friends of the Library when they do their book sales and bake-offs. She collects for March of Dimes, sells magazine subscriptions to raise money for the Cancer Society. She collects clothes for the Red Cross. She also has a part-time job.'

'Where does she work?'

'She does some shelf stocking at Dahlausen's.'

Dahlausen's was a country store and farmer's market on Granger Road. This information had not been in the initial report.

'She took the job so she could pitch in around here. Her older brother and sister are away at college now.'

'You mean pitch in financially?'

'Yes,' she said. 'Her dad is on disability.'

'May I ask what happened?'

'It was at his work. He's an iron worker. Local 207.'

'And there was an accident?'

'Yes.'

Ivy looked at the door to the bathroom. It had recently been widened, the drywall patched but as yet unpainted. A glance out the back door showed a recently installed ramp. Now Ivy recognized the sound she'd been hearing. It was the steady diaphragm pump of an oxygen concentrator.

'Tell me about the last time you saw Julie.'

Meredith went through the morning of the day her daughter disappeared. It seemed ordinary enough. When Julie left early that morning, on her bicycle, she was headed to Dahlausen's. She never arrived.

'Can you describe Julie's bike?'

Meredith did.

'What was she wearing the last time you saw her?'

'She had on her red cardigan. It has white trim around the collar and the two pockets.'

'Bright red? Deep red?'

'I can show you.'

The woman stepped out of the room for a few seconds, then returned. Ivy expected her to be holding a photograph. She was holding a red cardigan sweater on a padded hanger.

'I don't understand,' Ivy said. 'She was wearing this sweater?'

'Yes,' she said. 'I mean, not this exact sweater. One exactly like it. We always buy her two of everything.'

'May I ask why?'

'Julie was a twin, you see. We lost Janie when they were only three. She had a bad heart. Ever since, Julie has always insisted we buy two of everything. She always wears both sweaters, jeans, jackets. She alternates. I guess it makes her feel closer to Janie.'

'And this is the sweater she was wearing? One exactly like this?'

'Yes. She had it on when she left to go to her job.'

'May I take this with me?' Ivy asked. 'I promise to return it soon.'

'Of course.'

Ivy asked about the follow-up visits or calls from the Auburn Valley Police Department. There had been a few contacts made. Ivy knew everyone in the small department. They were competent, if not aggressive in their investigations.

Ivy left the woman her card, and sensed that Meredith Hansen had a little more confidence in her than she did in her local department.

Ivy hoped the woman's trust was warranted.

65

Detta had seen Billy three times in the past three weeks. Not one of their encounters had been planned because, apparently, Billy didn't make plans. Every time Detta wanted to bring it up, she'd stopped herself. She didn't want to seem needy or grabby. Their time together had been so easy and natural that she didn't want to spoil it.

She'd only fallen for a boy twice before, and those had been little-girl playground crushes. She knew that now. There had been nothing mature about the boys or the feelings she'd had.

This was different.

She never knew when she was going to see him. He seemed to just appear out of nowhere, then vanish after they'd spent some time together.

She'd taken a picture of herself in the peach ball gown she found in the steamer trunk in the basement and printed it off. Like an idiot, she gave the picture to Billy before she could stop herself. She'd thought he might reciprocate, but so far he hadn't offered.

The best part of knowing Billy was that he had, completely unbeknownst to him, inspired her. It was because of him she had begun to draw again.

She'd fallen for the work of Pieter Bruegel. Bruegel the Elder, as he was known. He lived in the Netherlands in the late sixteenth century. There was something earthy in Bruegel's work, she thought, the way he rendered peasant life without irony or judgment. There was even quite a bit of it that was rather risqué.

She often found herself up late at night, the coffee table book propped under a light on the desk in her room, her charcoal pencil in hand, sketch pad on her lap.

She didn't kid herself that she had much natural artistic ability, not really, but she was a good mimic on the page, and a few of the renderings she had done were not bad.

At least she wasn't moved to instantly throw them away.

When Detta got home she saw a note from her father on the refrigerator. He had another meeting with the department at KSU.

On the dining room table was an old book, a stack of photographs, and a leather-bound journal. She'd never seen any of it before. She wondered where her father had gotten them, if maybe they were one of the auctions he'd been to.

Detta slipped off her shoulder bag, went into the kitchen, put the kettle on. When she returned to the dining room she picked up the journal. It was very light, very dry to the touch. The leather was cracked and creased.

Inside the front cover of the journal was a single photograph. It, too, was dry and brittle. The picture was a portrait of sorts, of a young woman standing in the parlor of Godwin Hall. The top of the image was worn away, as if someone had touched the girl's face so much that it had all but disappeared.

While the picture itself was interesting, it was what the young woman was wearing that took Detta's breath away.

She was wearing the dress that Detta found downstairs. The ball gown that was now on a hanger in her closet.

She was also wearing the gold locket, the very one Detta had around her neck at this moment.

Eva Claire Larssen.

Detta took the journal, and ran up the stairs.

66

In the late afternoon Jakob walked the girl into the clearing. As they stepped into the glade the girl looked up, toward the sun. Jakob could see the tears collecting in her eyes. He knew that these were tears of wonder, not sadness. She had taken a cup of strong tea before they left Veldhoeve.

Jakob had taken a cup as well.

As she sat motionless beneath the tree, Jakob took a step back. He glanced at all the objects, items that he'd begun placing in the clearing years earlier.

It was perfect.

He knelt beside the girl, watched her eyes as the thorn pierced her pale skin. She had already grown so pallid over the last few weeks, barely tasting the meals he had prepared for her. It was not uncommon near the end, but still he worried about her.

He worried about the blood.

After he collected what he needed, he held her as she took

her final breaths. When her body was calmed, he took out his camera, and began to take his photographs.

He would soon take the flask to the girl's grove, and consecrate her orchard.

Minutes later, as Jakob prepared to leave, he heard stirring behind him. Heavy footfalls running through the forest.

'What are you *doing*?'

It was a man's voice. It was not a voice belonging to any of his fathers. It was of this time and this place.

As Jakob turned to face the intruder, he slipped the razor sharp *paardenmes* into his right hand.

Jakob knew the voice, but it seemed so out of place here, at this moment, in this time, that he hesitated. For a fleeting instant he could not separate that which was present with that which was past.

In that instant he had considered that the voice was in his head.

It was not.

You must stop this.

'I'm talking to you!' the voice demanded. 'What did you *do* to her?'

Jakob did not know what the intruder had seen. It might have been the small, delicate hands of Rinus van Laar, the dexterous and skilled hands of a physician. Perhaps it was Mads van Laar and his massive arms; Mads who once cleared a grove in a single afternoon, carrying the great logs to the river.

It mattered little.

There was only one task.

Stop this.

67

Ivy parked down the street from the Hansen house. She called Walt Barnstable, who had met the other family, with similar results. There had been no contact from the missing girl.

Ivy drove the two miles to Dahlausen's, interviewed the store manager and some of the employees. None of them had anything to add.

When Ivy left the store she retraced the route between the store and the Hansen house. She made the drive three times. It was all country road, with a series of wide, soft bends. Julie Hansen could easily have been taken at any point without anyone seeing the abduction. Ivy figured it might have taken the girl ten to fifteen minutes to cover this amount of territory on her bicycle. She checked on the weather that day. It was clear and balmy.

What happened in those ten minutes?

Ivy returned to the Dahlausen's parking lot. With Frankie looking over her shoulder, Ivy took out her iPad, opened Google

Maps. She studied the area. In satellite view it was almost all green.

Using the store as ground zero, she started to drive the area, looking for pathways that cut into the woods. There were not many cross streets in this area, and the turnoffs were few and far between.

For more than two hours Ivy drove with her light bar flashing, stopping every time she saw something that might have been an access road or path to a clearing she'd pinned on Google Maps.

It was all starting to look the same.

She returned to the parking lot at Dahlausen's, picked up a sandwich at the Subway next door. Frankie ate most of it.

Ivy looked at her watch. It was about an hour until sunset. She decided to pack it in. It had been the longest of long shots anyway. There were thousands of acres of forest in this part of the county. Not every clearing was visible from the air.

Still, Ivy put a pin in her mental map, deciding to take it up in the next few days. She pointed the SUV toward Abbeville. It was then that her dog sent her a clear message.

Frankie had to go. *Bad*. She'd been cooped up in the SUV all afternoon. Ivy had of course made sure she had water, which was probably the problem.

'Can it wait, baby girl? We're almost home.'

Frankie barked.

'All right, then.'

Ivy pulled over on the berm, checked her mirrors. Frankie was pawing the hatch door at the back.

'Relief is on the way, Francesca, *mi amor*.'

With leash in hand, Ivy had barely gotten the hatch open when Frankie was off like a shot. The dog was across the road and hightailing it for the tree line before Ivy could open her mouth.

'Frankie!'

The dog didn't break stride.

*

369

Ten minutes later, with no sign of Frankie, Ivy locked the SUV, trundled into the woods. It was thick forest, and getting darker by the minute, even though the sun was bright and hanging low in the western sky.

'Frankie!' she yelled.

Nothing. Just the whirs and clicks and chirps of the forest.

She continued on, ever deeper into the woods. Ahead she saw shards of late afternoon sunlight. She knew she was not deep enough to be emerging onto Warner Road.

When Ivy stepped into the clearing she saw Frankie on the other side, maybe thirty yards away. She again called her name. The dog took a few steps toward her, then turned around twice and barked.

'Come on, Frankie,' she said. 'I'm beat. No time to play.'

Another two barks. She was going to make Ivy work for this.

'I can still take you to the pound, you know.'

When she was halfway across the field she saw it. It was an unnatural color to be out here in the middle of the woods, a glossy royal blue reflecting the sun in an iridescent shimmer. She might have walked right by it, but it caught her eye in a way that something you've been hunting for in your house all day seems to do, stepping front and center in your world, daring you to not see it.

But there it was. In the middle of a field about a mile from any road.

A blue vase.

A yay-high, yay-wide blue vase with a gold rim.

Peggy Martin's vase. The only thing stolen in that break-in.

When it registered, Ivy realized what it meant. One hundred fifty years of history coalesced into that single instant. The random junk dumped in all these fields. It had never been random at all. She looked back across the clearing, where Frankie sat in place, on full alert, and knew.

The smear of white skin against the deep green of grass. The shock of blond hair. The red sweater with the white trim.

When Ivy saw this everything seemed to stop. The clouds overhead calmed, the gentle sway of branches came to a halt. Ivy could only hear the sound of her own breathing.

Because Frankie wasn't playing. Frankie was *working*. She'd picked up the scent from the identical red sweater in the SUV and now she was alerting.

'No, no, no, no,' Ivy said as she quickened her pace. She began to run. 'Please, God, no.'

When Ivy reached the spot where Frankie was sitting, her fears were realized.

The body was that of Julie Hansen. Her pale hands were streaked with blood. Ivy leaned over, felt the girl's neck for a pulse. She found none.

'God *damn* it!'

Frankie jumped at the sound of her shouting, took a few steps away, her tail between her legs, her head lowered. Ivy knew what she should do at this moment, that she should comfort the dog, utter some soothing words. It was important for duty dogs to know that they had done a good job. Ivy knew this but she was being selfish.

Why? Because she'd had the chance to save Julie Hansen and she'd failed.

Frankie cautiously walked back, sniffing the air around the girl. She sat down, again alerting to the presence of her quarry.

'Good girl, Frankie. Good girl.'

A few wags of the tail, but Frankie wasn't convinced. Still, she did not move; she had not been released.

Ivy reached for her shoulder microphone. It wasn't there. She had come without her radio. She fished her cell phone out of her pocket, fumbled with it a few agonizing seconds, punched in 911. When Dispatch answered, the woman asked her location. Ivy was lost. She couldn't remember where she was. She looked up, saw the top of the cell tower that she knew to be near the county line at the twenty-four-mile marker.

She relayed it, and asked Dispatch to contact the Sheriff's office and to call the main Abbeville PD number. She needed everyone and anyone with a pair of eyes and a gun. Before she signed off she told Dispatch that she would meet the EMS and officers at the road with her lights flashing.

The next thing she remembered was her training. There was still a threat. She drew her weapon.

'Frankie. Good girl. *Come.*'

The dog got up, circled Ivy's legs, sat near her feet. Ivy took a knee, one hand on the dog. She cocked her ears to the sounds of the forest. She heard nothing moving. No footfalls on leaves, no snapping of twigs.

Ivy kept her voice soft and calm and even, her hand firmly on the dog's collar.

'Is someone out there, baby girl?'

Frankie raised her ears. She put her nose in the air.

'Bad guy, Frankie?'

Frankie stood, strained against Ivy's hand. She was interested in an area due north of the victim. She began to dig her back paws into the earth.

'Frankie,' she said. 'Search.'

Ivy let go. Frankie was off into the woods in a shot. In a few seconds she disappeared from view.

It was then that Ivy heard the EMS siren rise in the distance, along with the siren of Walt Barnstable's cruiser, echoing through the canopy of trees. She hated to leave the victim's body, but she had no choice.

Keeping her weapon drawn, Ivy rose and began to make her

way across the field. Before she had taken three steps, she heard Frankie return, heard the sound of the dog's breathing.

Ivy turned around. It wasn't Frankie.

It was the girl.

Julie Hansen was alive.

68

The ambulance screamed toward the Geauga Medical Center, the nearest Trauma III facility. They were under a Highway Patrol escort.

Every so often Ivy would glance at the paramedic and make eye contact. What she saw there was not good.

When Julie Hansen was rolled into emergency ICU, Ivy called Walt Barnstable. Walt was on scene where Julie Hansen was found.

'How is the girl?' Walt asked.

'Critical. She lost a lot of blood,' Ivy said. 'How's Frankie doing?'

'She's okay,' Walt said. 'As you might expect, she's pretty amped up with all the activity around here. She wants to get into the game, but I think she's a bit scared.'

'Anything from BCI?'

'They dusted that blue vase. I think they pulled a half-dozen prints off it. The mobile unit is here. We should know any minute if there are any hits.'

'Ask them to—'

'Hang on,' Walt said.

Ivy heard some muffled conversation as Walt covered the phone. Before long, he returned to the line.

'We've got a name.'

'From the prints?' Ivy asked.

'Yeah. Dakota Rawlings. White male, seventeen.'

'Where is he from?'

'Lives at 2815 Mayfair Road.'

'That's not Abbeville,' Ivy said. 'That's Ashdale. Why is he in the system?'

'He's got two breaking and entering, one misdemeanor possession of a controlled substance. Pled all three, did community service.'

'How long ago?'

'All three were last year.'

'What was the controlled?'

'Hang on,' Walt said. 'I'm reading all this on an iPhone. Here it is. It was MDMA. Five hits.'

Ivy absorbed this. Kids broke into houses to get money to fuel their heroin or meth habits. Not so with ecstasy.

'Do we have someone en route?' Ivy asked.

'A deputy should be arriving at the subject's house right about now.'

'Did Frankie alert on anything else?'

'No,' Walt said. 'I've got her leashed right here.'

Ivy thought for a moment. 'When you get things under control see if you can get her to pick up a trail. Start where the vase was found.'

'You got it.'

At this Ivy saw the ER doctor standing outside the ICU. He was signing something on a clipboard. Ivy caught his eye.

'How is she?' Ivy asked.

'We've got her on epinephrine, whole blood, as well as a ventilator. What she has in her favor, at this moment, is her youth. I wouldn't have survived the ride here.'

'Can you say how long it was after the trauma that I found her?' Ivy asked.

'It couldn't have been too long. A few hours. Less.'

Hours, Ivy thought. If she hadn't been driving by. If Frankie had not keyed on that article of clothing.

'Did she say anything?'

'She did,' the doctor said. 'Just one word. It sounded like "Richard". She said it more than once.'

'Richard,' Ivy said. 'You're sure?'

'That's what it sounded like.'

'Doctor?'

They both turned to the voice. An ER nurse was calling him.

Before the doctor turned to leave, he looked back at Ivy. 'If you're a praying person, now would be a good time.'

Ivy found Meredith Hansen in the ICU waiting area. According to Meredith Hansen, there was no Richard in her daughter's life that she knew of. No family member, either immediate or extended. No close friends, no school or volunteer acquaintances named Richard that she had mentioned.

Of all proper male names, few had more nicknames and diminutives than Richard. Ivy walked Meredith Hansen through them all. Rick, Ricky, Dick, Dickey, Rich, Richie.

Nothing.

Within ten minutes Ivy dispatched Missy Kohl to the Hansen house to pick up Julie's school yearbooks.

Ivy watched the girl. She was hooked up to two IV lines, had on her face a ventilation mask. Every five minutes or so a nurse or a doctor would come in the room, check the numbers, check the fittings, watch, listen, write something onto a clipboard. Each time they met Ivy's gaze with a look of grim purpose, a flat-lined smile that communicated a shared hope, a cold reality.

When Ivy's phone buzzed, she nearly jumped.

She stepped out of the room and into the small alcove at the end of the hallway, looked at the screen. It was Walt.

'Hey, Walt,' she said.

'How's the girl? Any change?'

'No. Are you still on scene?'

'I'm about a half-mile north. Right near a cliff that overlooks the river. Do you know it?'

'I do,' Ivy said. 'What do you have?'

'I took Frankie over to where the vase was found. It took her about two seconds to pick up a scent. She led me here.'

'Anything?'

'Unfortunately, yes. We have a body, Chief. Looks to be male. By the looks of some of the scrub growing out the rocks, the snapped branches, he either fell off the cliff, or was shoved off. Can't see much from up here.'

'Who do we have en route?'

'Akron FD is the closest with the equipment we need. Their ETA is about forty-five minutes.'

'What can you see?'

'Hang on,' Walt said.

A few seconds later Ivy heard the tone that signaled new email. She looked at the screen, swiped over to the app. It was a photograph of the scene, the vantage looking down the face of the rock wall. In it she could see the legs of a subject: black pants, black shoes. The upper body was obscured by foliage. One arm was twisted at a brutal angle behind the body.

'Did you get the picture?' Walt asked.

'I did.'

'I'll update you when we get the body up.'

When Ivy clicked off she entered the room, walked quietly over to the chair next to the bed.

She thought:

I'll make you a deal, Julie Hansen. If you find the will to survive, to open your eyes and return to this life, I will bring this to a close. I'll do it for you and your sisters. My sisters. I'll do it for Josefina and Paulette and Elizabeth. I'll do it for all the girls who so innocently walked into the darkness, never again to emerge into the light.

Find the light, Julie.

69

The light was perfect.

In the dream she was in the ballroom of Godwin Hall. A string quartet was playing a waltz. She reached out a hand, touched the beautiful silk wall covering. In the dream it felt real.

Was she actually walking around Godwin Hall?

Although she would never admit it to her father, she'd had a few instances of sleepwalking. It was a common enough side effect of Ambien. She'd once read that some people had even gotten into their cars and driven while in a hypnotic trance, which was what Ambien did to you.

She couldn't remember if she had taken a second pill or not. It felt as if she had.

She had read Eva Larssen's journal, cover to cover. And then a second time. All the people seemed so real. Especially Willem. And Dr van Laar. Evil Dr van Laar.

But the great revelation was that Eva Larssen was an artist. The journal was full of wonderful drawings.

Detta found herself back in her bedroom.

Then came a sound. A scratching beneath the music.

She heard it again. It wasn't in the dream. It sounded like a tree branch, a real tree branch, scraping against the window.

Somehow she found herself standing at the window, peering onto the Fairgrounds below.

When she lifted the pane she saw that it wasn't a tree branch at all. It was Billy. He was standing just below her window, and he was wearing a suit. On the ground below the window were a handful of small white stones.

Is this real?

'What are you doing here?' Detta asked in a loud whisper.

'I forgot to tell you,' he whispered back. 'I have a midnight landscaping company. Just doing a little trimming.'

Detta tried not to smile. 'Not funny,' she said. 'You can't be here.'

'Now, did Juliet say anything like that to Romeo?'

'I think she did.'

'Yeah, well, how did that turn out?'

Now Detta did smile.

'There's something I want to show you,' Billy said.

'When, *now?*'

Billy stepped forward. 'Yes.'

'I can't.'

'Why not?'

Detta opened her mouth, but said nothing. She really didn't have a good reason.

'What are you wearing?' she asked.

'Do you like it?'

It was a dark suit. The shirt had a high collar.

'Is that a costume?'

Billy grabbed his heart, feigning an attack. 'A *costume*? This is my best finery, young lady.'

Detta laughed. 'Okay.'

'I'm taking you to the ball. You have to dress up.'

'The ball? I don't have anything fancy, Billy.'

'The dress,' he said. 'The antique dress you were wearing in that picture you gave me. You look beautiful in that.'

Detta ran to the closet, took down the peach gown she had found in the steamer trunk. Eva Larssen's gown. She slipped it on. She did not have any shoes that would be appropriate, but she somehow knew she didn't need them.

Detta took out her pen, tore a page from her Strathmore pad. She needed to leave some kind of note for her dad. She tried to think how best to word this. Her father was not as full-blown paranoid and nervous about her well being as he had been even a month earlier, but he did worry. If he came in her room and she was just gone, he would panic.

Went for a walk. Took a pad and some pencils. Hope to sketch. I have my phone. Text later. Love you!!

Detta quickly made her bed, put the note on her pillow, then stepped over to the window. As she slipped into the warm night Billy took her by the hips and carefully lowered her to the ground. She was amazed at how strong he was.

'You look beautiful,' he said.

'I'm so dead if we get caught.'

'We won't be long.'

She looked behind Billy. On the ground, behind him, was a beautiful wicker basket, wrapped in scarlet cellophane.

'What's this?'

Billy picked it up. Detta could now see that the basket was full of fruit.

'My gift to you.'

They hurried across the Fairgrounds, hand in hand.

More than once Detta turned around and looked at Godwin Hall, silhouetted in the moonlight.

It looked like something out of a Hawthorne novel.

70

The deputy securing the Rawlings address was young, perhaps twenty-five or so. Ivy didn't know how much he knew about the current cases, or the urgency of the moment.

Ivy pulled up, parked her SUV. She exited, showed the deputy her badge.

'Evening, Chief.' He pointed at the shack. 'No one in or out since I've been here.'

'Have you tried to make contact?'

'No, ma'am,' he said. 'Orders were to secure.'

Ivy looked a little more closely. *Shack* was being generous. The small structure looked to be no more than fifteen by twenty feet. The small front porch was caved in, with a half-sheet of plywood nailed over the opening. Even that was delaminating. The surrounding area was littered with junk.

'Hang tight,' Ivy said.

'Yes, ma'am.'

Ivy crossed the yard of shin-high grass and weeds, sidestepping the rusted car parts. She found a section of the porch that looked secure, stepped over to the door. She knocked. '*Police*,' she said. 'Need to speak with you, Mr Rawlings.'

Nothing. She knocked again, put her ear near the door. Just silence. No TV, no radio. No dogs, so far.

She walked around back. Once there she drew her weapon, shouldered open the back door, and stepped inside.

The interior made Lonnie Combs's place look like *Architectural Digest*. The main room had a pair of dirty mattresses on the floor. The kitchen sink was piled high with crusted dishes and flatware.

After a brief search she found that the house was indeed unoccupied. Ivy holstered her weapon, took out her phone. She needed more than one person to begin a grid search of the premises. There was something in here that tied Dakota Rawlings to that vase, to that clearing and, in some way Ivy had yet to determine, to the attempted murder of Julie Hansen.

There was little doubt that Rawlings was the burglar she had sought for a while. Scattered everywhere were small appliances, clothing, empty pill vials, DVD players and at least a dozen game consoles in some state of repair.

As Ivy made a note to check the pawn shops with Rawlings' picture, her phone rang.

It was Walt again.

'We've got the body up from the ravine,' he said. 'BCI just did a field print on him.'

Ivy knew what he was going to say.

'It's Rawlings, Chief. The body is Dakota Rawlings.'

Ivy looked at her watch. It was just after midnight. It was the beginning of the most hectic day of the year in her little village and there was a madman on the loose.

As she waited for her officers to show up, her phone trilled. She answered. It was a woman's voice.

'Chief Holgrave, this is Stella Eames.'

'Yes, Ms Eames.'

'Sorry to be calling so late. You said to call if I had any more information. I thought I'd get your voicemail.'

'Not a problem,' Ivy said. 'What do you have?'

'I talked to my stable master, John Gilman. We went back over the books and he told me that we did indeed get a delivery that day from an independent delivery truck. He said it was a white F-150.'

'Do you know why it wasn't logged on your calendar?'

'I do. The delivery was scheduled for the day before, but for some reason was delayed. John never updated it. It didn't seem important.'

'Does he recall what the delivery was for?'

'It was apples,' the woman said. 'Apples from Zeven Farms.'

71

They stood beneath the sugar maple in the center of the Fairgrounds, surrounded by the silent booths and stalls and kiddie rides that were set up for the festival the next day.

To Detta, it looked magical, a celebration frozen in time.

Billy spread a blanket on the ground. He opened the basket, reached in, removed one of the small apples. He handed it to Detta. When she took a bite she found it sweet and firm and juicy. She'd never had anything like it. Or maybe it was the moment.

'This is wonderful,' she said.

'I grew up on them.'

Detta looked down, at the now familiar Z logo on the cellophane that wrapped around the basket. She'd seen the logo around the village.

'So you *are* from around here,' Detta said.

Billy said nothing for the longest time.

'Okay,' Billy said. 'Confession time.'

'What?'

He pointed at the basket. 'This was already at your house.'

'It was?'

'It was sitting by your front door. I would have bought one for you myself, but I am, alas, just a poor country boy.'

'It's okay. I kinda thought that the—'

Billy leaned forward and kissed her. It wasn't a small peck like he had given her once at the library, but a deep, slow kiss.

When he pulled away he said, 'We were supposed to meet, you and I.'

'We were?'

Billy nodded, brushed a strand of hair from her forehead. He then reached into his pocket, removed something. Detta looked down. It was small, delicate feather. A white feather. He gently placed it in her hair, over her right ear.

'What did you want me to see?' Detta asked.

Billy waited a moment. He looked at his watch.

'This only happens once a year.'

'What does?'

'I want you to close your eyes.'

'Uh oh.'

'Trust me.'

Detta did. For some reason, she felt no fear, no apprehension. She closed her eyes.

Billy took her by the hand, led her a dozen or so steps to the left, toward the river. The grass was warm beneath her bare feet. She found that her heart was beating with anticipation.

'Okay,' Billy said. 'I want you to count to five, then open your eyes.'

'When do I start?'

'Right now.'

Detta counted slowly. Her mind raced with the possibilities. When she reached five she opened her eyes.

'Oh my God.'

At that moment the moon was directly behind the finial on the gable end of Godwin Hall. The tip of the pinnacle touched the moon at its center.

The beauty of it, the perfection, seemed magical, as if it was the work of a painter or sculptor. Or maybe it was the way she felt.

She turned to face Billy. 'I've never seen anything like—'

There was no one standing behind her.

'Billy?'

No answer.

Detta called his name a few more times. He did not respond. She walked down toward the river, back up the gentle slope. She was alone. Time passed, but Detta did not know how much. Everything had taken on a soft focus, a surreal quality.

Suddenly, a cool breeze swept over the grounds, ruffling the lace on her dress. It was the first chill of fall. In that moment the empty rides and silent booths took on a menacing appearance.

She heard a sound from just beyond the trees.

'Billy?'

A long shadow drew across the field.

'Eva,' came the voice from behind her.

Detta spun around.

It wasn't Billy.

72

The vendors arrived at just after 5 a.m. and began to put the finishing touches on their tables and stalls. They parked their trucks and vans in the diagonal spaces that crosshatched the outer rim of the Fairgrounds.

At just after 6 a.m. Will opened his eyes to soft sunlight filtering through the blinds, and the sound of a calliope.

Will dressed in his best country innkeeper outfit – LL Bean shirt, chino slacks, suede chukka boots – and walked upstairs to his daughter's room. He knocked.

'Honey?'

Nothing. He put his ear to Detta's door.

'You up?'

Silence.

Will edged open the door. His daughter's bed was made.

Before he turned to walk downstairs he saw the note on her bed. He crossed the room, read the note.

When had she gone out?

Will checked his phone.

There were no texts from Detta.

73

The music came to her first, sifting up like steam through a city street. It sounded like the soundtrack of an old movie, the kind of movie where the men wore suits while they ate dinner, and all the women wore beautiful hats and lace gloves.

Detta opened her eyes. She was in a field, a vast expanse in some strange, silvery world, a world that resembled Abbeville, but was clearly other. The shadows and highlights were overexposed, highly saturated. There was a forest in the distance, lined with trees that had shimmering platinum leaves. Above them was a bright sky with soft clouds.

But there was no color. The world was black and white.

How could she be living in a black-and-white world?

She turned her head to the right. This image was of a broad field, a meadow with low bushes and tall tufts of grass.

When she looked down at the ground she realized she was not outdoors at all. She was in a strange room that had bright, life-size images on all four walls.

She looked to her left, saw a beautiful tea service with delicate cups and saucers on a mahogany tray.

When she looked more closely at the cups she thought she had to be mistaken. She wasn't wearing her glasses, and had to be seeing things.

They were the same china cups that were in their house when she was small.

74

The Fairgrounds buzzed with activity. Every so often a horse-drawn carriage would circle the midway. It began its journey at Veldhoeve, circled to Godwin Hall, and back. The driver was dressed in period clothing from the early 1800s, complete with top hat.

In addition to the stalls and booths and games of chance there was an antique tractor tent, a wood carver tent, a midway stage that promised a variety of musical acts, as well as a milking parlor. In addition, any number of food concession stands promised everything from funnel cakes to fried cheese to prime rib on a stick.

Will had been to a handful of county fairs in upstate New York, but this was the first one in which he had participated, the first one in which he had any kind of stake.

Reuben and his brother had done a wonderful job creating the small kiosk for Godwin Hall. It looked a bit old-fashioned by comparison to the bright colors of all the other concessions on the midway, but that was probably a good thing. If this festival – one hundred fifty years old this day – was about anything, it was about a reverence for the past.

The fair was set to open at 10 a.m., and by nine-thirty Will had everything in place. He strolled the north side of the Fairgrounds, stopping to chat with a few of the vendors. Every so often he would scan the crowd looking for Detta. As he made his way around the far end of the midway he decided to poke his nose into the library and see if she was there.

She was not. In fact, he was told that the library would be closed for the day.

He typed up a text and sent it off. He found himself staring at his phone, waiting for a reply. His daughter usually texted back within seconds, as did almost everyone her age. After a full minute he began to type a follow-up text, then stopped himself. He was needlessly worrying. She'd left him a note, she was responsible, and he really had nothing to worry about.

Still, it was with a slight sense of unease that he returned to the Godwin Hall booth at the Appleville Festival, stepped behind the counter, and officially opened for business.

75

'What do you see?'

Detta spun quickly around. There was a man standing behind her. She had not heard him enter the room.

The man was elegant and slender, and wore a dark suit and scarlet tie. Even though she was a little afraid, there was something about his voice, in this place, at this time, that reassured her.

The man took a few steps toward her. He gestured to the wall to her left.

'These trees have had a very long journey to come to this place,' he said. 'As have you.'

'Where am I?'

'You fainted,' the man said.

'I did?'

'Yes.'

'Where is Billy?'

'The boy went for help when you faltered, my dear. He came to get me, and together we brought you here.'

Detta looked around. The quick movement of her head made her dizzy. 'Where is here?'

The man touched a panel near the door. In an instant, all four walls came to life. It was as if Detta was sitting in the middle of the Fairgrounds. All around her there was activity. Stalls serving food. Children running around. The sounds of a calliope.

Her father was standing next to the booth Reuben had built for Godwin Hall.

'Dad.'

'Yes,' the man said. 'I told your father where you are. He will come for you shortly.'

The man poured some tea into a china cup. It was white porcelain with a watercolor design of pink and yellow and lime green.

'Have some tea,' the man said. 'You will feel better.'

'These are our cups.'

'Yes.'

'My mom's china cups. I chipped one once and had to go to my room.'

Detta looked at the cup in her hand. It was damaged in the same place as the one she dropped. It *was* the one she dropped.

Detta took a sip. The tea was sweet and aromatic, just the right temperature. It tasted faintly like the apple she had eaten.

'Do you remember the day that you went to the library on a school trip?' the man asked.

'What library?'

'The majestic library on Fifth Avenue.'

He was talking about New York.

'When was this again?' she asked.

'It was six years ago. There was an old woman on the street.'

Before Detta could respond, the wall in front of her changed. It was now the massive steps leading up to the library's main entrance. The two enormous lions, Patience and Fortitude, kept watch. In the foreground, nine-year-old Detta stood next to the homeless woman. The memory came flooding back.

'Oh yes,' she said. 'I remember.'

'It was just before Christmas. There had been snow, but not much of it. Still, it was quite cold.'

Detta could suddenly feel a chill in the air.

'While all your classmates ran up the steps you lingered by the woman.'

Another photograph. She now had the woman's hand in her own.

'You spoke briefly with the woman. You did not give her money, but you passed a few moments with her.'

Detta recalled the encounter now with clarity. She felt something unmoor inside her. She had forgotten about this woman.

'Do you recall what you said?' the man asked.

'I do.'

'What did you say?'

'I told her she was not alone. I told her that she shouldn't be afraid.'

The man walked across the room, knelt in front of her.

'It was always going to be you, you see. From the moment you first drew breath, this moment was planned. And now we are here.'

Detta felt warm tears on her cheek. The man reached out a finger, collected a tear, brought it to his lips.

'There's someone who wants to see you,' he said.

Detta looked up, suddenly returned to the moment. 'Who?'

The man stood, crossed the room, and touched the panel near the door.

'I'll leave you two to catch up.'

As the man left the room, the wall in front of Detta, as well as the walls to her left and right, went black. She could see her own shadow from the light coming from behind her.

Detta turned slowly around, and what she saw took her heart. There was a woman sitting behind her, a beautiful woman with deep auburn hair and sparkling green eyes.

It was her mother.

76

Of all the feelings Jakob expected when he'd finally stood in front of the girl, when he'd at last fully tasted her essence, the emotion he experienced was unlike any other. What had for many years been lightless within him was now illuminated.

He felt different in his skin, as if he were not reliving the life of Rinus van Laar, but actually was the man.

The dead men lined the gallery.

'I don't know if I can do it,' Jakob said.

You must finish what you've started. You must complete the cycle that was begun one hundred and fifty years ago. You have no say in this.

But he did. Meeting her, touching her, *savoring* her, gave him the power.

Finish what you've begun.

Jakob began to pace the gallery corridor. Every so often he would glance up at the drawings. More than once he saw movement in them. The vices were stirring, as they stirred within him. He stopped, poured himself a sherry infused with mandrake.

The feelings inside him grew warmer, more vivid. His own voice rumbled.

Now is the time.

You will never again have this moment.

He had always thought of time passing in terms of seasons and years, each era clearly defined by numbers. But now he knew that the decades and centuries were not discrete, but one. From the first raindrop to the final harvest.

One eternal life, one thought.

Forever.

He now knew that he would not fulfill his legacy, and for that shame he would one day do penance. But for now, in this glorious and revelatory instant, he was free and he was complete.

He turned back to the gallery. The dead men were gone.

What lingered was the smell of mortality.

Beneath it, the essence of the girl.

One by one Jakob began to take down the drawings. He would take them and leave with Eva. He would build a new house, an even grander house than Veldhoeve. In the end there was nothing for him here. It was just brick and timber and stone and glass.

His sin was Pride, and had been all along.

Once all fourteen drawings were removed, and stacked at the end of the corridor, Jakob straightened his tie, found his bearings and began to descend the steps. He knew what he had to do.

He touched the newel post at the bottom of the stairs, as he had nearly every day of his life.

And that was when the doorbell chimed.

77

When Ivy rang the bell she didn't know what she expected. Probably a butler or a maid. In her whole life, indeed that of her mother and grandmother, the van Laars were always The Rich People.

For as long as she could remember the family was involved in just about every aspect of village life in Abbeville. There was not a charity board or philanthropy enterprise in which the van Laar family was not integral. But that's not to say they were highly visible. Just the opposite. Ivy remembered once, as a little girl, going to the county fair in Burton. Her mother pointed out the well-dressed man giving a speech to a number of business owners. She remembered a boy about her age sitting calmly and firmly and properly to the man's side. The man giving the speech was Sébastien van Laar.

In all the time since she had seen Jakob, perhaps, four or five times. To be honest, she didn't even know if the man was married or had children.

So, as she stood on the front porch at Veldhoeve she did not know what to expect. Perhaps the last thing she expected was the man himself opening the door.

'Chief Holgrave,' he said. 'How nice it is to see you.'

'Mr van Laar. Nice to see you, too.'

'Please come in,' he said. 'And you must call me Jakob.'

Ivy had never been inside Veldhoeve. She had been to the farm a number of times, had eaten in the restaurant, had visited the gift shop. All of those interiors were mostly modern in design and execution. Veldhoeve was like stepping into a painting. The foyer gave way into a great room. The floors were highly polished chestnut, as were the raised panels of the walls. A great crystal chandelier hung overhead. There was artwork everywhere.

'This is really beautiful.'

'Thank you,' Jakob said. 'When Rinus van Laar built Veldhoeve he entertained quite a lot, as I understand it. I'm afraid I don't find the time for guests these days as often as I'd like.'

The long hallway leading to the south end of the building was lined with framed paintings and drawings.

'May I offer you some coffee or tea?'

'I'm fine, thanks.'

Jakob gestured to a tufted leather loveseat. Ivy sat down. Jakob sat on the wing chair opposite her. He crossed his legs, smoothed the crease in his trousers.

'How may I be of service?' he asked.

Ivy flipped open her notepad, even though she knew what she was going to say.

'I just have a few basic questions about an investigation we are conducting.'

'I'll be happy to help in any way I can,' he said. 'I hope it is nothing too serious.'

'Just routine for now.'

'Of course.'

'Do you do any business with the Heritage Equestrian Center?'

'Yes,' he said. 'I believe my grandfather began supplying them with produce many years ago. It is a lovely place.'

'What do you supply them with?'

'Apples, of course. There may indeed be some other fruits. I would be happy to check for you.'

'What about Comfrey tea?'

'Comfrey tea? By this you mean *Symphytum uplandicum*?'

'Yes.'

'This is not something we sell. It is what's known as a dynamic nutrient accumulator. It is used to improve soil. Although the jury is still out in the study of permaculture, we have used it in limited tests here at Zeven Farms.'

'So, it's not something to drink? Something you serve at your restaurant?'

'Oh my, no. It can be quite toxic in quantity.'

'And you say that you use it here?'

'Yes.'

Ivy glanced at her notes. 'And you say you supply apples to the equestrian center?'

'We do indeed. Not in large quantities, mind you, but horses find apples quite the delicacy, if properly sliced and sized. Many times apples are used to mask the taste of medications.'

Ivy made notes. She moved on.

'Do you know a man named Chevy Deacon?'

'Chevy?' Jakob asked. 'Like the automobile?'

'Yes.'

He thought for a moment. 'I don't believe I know him. At least, not by name.'

Ivy reached into her bag, took out a mug shot of Chevy Deacon, his most recent. She held it out to Jakob.

'I do know this man,' he said. 'I don't believe I've ever spoken

403

to him, but he has done some work here. I'm not sure when the last time was, but I can find this out for you.'

'That would be great.'

'Let me talk to my day manager right now. Do you have a few moments?'

'I do.'

'In what time period are you interested?'

'Just the past four months would be fine for now,' Ivy said.

'Of course,' he said. Jakob stood. He gestured to a sideboard against the wall. On it was a beautiful silver tea service. 'If you change your mind about the coffee or tea, please help yourself.'

Coffee suddenly sounded good. 'I think I will. Thanks.'

When Jakob disappeared down a hallway at the other end of the great room Ivy poured a cup of coffee. She took a sip, walked the room. The hallways leading to the back of the house were lined with framed prints, artfully lighted. She was at a loss as to time period, movement or artist.

She could tell a Diane Arbus or Ansel Adams or Dorothea Lange from fifty feet away, but with drawings and paintings, not so much.

She took the opportunity to take a few pictures of the room with her phone, wondering how people who lived in such splendor did it. She wondered if she really could get used to it, then reminded herself that she would probably never have the opportunity to find out.

She'd just gotten her phone put away when Jakob returned, a pair of documents in hand.

He handed them to Ivy. Ivy took her glasses from her coat pocket, slipped them on. She scanned the document, saw what she needed immediately. Chevy Deacon logged four hours on the day in question.

Ivy held up the page. 'And this time sheet is accurate? By that I mean, his presence here during these hours can be verified?'

'Without question. We run a very tight ship. As you might imagine, there is a lot of transient work in this type of farming.'

'One last question for today, if I may.'

'Of course.'

'How was Mr Deacon paid?'

'I'm not sure I understand.'

'Was he on a payroll? Did he get paid a salary?'

'I see,' Jakob said. 'He is a day laborer, so not on salary.'

'Is it possible he was paid in cash?'

'This is not something we ordinarily do here at Zeven Farms,' he said. 'But some of our day workers insist on it.'

Ivy flipped through her notes. 'I think that's everything. I can't thank you enough for your time.'

'Not at all,' Jakob said. He opened the massive front door. The sounds and scents of the Fairgrounds flooded in. 'Quite the day in our village's history is it not?'

'Have you ever seen the white bird, Jakob?'

'I have. It was 1994. It came to light on the windowsill of my bedroom. It was absolutely radiant.'

'How nice.'

'What about you? Have you ever seen the white raven, Chief Holgrave?'

Ivy was just about to answer in the negative, but she stopped herself.

She had no idea why.

78

The photograph of her mother seemed so real. It was the one she had taken herself. The one with her mother sitting at the table at the *osteria*.

In the picture her mother wore the same green dress she had worn on the day that began the end of her life.

In here, though, in this place of old music and warm lights, this place with her mother's special china cups, Amanda Kyle Hardy was alive.

Detta stood, crossed the room, and touched a finger to her mother's face.

79

Business at the Godwin Hall booth was brisk, even though most of the early visitors to the Appleville Festival so far had been locals. While all of them were friendly and personable, offering Will an official welcome to the village, most taking a brochure, none of them seemed to have much interest in a romantic get-away weekend in their own town.

Miriam Yoder was helping out. The fact that she had baked a number of treats, and was offering them free to visitors, *really* helped.

'Good morning.'

Will looked up. It was Ivy Holgrave.

'Good morning.' Will gestured to the burgeoning crowd. 'You look like you have your hands full today.'

'Both hands and then some,' Ivy said. 'How are things going?'

'Not bad, I think. This is all pretty new to me.'

'These are good folks, as a rule. I think you'll meet some nice people, make some good contacts. People come to this festival from all around the state. Even further than that.'

'Have you seen my daughter by any chance?'

'Do you mean this morning?'

'Yes. She left me a note saying she was going out to do some sketching.'

Ivy looked around the Fairgrounds. 'I'm afraid I haven't seen her. Have you called her?'

'I have. Sent her a few text messages, too.'

'I'm sure she's just fine.' Ivy pointed toward the square. 'I'm heading back to the station right now. I'd be happy to look in at the Hall if you like.'

'I really appreciate it.'

'All in a day.'

As Ivy left, Will heard the clip-clop of the horse drawing the ornate carriage as it made its way around the Fairgrounds once more. When it stopped, a small group of giggling teenagers emerged.

Bernadette Hardy was not among them.

80

Will barely heard the sound. In fact, he felt the buzz more than he heard the tone signaling a new text message. He took the phone from his pocket, looked at the screen.

It was a text from Detta.

> I'm at Veldhoeve. The artwork is amazing!! When you
> get a break you have to come see it all. It's like being in
> a museum!!!

Will now felt a bit foolish that he involved Ivy Holgrave. He looked at the time stamp. It was from eleven minutes earlier. Why hadn't he heard this alert before?

He checked the switch on the side of the phone. It was on Silent.

Will got Miriam Yoder's attention.

'Do you think you could watch things here for a few minutes?'

'I'd be happy to.'

'I won't be long.'

Veldhoeve was on the far side of the Fairgrounds. Along the way Will was stopped by a few of the local merchants who wanted to buttonhook him regarding a co-promotion once Godwin Hall was officially open for business with paying customers. Will did his best to listen and not make any promises.

A few minutes later he stood on the porch at Veldhoeve. He found the doorbell, pressed it.

No one answered. He tried again. Still no response.

He opened the huge door.

'Hello?'

Silence.

'Mr van Laar?'

Will stepped into the foyer, closed the door behind him. In here it was cool and dim and quiet. He called out again, his voice absorbed by the dark wood and thick draperies.

He took out his phone, shot off a text to Detta.

I'm here. Where are you?

Almost instantly:

Up the stairs, down the hall to the right. In the gallery!!

Will climbed the winding stairs to the second floor, a bit taken aback at the opulence of it all. He'd thought the old house majestic when seeing it on his cycling rides around the Fairgrounds, but he hadn't imagined it like this. This was real money.

He stepped into the windowless room at the end of the hall. As he was about to send his daughter another text he heard another notification sound from his phone.

He looked at the screen. There was an email and a voicemail

message, both from Trevor Butler. Both had, apparently, taken time to download. Both were flagged urgent.

Will tapped on the email. The subject line was *Anthony Torres phone.*

The email had no fewer than a dozen photograph attachments.

Somehow, they were photographs of Will's family. Pictures of Amanda coming and going from the brownstone. Pictures of Will on the NYU campus. Pictures of Detta.

The last picture was of Amanda on the corner of Sixth and Washington. She wore her favorite denim jacket and black jeans, a white scarf.

For so many reasons Will's heart ached. He was seeing a new image of Amanda. He thought he'd seen them all, and that they were all gone. For the moment it didn't matter why they were on the cell phone of the young man who had killed the love of his life.

But as he took in the emotion of seeing his wife in a new picture, his heartbeat hammered in his chest.

In the photograph, Jakob van Laar stood behind Amanda.

Before Will could tap on the icon to call Trevor Butler, he heard a sound coming from behind him. Metal on metal.

He turned. The door behind him had closed. He tried the knob on the door.

It was locked.

81

Will tried the door again. It did not open. He turned, looked at the other side of the room, saw a second door. It was slightly ajar. He crossed the room, opened the door, which led to a short, dimly lighted hallway. At the other end was a staircase leading up.

He climbed the steps to the landing, turned, and climbed the remaining steps. He walked to the end of the corridor, pushed open the door. Here was a small square room, with two chairs near the center. Next to one of the chairs was a table covered with a white cloth.

Will stepped inside. On each of the walls were what looked like a live video feed of the Fairgrounds. The room had no windows, but was as bright as if he were outside.

'Welcome to *camera lucida*,' a voice said.

Startled, Will turned around.

Jakob van Laar closed and locked the door behind him.

'Where is my daughter?'

'In time.'

'*What*? Where is my *daughter*?'

Will took a single step forward. As he did this, Jakob lifted the white cloth from the table. Beneath the cloth was a ceramic plate and a single red apple. There was also a silver pistol.

Will stopped in his tracks.

Jakob held out a hand. 'Your phone.'

Will had no choice. He handed it over.

Jakob van Laar touched a button on a panel near the door. In an instant the four screens went dark.

'Where is my daughter?'

'You and I must settle the books today. Then I will take you to your daughter.'

Jakob gestured to the chair in front of Will.

'Please.'

Will glanced at the pistol. He sat.

Jakob turned his attention to the small, perfectly round apple, a deep red with an almost silvery sheen to it.

'Do you know what they call this variety of apple?'

Will had to keep the man engaged. He said, simply, 'No.'

'It did not have a name for many years. The naming of things is often quite complicated, an ordeal as complex as the creation of the fruit to begin with. God, of course, creates the fruit. We are merely instruments in his hands: the spade, the hoe, the rake.'

Jakob took from his vest pocket a small silver pocketknife. He unfolded it. The blade looked to be razor-sharp. He began to peel the apple.

'When my grandfather was a boy, a young man really, he worked in the orchard. It was his job, in those days, to help with the grafting for the new seedlings. It was that year when this apple – a variety that did not exist – was born. Every year, since that time, the trees have grown stronger, reaching ever towards the sky, beckoning the rain, producing more and more fruit.'

413

Jakob finished peeling the apple. He had done it in one long, perfect strip. He picked up one of the folded white cloths on the table, and dried the blade. He returned the pocketknife to his vest pocket. He then picked up the apple peel by one end and gently lowered the top onto the bottom. In this light, for one fleeting moment, the apple appeared to be once again whole. Will could not see where the cuts had been made.

Then, in an instant, the illusion was gone.

Jakob put the peel on the white plate. He continued.

'Consider this, if you will. Something that began its journey to our table centuries ago is here today for you and I to enjoy. In its flesh is a raindrop that fell when my grandfather's grandfather was just a boy. The very same. Without the inexorable turning of the earth, the seasons, the four winds, the equinox and solstice, it would not be as sweet. One cannot rush nature. We have tried this, and the results are not good.'

Will had to bring the man back to the moment. He tried to keep the urgency from his voice.

'Where's my daughter, Jakob?'

'We are all compost, in the end. We do not matter. The soil remembers. Think of Shiloh, Vicksburg, Ypres Salient, Omaha Beach. Dare we walk on that soil and not shiver with each step?'

Jakob touched a button on the console. On the wall behind him there was now an old photograph. In it stood a boy of maybe eighteen or so. He wore a white shirt that still had the creases pressed into it. When Will looked into the boy's eyes he felt something stir inside.

'His name was Willem Schuyler,' Jakob said.

Another photograph. This time, a girl. It was a picture of Eva Larssen, taken behind Godwin Hall. It looked to have been taken at the same time as the group photo Will had seen at the Historical Society. Except this one was a close- up.

He saw clearly for the first time Eva Larssen's beautiful face.

It was Detta's face.

Eva Larssen and Willem Schuyler were his blood.

'Rinus van Laar loved her dearly, you see. After he was widowed, he wanted her to be his.'

'He killed her.'

The man bristled at the word.

'He gave her immortality.' He gestured outward, toward the orchards and fields. 'He gave her the turn of seasons. The sun and the rain.' Jakob van Laar stood, took the pistol in hand. 'He raised his son, teaching him the ways of the land. Together they built Zeven Farms.'

Will stood up. Whatever was coming, whatever was going to happen to him, he was not going to let it happen while sitting down.

'You engineered all of it. You sent Anthony to me. You sent me that email as a man named Kessel.'

'Yes,' Jakob said. 'A small folly.'

'You *knew* I would take Anthony on. You *knew* I would try to help him.'

'We are all of our nature. It is nature that lights our way. Or, should I say, it is fire.'

'All these years. All these dead girls.'

Jakob said nothing. Will thought he saw a tell in the man's eyes, a flicker of something close to conscience.

'Why Paulette Graham? Why Josefina Mollo?'

'They were full of virtue,' Jakob said. 'Surely someone in your line of work knows how rare that is to find.'

Jakob stood on the other side of the room, near the door.

'The day your mother died,' Jakob said. 'What happened that day?'

For a moment, Will thought he did not hear the man correctly. '*What?*'

Suddenly, on the wall, was the article in the *Times*.

Fire in Dobb's Ferry Claims One.

The next photograph took Will's legs away.

It was picture taken of the thirteen-year-old Will Hardy standing outside the burning house.

'You were *there*,' Will said.

'My father and I. Yes.' Jakob continued. 'There were no guarantees that all these events would lead us to this day. You and I in this room. We plant our seedlings, prune our trees. We water and fertilize and cultivate. Still, sometimes, the trees do not bear fruit. The fact that we now stand together, with all the chance that may have conspired against us, must tell you that this was meant to be.'

Will again looked at the wall. It now showed the young Jakob van Laar next to the smoldering ruins of his house.

When Will turned back, Jakob was gone.

Will ran across the room, tried the lock, banged on the door. *'Open this fucking door!'*

As the four walls began to change, Will looked for something, anything, to pry open the door. On the walls, the photos now strobed between the house in Dobb's Ferry, the news articles about his father as a hero, pictures of Detta and her school class in Manhattan.

The only furniture in the room were the two chairs and the small table. The table was a mahogany pedestal candle stand with a wrought iron base.

Will upended the table, sending the ceramic plate crashing to the floor. He swung the table by the legs into the wall, over and over, until the top splintered away.

He ran back to the door, inserted the top of the base between the door and the jamb, just above the lock. It would not budge. He removed it, slid the base a few inches higher. With all his strength he pushed against the bottom until the door began to splinter.

For the next five minutes he continued to eat away at the door frame until he had the top of the lock mechanism exposed.

It was then short work to pry the mortise lock free. When he had the lock off he put his ear against the door, then immediately stepped back.

The door was warm.

Almost *hot*.

Will looked down, saw smoke seeping along the carpet.

Veldhoeve was burning.

82

There were no fewer than five mini-emergencies that Ivy encountered between the time she talked to Will Hardy and the moment she walked onto the front porch at Godwin Hall.

A five-year-old girl scraped her knee at the corner of Platteville and Jericho Lane, and Ivy directed her overreacting mother to the first aid tent on the Fairgrounds. An SUV decided that it did not want to pay for parking, and parked on the sidewalk in front of Uncle Joe's.

When Ivy finally stepped through the door at Godwin Hall she was immediately struck by her lingering sense of dread. She had not been inside since Delia disappeared, had indeed avoided looking at the structure, which had been shuttered all of her adult and professional life. The few times she had been called to the grounds – mostly to deal with trespassing kids – she had gotten onto and off the grounds as quickly as possible. She knew that these feelings were irrational, that whatever had happened to her sister did not live in the stone and mortar and timber of Godwin Hall, but that knowledge had never stopped the feelings.

'Bernadette?' she called out.

There was no response.

She looked around the first floor; the dining room, front room, kitchen, the small bedroom off the dining room. A quick scan of each space revealed nothing.

She stopped again in the kitchen. She put her hand to both the toaster on the countertop and the grates on the top of the stove. Neither were warm. Neither had just been used.

She crossed the foyer to the stairs, and called out once again before heading up.

There was no reply.

Of the six rooms on the second floor, Ivy quickly determined that five of them were set up to be guest rooms for when Godwin Hall opened. All five were simply laid out with a double bed, dresser, chair, writing desk. All had recently been plastered and painted. She checked each bathroom. Empty.

The door at the end of the hall was partly closed. As Ivy approached she found that she was holding her breath. She had no idea why. Maybe it was just being inside Godwin Hall for the first time in years. Maybe it was the fact that a number of teenaged girls had gone missing or had been attacked and left for dead.

Maybe it was the fact that, all those years ago, Delia had walked this very hall.

She called out one more time.

'Bernadette? It's Ivy Holgrave.'

Nothing.

She edged open the door.

What she saw was a completely benign, empty room. It was spare, by teenage girl standards. A queen-size bed, carefully made. Shoes arrayed beneath the side rail.

On one wall were drawings. Ivy recognized a few of the locations, landmarks around the Abbeville town square: the front of the library, the small, ivy-covered post office, the view coming toward the square from the south, on Platteville Road. They were all quite good, finely detailed, drawn with a sure hand.

There were only two posters on the walls. Museum reprints of Kandinsky and Paul Klee.

Ivy checked the top of the dresser. She saw the power cord for an iPhone. Wherever Bernadette Hardy had gone, it seems she had taken her phone with her. Ivy did not know too many fifteen-year-olds who left their phones at home.

She picked up the note on the bed, the note Will Hardy had referenced. She then noticed the large Strathmore sketch pads on the desk. She crossed the room, picked up one of the pads, began to turn over the pages.

Some of the drawings were extraordinary. Most were quickly drawn, but a few were quite detailed. These had what looked like a page number written in the upper right corner.

Beneath the pads was a large coffee table book. *Bruegel: The Complete Paintings, Drawings and Prints.*

She glanced at one of the sketches, at the page number. She turned to the corresponding page in the large book, and felt an icy hand close around her heart.

The seven discarded pails. The tied bundles of branches, the ladders.

It was the Paulette Graham crime scene.

Prudence.

She turned a few pages, to the section on Bruegel's vices.

In the first drawing, amid all the items scattered throughout, were the two dice, rolled to one and three.

It was the Lonnie Combs crime scene.

Sloth.

Next was another drawing. In this Bruegel had rendered a man with a drill bit through his head.

Chevy Deacon.

Gluttony.

Ivy took out her phone with a trembling hand. She scrolled down through the recent photographs, the pictures she had taken in Jakob van Laar's living room. The books in the bookcase.

There were two dozen books on Bruegel.

As Ivy ran down the steps it came to her.

Julie Hansen hadn't said *Richard.*

She'd said *orchard.*

83

In that moment he remembered it all, and it filled him with terror. The horrid smell of smoke, the fury of the blaze.

Photographs of his mother strobed on the walls around him. One of them was of the teenaged Sarah Hardy standing in front of Godwin Hall.

And Will understood.

None of the memories that had come to him since arriving in Abbeville had been his own. He knew these things about the village and Godwin Hall because of his mother's stories. She had told him of Daniel Troyer. She had told him of the needles and thread in the drawer of the breakfront in the dining room at Godwin Hall.

The concussion he suffered on the night of Anthony Torres killed Amanda had stolen the memories of his mother's girlhood remembrances.

Now they were back.

With them came the sense-memory of his father; the way

Michael Hardy would smell when he came home late from a job. Will could always see the weariness and fatigue in the man's eyes, but it was the smell that scared young Will. The smell of fire and death. No matter how many hot showers his father took, the smell never really left.

And now the fire was coming for him.

By the time Will got the door open the flames had begun to climb the walls. The heat was monstrous.

'*Detta!*'

He looked down the hallway to the left. The door at the end of the hall was open. Will tore off his shirt, held it over his mouth and nose.

Before long he couldn't see anything. He had gotten turned around and could not remember which way the stairs were.

Then, a fluttering, a flare of bright white light to his right. Paper cuts of sound across the air, like the sound of beating wings.

Will crawled in that direction, found the stairs. The smoke was so thick he could not see the bottom.

He tried to hold his breath as he pulled himself down, down. Behind him he could feel the flames at his back.

He blacked out for a moment, was brought back by the searing heat. When he reached the bottom he could no longer hold his breath.

Again the flash of white, disappearing into the flames to his right. He continued to crawl in that direction

He was now in the foyer. Fire filled the world.

When the front door blew open, Will saw something flutter out, into the darkening sky.

Then his world went as dark as the smoke.

84

When Ivy was halfway across the Fairgrounds she saw the smoke billowing from the gable end of Veldhoeve. She also heard the sirens.

By the time she reached the driveway she saw that there were two ladder trucks already on scene.

Walt Barnstable was herding onlookers away from the structure, out of the potential collapse zone.

Ivy looked across the front lawn and saw that one of the firefighters had Will Hardy. Within seconds the firefighter had an oxygen mask over Will's face. Ivy could see that Will was fighting with the man, struggling to stand up.

Ivy spotted the fire officer in command. He was with the Cleveland Fire Department. His crew had been on scene as part of the festival. Ivy introduced herself.

'Didn't expect to be working today, Chief.'

Ivy pointed at Will Hardy. 'Anyone besides him come out?'

'Not on this side,' he said. 'Not that I've heard.'

'There's a girl. A fifteen-year-old girl.'

'Sorry, Chief. Nothing yet.'

As the crowd from the festival amassed behind her, Ivy ran to the north end of Veldhoeve.

All she could do was watch.

Before anyone could put a hand on him Will tore off the oxygen mask and was across the yard. He was on the firefighter before the man could remove his helmet.

'Is she in there?' Will shouted.

The man shot a glance over Will's shoulder, back into Will's eyes.

What Will saw there ate him alive.

'Sir, I don't—'

Will grabbed the man by the front of his jacket.

'Just fucking tell me the truth! Is she in there?'

The man was Will's size, a few years younger. He did not fight.

'Look me in the eyes like a man and tell me if she's dead!'

Will felt hands on him, strong arms pulling him back. He fought as long and as hard as he could. The words coming out his mouth took on a guttural sound, an animal sound. He was taken to the ground.

Out of the sea of faces he saw Ivy Holgrave emerge.

'It's okay,' Ivy said. 'I have this. Let him go.'

After a few moments, the firefighters eased their grip.

'My *daughter*,' Will managed.

'Will,' Ivy said. 'She's not inside.'

With the fire contained and extinguished on the north side of the house, the fire officer cleared two deputies to search the other sections of the building, areas the fire had not reached. Five minutes later the Reese brothers emerged. Dale Reese caught Ivy's eye, shook his head. The house was clear. There was no one inside.

Ivy turned to the crowd. Just about everyone in attendance at the Appleville Festival had formed a semicircle near the front entrance to Veldhoeve.

'Did anyone see Jakob van Laar?' Ivy yelled.

Ivy scanned the faces in the crowd. No one responded.

'Anyone. Jakob van Laar!'

'I saw him.'

Ivy turned to the voice. It was Colleen Clausen.

'Where did you see him?'

'He was on that carriage. The old one that takes people around the Fairgrounds.'

'Was there anyone with him?' Ivy asked.

'Not that I saw, Ivy. There may have been someone inside. The door was closed.'

'How long ago was this?'

'I don't know. Maybe twenty minutes? Half an hour?'

'Which way did he go?'

Marge pointed south. Toward Route 44. Toward the forest.

Ivy got on her phone. She relayed the information to the Holland County Sheriff's office, who would in turn alert every police department in the tri-county area. She also put in a request for air assist. If there was a police helicopter available, she wanted it in the sky.

As she turned to head across the grounds she felt a hand on her shoulder. It was Will Hardy.

'You have to stay with EMS, Will.'

'No.'

'You took smoke. They have to clear you.'

'It's not up to them. He's got my daughter.'

Ivy searched the man's eyes, looking for the right words to say. There were none. He would not be consoled or persuaded. She took him away from the crowd, lowered her voice.

'I need you to go to Godwin Hall,' Ivy said.

'Why?'

'Get the book. The big art book on your daughter's bed.'

'I don't understand. We have to—'

'The answer is in there,' she said. 'Meet me at my house.'

'I don't—'

'*Go!*'

Will ran across the Fairgrounds. When he reached Godwin Hall it was as if he was entering the place for the first time. It was suddenly foreign to him.

He ran up the stairs, down the hall. When he went into Detta's room he felt the emotions surge. He had to calm himself. What would he counsel a patient to do?

Breathe.

He found the coffee table book on Pieter Bruegel.

He was down the stairs in an instant. He took his Cervélo from the foyer, jumped on. He left for Ivy Holgrave's house.

When Will burst through the door Ivy called him to the basement. She had a number of crime scene photographs laid out on the huge table.

'Look,' she said. She pointed to the crime scene photos from Lonnie Combs's apartment. The hanging body. The dice on the floor.

'The dice at three and one,' Ivy said.

It was all depicted in the drawing.

'Acedia,' Will said. '*Sloth.*'

'Yes.'

She pulled more photographs onto the table. These were from Chevy Deacon's trailer. The horrible close-up of the drill bit emerging from his temple.

'My God,' Will said. He flipped a page in the book, found it. '*Gluttony.*'

'Turn to the section on the Seven Virtues.'

Ivy tapped the first plate. In it were three urns. A ceramic rooster. A lantern.

'This one is Josefina Mollo,' she said.

More photographs. A dozen crime scene pictures of the Elizabeth Hollis scene. The spiral candles on holders, the peacock feathers.

Elizabeth Hollis was *Fortitude*.

In one motion Ivy cleared the large table of everything. She took one photograph from each crime scene and placed it on the table. She took the book from Will's hand and tore out the fourteen prints. Before long she had them all matched up.

'There is only one left,' Will said. 'One virtue and one vice.'

He tapped the final print. In it, a woman stood in raging waters. Around her were boats in distress.

'This is the one,' he said.

The last print was *Hope*. At the bottom of the drawing was the Latin phrase Will had found carved into the headboard. He now knew who had put the auction flyer on his door.

Ivy took a rifle from a mount on the wall.

'I know where he took her.'

85

She could hear the river. The sound was soothing.

It reminded her of the day she'd met Billy.

The man had told her that they would take a ride in this beautiful carriage and that she would meet up with her father.

When the door opened, and she took in the setting, the delta formed by the smaller river meeting the larger, she recognized it. It was the place she'd met Billy.

The man now wore a long coat and a wide-brimmed hat. His tie had in it a stick pin in the shape of an onyx raven. He held out his hand. Detta took it, stepped from the carriage.

'My dad is here?' Detta asked.

'Yes,' he said.

The man walked behind the horse, gave it a slight tap with a tree branch. The horse drew the carriage down the path, and soon disappeared into the woods.

As a gentle rain began to fall, Detta looked around. It was different from the day she'd met Billy. There were things scattered around the clearing. No, not scattered. The items looked *placed*.

Near the river bank was a shovel, along with a large anchor and something that looked like a sickle. Leaning against a wooden chair was an antique hand mirror.

It suddenly occurred to her. 'I don't know your name.'

For a long moment the man hesitated.

'Rinus,' he said. 'I am Dr Rinus van Laar.'

Detta knew the name. But from where? Then she remembered. It was from Eva Larssen's diary.

Fear gripped her heart. She looked down.

In the man's hand was a large, razor-sharp thorn.

86

In the moonlight Eva looked even younger than her years.

Rinus van Laar had dressed and redressed many times this night, fussing over his appearance. He felt shame in his age. He felt shame in the lines on his face, the scars and spots on his hands. He felt shame in his betrayal of his dead wife.

It was with these blackened feelings of disgrace and dishonor that he stepped from the shadows.

'Willem?' Eva called out.

In this word, this singular name, he knew his greatest folly and humiliation. Eva would never say his name thus. He knew that now. He knew it, and yet he could not stop himself.

'Where is the child?' he asked.

Her hand shaking, Eva pointed across the Fairgrounds, toward Godwin Hall.

'It is all right. I will raise the child as if it were my own. Our own. You and little May will never want for anything.'

He could see that Eva knew what was happening. In her eyes he saw the fear. She withdrew from him.

'Willem,' she said.

'Willem is dead.' Rinus held up the silver flacon. 'This is his blood.'

Eva's eyes fluttered once, then she collapsed to the ground.

Rinus carried her to the first grove. In the moonlight he saw the white bird circling, circling.

With the last of his strength he buried the girl.

It was there that her blood became forever one with the soil.

It was there that Rinus van Laar perished.

87

On the way into the forest, the rain had begun to fall in a steady downpour.

When they rounded the bend, Will saw the horse and carriage, standing on the side of the road. He was out of the SUV before Ivy could stop him. He threw open the door on the carriage. It was empty. Seconds later he found the path leading deep into the woods.

As he ran into the clearing the rain began to fall in earnest. Through the torrent he took in the horrifying scene.

Detta was seated on a wooden chair, just at the river's edge.

Her eyes were closed.

Jakob van Laar stood next to her.

In the man's left hand was something that looked like a silver flask. In his right hand was a sickle. Even from fifty feet away Will could see the keened edge of the blade.

When Jakob saw Will approaching, he stepped behind Detta. He held the sickle to her throat.

'Stop, Willem Schuyler,' he shouted.

'Jakob,' Will yelled. 'Don't do this.'

Will could now see a thin wash of pink on his daughter's wrists. She was bleeding.

'The word derives from the Old English *prud*,' Jakob said. 'Did you know this? It meant excellent and fine.' The edge of the blade was now an inch from Detta's throat. 'It also meant arrogant and haughty.'

My God, Will thought. He's talking about Pride.

Jakob van Laar is the last vice.

Will sensed movement in his periphery, but he dared not look away. He had to find the words.

'Pride is not a sin, Jakob. There is no shame in it.'

'Oh but there is. I am guilty of it.'

If you want to counter it, you feel hope. Hope, man. Her name was Eva.

These were Anthony Torres's words.

Will had to keep the man talking. He slowly continued across the clearing. Everywhere were placed items, items he'd seen in Bruegel's drawing.

'Why, Jakob?' he asked. 'Why do you say that?'

'I've taken credit for all that is Zeven Farms. I live in the grace of its bounty.'

Will could see movement through the trees to his left. The river began to churn. He did not take his eyes from Jakob.

'There's nothing wrong with that,' Will said.

'Is there not?'

Will took two more steps forward. Detta did not move.

'Because there is something to be found in this,' Will said. 'All of this.'

'Not for me. Not anymore.'

Will took one final step forward. 'What about self-worth, Jakob?'

434

Jakob looked north, toward the looming hulk of Veldhoeve. He lifted the silver flask. 'Each of my fathers knew when to sip from this. They knew when it was time. For the briefest moment I felt I could not join them. Now I know that I was wrong.' He tilted back his head for a moment, grimaced at the taste of whatever was in the flask. He dropped the flask to his feet.

Will gestured to the rolling hills in the distance, the vast and flourishing orchards.

'Look at all this, Jakob. This is something. You should feel something for all of this. For all that your family has accomplished. Don't throw it all away.'

Jakob looked out over the rain-swept orchards, back at Will. The blade trembled in his hand.

'What?' he asked. 'What is my legacy, Willem Schuyler?'

Will was now less than ten feet away.

'Dignity,' Will said.

Everything seemed to stop. Will saw the blade drop a few inches from Detta's neck.

Will had reached him.

A few moments later, whatever had given Jakob van Laar pause, whatever humanity flickered within him, was gone. He looked up, into Will's eyes, and mouthed the word:

'Hope.'

He lifted the blade.

In this instant Will saw the baby in Amanda's arms, pink and loud and healthy. He saw the toddler on Rockaway Beach, scooping sand into a plastic pail. He saw the teenage Detta Hardy dabbing her eyes during the closing credits of *Casablanca*.

In the next moment he saw the back of Jakob van Laar's head explode in a violent gush of blood and bone and tissue. His body shuddered once, then tumbled backward, into the raging river.

Will heard the delayed report of the rifle as he ran to the river's edge and took his daughter into his arms.

'I have you, baby. I have you.'

A few moments later the EMS paramedics reached them. Will turned his gaze to the rim of the forest, where Ivy Holgrave stood, the long gun in her hands.

They saw each other and, in that moment, knew it was over.

88

Ivy had rehearsed an elaborate speech for the girl, intending to shield her from some of the more terrible truths. On the way to the hospital she chucked it all. The girl had been through a hellish ordeal. She was probably tougher than some small-town police chief.

The good news for Bernadette Hardy, and her father, was that her wounds – her external wounds – were minor. The toxicology report would take a few days, so they did not know what she had ingested. When Jakob van Laar had attempted to pierce a vein with the large thorn, he had missed, and only lacerated the skin.

Ivy took note of this, and planned to revisit all the autopsy photos of the other girls. She knew that she would find this to be consistent with the other victims. The reason they had not found the murder weapons for all these years had been because the murder weapon had been organic.

Jakob van Laar's body was pulled from the Hoop River about

one hundred yards south of the clearing. He was pronounced dead at the scene.

Ivy took no joy or satisfaction in this. In her more than two decades in law enforcement, it was the first time she had ever taken a life.

'Tell me how it began,' Ivy said.

Detta took a few moments, arranging her thoughts. She told Ivy about the events leading up to the previous night. She began with her taking 20 mg of Ambien, and going to bed.

'Is that your prescribed dose?'

Detta flicked a glance toward the doorway, where her father stood. She looked back at Ivy.

'No,' she said. 'It's twice.'

'Tell me what happened next.'

'I heard something outside. At first I thought it was a tree branch scraping the glass. But it wasn't. It was tiny stones being thrown at the window.'

'Who was throwing the stones?'

'It was Billy.'

'What is Billy's last name?'

'I don't know.'

'Where does he live? Here in Abbeville?'

'I don't know that either.'

'Okay,' Ivy said. 'Where did you meet him?'

'I saw him one day in the library. But I didn't talk to him that day.'

'Our library?'

'Yes. Then a few days later I went down to the river by myself. I rode my bike down there, and Billy was just ... there. It was kind of like he was waiting for me.'

'Where by the river?'

'Right where that man took me.'

438

'Did you feel threatened by that?'

'Oh God, no. Nothing like that. In fact, whenever I was with Billy I felt safe. Really safe.'

Detta went on to tell Ivy about her further encounters with the boy.

'And in all this time he never told you his last name, or where he lived, or where he went to school.'

'We never talked about school.'

'Is there anything else you can tell me about him?' Ivy asked.

'I'm not sure what you mean.'

'Anything about a sister or brother? Anything about his parents?'

'No.'

'What about a distinguishing characteristic? Maybe a scar or a birthmark. Something like that.'

'There was something. On his right forearm.'

'What was it?'

'It was a tattoo,' Detta said. 'A tattoo of a white bird.'

89

Will found that he could not leave the hospital room. Even when Ivy was in there with Detta, he found that he could not step away. He hovered in the doorway. More than once, when orderlies and nurses tried to get in the room, he had to step to the side.

When Ivy was finished, she stepped out of the room. Together they walked to the end of the hall.

'Are you okay?' Ivy finally asked.

Will took his time. 'Not sure how to answer that.'

'I understand.'

They fell silent, listening to the sounds of a hospital in its midday hum.

'Was my daughter able to shed any light?'

'Some,' Ivy said. 'But this investigation is just beginning. There is no telling what we're going to find in Veldhoeve.'

The main house and all the outbuildings near Veldhoeve were

currently sealed off, as were all areas of the Fairgrounds leading up to the property. There were no fewer than a dozen forensic and investigative personnel on the grounds.

Ivy lowered her voice.

'I hope you're not blaming yourself for any of this,' she said.

'Yeah, well, I'm afraid that's going to take some time, too.'

'You talked the knife down, Will. I saw it. We all saw it.'

Will shook his head. 'If I had done that, he would still be alive.'

'That was his choice, not yours. You know that.'

Will didn't look convinced. 'It's a lot to take in, Ivy.'

'I know. But you have your daughter and your life together. You have all the time in the world.'

The nurse exited Detta's room with her cart. She offered a half-smile meaning: *Vitals are good.* When she made her way into the next room, Will asked:

'How did you know?'

'Know what?'

'How did you know where he was going to take her?'

It was a longer shot than Ivy would ever admit to anyone but Will Hardy. 'That part of the river? Right where that small tributary snakes off toward Zeven Farms?'

'What about it?'

'That's where Rinus van Laar landed when he came here. He named the stream Hoop River. It's not on any map.'

'I don't understand,' Will said.

'Hoop is the Dutch word for hope. It's about the first thing you learn in grade school around these parts.'

Ivy saw the ER doctor coming down the hall, making his rounds. She knew that Will would want to talk to him. She glanced at her watch. 'I should get back.'

'What about you, Ivy?'

'What do you mean?'

'How are you holding up?'

Ivy had no idea how to answer this. It was all new to her, too. 'I'm okay.'

'I have some experience with this, you know.'

'Experience with what?'

'I've counseled more than a few police officers at times like these.'

Ivy now understood what he meant. There were any number of protocols in place in large city police departments regarding the aftermath of an officer-involved shooting. Not so in her little village. 'Thanks,' she said. 'I might just take you up on that.'

She slipped on her jacket.

'I do have one question for you, though,' she said.

'Sure.'

'If I see you as a patient, do I have to call you Dr Hardy?'

'Only if I have to call you Chief Holgrave.'

'I think we can work something out.' Ivy touched the door to Detta's room. 'If you or Bernadette need anything, you've got my number. Day or night.'

'And you've got mine.'

Ivy had every intention of turning and walking down the polished hallway at that moment, of returning to the station and the madhouse that awaited her, of taking the first steps in the long healing process for her little village.

Instead, she found herself pulling Will Hardy into an embrace.

The hug was brief, but it meant a lot to Ivy.

It was the one she wanted to give Jimmy Benedict on that day nearly twenty-five years ago.

90

In the month following the Appleville Festival the evidence of nearly two centuries of crime was slowly gathered, processed, studied and catalogued. The arduous and painstaking process was undertaken by the FBI, with assistance from the Ohio State Police, Holland County Sheriff's office, BCI, and the Abbeville Police Department.

The three hundred acres that were the now-shuttered Zeven Farms were divided into quarter-acre sections, and would be scanned with methane probes. The process would take more than a year.

The boy that Rebecca Taylor had seen with Josefina Mollo, near the entrance to Calvary House, was Dakota Rawlings. Evidence found in the Rawlings house tied him to Jakob van Laar when Jakob had traveled on what looked to have been a buying trip the year before.

When shown a photograph of the boy, Detta Hardy recognized Rawlings as a boy called 'Cody' she had briefly met at Uncle Joe's Sweet Shoppe.

Among the items taken from Will and Amanda's brownstone in New York, removed just before Anthony Torres killed Amanda, was the china tea service, and a large album of family photos. The album was found in a safe on the first floor at Veldhoeve, and survived the fire. It was safely returned to Will and Detta Hardy.

Julie Hansen recovered fully. She told investigators a chilling tale of her time in Veldhoeve. She spoke of fourteen framed prints that Jakob van Laar told her were preliminary sketches drawn by Pieter Bruegel himself.

The drawings were never found.

Among the myriad grotesque and bizarre findings regarding Jakob van Laar's madness were the items found scattered at the crime scenes. It seemed he had collected objects for many years, carefully placing them in the clearings where the girls would be found, objects exactly mirroring the collection and placement of objects in each of Bruegel's drawings.

Toxicology reports showed that the liquid in the silver flask Jakob had ingested was from a plant grown in a small hothouse on the grounds of Veldhoeve called *atropa belladonna*, more commonly known as deadly nightshade.

The hallucinogenic drug in the apple Detta Hardy had eaten that night, as well as the tea she had ingested, was a unique strain of *mandragora officinarum*, also known as Satan's Apple.

The most surprising fallout was that Jakob van Laar, having no living heirs, ordered that his estate be divided between seven different charitable organizations upon his death, each to be distributed by a law firm in Columbus, each donation to remain anonymous.

The amount was close to four million dollars.

Even with the resources of city, county, state and federal databases, Ivy could not find any trace of a local boy named Billy.

When the story broke wide, Ivy began to get calls from

444

everywhere regarding girls who had gone missing as far back as the 1950s.

While Ivy was invested in each and every case, had sworn an oath to do so, there was one piece of evidence she sought in the dark recesses and eaves of Veldhoeve.

She did not find it.

By the first day of spring, Ivy finished restoring the photograph of Delia Holgrave in the Fairgrounds. On that night Ivy opened a special bottle of bourbon, one she'd been saving for the moment. She poured herself a few inches, and raised a glass. From across her basement room she could finally see what had been there all along, waiting for her like some long-hidden cipher.

Sitting on the branch overhead, on the day Delia Holgrave disappeared, was a white bird.

91

Detta sat near the huge apple tree by the river, feeling the warm sunshine on her face. The area had weeks earlier shed all remnants of that terrible day; all the yellow tape had been cut down, all the strange objects Jakob van Laar had placed near the riverbank had been collected by the police and sent to wherever it was things like that went.

For the first time in months it looked the way it did the first time she talked to Billy.

She glanced out over the river. The late afternoon light was milky and even and perfect.

It had been weeks since she'd thought of New York, and their life there. There were moments when she could not recall much of anything about it. And that was okay. She'd come to believe that it really didn't matter where you were, in the end, but who you were.

She had made some good friends at Carver High. The school had a pretty good art department. There was an art show coming up, and she had a few pieces ready.

Before she gathered her things, she looked at her new drawing. In it, the huge apple tree seemed to reach to the heavens.

She decided to keep the lowest branch empty, for now. She never signed a work until she was done with it, and she knew that she might not be finished with this one for a while.

She packed her pad and pencils and easel into her bag, stood up and headed down the riverbank, toward Godwin Hall.

I know who you were, Bernadette Hardy.

And I know who you were, Billy.

I know.

92

Godwin Hall's first paying guest sat with its owner and proprietor on the second-floor balcony overlooking the Fairgrounds.

The first sweet burst of April was upon Holland County, Ohio. Godwin Hall was booked every weekend through Labor Day.

Down below the balcony, the year's inaugural spring festival, the Holland County Maple Syrup Fest, was well underway, with a few hundred visitors already on the green.

The Godwin Hall exhibit, with pancakes and French toast served by Miriam Yoder, assisted by Bernadette Hardy and Ivy Holgrave, was particularly popular.

Detta and Ivy had become close friends over the winter. They had a bond that Will knew he would never be part of.

Ivy had introduced Detta to the basics of photography, as well as the fundamentals of restoring an old photograph in Photoshop by enlarging and working on it pixel by pixel.

Detta, in turn, had introduced Ivy to the pointillist painters; Seurat and Signac and Georges Lemmen. Detta had more than once remarked to Will how interesting it was that the two art forms could meet in the middle.

Ivy and Detta had twice watched the Blu-ray of Antonioni's 1966 film *Blowup*, at Will's recommendation.

As the festival crowd began to swell, the two men on the balcony sipped their Maker's Mark, Will Hardy's new favorite.

'Is she married?' Trevor asked. 'I didn't see a ring.'

Will didn't have to ask who Trevor was talking about. He saw Trevor's eyes light up the minute he introduced the man to Ivy Holgrave.

'She is not.'

'You know I love a woman in a uniform.'

'Yeah, well, I don't think you'd get away with anything with her,' Will said. 'In fact, I'm sure of it.'

'I think you're right.'

The two men sat in comfortable silence for a while.

'Do you miss it?' Trevor finally asked.

'Miss what?'

'Teaching. The city. The life. New York.'

Will didn't have to think too long about it. 'I really don't, Trev. I know there's a position waiting for me nearby if I ever have the urge to get back to teaching. As to the city, it seems like someone else's life right now. I know Amanda isn't in New York. She's here with us.'

Trevor just nodded.

There was a lot both men wanted to say. There was a lot of sorting through regarding the madness of the last year. They would, in time. For now, there was the warm spring breeze, and the sound of children on the green.

'I can't believe I forgot,' Trevor said.

'Forgot what?'

'There might be a new season of *Broadchurch*.'

'Awesome. Will David Tennant be in it?'

'Therein lies the mystery,' Trevor said. 'And, by the way, I finally figured out why you like that show so much.'

'Have you now?'

'I have. I'm a detective, after all.'

'Okay,' Will said. 'Why do I like it so much?'

'The main character's name is DCI Hardy.'

'I never noticed that.'

Trevor laughed. 'I think you may fold under further questioning.' He tapped his empty glass. 'Another round, innkeeper.'

Epilogue

Astor Shores was a county-run elder care facility near the Lake County border, a four-story brown brick building overlooking Lake Erie.

Ivy sat in the parking lot for a long time, trying to talk herself out of what she was about to do. She could not find a single reason to move forward. There was every reason to let this part of her past, their past, fade into memory.

Before she could stop herself, she exited the SUV, crossed the parking lot, and entered the building.

Ivy stepped into the day room. Before long the woman's face drifted into view, achingly identifiable.

Ivy allowed the woman a few moments to find her, to place her in time, if that was still possible. When she was certain the woman had seen her, Ivy slowly crossed the room to where the woman sat.

Arcella Richards watched her every move.

'My God,' the woman said. 'It really is you.'

451

'It is.'

The woman studied her. 'Has it really been twenty-five years?' she asked.

'Yes, ma'am.'

Arcella Richards had just celebrated her eighty-second birthday. Ivy did the math on the drive to Cleveland. The woman had been only fifty-seven years old on that terrible day. It was a number that seemed ancient to Ivy at the time. It was a number just beyond her grasp now.

They spoke of the weather. They spoke of the city. They spoke of everything except what put them together on this day, in this room.

Arcella reached into her handbag, produced a faded school photo of her grandson, a gap-toothed boy wearing a too-large Cleveland Browns jersey. Number 32. Even at the time the photograph was taken, years after Jim Brown had retired, boys wore 32. Ivy still saw them from time to time.

'Went to a game once, Terrance and me,' she said. 'He was about eight years old. It was right around Thanksgiving, but it was awfully cold. January cold. His daddy was already in the ground, his mama run off. The wind came off the lake that day like enough to kill you. Played the Cincinnati Bengals.'

'Did the Browns win?'

Arcella nodded. 'They did. Score of twenty-four to six. Terrance was so happy. Got that Ozzie Newsome's autograph.'

They fell silent as the staff at Astor Shores started gearing up for dinner.

'I watch the shows, you know,' Arcella said. 'On the TV.'

'Ma'am?'

'They all talk about the how and the why of things. Why boys go bad, what we all should have done, what we all should do so they don't go bad again. None of it makes any sense at all. Not to me.'

Ivy had no answers for the woman. It was a question she'd asked herself since the day she first put on a uniform and a badge.

Instead, she took the woman's small hand in hers, and together they looked out the window until the sun began to set over the shore.

The stereo played *Patsy Cline's Greatest Hits*. It had been such a long and emotional day that Ivy figured she'd go all in.

Frankie sat at Ivy's feet, reading her mood.

'We're in this for the duration, aren't we?'

Frankie raised a paw to shake. Ivy obliged.

A few minutes later Ivy stood, crossed the room, reached into the closet, and removed the large plastic bag. She went back to her chair.

Frankie nosed the air. She was dying to know what was in the parcel. Maybe she already knew.

Ivy unzipped the bag, took out the clothing. Frankie leaned in, sniffed the sweater. It was Delia's favorite.

'This one isn't going to be easy, baby girl.'

Frankie wagged her tail. *Try me.*

On the way to the back door, Ivy slipped on her jacket. She took the long leash off its hook.

Twenty minutes later Ivy and Frankie walked across the Fairgrounds to the stone gazebo at its center, then beyond, past ash and beech and box elder, past the whispered secrets of two great houses, into the dark and silent forests of Holland County.

Acknowledgements

With deepest thanks to:

Meg Ruley, Rebecca Scherer, Danielle Sickles, Christina Prestia and all at Jane Rotrosen Agency;

Ed Wood, Thalia Proctor and the brilliant team at Little, Brown UK;

The Dalt Gang, Kathleen Heraghty, Robyn Morris, Michael Krotz, Michael Caticchio, Gary Wilgus, Dan McClelland, James Hyland, Douglas Bunker, Ronald Cimaglio, Kathleen Franco, and the inscrutable Mr. Z;

My father, Dominic, for looking in on me when I've been quiet too long. Full circle, Pop. I love you.